THE WIDOW OF DESIRE

THE
WIDOW OF DESIRE

JUSTIN SCOTT

BANTAM BOOKS
NEW YORK · TORONTO · LONDON · SYDNEY · AUCKLAND

THE WIDOW OF DESIRE

A Bantam Book / April 1989

Grateful acknowledgment is made to the following:
WHO AM I ANYWAY? *excerpt on page 77 by Marvin Hamlisch*
& Edward Kleban from "A Chorus Line" © *1975, 1985*
MARVIN HAMLISCH, INC. *and* EDWARD KLEBAN. *All Rights Controlled*
by WREN MUSIC CO. *and* AMERICAN COMPASS MUSIC CORP. *International*
copyright secured. All Rights Reserved. Used By Permission.

Jacket photo fur courtesy of Goldin-Feldman;
hat courtesy of Lenore Marshall.

Library of Congress Cataloging-in-Publication Data

Scott, Justin.
The widow of desire.

I. Title.
PS3569.C644W54   1989   813'.54   88-7809
ISBN 0-553-05351-5

PRINTED IN THE UNITED STATES OF AMERICA

WKO   0 9 8 7 6 5 4 3 2 1

To Gloria Hoye,
my love, my beauty, my friend,
and for our daughter Laura Patrick,
who gave me a fix on Natalie

PROLOGUE

OCTOBER 1987

WALLACE & NATALIE

When the gossip, laughter, and shrieked greetings drowned out the music, Natalie agreed Wallace had been right to enliven Cotillion's annual champagne cruise by inviting their favorite furriers and designers, a colorfully irascible mink farmer, and a clutch of high-powered fashion editors. Wallace conceded that the view didn't hurt either, as *Panache*—the dowager 150-foot motor yacht he had acquired from a bankrupt Romanian the year Natalie was born—steamed down the Hudson River.

They were holding court beneath a chandelier in the middle of *Panache*'s enormous main salon—a floating ballroom of polished wood and beveled glass—for two hundred Cotillion Furs franchise owners and spouses who were *oooing* at the Statue of Liberty, etched like a cinder against a fiery autumn sunset, and *ahhhing* at the Manhattan skyline, which had begun to twinkle beneath a freshly minted evening sky.

Waiters pressed champagne and smoked salmon on these guests of honor. The furriers dutifully chatted up lonely women. The designers cavorted outrageously. The mink farmer, pretending rusticity in a flannel checked shirt from Milan, informed all who would listen why his furskins were environmentally sounder than fake furs, and the fashion editors affirmed their importance by talking only to each other.

3

A success, thought Natalie, and Wallace agreed. When the models showed Cotillion's new collection, everyone would be in a mood to order lavishly. No one in the fur trade did shows like Cotillion. Not Ben Kahn. Not Revillon. Not even Jindo Furs, their hottest foreign competitor.

She felt very proud of Cotillion tonight. And very happy. Wallace was beside her, home safe from a ten-day fur-buying expedition, the collection was ready, and good, and all seemed right in her world until she spotted an elegant blonde in a halter-top gown roving the edges of the crowd with the studied sangfroid of a gatecrasher.

"Darling, who's the blonde with the shoulders?"

She directed his gaze with a discreet nod. Wallace knew everyone in the fur trade and he was also an ebullient last-minute inviter, but before he could fix on the stranger he was distracted by a woman to whom Natalie had sold Cotillion's biggest West Coast franchise. Arms and hair flying, she enveloped Wallace like an octopus. "Great party, Wallace. Love your boat."

"Ship," he corrected, responding hug for hug and kiss for kiss. "Fred the Furrier owns a boat. Cotillion aspires to higher things. You know Natalie, of course."

"Sure."

"Welcome aboard," said Natalie, losing sight of the blonde and wondering where she had come from. An army of security guards, camouflaged in evening gowns and dinner jackets, should have stopped anyone without an invitation. And once *Panache* was under way, half a mile of Hudson River could be presumed to keep a private show private. Yet she was certain the woman had crashed. Having spent many a school holiday and summer vacation as the extra cousin parked with relatives while her foreign service parents were overseas, she knew an outsider when she saw one.

It was, however, a small problem in a big evening, and with one final glance in the direction the blonde had disappeared, Natalie turned her attention to the woman from Los Angeles who was coming on to Wallace under the guise of showing interest in the Soviet Union, from where he had just returned.

"Is *glasnost* a crock?" the lady demanded.

Wallace defused her with a practiced smile that opened their conversation to the circle gathered around them, and Natalie would always remember him in that moment. He had a handsome head of silver hair and he stood like a horse soldier, tall and straight. Yet there was nothing stiff about him, or old, because he was charged with a young man's restless energy that made his eyes glint like sequins in his lined and craggy face. The Jews and Greeks of the New York fur trade called him, with great affection, "the Cossack."

"*Glasnost* is real. Call it publicity, call it openness, Russia is *boiling* in self-examination. Lucky for Gorbachev, because *glasnost* gives him a clearer picture than Soviet statistics of the mess he's inherited. Lucky for all of us. What he's stirred up could be the most important event of the twentieth century. His real problem is *perestroika*. Love of change is about as Russian as humility is American. So even if the Communist Party reforms the Soviet bureaucracy, they'll still have to deal with the Russian people. . . . For instance, when I was in Moscow last week, GUM announced a sale of fine Italian leather boots."

Natalie looked at him. She thought he had spent the entire trip in Leningrad. Wallace returned an all-but-invisible wink, and his voice dropped to a seductive baritone. A dozen people pressed closer to hear over the din of the party.

"Well, winter is coming, so long before dawn a *million* Soviet citizens were jammed into Red Square, waiting for the department store to open. I've never seen anything quite like it. *Masses* of shivering humanity that stretched the length of the Kremlin Wall from St. Basil's almost to Marx Prospekt. They spilled onto Revolution Square and even perched on Lenin's mausoleum. Waiting. At first light a hard, cold rain began to fall and soon the air was thick with that peculiarly Russian odor, the scent of wet wool."

Natalie, a tall, slender, dark-haired young woman with a coat model's shoulders and a banker's collected gaze, quietly closed her hand around her husband's, a reminder that here in New York, they also had a mob waiting, which would soon be too high on Perrier-Jouët to find their order books. Wallace squeezed back—message received—without missing a beat.

"GUM's doors failed to open at the appointed hour. The temperature fell, and the rain began to freeze on the citizens assembled. Finally, the door opened a crack and a store manager strutted out.

" 'Comrades,' he addressed the masses. 'There has been an overestimation of the shipment of Italian leather boots. It has been judged there will not be enough boots to go around.'

"An anonymous muttering of discontent drifts across Red Square, trailing an expectant, if not very hopeful, silence. After all, they know the Soviet language. *There has been* and *it has been judged* are familiar phrases that relieve *everyone* of responsibility. Happily, however, the GUM manager has a plan to alleviate the shortage. It is brilliant. Indeed, the perfect solution. The GUM manager says, 'All Jews waiting to buy fine Italian leather boots must go home.'

"The Jews shrug their shoulders and wander resignedly from Red Square. . . . Nonetheless, GUM's doors remain shut. The freezing rain turns to sleet. At last GUM's manager reappears. 'The shipment of fine Italian leather boots has been overestimated. There are still not enough. Therefore, all Soviet citizens of the Central Asian Republics are ordered to return to their homes.' So," said Wallace, "Turkmen, Uzbeks, Kazaks, and Kirghizes shrug their swarthy shoulders and go home."

Natalie gave him a stern look and Wallace cut to the chase.

"The sleet changes to snow and the disappointing announcements are repeated periodically in the darkening winter afternoon. Siberians are ordered to leave. Georgians, Armenians, Caucasians, Finns, Tartars.

" 'All Soviet citizens of the Baltic States.' And Latvians, Estonians, and Lithuanians trudge home through the deepening drifts. We are down to Slavs, and soon even Ukrainians and Byelorussians are ordered to leave.

"I've been ducking into the National Hotel for a morning drink, lunch, an afternoon drink, and when Leningraders are dismissed en masse, I retreat for dinner. Late that night I venture once more into the storm. Wind-driven snow is blasting horizontally across the city. It is so dark it could be the sixteenth century.

"Red Square is empty, but for the snow and two old men, eyes fixed on GUM. These are *Russians*. Great Russians whose people have lived in Moscow for a thousand years. Under a glaze of ice I can just make out the rows upon rows of medals on their chests. War heroes. There is no one in the Motherland more worthy of fine Italian leather boots than these old veterans of the Great Patriotic War. When Hitler invaded they fought the *Wehrmacht* in the suburbs of Moscow. They stopped Nazi panzer tanks with their bare hands.

" 'Comrades!' GUM's manager sticks his head out the door. The veterans stiffen to attention. At last. 'GUM is forced to announce that due to conditions beyond its control there are no fine Italian leather boots.' *Bang*, the door slams.

"For a long time, the two old men stand alone and silent. Finally, one speaks: 'You know what makes me angry? I mean really, really angry?'

" 'It's always the same,' his comrade commiserates. 'The Jews get to go home first.' "

Natalie spotted the blonde in the halter-top gown again. She pointed her out to Wallace, who caught a distant glimpse of her bare back, which he pronounced "Attractive but not familiar. Somebody's girlfriend," he ventured. "Excellent wig—wait a minute! Speaking of unwelcome, who invited that son-of-a-bitch Stevie Weintraub?"

"Stevie showed me some dynamite fox jackets while you were in Russia."

"I bankrolled his grandfather. What does this *schlock* artist do? Shuts down the family's third-generation factory to import finished coats from Hong Kong."

Natalie was still learning the risks of ignoring the feuds that ran deep in the small, tight-knit international fur community, but she wanted those jackets.

"First of all, even you are not that old. You bankrolled his *father*. Second, Stevie's the biggest importer in New York, so he has access to more than *schlock*. Third, his fox jackets are perfect for the Diana Darbee line." On the other side of the yacht's salon, Diana, star of the long-running primetime television soap opera *Parmalee Canyon*, and a blonde best described in her own words as "drop-dead gorgeous," was entertaining a crowd of enchanted men with anxious wives. Natalie turned Wallace toward a *Women's Wear Daily* photographer. "Smile."

"We don't sell imported coats." Wallace smiled.

"We sell Canadian imports," she reminded him. "Coats from your Russian skins." Since American law forbade importing Russian mink, Cotillion bought some of its coats from Canadian factories Wallace supplied. His "Buy American" campaign was less nationalistic than pro-labor. "Here comes Stevie. Be nice."

"I don't buy from sweatshops, Natalie. They've got whole families over there making coats for a bowl of rice a day. I'm a union man. Since I was fifteen."

"You're a union millionaire," she reminded him, touching his ear where a silver lock had strayed.

Ignoring the party, which was roaring and surging about them, Wallace caught her hand and drew it tenderly toward his lips. Natalie was uneasy with public displays of affection, but when he kissed her palm a little electric tremor began to wander down her spine.

"Hey, Wallace! Your boat's a regular pleasure palace of Kubla Cohn. Ha. Ha. Ha. Gas cost much?"

"You want to buy coats from this peasant?" Wallace muttered. Then he greeted Weintraub, a young man with a black mustache, a shiny Korean leather jacket, and a heavy gold bracelet on his hairy wrist. "J. P. Morgan was right, Stevie."

"About what?"

"If you have to ask what it costs to run a yacht, marry your investment banker. I stopped worrying about gas when my beautiful wife turned Nevsky Russian Furs into Cotillion Furs, Limited."

Natalie rated that a classic Wallace Nevsky statement—an armor-piercing admixture of truth, exaggeration, and high drama—and she loved him for it, even though he was undercutting the work she had done to do a deal with Weintraub. In reality, even the Pentagon would have questioned the sanity of maintaining *Panache*'s polished brass, gleaming woodwork, and aging machinery. As for creating Cotillion's national salon chain, Natalie thought she deserved half the credit, although for reasons she couldn't fathom, it pleased Wallace to boast she had done it all.

When Weintraub stalked off, she said, "You forgot to be nice."

"Forgive me. He'll be back, I promise. He needs Cotillion. *We* don't need him."

Natalie did a quick take on a couple of name tags. "Darling, here are Bryce and Judy Hatch, from Idaho."

"Welcome aboard. Natalie couldn't stop talking about how exciting you made her stay in Boise."

Mrs. Hatch was bright-eyed on champagne. "Did anyone ever tell you your wife looks like Cybill Shepherd with dark hair?"

"Often," said Wallace. "But Natalie's so much prettier." He always said it with such conviction that Natalie almost believed him. She had the height, and the shoulders, but she considered her face much too angular to rate the comparison.

"I've been watching you two run your party. You're the most romantic couple."

"Actors," Wallace whispered. "Cotillion hires us for the image. The real Wallace and Natalie are watching TV in their stateroom."

As the franchise owners departed, Natalie murmured, "They're not watching TV."

"Making love like minks?"

"They're having a fight about business. He's a real conservative senior citizen type. She's an air-headed yuppie who—Darling, there she is again! By the companionway. Oh, you missed her." She had a disquieting sensation that the woman had plunged into the crowd to hide.

"Maybe a model escaped."

"She's not a model." One of the first things Natalie had learned in the fur trade was that elegant fur models were black or Chinese. Blondes played businesswomen and housewives.

"I better find out who she is."

Wallace caught her arm. "That's what we pay security for. Delegate. They catch the crashers. We run the party."

"Right. Delegate."

Delegate was their latest catch phrase. They had expanded business to the extent that they had to stop pretending Cotillion was a mom and pop operation and get organized. That meant hiring managers, but so far they were still in the talking stages, despite warning rumbles from their banks and investors who had begun to express a strong interest in running things properly.

"There she is! I'll get security. No, I'll let security find her."

Wallace said, "Here's Leo."

A short round furrier swaggered up, sporting three badges of success: a mahogany Florida suntan, an immense cigar, and a fat diamond pinkie ring. If Stevie Weintraub's *schlock* imports represented the pits of the modern fur trade, Leo Margulies's quarter-million-dollar Russian lynx coats were the ultimate in quality and design. Despite a certain undeniable grossness in his manner, Leo was that rarest of artists—a craftsman with taste.

He and Wallace had been friends and occasional business partners for close to fifty years.

Ignoring Natalie, he barked, "What the hell happened in Leningrad?"

She knew that the old-timers in the New York fur trade considered Wallace the real furrier and her an outsider who just happened to have a talent for selling franchises. Being half Wallace's age didn't help her image. Coming from an old New York WASP family confused them. Marrying him made some think she was a fortune hunter. Now and then, it hurt.

Wallace noticed and galloped to the rescue before Natalie could stop him. "Leo, if you can't greet your hostess, and if you won't say hello to my wife, will you at least, please, stand on your tippity-tip toes and kiss the cheek of the smartest furrier aboard my yacht?"

Leo blinked at the very thought of Natalie as a furrier. An innovator in retailing, he might agree. Not that he was into mass market. But when it came to acquiring and dressing pelts, or the intricate manufacturing processes, or even the arcane financing—more akin to a medieval ghetto than a billion-dollar business—Natalie's knowledge was like a newspaper reporter's, acquired rather than absorbed.

She had read, haunted the workrooms, and even traveled to auctions when Wallace was bidding elsewhere. She had learned that let-out skins were halved down the *grotzen,* that *grotzen* was Yiddish for "backbone," and that the halves were sliced apart and resewn to make them long and supple; but Wallace, Leo, and Stevie Weintraub's father had refined the process with their own hands for decades. She could detect color blending with a magnifying glass; Leo could spot a tip-dyed coat across Carnegie Hall.

"As a furrier, honey," Leo said, standing dutifully on tiptoe to reach her cheek, "you're a hell of a banker."

Wallace rounded on him with a dangerous smile. Leo had gone too far, for which he would pay.

"It was the best Russian lynx auction I have ever attended," Wallace said. "I bought skins as white as angels' hearts. Skins you would kill for."

"Terrific."

"Well, not so terrific."

"What?"

"I'm afraid I have to cut you out this time."

"*What?*" Leo's tan turned purple. He pulled the cigar from his mouth and stepped closer, his nose almost touching Wallace's chest. "What do you mean, cut me out? You're my broker. Don't joke, Wallace. I need those skins. You marked them for *me.*"

Wallace was the leading broker of luxury wild furskins on the international fur auction circuit. Shuttling between Leningrad, Copenhagen, Ontario, and Seattle, he examined hundreds of thousands of pelts a year and bid on those he had "marked" in his catalog. He also bought Cotillion's ranched mink and fox, and marked for other furriers on commission, but his first love, and great skill, was selecting wild Russian furs for specialists like Leo.

"Sorry, Leo. I marked them for Natalie."

"Right," said Natalie, returning a grin over Leo's head. "Cotillion gets first dibs."

"*What?* Your customers wouldn't know a Russian lynx if it jumped off a tree and bit 'em on the ass."

"On the contrary, Leo," she said. "We're going to float some big ticket items in the Diana Darbee line. I'm hoping you'll make me some tiny little capes we can sell for less than a BMW."

"Listen, you two. Women who wear Russian lynx have rich boyfriends. Your yuppie girls are too busy making careers to even *meet* guys like that."

"Not true, Leo. Natalie's latest market research projects that one out of a hundred Cotillion customers has a two-in-five chance of meeting one of your guys on a business trip."

Leo was not sure he was being put on. The Cotillion empire, after all, was founded on the buying habits of young urban professionals. "No problem. You're not the only broker buying skins for Leo Margulies."

"Wallace saw him marking mink with a muskrat eye."

"Gimme a break. I'll go back to Leningrad and buy my own, like I used to."

Wallace encircled Leo in a long, thin arm. "You're too rich and lazy to go to Leningrad anymore," he said affectionately. "I'll make it easy on you. Have lunch with Natalie. Talk about capes. Come back to the office and we'll talk lynx."

"How is it you two make me feel like a Ping-Pong ball? I ought to sue."

"I'm offering lunch with my beautiful wife and you're talking lawyers? You ought to sue the surgeon who rearranged your prostate."

"Wallace, that's disgusting."

"Sorry, darling."

"What'd he say?" asked Leo.

On Wallace's command, *Panache* ran before the wind and he and Natalie led the party on deck to see the Statue of Liberty so the crew could set up folding chairs and a runway for the models. They slipped off for a moment alone on the wing that projected from the wheelhouse. Wallace shivered in the evening air and Natalie put her arm around him.

"Tired?"

"Dead. What a flight." He had literally just gotten off the plane and Natalie knew he was running on nerves.

"Let's go in before you get cold. You're on in a minute."

Wallace took her by the shoulders. His strength always startled her. She often felt ungainly, yet he could move her body like a dancer. He kissed her tenderly on the mouth.

"What was that for?" she asked, not ready to forgive him for screwing up her Stevie Weintraub campaign.

"I missed you."

"Take me along, next time."

"I can't take you to an auction. There's too much pressure. I've got to mark skins and eat and sleep on my own schedule."

"But I haven't seen Russia since I was three. About all I remember is cabbage soup and cigarette smoke."

"It's much the same, except the girls are younger."

She had tried to go back as a student, but in the unhappy aftermath of détente, Brezhnev's Soviet Union had not welcomed frequent visitors or even former foreign residents. For years she had cherished a vivid memory of toddling down a broad and endless boulevard eating ice cream in winter with her beloved babushka, until her father had explained acidly that cheery old Nini had spied on the embassy for the KGB.

"I want to see you there," Natalie persisted. "Something there makes you tick."

"You make me tick."

"How about Christmas?" she asked, brushing him softly with her hip.

"We'll talk. Tonight."

"I've heard that before."

"I promise," he said, and she believed him.

They returned to the salon, arm in arm, and their guests followed. Wallace regained his energy, as he always did, and they gave him a big hand when he bounded onto the runway.

Natalie loved to watch him work a crowd. There was plenty of salesman in him, but the hustle was tempered by his natural grace, for he was deeply civilized, as if he had seen much more of life than most men, yet somehow managed to love it all.

"Raise your hand," he commanded, "if you attended Cotillion's first collection."

A scattered ten hands shot proudly in the air. Natalie turned around to acknowledge the pioneers and noticed that the blonde with the bare shoulders had found an aisle seat in the eighth row. She had a Hermès clutch, stunning diamond earrings, and a large, single stone suspended between her breasts. The diamonds were old, rose-cuts, undoubtedly genuine, which deterred Natalie from alerting security. Stranger she might be, but hardly desperate.

"Remember? Crammed into that little suite at the Waldorf? Now look at us. Five years later, we're a hundred franchises strong. Coast to coast. How did this happen?

"Like this, ladies and gentlemen. Vintage Cotillion—quality furs for the affluent working girl." Music boomed from the speaker stacks. And Cotillion's models streamed into the light.

Mink, dark and classic, was the heart of the Cotillion empire because Natalie Stuart had earned her fortune selling conservative quality coats to conservative young businesswomen. She watched proudly as the models paraded the line. Dancing to a sensual rock club beat, they twirled the dark furs into airy folds that seemed to float above the runway. She knew her customers from her own investment banking days. She knew the life and knew the rules. Cotillion coats were in and out of corporate reception rooms, airplanes, and business hotels.

A pony-tailed photographer in a leather vest with no shirt and spandex stretch pants pushed to the front, his strobe light blazing. Natalie ground her teeth. No matter how stylish the fashion event, no matter how carefully choreographed, there was always some photographer or disk jockey who looked like Mick Jagger just off his motorcycle. She recognized this one as a star from *Vogue* and smiled politely as he strutted by, flexing his glutes.

Of course, the new line paid homage to the wealthy look the luxury designers were selling this season, but she had persuaded her stylists to raise hems and tone down the big shawl and wing collars to match the pocketbooks and traditional tastes of her earnest customers, who were not yet rich, but working hard at it.

"Boring," Wallace would tease. "Where's their excitement?"

"Weekends."

The last coat of the main line was a lavish, light mahogany hooded mink, which they both knew wouldn't sell, but couldn't resist showing. As the model whirled it away and Wallace returned to center stage, Natalie rated the franchise owners' applause midway between gratifying and reassuring, not bad at all for a season that had them nervous.

Wallace opened the lions' cage door, saying, "I keep hearing rumors about price wars and foreign competition and our old boogeyman, another recession. Stop worrying. Recessions come and go, but Cotillion women don't lose jobs, they make jobs. And price wars are for *schlockers*. That's a Yiddish word that means discounters who sell cheap, shoddy foreign furs." He looked straight at Stevie Weintraub and at that moment Natalie thought she could cheerfully shoot him.

"But we've invested millions in national TV advertising to reach Cotillion customers who demand American quality."

Natalie glanced around at the franchise holders, wondering how many would be delighted to sell imports, what with Fred the Furrier and a hundred imitators breathing down their necks.

"So grab a glass, ladies and gentlemen, because we're going to toast 'Cotillion Furs, the Smart Woman's Furrier.' "

Salon owners roared to their feet, cheering for the advertising slogan that had made them all a lot of money. Wallace called for Natalie and she joined him reluctantly on the runway, shying from the crowd that surged about them. A forest of arms stretched for glasses as the waiters popped champagne corks off the ceiling.

"How're we doing?" Wallace whispered.

"*I* believe."

"You wrote it."

The blonde in the halter-top gown pushed through the crowd and emerged suddenly in front of them, two steps below the makeshift runway. Natalie's eye was drawn to an Art Nouveau rose-cut diamond bracelet on her bare arm. She wore a black glove. Nestled in the glove was something impossible—a small gun rising darkly toward Natalie's face.

The gun was half-hidden in the glove, lost where the gown swelled over her hip, and no one but Natalie saw it. Her guests were straining toward the waiters popping corks. Her husband was reaching for a glass to make his toast. In terror, she felt time freeze. Conceding that what she saw made no sense, surrendering useless why's, she gained the focus to distinguish each minute detail of the attack.

Fine muscle rippled in the woman's sleek arm. Her eyes narrowed. Anger stretched her lips like steel mesh across her teeth. The split second soared toward climax. Natalie heard music, laughter, and Wallace's voice. She drove her hand at the gun.

It swept past as if her fingers were made of air. Too late, she realized that the woman was aiming at Wallace, not at her. The gun jumped. It made a champagne *pop*. Popped again. Wallace coughed and turned to Natalie. An astonished expression crossed his face as if he realized he had made a terrible mistake.

The woman whispered something, lowered her gun, and turned into the crowd, which was still oblivious to the attack. Sad, weary lines gathered around Wallace's eyes and a look of infinite regret seemed to spill over his face like a glaze.

Natalie caught him as he fell and someone laughed.

"Look at those two, always kissing."

BOOK ONE

WIDOW'S WALK

1

The part of Natalie that believed Wallace was dead was nearly dead itself. The part that could not believe it handled the police. Each new detective they brought to her stateroom started with the same mistake. "Your father—"

"My husband," she corrected patiently, as if shock and horror could be contained in a cage of proper behavior. "My husband," she repeated. "My husband. My husband."

"Excuse me. How old was Mr. Nevsky?"

"Wallace was in his sixties."

The detectives walked around the cabin, running their big hands over the racks of fur coats. The models had used the owner's cabin because its bathrooms had mirrored dressing tables. They had left debris: an eyebrow pencil on Wallace's night table, sprinkles of powder, and long cigarette butts ringed with dark lipstick.

"And, uh . . ."

"I'm thirty-two."

They exchanged looks and zeroed in on age. "And how old did you say the woman was with the gun?"

"Twenty-five, I'd guess."

"Did you recognize her?"

"No."

"Can you describe her?"

She had already described her for the police computer artist, but she answered patiently because their questions, dreamlike in their familiar pattern, seemed out of books and movies, which suggested nothing real had happened.

She would go home and Wallace would be waiting, tired from his long flight, comfortable in a cashmere robe. . . . Brandy and warm milk . . . Bed . . . Bed.

"Mrs. Nevsky?"

"She was a very attractive blonde. She had broad features. I thought her gown was European. Oh, I just remembered. Wallace thought she was wearing a wig."

"Grand," muttered a detective.

"What do you mean he thought? *Was* it a wig?"

"I missed it. If he said it was a wig, it was a wig."

"How could a guy spot a wig you couldn't?"

"A man who sells furs for fifty years knows more about women than women."

"Do you have any idea why a stranger would shoot your husband?"

"No."

"Did Mr. Nevsky recognize her?"

"I don't think he saw her face."

"Can you think of any enemies he had?"

"He had no enemies."

"Excuse me, Mrs. Nevsky, but a furrier fifty years makes enemies. I know, my old man was a furrier."

"Ask your father about Wallace Nevsky. Ask him about the Cossack. He was loved." She turned eagerly to the others. "Wallace was a fur broker. He bought skins at auction for other furriers. He deals in fortunes over a handshake or a promise on the phone."

"A broker's got all kinds of ways to finagle," the furrier's son insisted. "Plenty of chances to hold up a manufacturer."

"There isn't a furrier in New York who wouldn't trust Wallace with his last dollar," Natalie said flatly.

"Okay. Could this be maybe related to the company you own? Burned investors. Somebody thinks he's owed?"

Natalie shook her head. "I'm president and chief financial officer. No one's lost an investment. No one's been cheated."

It was the third or fourth detective—she was losing concentration by then—who repeated with an emphasis Natalie missed at first. "No one?"

"Wallace Nevsky was an honest man."

Detective Lieutenant Kunitz, who had been pacing, sat in the armchair opposite Natalie's and looked through his notes, as if wondering what to ask next. He motioned his partners out of the cabin. They left, closing the door. He was a big bear of a man, his manner direct, but his voice gentle.

"If you're up to it, Mrs. Nevsky, I'd like to go through the hours before the shooting." Natalie nodded. "According to his driver, Mr. Nevsky arrived JFK approximately three o'clock, stopped a moment at your apartment on Central Park West, and got to the boat just before five."

"I wasn't aware he had stopped at the apartment."

"He also stopped at a pay phone on Riverside Drive. Was it you he called?"

"No. Why would he use a pay phone? There's a phone in the car."

"He told the driver it wasn't working."

"No, he didn't call me."

"Any idea who?"

"It could have been anybody. He'd have bought skins in Russia for a dozen manufacturers, at least."

"So, he got aboard and the boat left the slip. Then what?"

"Wallace ran below to change into his dinner jacket."

"Did you see him?"

"Of course. We said hello. And he ran—"

"Just hello? He'd been away two weeks."

"We were giving a party for two hundred people. We kissed. I told him I'd be down in ten minutes to help him with his cuff links."

"Was that the next you saw him?"

"I went down. He had dried off from a shower and was putting on his dress shirt. He had already done his studs and he had the links in one side. I put them in the other side."

"What did you talk about?"

"We really didn't have much time."

The detective consulted his notebook, a little pad in a leather slipcase. Natalie knew her mind was barely working, but she had the impression he had checked his notes for show. "People saw you enter the main salon together at five twenty-five, five-thirty. You were down here in the stateroom for fifteen or twenty minutes. . . . So what did you talk about?"

She still fought not to cry, and it was equally important not to surrender her and Wallace's privacy, but the veneer of correct behavior was proving thin as November ice. "We didn't talk."

"For twenty minutes? I don't understand. What am I missing?"

Natalie's chin came up. Her eyes darkened and her voice became mechanically clear. "We made love."

"Christ, I'm sorry. It didn't occur to me with all those people waiting."

Memory seized her voice and started to gallop away from her. "I just kissed him when I did his cuff links and he picked me up—this really isn't any of your business."

"Right," said the detective, glancing at the bed that the models had rumpled.

In fact, they had never reached the bed. Wallace had lifted her in both hands and backed against the dressing table as they glued themselves mouth to mouth and pelvis to pelvis, kissing wildly and arching their backs, at first, like a pair of cats so as not to wrinkle his shirt and her dress.

"This makes my next question easier." The detective looked embarrassed as he handed Natalie a clear plastic bag that held a pair of her white silk panties.

Ordinarily she would have felt embarrassed. Now she said simply, "Wallace liked to tease me. He put them in his pocket like a handkerchief."

"Keep 'em," said the detective. "I think I can build a case without them. . . . What was he like—I mean his state of mind."

Triumphant, Natalie recalled. She had seen it in his face when he ran up the gangway. High and happy. Glad to be home. Exuberant. Excited. And . . . hungry. Here in their stateroom, hungry like a warrior who had won in the world and come home to claim his reward. These were not things the detective would understand. She didn't understand them herself, but Wallace was never an easy read.

"We were happy to see each other. . . . We always were." Her voice caught in her throat and she swallowed hard, staring at the floor.

"Did he say anything about his trip?"

"Just that things went well."

"Did anything strike you as unusual?"

Natalie looked at the dressing table. Standing up, fumbling like kids, beating against each other like two hands clapping . . . and then the surprise. A quickie was, by definition, fast. She had not expected any sort of earth-moving orgasm, not with two hundred people waiting for a fashion show that would make or break Cotillion Furs in the year to come. Wherever they left off, they would pick up later, at home in a proper bed. But Wallace had surprised her.

Something in him—that primitive sense of victory, perhaps—had pierced her deeply, shearing through distractions, obliterating time. Forgotten were guests, purpose, even wrinkled clothes. His body met hers in a long, hard line from their lips to their thighs. She remembered screaming. . . . She looked up, half expecting to see the cry still circling the cabin walls. When it was over they clung to each other, trembling violently on watery knees.

"Nothing unusual."

"Did he seem different?"

"He was always different. Every day was new."

"Did he seem worried?"

"Not at all."

"Was he distracted?"

"Not in the slightest. Wallace was rarely distracted. Whatever he did he did fully. In the moment. It was a gift he had. . . ."

"Did the woman say anything?"

Natalie stood up and retreated to the pipe hangers where the coats were. Mechanically, she stroked one, the luxury mink, the natural, hooded model she and Wallace knew wouldn't sell.

"Mrs. Nevsky?"

Too expensive for their customers. Too extravagant for a young woman who was starting out and needed to appear serious.

"*Mrs. Nevsky!* You've been wonderful. Can you hang in just a little longer? What did the woman say when she shot your husband?"

"I wish I had stopped her. She moved so fast."

"Don't start blaming yourself. Nobody stops a gun with her hand. Most people don't even try. What'd she say?"

"How did she get off the boat?"

"We don't know yet. But that wig probably helped. What did she say? What'd she say," he coaxed, somehow communicating with the sound of his voice that he knew and it was safe to tell him. But her natural sense of privacy resisted seduction. It was not her way to discuss secrets. Particularly secrets that menaced her belief in herself.

"What did she say, Mrs. Nevsky?"

It was frightening how the man seemed to read her mind.

The woman had whispered one word, *Traitor*. Spit it, as she pulled the trigger. *Traitor*.

"What did she say?"

"Nothing."

"Are you sure?"

"She said nothing."

"And you say he never cheated."

"Ask anyone in New York, London, or Leningrad."

"I meant on you."

Natalie let go of the coat. "I've given you my statement. I'm going home."

"Did he cheat on you?" the detective repeated. "Am I looking for the other woman?"

"You wouldn't ask that question if he'd been shot by a man."

"Not right off," he admitted. "But your husband wasn't shot by a man. He was shot by a beautiful woman, even younger than you, Mrs. Nevsky."

"I told your artist what I saw. You've got the computer sketch, right there."

The killer's face stared emptily off the page. Missing, Natalie knew, were both her intensity and her rage. The former had been beyond the artist and his machine. And Natalie had been unable to bring herself to describe the rage. Like the whispered *Traitor,* the anger shrieked of a personal connection she refused to admit to the detective, or herself.

Natalie picked up the ship's intercom. Joannie Frye, Cotillion's administrator, answered, "Yes, Natalie."

"We're going home. Please get a car."

"You're hiding something," the detective persisted, but her resolve had hardened. This was between her and Wallace. She would never tell a soul.

"I am hiding my tears. I have answered questions for hours. I have a right to cry alone."

"Of course."

He walked her off the boat to the waiting limousine. Outside the pier gates, reporters clamored. "We'll need to talk in a few days."

"My office will know where I am. This is Joannie Frye. She can always find me." Joannie and the detective measured each other until both were clear that from now on all calls came through the tough and capable young woman from Queens.

"Is there someone who can speak for you? A lawyer, maybe."

That stopped her because she found it impossible to plan the next sixty seconds. She thought of Greg, who had introduced her to Wallace. "My cousin Greg Stuart lives in Greenwich."

He closed the door. She didn't remember getting in the car. A thought hit her and she lowered the window. "My husband was Jewish. I think he's supposed to be buried by sundown."

"I'm afraid with a homicide it will be a few days with the medical examiner. Was he religious?"

"No. But he liked ceremony."

Reporters trailed her car uptown to their Central Park West apartment. Wallace had lived there since the early fifties. When they married they had agreed it would be wise to start new with their own place, but Cotillion had kept them too busy.

"There's more of them," said Joannie. "Dammit, I tried to get Kenny over here but he's still with the cops." Kenny Wilson headed Cotillion's merchandise security department. Reporters and photographers mobbed the car as it pulled up to the canopy, overwhelming the doorman and her driver, screaming questions through the glass.

"Who was she? Did you know her?"

Natalie stared back blankly, distantly aware that she had lost control of everything happening around her.

Suddenly they scattered. An old Puerto Rican porter had come up from the service entrance, dragging the hose he used to wash the sidewalk, and was solemnly spraying the reporters, thanking Wallace, Natalie knew, for getting his children into the union.

"Get the vultures," yelled Joannie, throwing an arm around Natalie and hustling her into the building.

Natalie tried to remember the last words he had said to her.

"I'll come up with you," said Joannie.

"No. Get some sleep. You'll have your hands full at the office tomorrow." Joannie tried to hug her, but Natalie pulled away and fled into the elevator.

Upstairs, alone in the big empty apartment, she wished she was still answering questions for the police. She wondered if she could sleep, forget, and wake up with everything as it used to be. She headed for their bedroom, walking familiarly through dark rooms. She felt her body start to desert her and was abruptly too tired to undress. She dropped a shoe and climbed onto the bed and lay back against the heaped pillows. Something hard was in the way.

Reaching for the light, she found a big box on the bed wrapped in silver paper and bound in ribbons. The limo driver had told the detective that Wallace had stopped at the apartment between the airport and the boat. She opened the envelope slowly, nursing the frail connection to a moment of his life.

He had folded a note around a pair of Aeroflot tickets and some Intourist vouchers for the Astoria Hotel in Leningrad, the National in Moscow, and the *Red Arrow* night train, which connected the cities. "For my Natasha, from mysterious Russia, with all my love, to keep you warm when we go this winter."

Natalie's heart soared. He loved surprises, so he hadn't told her at the show, intending to surprise her tonight. He was taking her to Russia, after years of pleading that she wanted to see him in the country that seemed so much a part of what he was. Memory smashed into her like a stone. Too late.

His hand was shaky and she had to turn the paper to the light to read the rest. "Should we start a baby in the City of the Czars?"

"No," she whispered. "It's not fair." What could have changed his mind? Dead set against children, he had argued he was too old. A stranger might have written that. But the last line, a postscript, was pure Wallace Nevsky.

"P.S. Dare you to wear it to a Junior League lunch with your mother, you uptight Wasp."

As if he were alive with her in the bedroom, she said, "Wallace, what have you done?" and she tore the silver paper. It was a Leo Margulies box, which meant he'd bought the skins on the last trip and given them to Leo, the best mechanic in the business. She opened the box with a startled, "Oh, my God!"

Wallace had gone wild. The coat spilled out in the light. Russian lynx, fashioned from pure white bellies, which were speckled with subtle black markings like dry leaves fallen on an early snow. Junior League? The Saudi oil minister's concubine would have blushed to wear it to Nell's. The gift was so Wallace, and so emblematic of their marriage. She could never wear such a flamboyant extravagance unless she was out with him.

Burying her face in the silken fur, rocking back and forth on the unopened bed, she thought she would cry. But the tears wouldn't come. Battered by the terrible night, she extinguished the light, curled her long arms and legs into a tight ball, and huddled under the fur.

For hours, events raced before her eyes, *Panache* in the sunset, the party, the game they played with Leo, the show, Wallace's performance, the gun, her husband dead in her arms. And the police. *And you say he never cheated. Ask anyone in New York, London, or Leningrad. I meant on you.*

Sometime before dawn, she got angry.

She climbed off the bed. She removed her wrinkled gown, stripped off her clammy lingerie and stockings, and took a long, hot shower. First light found her standing in the window, wrapped in the lynx coat, staring at the park.

"Who is she?"

Only then, when she realized that Wallace could never answer, much less explain, did Natalie Stuart Nevsky finally cry.

2

The morning of the funeral she stood alone with his casket in a private chapel at Riverside, still struggling to make nonsense of his murder because anything more than nonsense shrieked of involvement between the man she loved and the woman who killed him.

Had Wallace known her?

It was a terrible question. Like a glacier, rumbling between Wallace in death and Natalie in life, it threatened to flatten everything they had shared, grinding love and passion and trust into lies. Loving him, trusting him, weeping for him, she struggled for an answer.

Maybe the woman had mistaken Wallace for her intended victim. Maybe she was a professional killer. But there was no mistaking her anger. And what did *traitor* mean? Perhaps the woman *was* a crazy. Certainly Wallace had been a public figure, with his picture regularly in the trades to draw the attention of the strange and bent. But there was no irrationality in the coldly executed attack and the neat escape. The police had even dragged the harbor, an exercise as futile as questioning all two hundred people on *Panache*, but the "Mystery Blonde," as the newspapers called her, had simply vanished. The police made noises about an accomplice in a boat, though no boat was found. A newspaper cartoonist whose work she ordinarily enjoyed had joined the circus, depicting a sexy mink swimming from the yacht in scuba gear.

She was losing the strength to fight logic. All she could do was repeat to herself what she had told the detective. Had Wallace's killer been another man, instead of a young woman, they would ask more than *had he cheated?*

There was a knock on the door and someone entered softly.

Her hands flew to the casket. "I'm not ready."

But it was not the morticians come to hurry her along. "You've got a minute," a familiar voice assured her. "They're still coming in."

Her cousin Greg Stuart had taken firm charge of the funeral, procuring a swift release of Wallace's body and shielding her from the details. They had been friends almost as long as Natalie could remember, since the Vineyard summer when she was twelve and Greg, a lordly eighteen, had allowed her to crew on his sailboat.

A fair-haired, fine-featured man, he was dressed for mourning, this terrible day, in a charcoal suit and somber tie. But she would always see Greg as she had through an adolescent gaze—a suntanned college student, impossibly adult, with a quick wit, golden hair, and eyes as blue as the Sound.

He closed an arm around her shoulder. Natalie sagged gratefully against him. "You're a godsend. I couldn't handle it."

"You're not expected to."

"Isn't it strange? You introduced us and now you're picking up the pieces."

"I wish I could."

"I have to know why he was killed."

"Of course, Natalie. But first, let's just get through today. And remember, whatever you need, come to me."

"Thanks, but the office is running itself, somewhat. I've got good people."

"Or if something crops up outside of business. There's a number on this card. I'll be down in Washington. They can find me anytime. I want you to promise to call me if anything unusual should come up. Anything."

"It's just this woman. But you can't help me with that."

"No," Greg agreed. "Let the police do their job."

"What's all that noise out there?"

"Diana, mourning. With entourage and stampeding paparazzi."

"I wish she hadn't come."

"Old girlfriends never die," said Greg. "They just hang around."

He laid a hand on the polished casket and when Natalie looked up at him, tears were streaming down his cheeks. "It's all right," he said heartily, but the firm line of his mouth was crumbling.

"Whatever you need," he repeated, and she had a funny feeling that Greg shared a bond with Wallace she hadn't known about until this minute. Before she could ask, the chapel door flew open and Diana Darbee burst in, trailing clouds of blonde hair, black silk, and the perfume that bore her own label, the best-selling Diana.

"Oh, Natalie, you poor thing."

If private school, dancing class, and tea with grandmother amounted to anything, it was preparation for moments like this. "Hello, Diana. Thank you for coming."

"If only I had been standing next to him, I could have done something."

"There was nothing to do."

"I would have stopped her if I had seen her."

"I tried. It happened very fast."

"Could I be alone with him, for a minute?"

It cut like a knife. Diana and Wallace had remained friends, kidding-around pals, maybe more. Natalie had been afraid to ask, afraid she would see him lie. That admission made her angry and she said, "No. No. I'm sorry."

Greg advanced surely on Diana, indicating the door, and his face brooked no resistance. The actress's mouth tightened angrily, but when the bright light left her eyes, she looked as if she would cry. Natalie relented.

"Of course. I'll leave you for a minute."

She went out with Greg, then stood by the door, counting sixty seconds. "Greg?"

"What?"

"Ride with me to the cemetery?"

"Of course, but what about Mike and your parents?"

"My brother's got a look in his eye that says that men aren't shot by blondes they don't know. And I will not sit with my mother and father pretending they didn't look down on my husband the furrier."

They went back into the chapel.

Diana had recovered. "Christ on a crutch, what a waste. He'd have kept going twenty more years."

"They're ready to start."

"Hang on. I want to talk to you a minute."

"We're running late."

"Hey, no one's going anywhere without Wallace. We have to talk."

"Diana, what do we have to talk about right now?"

"A group of Cotillion shareholders asked me to throw in with them."

"What for?"

"Against you. They don't believe you can run Cotillion without Wallace."

"I run it already."

"You run the franchises. Wallace bought the skins and hired the manufacturers. You're sales. He's production."

"They think I don't know the fur trade?"

"Do you?"

"I'm learning," Natalie replied seriously. Whatever else she thought of Diana, she respected her as a businesswoman who had turned television stardom into a multimillion-dollar label-licensing enterprise.

"I'll call a board meeting tomorrow."

"Too soon," said Greg. "Let it wait."

"Do it," said Diana. "You've got my proxy for the moment."

"What do you mean, 'for the moment'?"

"If these 'Blonde Shoots Furrier' headlines don't quiet down real fast, I'm pulling my name off your new line."

"What? You can't."

"I came to the funeral for Wallace. I had to. But I'm not losing ten years' work getting my name on bathing suits and perfume bottles to some bimbo with a gun."

"What are you saying?"

"Natalie, I'm *Diana Darbee*. I'm a fucking institution. Look why you hired my label. I'm smart, sexy, and honest. That's what I sell. I can't be connected to some love triangle. People in love triangles are dishonest and stupid."

"It wasn't a triangle. I didn't even know her."

"That old *macher*. Always had to cut one more notch."

"No! Not with me."

"Sure about that? Natalie, if you have what it took to keep Wallace Nevsky home, I would suggest retiring from the fur trade and bottling it." She rapped her knuckles twice on the casket. "Or were you losing it, Wallace?"

"He lost *nothing*."

"Then we've got a problem. Because if they catch the bimbo and there's a trial, Diana's going to walk."

"We're shipping coats."

"Sorry."

"What about our ads? I have a whole campaign built around you."

"Pray she gets clean away."

"We have a contract, Diana."

"Read it. I get bounced if I'm a bad girl. I walk if you're a bad boy."

Wallace, Natalie thought bleakly, would have had a quick answer, but she did not, not today. She reached for Greg. They still had to bury him.

"It's business," said Diana.

"Is it?"

"What is that supposed to mean?" Diana crossed her arms and smiled. "Oh, yes. You think I'm doing this for revenge for your taking Wallace."

"I didn't take him."

Diana shrugged.

"How could I—a boring investment banker, that's what you called me—how could I take a man from Diana Darbee?"

"I have often wondered. But then again, Wallace was full of surprises, wasn't he?"

3

I keep thinking of the day you introduced us," Natalie told Greg as Wallace's cortège moved up the Henry Hudson Parkway. "Like I'll discover a clue. Like whatever went wrong was already going wrong that day."

"A clue?" Greg echoed solicitously, but her thoughts had already volleyed at another angle.

"I didn't take him from anyone. He took me."

"Diana knows that. Wallace was drifting till he found you."

"I thought I was the one drifting. . . . I was so cold and empty. You know, sometimes I'd wake up beside Wallace and think, what if I hadn't gone to Greg's party? What if I'd gone to the beach, instead, or stayed home in the air conditioning? I'd move closer to him, feeling so grateful. To you. To God. To whoever sets these things up. . . . Now it's like a dirty trick," she whispered bitterly. "I can't believe we only had five years."

She started to cry. Greg put his arm around her. "I think the thing you will remember is they were a unique five years. You two enjoyed things most people never have in a lifetime."

"We did, didn't we?" she said eagerly. "Right from the day we met. . . ." She pulled away from him and stared at the window. "Full circle, Greg. Here we are again. I don't know what's going on and you're so wise. What went wrong, Greg? Was it already wrong that day?"

*   *   *

She had had a fight with her father, their typically understated brand of fight that lingered like ice in her veins. Beating a pair of cousins on the tennis court in straight sets of Canadian doubles had not helped much. Nor had some angry laps in the pool. She had turned to champagne and finally, buzzed on Moët and the late summer sun, to Greg, who was hosting the Stuarts' end-of-summer party from a chaise longue a safe distance from the croquet lawn.

Greg had a cold bottle and a cordless telephone close at hand. He was, that year, working with the National Security Strategy Group, and awed children told Natalie that he had fielded two calls from the White House. Now his eyes were on his own children, a two- and a four-year-old tumbling on the grass and running to him with their discoveries.

"My father just hailed you as a paragon of civic virtue," she told him.

"He probably meant it as a compliment."

The annual party was a family tradition that anteceded Labor Day by generations. Ordinarily, they gathered at The Birches, the rustic family place high in the Berkshire Mountains, but Aunt Louisa, the matriarch who maintained it, had died in July, so Cousin Greg's wife, Sally, had offered her Greenwich home as a logical substitute until stewardship of the Berkshire place was sorted out.

Nearly a hundred Stuarts of the four generations were swimming, romping, lofting Frisbees, arguing over croquet, and playing tennis. Natalie had changed into her bathing suit in a mirrored cabana, had a swim, and discovered that Greg's wife had introduced champagne to an event that had survived a hundred years on beer and wine. Pausing for a refill at one of the several bowered bars maintained by the servants, she had gone for a look at the grounds.

A great deal of money had been spent in a hurry. Brilliant green lawns and gray stone terraces spilled down from the house to merge around a huge swimming pool into which stone flamingoes spewed water. The landscaper responsible for the flamingoes had presumably been the one to scatter French street lamps about the property, creating the odd effect of a privately held Central Park.

She had found her parents observing from the shade. Martha Stuart wore a plain white summer dress and no makeup. She had calm, steady eyes, which could turn very cold in defense of her husband or correct behavior, and was easily the most beautiful woman at the party. Natalie's father stood behind her chair, one hand on her shoulder, nursing a tall watered scotch. After forty years in the foreign service, Richard Stuart could make a single tall watered scotch last a week in Indian country, and while neither commented, Natalie knew that any place with flamingoes around the pool was Indian country on their map.

"Congratulations are in order, I suppose," her father had greeted her. "Vice-president. My, my."

Their tight-lipped fight had followed, as naturally as water runs downhill, and she had fled to the tennis court, the pool, and then the bar, heading ultimately toward Greg, but bumping first into Sally, who was as high as she was, and who complained, "I've shocked your family again. How the hell am I supposed to know they don't drink champagne on picnics?"

"They do when they can afford it," Natalie replied. "Personally I think champagne's a great idea."

Greg's wife was a mystery to her. A poised and sensual beauty— the spoiled only child of an indulgent father who had accumulated one of the great American fortunes in his own lifetime—why should she care what Greg's family thought of her?

There was no polite way to say, Don't try so hard, so she advised, instead, "Blame it on our missionary genes. You know, if it tastes good, it's probably bad. This tastes wonderful, by the way," she added, illustrating the compliment by draining her glass.

Sally propped her perfect chin in a nest of jeweled fingers and regarded Natalie with a mocking smile. "Maybe they don't like me because they think Greg married me for my father's money."

"Sally, we're both a little high, but Greg—"

"Maybe they think Greg doesn't love me."

Natalie was stunned. Two more beautiful-looking people had never walked into a room together. Greg and Sally were *the* couple.

"Easy there, little girl. I'm just kidding." Sally grinned. "Maybe they think the guy's supposed to take care of the girl."

"I don't," Natalie denied staunchly. "I'd rather take care of myself."

"I'd rather take care of myself," Sally echoed with another mocking smile. "Them missionary genes run really deep, don't they? Everyone's worried about paying the bills. But what they should worry about is how they get taken care of in their hearts. So they don't feel alone. Do you know? . . . You don't know, do you?"

Natalie flushed. Sally was gorgeous. Sally was wealthy. And now Sally was making her feel like an idiot.

"Have some more champagne, Natalie. Enjoy the party."

Before she could think of an answer, Sally had drifted toward the pool. Natalie had started after her, but changed her mind. Then, annoyed that her cousin's beautiful wife—like her own father—found her lacking, she had wandered on to Greg with her empty glass.

"Got a refill?"

Greg gave her maillot an appreciative look, hauled his bottle out of the ice, and glanced at the children who had crawled out of earshot to maul an enormous dog. "I wondered when you'd alight. We haven't talked since Christmas. Why did your papa compliment me?"

"Informed that I made associate and vice-president at Stuart, Malcolm and Hardy, he begged me to follow you into public service."

"The last refuge of the declining classes."

"Our same old argument: 'Good Christ, Natalie, turn your education and experience to something more important than raising capital for dubious mergers. You're a foreign service brat. You've lived our life. You speak tolerable French and excellent Russian.' The funny thing is, I'm actually thinking of quitting banking."

"Summer talk," Greg said mockingly. "A typical end-of-August, or Sunday night, or anytime-in-the-Caribbean career statement if I've ever heard one."

Natalie drained her glass. "I'm serious."

"I've never met an investment banker who wasn't serious about quitting. Nor have I ever met one who did. Lassitude about your victories is a perk, like limousines and dinner on the client."

"Lassitude suggests a loss of energy, which I am not suffering," she snapped. "I'm fed up making money for other people. I want my own business, something I can touch. So stop patronizing me."

"I am merely sharing the wisdom of a man below the fray. As an underpaid civil servant, I find it hard to believe you would walk away from a successful career. In the crunch, no one loses their zest for survival."

"*Below the fray?* If marrying well includes a French chateau imported stone by stone to thirty acres a short limo ride from Manhattan, then you are one underpaid civil servant who has married very well."

"Ah, but the price, the price."

"Tell me you've sold your soul?"

"Never! But the woman demands I sleep with her."

Natalie cast an envious look toward the pool where Sally had draped her exquisite body over the diving board like a poster for a Helmut Newton retrospective.

"That bathing suit looks like it was bonded on by Japanese technicians."

"Not to worry, they left plenty of solvent."

"How do you stand it?"

To her surprise, Greg's grin clouded. She had hit where she hadn't aimed and she said, "I'm sorry. I've had way too much to drink. Sally is very nice."

"She's not," he said, shortly, closing the subject with a counterattack. "Tell me, was this promotion for brilliance, hard work, or connections?"

"By connections, do you mean the family name on the door or a certain senior partner in my bed?"

Greg did not flinch. "I heard the partner's been barred from your bed. Something about getting too serious and leaving his wife?"

"You heard that in Washington?"

"I was referring, however, to our name on the door."

"Are you kidding? You know damned well they've kept the Stuart name for historical value, period. Old line and all that. I'm the first Stuart to pull her weight since the Crash of twenty-nine. Not that it makes much difference. Mr. Baker, our sterling chairman of the board, for whom I have worked for the past five years, lurched up to me a minute ago and asked about the drought in Chad."

"Chad?"

"He thinks I'm Jennifer in the Peace Corps."

"Don't take it too hard," Greg laughed. "I'm told RB is routinely carted from dinner with the soup."

"Then he called me an 'entrepreneuse.' Do you believe that?" Her uncharacteristic desire to confide was paling rapidly. "I'm monopolizing you. You ought to see to your other guests."

"It's the host's privilege to entertain his most attractive guest."

Natalie looked at him sharply. She felt, by comparison to Sally, an ungainly jumble of long arms and legs and wondered if Greg was making fun of her. "Was that a compliment or a pass?"

"A passing comment." He raised his voice to caution a child. "Jason, if that animal bites you for doing that to him he will be right and you will be wrong."

Natalie glanced apprehensively at the writhing tangle of child and dog. Greg noticed and patted her hand. "Don't worry. He doesn't bite. And if he tried his teeth would fall out."

They shared a smile and she decided to take Greg's remark as a compliment, which, along with the wine, made her feel bold. "How come I don't know you better?"

"We are distant cousins in a very large family." Greg watched his children release the dog and toddle like miniature drunks in the direction of their great aunt, who was moderating a vociferous croquet game from a fanback chair. "We have amusing chats at the summer party and Christmas. And we flirt a little—yes, we do. Don't turn away." Greg laughed. "In fact, I recall one Christmas when it got interesting. . . . Remember?"

Blame it on the champagne, she thought, but he was very beautiful to look at. The sun, which was angling across his tan face, seemed to light his blue eyes from within. He had a great mouth, which was full with a smile. Natalie was inclined to pursue "flirt-a-little" further, but not frontally. "Remind me."

"Da! Da!" Greg's little daughter ran up, pointing at the sky where a white new moon had risen like a slice lopped off a cloud.

"Moon," said Greg, scooping her into his arms. "That's the moon."

Young parents, an exasperated Natalie reflected, not for the first time, were maddeningly mercurial: one moment she and Greg were trading significant glances and perhaps edging toward a new stage of the titillation they had enjoyed since she was a teenager; the next moment she had ceased to exist as her handsome cousin broke into song.

Mr. Moon, Mr. Moon,
You're out too soon,
The sun's still up in the sky.

Greg accompanied these lyrics with extravagant gestures, which drove his daughter wild and left Natalie feeling grateful that at twenty-six she had many childbearing years to go before she had to make that particular decision.

"More," Fiona roared.

Go back to bed,
And cover up your head,
Until the day goes by.

When the child departed at last, Natalie said, "Now I remember that Christmas. You recited our genealogy."

"I was merely explaining that we are distant enough, cousin-wise, to bear children no more idiotic than ourselves."

"Children? You didn't even kiss me."

"I had the impression you seemed more kissable than you were. No, what we mostly have in common is a droplet or two of blue, blue New York blood and perhaps a vague sense of dissatisfaction."

"I thought you were happy in Washington."

"Oh, I *am* happy. In Washington. As the senior senator from Mississippi praised me the other day, I'm like a catfish in mud, too prickly to eat and growing bigger every year."

"Ambitious?"

"I'm sure you don't believe we're all as high-minded as your father. Which brings us back to why you're so ambivalent about your associateship."

"I'm a servant, just a middleman. I want to do something real."

Just then, Natalie's brother Mike came padding across the lawn, approaching hesitantly, as if acknowledging a certain contained aura around Greg and Natalie that should not be disturbed.

He was balancing six champagne glasses, three in each hand, a skill he had learned while bartending the summer before on Cape Cod. Natalie thought the job had been a brave, if small, attempt to step beyond their cloistered world, but their father had disparaged it as a descent into the ordinary. This summer he had demanded that Mike take a job at State, but Natalie had encouraged her brother to draw the same line she had several years before, and Michael had interned, instead, at her own firm, SM&H. What he didn't know yet was that that line had to be redrawn almost daily. Natalie could only guess as to whether he was up to the fight, although she feared that her mother, who lived quite comfortably by basic axioms, was probably right when she rated her son as a typically aimless second child.

Mike, like Natalie, had inherited their father's height and dark hair, but flesh clumped to his frame, and self-indulgence marked his soft face.

"Excuse me. Message from Mom. Dad's over his mad."

"Grow up," Natalie snapped, annoyed at the interruption. "You're too old to carry her messages."

"She didn't tell me. I deduced it from the subtext."

He squatted beside them, red from the sun and smiling goofily from the champagne. Natalie noticed he was getting fat again. She poked his gut, leaving a white spot. "You're burning. There's lotion in the cabana."

"Your sister," Greg said, "wants to give up banking for something real."

Mike grinned, surer of his welcome. Now that he had spent a summer on Wall Street and was about to start his third year at Wharton, observations upon the business world slid freely from his tongue. "Doing something 'real' is every banker's dream. Instead of earning billions for other people, you think, 'Hey, I'm going to find a nice company, work a no-cash leveraged buyout, pay the interest out of earnings, and run the business myself.' Only trouble is, investment bankers aren't managers. You don't know the first thing about business, marketing, inventory, managing people."

"Nothing I can't learn."

"Sure you can. Until one day you're negotiating across the table from a pack of union radicals when the telephone rings—the truck that left Cleveland last week seems to have meandered to Mexico. At that moment the cops knock on the door to inform you that the rock star who promotes the new product is facing ten-to-twenty for molesting some of his younger fans. Then your accountant reports that your comptroller seems to have resettled in Brazil. And by the way, your rights and permissions department screwed up, so customs has seized the Hong Kong shipment and you're being sued for counterfeiting knockoffs. Marketing, meanwhile—"

"Mike, go away."

"Right." He rose unsteadily and lurched toward the trees.

Natalie turned eagerly back to Greg. "I specialize in retail clients—dress chains. A lot of franchises. The department store deal I just put together, that got me the VP, taught me a ton about the fur trade."

"Fur?"

"I love it. It's beautiful and sexy. They sell fantasy, but making the coats is a real nuts and bolts business. I'm just thinking, wow, that's a way to have fun going to work in the morning, and get rich. You're staring. Do I have a bee on my head?"

"Do you know Uncle Wallace?" Greg straightened up and put down his glass.

"I don't think so."

"Wallace Nevsky."

"Oh, yes. The old Russian guy on your father's side, isn't he? I have a vague memory of my parents whispering his name when we were kids."

"That's Wallace, all right. Half Russian Cossack, half Russian Jew, adopted in 1922 by my great-grandfather James."

"I've never met him."

"It was an unhappy adoption. He avoids the family. But he's been in the fur trade for over forty years."

"Really? I should talk to him."

"I'll set it up."

Greg fished in the grass under his wicker chaise. Natalie extended her bare foot and nudged the cordless telephone into his fingers. "Oh, God. More champagne, please. Here come my parents to make up."

She noticed that for the first time since they had been bantering, Greg's languid face had become bright with purpose.

"He's calling Uncle Wallace," she announced to her parents. "To set me up a meeting about the fur trade."

Her mother blanched. "In the garment district?"

"Not on Labor Day," said Greg. "He's probably just home from the parade."

"I don't think that's a good idea," Natalie's father said sharply.

"Sure it is," said Greg. "No one knows more about fur coats than Wallace Nevsky—Wallace! Greg . . . Yes, I know you told me you weren't coming." He winked at Natalie and slipped into a creditable imitation of a Yiddish accent, "But do I have a girl for you. . . . My cousin Natalie. . . . Jewish? Where would I get a Jewish cousin? Seriously, she wants to be a furrier. . . . Tell her yourself. . . . Beautiful. Very, very beautiful."

Wallace, apparently, still demurred.

"Not only is she beautiful," Greg insisted, "she speaks Russian."

That did the trick, for some reason she never thought about until years later.

"He'll be here in an hour," said Greg.

"You built me up too much. He'll be disappointed."

"Of course you speak Russian."

Wallace Nevsky had arrived at Greg's party in a linen suit. Natalie had been expecting a round old man with a pinkie ring and a fat cigar, but he was quite another thing.

"The furriers call him 'the Cossack,'" said Greg. "Looks like a cavalry officer, doesn't he?"

Natalie studied him as he sauntered down the sloping lawn. "No. He looks like the character in a Fitzgerald novel that the narrator wants to be."

"I thought you'd like him."

"How old is he?"

"About sixty."

"I would have said fifty."

"He'll love that."

"Is he married?"

"Widowed," said Greg, "before you and I were born."

Wallace greeted her parents and Greg, inspecting Natalie sidelong as he did. When they shook hands, she was jolted by a glimpse of raw sensuality smoldering like a fuse in his eyes. Then a humorous smile warmed his craggy face.

"The last time I saw you, young lady, you were flat on your back clutching a bottle."

A blitzed-out weekend at Brown flashed through her mind.

"Oh, you mean Moscow. Mother said you visited the American compound. I was a baby."

"The years have been kind. You've undergone a remarkable transformation."

She was thoroughly dazzled and couldn't think of anything brighter to say than "What were you doing in Russia?"

"On my way to a Sojuzpushnina lynx auction. Greg says you want to be a furrier. I don't recommend it. Furriers are crass and argumentative. Why do you think their children become bankers? But you're already a banker."

Natalie had used the hour it had taken him to drive to Greenwich to take a sobering swim, change into a long dress, and order the thoughts that had been percolating in her mind. She said, "I have an idea about franchising fur salons to sell to young professional women like me."

"So does Fred the Furrier."

"I'm thinking more upmarket. A preppier atmosphere, but not scary like Revillon."

"Reginald the Furrier?" Wallace asked, and they both smiled.

Wallace glanced about. "There's a path through those woods to a pretty pond. If we could persuade Cousin Greg to part with a cold bottle and a couple of glasses . . ."

"I'd rather talk this out with a clear head, if you don't mind."

"Not at all. It's just that what you're suggesting clangs like an idea whose time has come. I thought after we settled some details, we might want to toast a partnership."

"Just like that?"

"You've got a grand idea and the ability to attract investors. I can supply the coats. We could bounce it around for a year, or we can get started this afternoon."

Greg produced the glasses and a bottle dripping from the ice and they walked down the lawn and into the woods. Natalie's ankle had tightened up from the tennis and she found herself quite naturally taking the arm Wallace offered, providing a budding teenage Stuart photographer with a romantically out-of-focus picture of a couple in white, and the rest of the family with gossip to last until Christmas.

The parkway ahead curved, bringing the hearse into Natalie's line of vision. "Do you know what kills me? I can't grieve. I'm not just a widow. I'm a suspicious wife. Wallace is dead, but I don't know why. What was he doing? Those dumb newspapers with 'Furrier Shot by Other Woman???' headlines are asking my questions. I've lost the most important human being in the world. But I don't know if I was his most important human being."

"You'd ask different questions if a man had shot him."

"That's what I told the police," she said bitterly. "They made a real effort not to laugh. I don't know if I should trust him. . . . Is this horrible of me?"

"Grieve for the man you knew."

"Who?" she cried. "Maybe I don't know who he was. Maybe Diana's right. Maybe Wallace was full of surprises."

"Then grieve for the man you loved."

Greg's words hit home. They flattened her anger and lent shape to a pain so sharp that she brought her hands to her body.

"I'm sorry," he said. "I don't mean to hurt you."

"No. I want to hurt. I don't want to be angry. What you just said . . . it's as if you gave him back to me, for a moment."

4

U nable to sleep, Natalie arrived early at Cotillion Furs' 333 Seventh Avenue headquarters. It was the day after the funeral, five days since he had died. Weary of speculating, drained and exhausted, she had fixed on the shareholders' meeting as her only distraction from Wallace's murder.

Now, she worried that it was too soon to handle business. On cue, her elderly great-aunt Margaret tottered into the boardroom, swathed in ancient silks and wondering aloud, "Isn't this a bit soon?"

"I just want to reassure the shareholders," Natalie explained, taking her seat at the head of the table. She put her briefcase on Wallace's chair, as she had on the rare occasions when they had held a meeting during one of Wallace's trips to the furskin auctions.

Aunt Margaret plunked down a stack of antifur literature. "My animal rights friends are quite put out with me. The latest charge is I support minks being caught by smearing grease on cold metal so their tongues freeze to it."

"Our minks are raised on farms, Aunt Margaret."

"*I* know that," the old lady cried. "I visited one."

"You did?"

"I was rafting down the Snake River. Got off at a mink farm and chatted up the farmer. Those animals live in luxury for nine months. I should be so lucky to die as fast as they do in the gas chamber."

"Aunt Margaret, has anyone tried to buy your shares?"

"How are you, dear? I'm worried about you. I liked your marriage."

"I'm all right, thank you. Has anyone tried to buy your shares?"

"I don't like most marriages," the old lady went on. "So much jockeying for position. You and Wallace seemed above that."

"Wallace was patient."

"At his age he should have been. Have the police made any progress catching that woman?"

"The investigation is winding down, I think." In fact, "zilch" was the detective's assessment of what they had on the woman in the blonde wig, even after questioning most of the models in the fur trade, and several indignant furriers' wives. "Excuse me, Aunt Margaret. I've got to check something in the workroom. Joannie'll bring coffee."

She fled down the iron spiral stairs to the enormous loft on the twenty-second floor where the original Nevsky Russian Furs factory manufactured coats for Cotillion. It was one of the last big operations in Manhattan. There were a few old Jewish mechanics left, but most of the workers were black and brown now—from the Caribbean and Central America. Here and there shone the smiling face of a Russian refugee Wallace had adopted in Brighton Beach. A radio was tuned to a loud Spanish station.

Her appearance in the open workroom drew curious looks and shy smiles of sympathy. Natalie wasn't comfortable with the workers the way Wallace had been, and today she felt especially awkward, but she managed to say, "Good morning, everybody. I just wanted to thank you all for the flowers. Our apartment looks like a garden."

She got a Styrofoam cup of coffee and wandered through the workroom. They were watching, expectantly, but all she wanted was to be where Wallace had given her her first tour of the furriers' trade. She ran her fingers through a bundle of dressed mink pelts that had been delivered from the Brooklyn tannery, and pulled a single pelt from the bundle. It was a long, hollow tube. She snapped it like a whip, as Wallace had taught her, ruffling the fur, then blew into it to examine the soft, wooly underfur. The outside guard hairs that covered it completely were long and silky. They were a natural mahogany color and impressively uniform. Without Wallace, Cotillion was going to have great difficulty acquiring such quality for the money.

She wandered among the worktables where mechanics were letting out the skins. They cut them the length of the *grotzen,* then placed the halves, fur side down, in a machine that sliced the leather in diagonal strips every quarter inch until the half-pelt lay in ribbons. At Leo's workroom they still cut them with a razor knife, by hand.

She paused beside a sewing machine where a Spanish woman with a gold tooth was whipstitching the cuts back together. By slightly canting the cut edges, she made the finished piece longer and narrower than before, with the *grotzen* running evenly along its length. Her thread was thin as a spider web. A hair would just fit between the stitches.

In addition to lengthening and narrowing the shape of the skin, the letting-out process made it more supple, Wallace had explained on that first tour. "Imagine each sewn cut as a miniature hinge. When a *schlocker* cuts coats with wider slices, the coat is stiff and the woman looks like she's wearing a bell." In that description of what made a garment supple were the keys to his success: he loved craft and he loved women.

"*Señora?*"

The woman's gold tooth flashed between bright red lips.

"Yes?"

"Is there word, *Señora?*"

Mechanics stapling wet let-out skins to plywood pattern boards, seamstresses who'd been chattering in Spanish while they sewed sleeves and pockets, and finishers stitching linings, all stopped work to hear Natalie's reply.

"Well, frankly, the police have no leads."

"Ah. . . ." The sewing machine operator bowed her head a moment, then raised anxious eyes. "I mean, *por favor,* about the factory."

Everyone in the vast loft seemed to be staring at Natalie. The music sounded very loud. "Oh," she said. "Well, I do think it's a little early to concern ourselves with that just now."

Pete Kastoria, the foreman, intervened. He was a neat, balding Greek with a trim mustache and dark, unblinking eyes that radiated dignity. Wallace had hired him twenty years ago, off the boat, and if there was deference in his voice, it was more for Wallace than for her as he explained what should have been obvious. "They're worried, Mrs. Nevsky."

"Of course, Pete, of course. I'm sorry. Tell them—" Pete was looking at her strangely. "No. I'll tell them."

"Thank you." He raised his voice. "Listen up, everybody! Mrs. Nevsky has something to say."

Someone turned off the radio.

She saw a sea of faces, dark with worry, and suddenly felt her own cheeks burn. She knew she wasn't functioning normally, but this particular lapse was inexcusable. How many times had Wallace explained that these were people who spent every penny they earned on rent and food and school for their children? Once when she had complained about a payroll, he had said, "They don't drive Cadillacs, Natalie." Of course they were afraid now. Jobs were galloping out of Manhattan.

Stiffly, too stiffly, she said, "Cotillion Furs has many orders to fill. We'll be reorganizing the company at the top, to replace Mr. Nevsky, but here on the floor it will be business as usual until further notice."

She forced a smile, but no one looked especially reassured. Pete Kastoria nodded, demanding that she go on. She felt she couldn't, but she had to try. Censure was gathering like smoke in the foreman's dark eyes.

"What's important right now," she stammered, "is that we maintain the quality Mr. Nevsky was famous for."

Wallace would have said more. She wanted to promise they would keep their jobs, but she couldn't think how to say it. "We'll be fine," she murmured, turning away. "We'll be fine."

Pete walked her back to the spiral stair. "Thanks for coming down. They're really scared. They know darn well Mr. Nevsky's going to be tough to replace."

Survive, she thought on the stair. I should have said, We'll survive. But she didn't have the strength to go back.

She fled back to the boardroom just ahead of the shareholders, who arrived en masse as she took her seat.

Aunt Margaret asked, "Who's that fat little man?"

"Leo Margulies. I've asked him to help us."

On those occasions when all its members attended, Cotillion's board was large and unwieldy—the disparate shareholder-directors a mismatched group of money men, furriers, and family. In common with other privately held companies' boards that Natalie had encountered in her banking days, it reflected the leaps and bounds of Cotillion's rise.

She had tapped a diverse group for start-up money in the beginning, inviting the larger investors to form the board. To balance the money people and establish more clout with suppliers, Wallace had drafted a gang of furriers to serve as directors, most of whom became investors, too, as Cotillion prospered.

For some time, Natalie had continued to don her banker's hat to finance expansion. But when Cotillion launched its chain of wholly owned freestanding salons in the ritzier shopping malls around the country, she had considered turning to her old boss at Stuart, Malcolm and Hardy for further financing. She was simply too busy selling franchises and helping Wallace manage the business. At that point her brother Mike, who appeared to be flourishing on Wall Street, offered to sell shares to various members of the Stuart family.

It had seemed like a good idea at the time, and, she had to admit, it was extremely satisfying to demonstrate to cousins, aunts, and uncles how well she was doing. Best of all, Cotillion got the money with a minimum of investor interference. Few family directors, other than Mike, bothered to attend board meetings, assigning Natalie their proxies instead, as Wallace's furriers often assigned Wallace theirs.

But such, Natalie noticed, was not the case this morning. All eighteen directors—money men, furriers, and family—were shuffling in, eyeing Natalie cautiously and casting curious glances at Leo, who sat beside Wallace's empty chair. She was suddenly grateful to whatever business instinct—operating on some level above, below, or beside grief—had prompted her to invite her great-aunt to sit beside her on her left. Aunt Margaret owned the largest single block of shares in the company.

"Thanks for coming on such short notice," Natalie said, as soon as they had taken their seats. "I will make this brief. As most of you know, Wallace has essentially left everything that was ours to me, as I would have left everything to him. I own his shares and his voting rights, as he would have owned mine had I passed on first."

She hesitated, derailed by his absence. She always conducted board meetings, but Wallace sat beside her, quick to team up against anyone who gave them trouble.

"So I have the same problem Wallace would have had, had I died: how to fill the empty spaces at Cotillion. Actually, I have two problems because I'm told that someone is trying to buy our shares. So, while I put my immediate energy into preventing a takeover, I'm asking Wallace's old friend, Leo Margulies, to oversee supply and production until we can hire a couple of people to replace Wallace. I asked Leo here to answer any questions."

"Slow down, Natalie."

At the far end of the table her brother had hunkered down on his elbows. "What's the matter, Mike?"

"Leo's a specialist. He manufactures luxury coats. He's not a boss like Wallace."

"The hell I'm not. I've run my business forty years."

"You're making two hundred of the best coats in the world per year. We're selling twenty thousand."

"Hey, I'm doing a lot more than two hundred since my sons came in with me."

"I thought they went to law school."

"They got bored, they came home. We're doing two hundred, two hundred and fifty mink alone. We're doing a lot of sable."

"How many sable?"

"A lot. We're doing fisher. Baum marten. Leo Margulies is getting big."

"So where do you find time to help Natalie?"

"For one thing, I make the time for my friend's widow. You'd do the same thing yourself," he added, with a look that suggested Mike might not. "For another, I got three sons. They got expensive wives. So they work their tails off. Okay?"

"All I'm saying—"

"And one of those wives is a business school graduate who can straighten us out."

"Thank you," said Natalie. "Can we agree that temporarily Leo is a real asset?"

"We appreciate Leo's help," Mike replied, "but the board feels that we can't risk a management breakdown."

"The board?" Natalie asked incredulously. "The board is right here. Who are you speaking for?"

"Myself. Andy."

Natalie glanced at Andy Stuart, scion of the last branch of the Stuarts that could luxuriate on private incomes, but the vapid young man looked away. "Who else?"

"Joe Karapoulous, Ronnie Kossar."

Those furriers named looked uncomfortable, and when Wallace's old friend Al Silverman said, "Fastest thing that'll kill you in this business is bad word of mouth," Natalie realized, belatedly, that she had an insurrection on her hands.

"Where are you taking this, Mike?"

"Some of us feel that Cotillion needs a manager."

"You're looking at her," Natalie shot back.

But in truth, she feared that she had been caught. She thought of herself as a normal woman with normal doubts, yet some nights, when she lay awake questioning her success, those doubts cut to the bone. Reduced to the coldest reality, what was her great success but a single bright idea, now six years old? Seen with a cold eye, or weary eye, Wallace had made Cotillion, run the factories, negotiated with the manufacturers, bought the fur skins. Wallace had made it all happen, as they had just reminded her downstairs in the factory.

"You're a deal maker." Mike zeroed in, with devastating accuracy. "Not a manager."

"I put together the deals that made this company. And I continue to do the deals that expand it by thirty percent a year."

"You're a gunslinger, for Chrissake," Al Silverman retorted, and Wallace's other furrier friends nodded solemnly. "You ride into town like the Lone Rangess, sell the locals a fur franchise, and ride on. You're a saleswoman and a goddamned good one, but you're a loner, not a manager, and we can't afford to wait for you to learn on the job."

"Too true," said Ronnie Kossar.

"We've got to set up systems and delegate authority, which neither you or Wallace, God bless, ever learned to do. Joannie scrambles around picking up the pieces, but the operation is a disaster, which is getting apparent now that business is flattening out. You've been so busy hustling new franchises you haven't seen what's gone wrong with the costs, and competition. The importers are killing us. We've overinvested our own money in the malls. I know it was Wallace's idea, but—"

"Leave him out of this."

Silverman and Kossar went on and on, interrupted occasionally by the money men reminding her they would lose Diana Darbee and alluding to what they called adverse publicity. Natalie stared at the table until she felt an odd half-smile tug at her mouth. She stroked the silken wood. A Canadian furrier, in debt to Wallace for a purchase of Russian mink and karakul, had defaulted, so Wallace Nevsky had attached the furrier's inlaid yew wood conference table, his brass-studded leather chairs, and a mirrored armoire. Fresh from investment banking, Natalie had never connected actual objects to numbers, and when she called the furniture symbolic of reality, Wallace had laughed. "It is reality. The guy stiffed me, so he lost his furniture."

". . . And meanwhile, in the cities, our franchises are getting undercut by local chains selling cheap imports."

"Cotillion customers have been educated to spend a little more for quality."

"Fred the Furrier's gone upscale," her brother chimed in. "They can spend with him." The furriers nodded emphatically and the money men looked thoughtful.

The argument was so familiar—Natalie and Wallace had been over this territory a thousand times, but this time she was taking his position.

She felt her mind start to drift again. Then she remembered her dismal performance downstairs with the workers. The mistrustful expressions on the directors' faces were alarmingly like those that had challenged her in the workroom. If she could not seize the reins in the next sixty seconds, she would lose control of Cotillion, here and now, in this room, to these people.

Fear and grief could not march together, and in that instant, *for* an instant, fear forged ahead and she was suddenly, fully Natalie Stuart Nevsky again. Dismissing Mike with a lightning change of subject, she took the initiative, telling the group at large, "I need time to examine everything Wallace and I were doing. I need time to set up new management."

Now she addressed Aunt Margaret, directly. "How much time will you give me?"

"Of course you must have time. My God, what you've been through."

"Give me three months then. With Christmas coming and all, let's say early February. Three months." She saw a way to get another week and took it, with a grim smile. "In fact, why don't we say Valentine's Day? February fourteenth. That's a Saturday, so we'll meet the sixteenth." She knew the day because she had secretly reserved a room for her and Wallace at the Boxtree Inn.

She saw some hesitation.

"I'll make an interim report in January. I will implement changes as I see we need them. For the moment, we've got Christmas coming, so let's sell, sell, sell what we're shipping to our stores."

"But Natalie," Al Silverman objected, "we've got major bank notes due in a month. The banks will demand a manager or they won't renew."

"They *will* renew if this board goes along with its largest share-holder, who has just offered me three months." She stood up. "Let's break for ten minutes. Joannie's called out for bagels and lox. We've got coffee. Mike, could I see you?"

They found a quiet spot in the hall. He couldn't meet her eyes.

"I'm missing something," she said. "What is going on?"

"Nothing I didn't talk about in there."

"Are you leading the attack?"

"No."

"Why this sudden interest in the fur trade?"

"I always attend board meetings."

"But you don't tell me how to run my business. What's going on?"

"Hey, I got my own problems." He struggled and failed to look at her, then addressed a quiet confession to his shoes. "I got creamed in the crash."

"So did half of Wall Street."

"They fired me."

"Oh, Mike."

Natalie felt like sagging through the wall. At times, she thought, it seemed that failure lurked around their family like a spy at the door. Their father losing battle after pointless battle at the State Department. Mike, brilliant and erratic, quitting business school, where he had excelled in management studies, blowing law school, then abandoning a promising investment banking career for a trading job, which was ordinarily a license to print money. And now Cotillion slipping from her grasp.

"But what do you want from me?"

"I don't know." He looked up with an anxious grin. His mouth was trembling. "A job, maybe?"

"A job? You just finished telling me and the board what a mess I've inherited. Why would you want to work here?"

"I could help you."

"You're certainly not helping today. How goddamned self-centered can you get, Michael? My husband is dead and you just set off a firestorm against me!"

"I didn't mean to. Listen, I could handle things for you, maybe, while you recover."

"No, thank you. I will 'recover' right here at my own desk." Her mind started reeling again. Wallace. Wallace always said weak people were the most dangerous. An awful thought staggered her, a connection she would have picked up much sooner had she been functioning properly.

"Michael," she breathed. "You let Silverman and Kossar talk you into fronting for them."

"No. We just talked and I—"

"Those bastards. They know the money guys will stay with me for a little while, if I don't fall apart. And they know the family won't desert me, not for a while, anyway. So the furriers got *you* to break up my family support. You are really—oh God—you're doing coke again?"

When his eyes slid away, Natalie's heart slipped a final notch.

"Where'd you get that idea?" he blustered.

She had been staring at the evidence all morning, but she had been too distracted by grief to notice.

"You were too aggressive with Leo," she explained. "And then you weren't sharp enough to realize that's the wrong way to handle him. You're better than that, Michael, at least when you're straight."

Mike grinned ruefully. "The good news is I can't afford much."

"Does Anne know?"

"No!"

Recently, he had been seeing a remarkably self-assured nurse who worked at Beekman Downtown. He had met her in the emergency room where he had gone with heart palpitations following a heavily coked-up day on the trading floor. When Natalie and Wallace had had dinner with them, they had come away convinced that Anne was the best thing to happen to Michael since he had finally left home.

"You can't fool Anne, you know."

"I know. I know. She'll nail me. She'll leave me. I'm stopping. I swear I am."

"Please, Michael, don't fall apart on me now. I can't handle any more."

"I won't. I won't."

"And stop undercutting me in there. They're ready to dump me. You're making it easy for them."

"Hey, I'm not a villain."

"You're not? Then support *me*, not those damned furriers."

"I was only thinking you'd be better off out of it for a while. Give yourself time to get over what happened."

"No, Michael, all I want is my husband, and since I can't have him,

I am certainly not going to surrender our company. It's our *child,* Michael. We made it together. Now it's mine."

Mike looked away. "I guess I never saw it that way."

"Do you still want a job?"

"Yeah, I could use a job," he said sullenly. "I told you I'm nowhere. My big sister's the last person in New York who'll give me a job."

"Don't count on it."

"What?"

"When you can look me in the eye and say you haven't touched dope, or booze, for two months, then you've got a job with Cotillion Furs."

"Two months?" he echoed, trying to look brave, and Natalie, mired in sadness and despair, did not at that moment believe he would make it.

The shareholders watched Mike and Natalie anxiously as they returned. Natalie went to the closet and reached for her Cotillion mink. Next to it, the Russian lynx coat blazed like a snowstorm. She had brought it in this morning to store in Cotillion's vault. On a sudden impulse, she swirled it around her shoulders.

The directors were not the problem. She was the problem. She had to prove herself, again. Alone.

"I'll see you all, back in this room, on February sixteenth."

"What about the interim report?" asked Al Silverman.

"Of course, anyone who wants to come by in January is welcome. I'll have Joannie inform everyone of the date. I ask one favor, in the name of my husband. If anyone tries to buy your shares, sell to me first."

They were staring at the coat.

"May I have a vote of confidence before I adjourn this meeting? Three months, to run my company? All in favor say aye."

"Aye." It was a ragged chorus, loudest from the Stuarts, led by Margaret and Mike. The money men mumbled assent, which Natalie had expected. Three months gave them time to search out new investments. In the meantime, from their point of view, it was better not to get involved in messy battles. The furriers were grimly silent, but at least no one protested when she said, "The ayes have it."

She stalked out, imagining that Wallace would have cheered the dramatic gesture. But she knew in her heart she had won no more than a temporary reprieve. Three months and a week was hardly time to prove herself, and already she was berating herself for not having the courage to demand six.

She suddenly missed Wallace so much that it hurt physically. She had work to do, phone calls to make. To be close to him, she would make them from his boat. Clutching the lynx about her like armor, she fled toward the elevators.

A man was sitting in the reception room. She caught a glimpse of blue worsted trousers and handmade English shoes before she lowered her eyes and tried to forge past him. But he bounded to his feet and blocked her escape. He was built massively—a pyramid of hard muscle—and with his sturdy arms spread wide to greet her, he seemed to fill the reception room like a truck.

"Eddie? What are you doing here?"

"Sorry I missed the funeral, darlin'. I was in Taipei for a client, may his breath congeal."

"I got your telex. Thank you."

Eddie Mayall—president, founder, and sole partner of Edward R. Mayall Capital—had been more Wallace's friend than hers. A recent friend, and Natalie had never entirely trusted his motives for courting them. He was one of those New York anomalies—the independent, private investment banker who hustled in the shadows of the billion-dollar institutions, sharing modest office space with other unruly mavericks while he juggled a covey of small clients and stalked the big score. His main asset appeared to be an expensive suit; his chief operating expense, his telephone bill.

Wallace had attributed her mistrust to the Wall Street organization woman's wary awe of the entrepreneurial lone wolf, which Natalie admitted was possible.

Not that Eddie Mayall needed her approval. Only last year, he had assembled a remarkable public offering that enabled an obscure Seventh Avenue importer of ladies' knits to sell a sweater to every third teenager in America. Wallace had enjoyed him. The burly former Airborne sergeant was the only man she had ever heard him trade war stories with, and no one could make Wallace laugh louder. He had once likened Eddie's voice to the crunch of paratrooper boots on wet gravel.

"Trouble in the zoo?" he asked, inclining his massive, closely cropped head toward the boardroom.

"Nothing I can't handle." She was still shaken by the insurrection, shaken and wary. "What are you doing here?"

"Just stopped by to say don't hesitate to call on me."

"What do you mean?" she asked, only half-aware that her voice was rising. "For what?"

"For anything you need, darlin'."

"We won't go public. Wallace told you *ten times* we won't go public."

"Darlin'—"

"He didn't want to take Cotillion public and neither do I. We prefer our control and our privacy. We don't want stockholders. We don't want public scrutiny. We don't want the SEC telling us how to do business, and we definitely don't want to become a target for some sleazy buyout artist. Is that clear? *Is it?*"

She pushed past him, out the double glass doors, and stabbed angrily at the elevator button. Eddie lumbered after her and planted himself in front of the elevator. He raised both hands, palms out. They were pink and veined white like a pair of hams. "Natalie. If I had checked out first, Wallace would have been on Danielle's doorstep offering what he could. I'm on yours. Anytime you need me. Is *that* clear?"

She glared back at him and in so doing finally saw the sad light in his eyes. "I'm sorry," she whispered. "Oh, I'm a mess."

"Don't apologize. You don't owe apologies for at least a year."

"I thought you were pitching to take me public."

"I'd love to, but not 'til you're ready."

"*Never.*"

"Can I buy you lunch?"

She shook her head and turned aside to hide her tears. "No, thank you. I'm on my way to Wallace's boat." The elevator arrived and Natalie headed down, grateful that Eddie Mayall had the grace to let her ride alone.

They gave her a funny look at the marina gate, which she attributed at first to the shooting. Then she saw that *Panache*, moored at the end of the main pier, appeared to be moving. A blast from her horn shook the air. Black smoke issued from her stack and to Natalie's astonishment, the long, white yacht started backing into the river.

She broke into a run, the lynx coat flowing in the wind, but in the seconds she took to reach the gangway, a broad stretch of riled water had swelled between her and Wallace's boat.

"Where's she going?" she yelled to the marina captain, who was speaking into his walkie-talkie. He answered with an uncomfortable shrug, "I don't know, Mrs. Nevsky. They didn't say."

"Who?"

"The owner."

"What owner? My husband—*I'm* the owner."

The marina captain shrugged again. "The paperwork's in my office. They had a court order to repossess and a city marshal to explain it."

"Where's my crew?"

"Paid them off. Paid off Mr. Nevsky's arrears, too."

"What arrears?"

"Few months' dockage and maintenance. I wasn't worried."

"But—"

"Once they paid me, I had to let her sail."

Panache backed clear of the pier and pivoted through a stately half-turn until her bow was facing south. Another oily puff from her diesel stack and she started down the Hudson, her bright work alive in a cool, pale sun. In moments, it seemed to Natalie, the boat grew small. "Why didn't you call me?"

"I called your husband's lawyer. I mean, with everything happening to you, and it was Mr. Nevsky's boat, I figured—"

"May I use your phone?"

When she finally got through to Wallace's lawyer, he said, "I just got served with the papers."

"Why? There's no lien on his boat. There's no mortgage. What about probate, Sol? They can't just seize his estate's assets."

Sol Levy allowed a long silence to gather. Natalie waited until she couldn't stand it anymore. "Sol? What is going on? Wallace is dead. Why would the city marshal allow a creditor to take the boat?"

"Listen, you're backing me into an uncomfortable corner here. I was Wallace's lawyer."

"I'm his widow," she shouted. "That boat's mine. Wallace left it to me."

"It wasn't his to leave."

"What?"

"He sold it to a guy who leased it back to him."

"That's crazy. He loved owning that boat."

"Apparently he needed money and that's how he raised it."

"When?"

"Five—six years ago."

"He told me he owned it," she whispered.

"Maybe that made him feel good."

"That is crazy. We didn't have secrets from each other."

Sol's silence suggested otherwise. When he finally spoke, it was like a wary act of charity. "When Wallace met you, I think he kind of felt he had to impress you."

"Me?"

"Being so young, I think. He had to talk a good line to catch you."

"He caught me the second I saw him smile."

"Maybe you shoulda told him."

"I told him."

"Maybe he shoulda listened."

"He listened and he heard. No, Sol. There's more to this. Something doesn't compute. Who'd he lease it from?"

"Looks like a front operation."

"Find out who owns it, please." Better Sol than her own lawyers, who would have their hands full fighting the threatened Cotillion takeover. More important, as she had to prove herself capable of managing Cotillion, it would be foolish to draw attention to another strange situation. Wallace needed money, Sol had said. She wondered what for. Five or six years ago. Around the time they were setting up the business. But she had raised the money; she knew the source of every dollar. It had to be something else, some serious setback Wallace had suffered, separate from Cotillion. Raking her memory, she could only think that one of his private furskin deals had fallen through. And broadcasting that wouldn't help Cotillion's word of mouth in the fur trade.

She stood for a while with the phone frozen in her hand. Abruptly, she dialed the homicide detective and demanded a report in a voice even she could hear belonged to a shrill stranger.

"We've got a wig washed up on Staten Island," Kunitz said.

"What does that mean?"

"Mostly it means your husband was probably right about her wearing a wig. It's made in Europe, which goes with the gown you mentioned. I wish I could tell you more."

In a daze, she took a cab to Fifth Avenue, where she walked without purpose, staring sightlessly at shop windows, wandering in and out of stores. She was vaguely aware she was leaving Bonwit's, which she had entered through the Trump Tower, when bells started ringing. Uniformed store detectives descended on the door. Natalie stepped aside.

"Excuse me, Miss. Could we see your bag, please?"

"What?"

"Lady, the alarm got you. Let's see the bag." They surrounded her, two dour men and two women with bad haircuts.

"You think I'm shoplifting?"

It was so funny that she started to laugh. Four uniforms staring at her like a criminal. The laughter got away from her, fast, like a ball bouncing downhill.

The store detectives exchanged anxious glances. The women reached for her arm. Natalie backed away. Then she heard a strange barking sound in her laughter. Sharp and brittle, it frightened her. But when she tried to explain, she sounded like a drunk at a party. And she couldn't stop.

"You don't understand what's funny, do you? You see, my husband died. Actually he was shot by a woman. And the shareholders are trying to take my company. And somebody took his yacht. And now you're arresting me for *shoplifting?*"

She started laughing again. "I don't believe this. Don't you get it? It's like the plagues in the Bible, only mine are in reverse order." The laughter stuck in her throat. Suddenly, she was crying. Shoppers began to collect around the wild-eyed young woman in the magnificent white fur because she looked terrified and tears were streaming down her face. Bonwit's did not encourage such scenes and the detectives tried again to coax her upstairs.

"Don't touch me!"

"It'll be easier if you come with us."

Natalie yanked free. The store seemed to spin around her. She closed the lynx and gripped it tightly to her body. The gift made her think of Wallace and how he would handle this. Laugh, probably.

"Get Rona Smith down here right now! Tell her it's Natalie Stuart."

The detectives exchanged looks. One spoke quietly into his radio and they waited until Bonwit's senior store manager hurried to the door. Rona had a pencil stuck in her gray-streaked black hair and a Tiffany watch pinned to her blouse. "Natalie! You poor thing.

I just wrote you a note about Wallace. . . . What are you doing here?"

"I was taking a shortcut through your store when these people stopped me for shoplifting."

"What?"

Rona Smith whirled on the detectives. "This lady is Natalie Stuart Nevsky. She owns Cotillion Furs. For three years I have been trying to convince her to leave Saks to Revillon and let Bonwit's sell her coats."

"But she tripped the alarm, Ms. Smith."

"Mrs. Nevsky does not shoplift. And, frankly, if she did, she'd be welcome to. Please apologize and go away."

"I'm sorry. But something tripped the alarm."

"This one's real sensitive," volunteered one of the women.

"It's *what*?"

"Well, I mean, it always rings before the others."

"Fix it!" Rona hissed. "And I'll see you in my office. Natalie, I'm so sorry. It's something electronic. They put little wires in the garments. Well, you know, you probably do it in the coats."

"This is a Leo Margulies made of skins Wallace brought from Russia. I doubt Leo was worried about shoplifting."

"No, no. I don't mean that."

Natalie thrust her handbag at Rona.

"I want you to look in my bag, Rona. I don't steal. I've never stolen a thing in my life. Ever!"

"It's not necessary."

Natalie started crying again. "I really didn't take anything," she sobbed. "I'm very honest."

"Come upstairs, dear. Have a drink or something."

"No. Forget it. I want to be alone."

"Let's go fix your face," Rona pleaded.

"No." She couldn't stop crying. "I want to go home."

Rona snapped her fingers and three detectives bolted out to Fifty-seventh Street whistling for taxis. As Natalie went out, the bells started ringing again. "Turn it off," Rona yelled.

Natalie felt something in her take hold again, like the gear shift on her car locking into first. She patted Rona's hand. "Hey, it's okay. It's almost funny."

There were police cars outside her building and cops in the lobby. A detective was waiting in her foyer. Wallace, she thought. They found the woman. Then she saw three kitchen knives scattered on the front hall table. Her housekeeper, Bernadette, sat weeping on a chair. It occurred to Natalie that she had never seen her sit down except to eat lunch or polish silver.

"It's okay, Mrs. Nevsky. It's okay. Don't worry."

"What happened?"

The plainclothesman explained that Bernadette had surprised a burglar ransacking the bedroom.

"What are those knives?"

"It's the thief saying he's here. Your maid was smart enough to run screaming. The guy took off."

"Nobody hurt. Nobody hurt. It's okay, Mrs. Nevsky."

"Your maid got scared silly, but she's more worried about you because of what you've been through. You know, with your husband and all."

"I can't handle this," Natalie said in a brittle voice. "It's one too many."

"I don't think they got anything. Just messed the place up a little bit. She says your jewelry's okay."

"Why now?"

"They read the obituaries for empty apartments," he replied, treating her bewildered plea as if it were a sober question.

"I can't handle this," Natalie repeated, and pushed blindly out the door.

"Mrs. Nevsky," Bernadette wailed.

"I'm going to the country. I can't stay here. I'll be okay. I'll be okay."

She got as far as the Ninety-sixth Street entrance to the West Side Highway before she fell apart. For several long minutes she sat on the merge, incapable of making Wallace's Cadillac enter the whizzing traffic. She had taken his car for the same reason she had gone to *Panache,* to feel near him, but it hadn't worked. She was hideously alone and bewildered.

Headlights blazed behind her, horns blared. Cars pulled around and blasted past, drivers yelling, but she could not move. A man approached on foot. Frightened, she put the car in reverse and backed toward West Ninety-sixth Street. The tires squealed and the man jumped out of her way. She turned around, her mind whirling, and raced across town, through Central Park, with the vague intention of trying again on the FDR.

The boat troubled her worst of all. Wallace had always maintained his own checking account, just as she did, but selling the yacht was not the kind of secret a man kept from his wife. Money troubles made her think of loan sharks, who flourished in the fur and garment districts, but loan sharks didn't kill people with assets. The crazy, sad thing was she almost wished it had been a loan shark, because if Wallace had been shot by a professional killer instead of a lover, at least the woman couldn't kill their marriage, too.

At the crest of Second Avenue and Ninety-sixth, with the FDR glowing frighteningly in the distance, she stepped on the accelerator and wove the big car through the traffic lining up for the highway. Compared to her 320i it was like trying to drive a train. Cut off by a swiftly moving Porsche as the signal turned yellow, she careened into the empty right lane and was gunning for the light when a Brownie traffic cop blocked her, pointing at a Right Turn Only sign.

Forced off the entrance ramp, she found herself heading down York Avenue in the wrong direction. Sobbing with frustration, she slammed the brakes on, dumped her bag on the seat, found Greg's card with the Washington number, and stabbed frantically at Wallace's cellular car phone.

"Greg! Greg!"

"Natalie. Yes, I'm here!"

"Greg, did he have affairs?"

"What?"

"I don't know who I am if Wallace lied to me."

"Calm down. Where are you?"

"Greg, tell me honestly. Do you have knowledge of a single affair Wallace had while we were married?"

"No."

"Not even Diana?"

"No."

"But that doesn't prove a thing."

"Where are you?"

"Greg, help me find that woman."

"The police are looking."

"They'll never find her. She's the only one who can tell me the truth."

"Natalie, please, where are you? Calm down. Tell me where you are."

"I have to know," she sobbed.

"Natalie, let's get real a second. The woman who shot Wallace is not a likely candidate to tell the truth."

"Help me."

"First stop crying. . . . Just take deep breaths. . . . That's better. . . . Now where are you?"

"I have to know if he was sleeping with her."

"We are stepping into weird territory. Can I ask you something harsh?"

"What?"

"Why is Wallace's faithfulness so important?"

"Because if Wallace and I weren't the couple I thought we were, then I'm just a face in the dark."

"You are not a face in the dark," he said gently. "No matter what happened, you're still Natalie. You were Natalie before I introduced you to Wallace and you were Natalie married to Wallace, and you're still Natalie."

"I was much more than just Natalie when Wallace loved me. I was Natalie and Wallace. I was this woman Wallace said he loved. I was who Wallace thought I was. If Wallace cheated, then he made me nothing."

"You're not nothing."

"His cheating denies what we were and what I was."

"You're putting too much freight on fidelity. The man was more than sixty years old when you met. Women loved him. He had habits of a lifetime, but they don't make you nothing."

"You're admitting he had affairs."

"I am not! And *you* are not nothing."

"That's your opinion," Natalie sobbed. "I have to know Wallace's opinion. I can't sleep. I can't think. I have to know they weren't lovers."

"Another person's opinion—even Wallace's—isn't you."

"If you believe that, then you've never been in love like we were."

"So be thankful you're one of the lucky ones. . . . Now where are you?"

The bleakness in his voice hit her like cold water. "Are you okay?"

"Of course I am. You're the one crying."

"I'm better now. Thank you."

"What are you doing?"

"Driving to the country."

"Will you be okay there?"

"I'll be fine as soon as I get in the house."

The house, unlike Wallace's apartment and the money-pit *Panache,* was theirs alone, their honeymoon cottage, paid for by Cotillion profits. But it occurred to Natalie that the house would be empty, silent, and maybe, in the middle of the night, scary. "No," she said firmly, refusing to allow any thought of being afraid in the house they had loved together. "Enough. Not in our house."

"What are you talking about?"

"I'm going to build a fire when I get home. I'll open a window for the draft. And I'll listen to the waterfall. I'll watch the flames in the fireplace. I'll look at the stars and then I'll go to bed. But first I'll call my lawyer and ask her to come up for a strategy session tomorrow."

"Why so soon?"

"Anything not to think."

"I guess that sounds pretty good," Greg said dubiously, "if you think you're all right up there alone."

5

She couldn't get a fire started. The wind kept blowing smoke back down the chimney and extinguishing the kindling before it ignited the logs. The sitting room fireplace had a better draft, but she had shied away from the big room. The kitchen, with its low ceiling and warm shutters, was a better place to be alone.

What was it Wallace always said? One log can't burn. Two logs won't burn. *Three* must burn. She was forgetting something, but she couldn't remember what it was. He always built the fires.

She was kneeling on a hearth rug they had bought at auction. Her gaze fell on the pine woodbox they'd spent a weekend stripping of yellow enamel. The ticking of a Regulator clock—Aunt Margaret's housewarming gift—grew loud in the silence. She wanted to scream, to keen, to wail her lament, but in her confusion, all she could do was cry. She left the kitchen and wandered the other rooms of the big old house, turning on lights. Back in the kitchen, desperate for release, she picked up an earthen vase and forced herself to throw it.

It smashed on the cold hearth. She stared at what she had done. They had bought it at a tag sale. She swept the shards off the brick and picked up the splinters with a wet paper towel. Mechanically, she mopped the floor, but it, like everything else in the kitchen, was spotless already. Suddenly she lacked the energy to put away the mop. But as she wandered, her eye kept returning to the grotesque contrast between the mop's hideous turquoise handle and the ancient chestnut floors.

At false dawn, bursting with pain and still unable to release it, she broke an old habit and swallowed one of Wallace's Valiums. She lay down on their bed, under his robe. Half asleep, she remembered that Wallace always crumpled an extra piece of newspaper on top of the fire, which he lit before lighting the bottom paper, to send a warm draft up the chimney.

She awakened, minutes later it seemed, with the sun in her eyes.

She felt terrible and she looked awful, her eyes red and puffy. She had to get hold of herself. She needed a plan for the day. One moment at a time. She would get off the bed in a moment and shower. Lynn Brown, her lawyer, was coming at noon. She had frozen quiche for lunch, but she'd have to run into town for salad greens because the frost had killed the garden. That left three hours to work outdoors before she had to change. There were, as always, a million chores to do, but this first day home, alone, was not a time for maintenance. She wanted to improve or try in some small way to finish what they had started.

Fine-tuning the views of stone and green lawn and the flash of water moving from pond to pond would make it easier to remember good things about Wallace. Here, cherishing and nurturing the place, they had grown close through compromise. Wallace had wanted this vast, glass wall in the bedroom. She protested maiming an eighteenth-century house. Together, they devised a plan: a housewright removed posts, beams, and clapboards with loving care, and stacked them, numbered, in the barn for some future purist owner to restore the wall with.

She dressed in loose jeans, a sweatshirt over a tee shirt, clogs, a straw hat to protect her face from the sun, and gloves for her nails. In her work shed she found a carton of Breck's daffodil bulbs they hadn't had time to plant. Covered with a brown, flaking, curling skin, they were fat with promise and she was suddenly certain she wanted to spend the morning adding to the daffodils behind the main pond.

Wheelbarrowing her tools along the shore, she made her regular apprehensive check for muskrat tunnels. Thankfully, she found neither holes in the banks, underwater trails, nor floating vegetation. The garden-wrecking rodents were cute to watch, which made going to war with them even more traumatic, and they were too smart to fall for a Have-A-Heart trap. After catching and releasing a dozen bemused raccoons, she had undertaken what Wallace had laughingly called "The Furrier's Solution," the memory of which still made her shake. She sidestepped the little monster's grave and went to work in the garden.

They had started the bed four years ago and by now the old brush roots had rotted so the soil was soft and planted easily. The trick was finding spaces among the existing daffodils and hybrid lilies. She had been at it about an hour when a dog started barking nearby.

Natalie picked up a long rake and went to investigate. She found an enormous ancient red setter barking at a tennis ball that had escaped from the court. Steadying herself with a single deep breath, she spoke to the animal. "Hey, you're back."

When she was eight years old, one summer at her uncle's house on Martha's Vineyard, she had not realized that a dog flattening its ears was dangerous. Moving from overseas post to overseas post, her parents had not kept pets, nor could she have them at boarding school. But the sort of generous people who invited "orphans" usually had dogs and cats roaming at will. And when she leaned too close in wide-eyed inspection, one of them had bitten her face.

The best plastic surgeon in Boston had erased the wound, though not the memory of sudden pain and ruthless violence, which had left her ever since both afraid of animals and oddly fascinated by them as well. They provided her images of people. Her brother was an amiable frog, her mother a snowy egret, her father, for reasons she did not investigate, a snake. Wallace had been a handsome bluejay, quick, bright-eyed, jagged on the wing, though sometimes when they made love she fantasized they were lions.

Always her own sternest judge, she had gotten a dog, as soon as she was living on her own, to force herself to overcome her fear. A German shepherd, with which she spent a terrifying month, afraid to sleep, until sanity prevailed in the form of Mike, who traded it in on Muffin the poodle. Less animal than companion, the little dog, who had died last year, had quickly ceased to be a valid test. Similarly, the old red setter, while fearsomely huge, was so old and so tame that Natalie had needed only one stiff command to her stomach to summon the courage to greet it.

It came from a farm through the woods, and would appear on occasion for a drink from the pond. Its muzzle was whiter every time, its long, shaggy coat faded like fallen leaves. She was sure each visit would be its last, but this crisp fall day, it even had the energy to bark at a ball.

"Okay."

Natalie threw the ball. The dog yelped and shambled after it like a cheerful bag lady. Natalie headed back to the pond, but the dog caught up with the ball in her yellow teeth, dropped it at Natalie's feet, and started barking again.

"Shut up."

It wouldn't. She threw the ball as far as she could, toward the barn, and headed for the daffodils. Shortly, the dog resumed barking. She found it barking at the barn. "Okay, I'll drive you home."

It nosed up to the footing and barked at a hole between the stones where the tennis ball had apparently disappeared.

"I'm not putting my hand in there."

The dog moaned as if it would die. Natalie put on her garden gloves, stretched on her stomach, and reached in. She was feeling around, wondering what lived inside, when she heard a thin, reedy whistle overhead, like a late summer insect.

The whistle repeated in measured cadences. It sounded like one of the Radio Shack phones at the house and she stood up before she realized she was too far from the house to hear the phone through the closed windows. This sounded close, overhead, as if there were a telephone in the barn, which there was not.

She went around the front, slid the big door open, and went in. It was cold and dark. Light streamed from the tack room, where Wallace had kept a little office. She went to it and stood in the doorway, puzzled. It had no telephone, not even electricity. Just the window for light, an oil lamp, and a potbelly stove Wallace had had installed.

But she had traced the noise to his office. When it stopped, she stepped in and looked out the window. Below was the grass where she had lain trying to get the ball out of the foundation. She glanced at his rolltop desk. The top was locked, but the key was in the latch and when Natalie lifted, it rattled easily in polished tracks. The desk smelled inside of pungent oak, dry rot, and Wallace's cologne. One cubby was filled with little scraps of paper. Natalie hesitated. Then she sat in his swivel chair and reached for the papers.

He had never said, Don't use my desk, just as she had never said, The desk and the tack room are yours and the birthing room in the house is mine, but she knew she was intruding in his private place. Once or twice a month he sat here. She would trundle a garden cart past and glance at the window and see him staring into space, or reading, or gazing out the window at the ponds and gardens and his wife. She had assumed it was his way of refueling much the same way she did by digging holes in the ground or stacking stones on a wall.

The paper scraps caused her heart to ache. They were notes she had written him. Home at four . . . Home soon . . . Shopping . . . Love you . . . Let's eat home tonight . . . Love you . . . Nursery . . . Tennis . . . See you soon . . . She had signed them with a heart and sometimes a squiggly dog. Love you . . . love you . . . love you . . .

Natalie broke away and lit a fire in the potbelly stove. She stood by it, staring at the bright flames until they had begun to eat into the bigger logs and the heated metal had driven the chill from the room. Then she returned to Wallace's desk and browsed.

She found a box of paper clips and a few Mozart cassettes for the little battery tape recorder he kept in the bottom drawer, some years-old calendars, the current *Old Farmer's Almanac,* a four-inch Schrade pocketknife, a Players club ashtray filled with thumbtacks and paper clips, an empty stapler, a stamp pad with no stamp, and a drawer crammed with mail order catalogs. The bolder she became and the deeper she probed, the more she felt like one stranger sifting through another stranger's past, like opening drawers and boxes in a collectibles shop. But then an open pack of Trues made her angry at him for sneaking cigarettes. And a three-by-five card listing her sizes right down to gloves and shoes made her cry.

The whistling started again, unmistakably near. When the wood vibrated against her knee, she knew it was in the desk. The bottom right drawer held the tape player. The middle drawer held used manila envelopes. The top drawer, the catalogs. The drawers on the other side were empty. She pulled the catalog drawer open again, saw it was short, and yanked it out of the desk. Hidden in the space behind it was a shelf on which was whistling a flat brown Radio Shack telephone.

6

It stopped ringing.

Natalie pulled out the telephone and held it to her ear. Dial tone. Mystified, she drew enough slack in the wire to put it on the desk. Then she picked up the drawer. The back had been neatly sawed off and rebuilt, duplicating the original mortise joint, and dirt or dust had been rubbed into the fresh cuts to make them look old. She felt inside the desk, found the phone jack and a hole cut where the wire exited. Crawling behind the desk, she found the wire stapled to the inside of a leg. It disappeared between two floorboards.

Natalie rocked back on her heels. Wallace had installed a telephone line, without telling her. He had hidden the telephone, well and deliberately. She had found it by sheer accident, thanks to the dog. Mechanically, she gathered up the scattered catalogs. Orvis, French Creek, Damart, L. L. Bean. Under the heap was a paperback book, which she hadn't noticed. She turned it over and stared, for a second time, in astonished disbelief. It was a Grove Press edition of *The Pearl*.

On the cover was a dark photograph of a nude in a boudoir chair. *A Journal of Voluptuous Reading. The Underground Magazine of Victorian England. Three Volumes Complete in One.* Natalie turned it over with shaking hands. Cracks in the binding and thumbed pages showed it was well used. She threw it suddenly across the room, crying, "What is your problem?"

The dog lumbered after it. Then the telephone whistled. Once. Twice. Three rings.

Natalie snatched the flat handset off the desk and pressed it to her ear. In her haste, she touched the plunger to her chin, accidentally breaking the connection. A jumble of clicks set off a dial tone. She put it back on the desk and tried to settle down. In seconds it rang again. She took a breath, picked it up, and placed it gingerly against her ear. She heard the *blip-blip* of an overseas call. "Vassily," a woman breathed. "The Millionaire laughed when I said Valentine's Day. Did I do wrong?"

"Who is this?"

She heard a startled breath. The phone clicked and the line went dead. A woman, she thought, as much in sadness as in anger. A woman calling her husband on a private—make that secret—telephone. Blinking at tears, she stared out the window, hardly aware the dog had laid its head on her lap.... A woman who didn't know Wallace was dead ...

"Natalie!"

Startled, she saw Lynn Brown, her lawyer, marching across the lawn in a business suit and Reeboks, waving her briefcase and trailed by two identically attired assistants. Natalie ran to intercept her before she came in the barn, drying her eyes on her sleeve.

"Hi. Sorry, I was working."

"I saw the smoke in the chimney. How you doing?" Lynn slipped an arm around her waist and they started up to the house, trailing the assistants, who had veered aside to let the friends talk.

"You got a dog?"

"Company."

"Good move. Who's going to walk it in New York?"

"No. She doesn't live—"

Natalie stopped. Lynn bumped against her. "What's wrong?"

The woman on Wallace's secret telephone—the woman who didn't know Wallace was dead, despite the hysterical *Post* and *News* headlines—had spoken Russian.

Va-SEE-lee. Vassily. Wallace. *Did I do wrong?* All in Russian.

She had been so shaken by the existence of the phone and the porn book, it hadn't registered. Besides, Wallace would occasionally say something in Russian and she would answer easily from the years of study or childhood recollections of talking to Russian house servants. It was a sexy language, in bed.

Vassily—

"Natalie? You okay?"

"Yes. Listen, I forgot. I left my notes. Go up to the house, I'll catch up."

"That's okay. I'll walk you."

"No. Listen, can you send someone for lettuce? I've got a quiche, but no salad."

"Don't worry about it."

"I want a salad." Natalie turned toward the barn, which seemed to loom very large against the thinning trees. "Lynn, we'll work in the dining room. Spread out on the table. I'll be right up."

"Can I make coffee?"

"Right. Make coffee."

The dog raced her to the barn, barking. She tore into Wallace's office, slammed the door, and sat at his desk. The phone's number slot was blank.

Natalie extended her index finger to press 0, to ask the operator in whose name the phone was registered. She was in motion, when her eye fell on the redial button and she remembered that these phones stored in memory the last number dialed. If she pressed that, she would repeat Wallace's last call. Hands trembling, she pressed the redial.

Laboriously the phone clicked through a series of numbers. It went on so long that she realized it was out of the 203 Connecticut area code. Lines engaged. It began ringing. A woman said, "Four-six-three-five."

"Uh, who is this?"

"This is an answering service. Do you want to leave a message?"

Then it hit her. "Four-six-three-five?"

"Do you wish to leave a message?"

"Is this two-one-three code? California?"

"That's right. Do you wish to leave a message?"

Natalie slammed the phone down on the desk. She remembered the number all too well. It was the last four digits of an unlisted telephone in Diana Darbee's Malibu beach house.

Now she dialed the operator, and asked, "What number is this?"

"Four-two-six, two-five-four-eight."

"And to whom is it listed?"

"I can't tell you that."

"Is it unlisted?"

"I don't have that information."

"How can I get it?"

"You can't. The telephone company doesn't give names for numbers. If it's urgent, call the police."

Natalie broke the connection and stared at the phone. She should, of course, inform the police; it might bear on Wallace's murder. But she dreaded the ramifications. The detectives would love a secret telephone and leap to conclusions if she admitted that a woman had called. They would twist it into evidence that Wallace had been shot by a lover. When the reporters picked it up, there would be front page headlines again, more embarrassing speculation, another threat to the business, and new attacks on their marriage.

Yet, there could be a clue in the phone.

"Delegate," Wallace had nagged her. "Delegate."

She thought a moment and called Kenny Wilson, the retired FBI agent who headed Cotillion Furs' security department. Ordinarily, he was a steady, affably loquacious man, but today he started with an apology. Natalie stopped him. "I meant what I told you that night, Kenny. And the police agreed. Your people were there to protect the goods, not to be bodyguards. I don't blame you."

"I appreciate you saying that, Mrs. Nevsky. It's damned nice of you. Is there anything I can do for you?"

At that moment it struck Natalie that it was not in her business interests to share with anyone at Cotillion Furs that her husband had maintained a secret telephone. Not with a shareholder fight looming and doubts about her leadership. She'd have to find the number another way.

"Just calling to touch base, Kenny. I'll be in the office in a few days. Any problems?"

"A little hijacking. I would have called you but we got the stuff back."

"Was anyone hurt?"

"No problem. The truck broke down, they bugged out. Happy ending."

"I guess we got lucky."

"Actually," Kenny said, "it's rigged to break down if the wrong guy's driving. By the way, I just walked the insurance investigator through your apartment, Mrs. Nevsky. Nothing's missing."

"Bernadette came in before they had time."

"I don't know. They sure tossed the bedrooms. Right down to the mattress. They were looking hard."

"Looking?"

"Hey, don't let me worry you. I just wanted you to know nothing's taken."

"Yes, but what do you mean, looking? Like searching? For what?"

"Mrs. Nevsky, you live in a rich neighborhood. When they don't find a wall safe, they check under the mattress. Lousy timing, but it coulda been a lot worse."

"You're right, Kenny. Thanks a lot. See you soon."

She hid the phone behind the drawer again, wondering vaguely where Ma Bell sent the bill, but when she closed the drawer, she felt right to keep this particular secret to herself. She wished Kenny hadn't used the word "looking." Somehow it implied a deeper invasion than plain thievery.

The telephone whistled.

Natalie yanked the drawer, seized the phone. *Blip. Blip.*

"*Zdrah'stvooite!*"

Silence. Static.

"Hello?"

"Is Wallace Nevsky there?" the woman asked in English.

"Who is calling?"

"Tell him Luba."

"May I ask in reference to what?"

"Just tell him Luba."

Luba. The Russian diminutive of Ludmilla. She tried to picture the caller. A Russian accent. She sounded young. And she sounded afraid, a frightened woman fighting to maintain control.

"Is Wallace Nevsky there? I can't stay on the line."

"I don't know how to tell you this—I don't know what he means to you. But Wallace Nevsky is dead."

"That's not possible."

"Who are you?"

Her demand drew silence at first, then a muffled noise. A sob, Natalie realized, with bitter rage.

"How did he die?" the woman whispered.

"He was *shot*," Natalie said coldly. "By a woman."

"Oh, my God."

"Wallace was my husband. Who are you?"

Silence again, stretching like a spider's web. Then a keening, cut short by grim resolve: "We shall meet tomorrow."

"Why?"

"In Connecticut I am being tomorrow."

"No!" Natalie was horrified. Connecticut was too close. The woman was a disembodied voice in a distant land. Here was home, their home. "No. I can't meet you." Through the window she saw Lynn striding toward the barn again.

"Please," Luba begged. "We must talk."

"I don't *want* to meet you," Natalie raged back at her. "I don't want to know you. Can't you see that?"

"Where is house?"

"You don't know?" Natalie's heart soared. She didn't know the house. Wallace hadn't brought her here.

"Natalie!" Lynn called.

She covered the phone. "I'll be right there."

"Where can we meet?" Luba said.

Lunch, she thought. *I can handle this at lunch.* Somewhere she wasn't known . . . "There's a place called the Hopkins Inn. On Lake Waramaug. Above New Preston."

"Noon, tomorrow," said Luba, and hung up.

"Natalie!" Lynn called, waving up at the window.

"Yes, coming."

"Hey, guy, if you want to keep owning your company, we've got work to do."

"Right."

Both assistants had been dispatched to town, giving Natalie and Lynn some time alone. They settled around the dining room table and Lynn said, "In a perfect world, you'd have a few weeks to grieve in peace, but I don't think it's going to work out that way. You've got three serious problems. Debts, nervous shareholders, and Diana Darbee."

"Four problems," Natalie interrupted. "My biggest problem is supply. Without Wallace, I don't have a steady supply of the quality coats I need. And that's what the shareholders are really worried about."

"Four problems. Which means there's one decision you've got to make right now. And I don't know if you're ready for it."

"What do you mean?" Luba said she didn't know where the house was. So Wallace hadn't brought her to their bed upstairs. He hadn't used the bed they'd bought together in a Montreal antique shop. So what did that mean? He'd taken her to the apartment instead? To hotels? Or gone to Luba's place, wherever that was?

"I mean, if I weren't your friend and I weren't your lawyer, if I were looking at you from the other side—like one of your banks, or a takeover attorney—I'd say, this woman's kind of flaky now, kind of hurt and confused. I'd say she hasn't just been widowed, she's been screwed."

Natalie returned a shaky smile. "Do me a favor. Don't tell anybody."

"Well, I am on your side."

"So what's this one decision I've got to make right now?"

"Do you want to fight?"

"What's the alternative?"

"I can get you out of this sitting pretty. If those shareholders want it, they can have it; I can turn your and Wallace's shares into some fairly serious money."

"No."

"No what?"

"We made Cotillion. I'm keeping it."

"It means going to war right now. This minute. And you *are* flaky, dear. You're worse now than at the funeral. It's sinking in. I hate talking to you this way, but I have to. Because if you fight and lose, you'll lose it all. . . . Look at the numbers. I'll get some coffee."

Lynn headed to the kitchen, Reeboks squeaking tracks on the waxed chestnut floors. Natalie couldn't think. She got up from the table, drifted to the back parlor window and stared at the barn, wondering about the woman on the telephone. Luba was a stupid name. It sounded round and fat and sloppy. But she was sure Luba was none of those things.

Pleading exhaustion, she got rid of Lynn at three o'clock, but as soon as the lawyer's car had rounded the first curve of the driveway, Natalie ran back to the barn. It was getting cold. She stoked the embers in the stove and fed it split logs. Then she sat in Wallace's swivel chair, propped her feet on his desk, and scrutinized the wooden room, wondering what else he might have hidden here.

She was thinking of things like small presents the woman might have given him, or letters, a pressed flower, maybe receipts from restaurants or hotels. She did not want to find any of these proofs, but she had to look for them, to establish their absence. The secret telephone was so bizarre, so incriminating, that she found it difficult even to wish for his innocence.

She scanned the boards that sheathed the walls, looking for cracks where a board might swing open or a letter might be stashed. The room had a tin ceiling, like an old New York saloon, and she wondered where the farmer had found it. She stood on the desk and tugged a bent corner, but it held firm. She went down into the cellar again, under the tack room. Here and there, light glinted in a crack in the floorboards, but anything that had slipped through would be lying on the dry earthen floor.

Back at the desk, she inspected the back of all the drawers. When she found his tape player, she thought she would listen to music. Wallace had been listening to Mozart divertimentos. She pushed the play button and out came the haunting theme that reminded Wallace of *A Chorus Line*. "Who am I anyway?" he would sing to Mozart. "Am I my resume?"

Natalie began to cry. Hurt and angry, she pawed through his other tapes and inserted Agustin Anievas playing Chopin ballades. But no. Chopin would set off memories—the C sharp Minor Fantaisie Impromptu invariably set Wallace to singing, "I'm always chasing rainbows," as surely as *Swan Lake* provoked songs from *West Side Story*.

She ejected the Chopin tape. It felt funny. The label was thick. She held it to the window and saw in the fading light that a Philips prerecorded tape cassette label had been glued on to a blank tape. The knockouts that prevented recording over were still in place. Her hands shook as she inserted the cassette in the machine and pressed Play. Wallace's voice jumped out, bright and lively.

"When Russia sneezes I catch cold."

7

My entire life, from my conception to this October morning, has moved in Russia's thrall. Like a serf, my fate is my master's fate, but I'd be a schmuck to complain. Thirty million Russian people have died violently during my lifetime, and even as I speak, their country reels again on the brink of violent change.

"Meanwhile, I survive, nattering into a tape recorder on a farm where not a shot has been fired in anger in two hundred years. Outside the window my beautiful wife beds peaceful gardens for the winter. Tonight we drive to New York and dine with friends. Tomorrow, work. How marvelous to be an American. But I'm also a child of the Revolution, and that breeds responsibility.

"I'm recording this oral history for my children. They're not born yet, but I can't risk waiting. Too many gents my age keel over with a coronary while enjoying their contribution to the birth process. Also, as I'll explain, my past is not dead. I live very much in the present, and at present, Russia is awakening to change. But in Russia, with her seventy-year history of gangster rule, change threatens. For every good and honest Gorbachev espousing perestroika, there is a resentful Ligachev or Lapshin dragging his feet. For every ardent reformer, a troglodyte defending his cozy cave, or an anti-Semitic reactionary member of Pamyat. For every supposed friend, a secret enemy. This

*is, after all, Russia I'm talking about, and Russia breeds as many
children as she needs to man her guns and hunt down her enemies,
both real and imagined. A bullet makes no distinction, which is why,
after all these years, I have a permanent crick in my neck from
looking over my shoulder."*

Natalie stared at the little machine. He had practically predicted his
own murder. She stopped the tape, rewound to the beginning, and
replayed the part she had heard, but it came out sounding the same.
Wallace Nevsky knew he was in danger. She let the tape continue
playing as she wondered what he had done to be mistaken for an
enemy.

*"Incidentally, kids, I rejected the idea of doing a video because I
don't want you to get hung up on an old man's face. This is a modern
story, going down right now. So here we go. And believe me, Dad's
told a lot of lies in his time, but this is the true life story of an
American Russian. Honest Injun.*

*"It starts in 1905, seventeen years before I was born. There was a
revolution in Russia, which failed. The czar sent a punitive expedition
into the countryside. The guilty, the innocent, revolutionaries, criminals, and the mass of quiet little men who love their wives felt the
terror.*

*"A little girl named Rachel Klimovitzsky, your grandmother, saw
her father flee Cossack justice. It's been said he fled for political
reasons, but simple fraud was more like it—cheating the czar's fur
monopoly. Rachel's father was a furrier, buying illegally from the
sable trappers. The politics came later, as usual.*

*"Rachel's father got away, but the Cossacks burned their izba, and
raped and killed her mother. Rachel and her brother were raised by
the landowner, a decent sort by local standards, who controlled that
region of Siberia. Rachel grew into a very beautiful young girl, and
quite passionate—Dad didn't develop his proclivities from thin air—
and the inevitable happened. The landowner fell in love. Rachel's
brother came home unexpectedly—expelled for revolutionary activity
from the university the landowner had sent him to—misconstrued an
afternoon tryst on the billiard table as rape, and brained the landowner with a cue stick. The times and animosities being what they
were, a simple tragedy was appropriated by conflicting sides for their
own goals. Her brother was shot, but Rachel escaped with the help of
the radical Social Revolutionaries.*

"The Social Revolutionaries moved her by a sort of underground

railway to Moscow and on to St. Petersburg. The trip took about a year. She became thoroughly indoctrinated in the principles of Communist revolution as practiced by that particularly violent wing of anticzarist Bolshevism, and embraced the movement with the same passion once reserved for her guardian.

"The Okhranka, the czar's secret police, were so powerful that even the most noisome of St. Petersburg working districts wasn't safe for Rachel.

"Among the many things that never change in Russia are the cops. You have a better chance of getting followed by the cops—the militia, the KGB, the GRU, what have you—in Russia than of getting mugged in America. It's kind of fun, when you get used to it. And sometimes they can come in handy. My flashlight died once while I was trying to locate a door in a pitch-black courtyard, so I borrowed one from the not-so-secret policeman on my tail. I've often wondered who dined out longer on that story, him or me.

"Anyway, the SRs got Rachel out of the country, over the Finnish border, and onto a Norwegian mailboat to Newcastle, England. From there she was on her own, though an SR welcome awaited her in New York City, if she could only get there. She made her way to Liverpool, found work sewing hats, as she had for her father, and earned the money for a steamer ticket. Imagine your grandmother at eighteen, kids, in mid-Atlantic. Steerage was not for her. So she began sneaking past the barriers for a stroll at night on the third class deck, a peek at second, and one night a heady walk on the first class promenade. She owned one thing of value, a gorgeous sable hat her father had left when he ran. When darkness hid her shabby greatcoat, she waltzed past the stewards with the beauty, the bearing, and the hat of an aristocrat.

"I don't mean to make light of her leaving, incidentally. Exile is the worst punishment a Russian can suffer. Happily, she returned, but I'm jumping ahead.

"Along the first class promenade strolled James Stuart—your mother's great-great uncle and Cousin Greg's great-great-grandfather—a callow youth of no proven merit beyond the good fortune to be born into a family that rewarded its young men with an education, a grand tour of Europe, and a functionary's job in the family bank. Young James struck up a conversation with this exotic Russian beauty, adept at handling men ranging from Russian aristocrats to revolutionary fanatics. Upon arriving in New York, Rachel was reunited with her

father making fur coats on the Lower East Side. Soon, James Stuart was calling on her, to the astonishment of Delancey Street and the horror of his family.

"Secretly, Rachel also joined up with an SR cell in New York, whose members were quick to notice the advantage of her liaison with James Stuart."

Natalie smiled, remembering that Wallace had told her this on their first date. She had professed astonishment. "Wait. Your mother was a Socialist. That means that Greg's great-grandmother was a Socialist?"

"Your great-great second cousin twice removed, or some such."

"I never heard this before."

"Ask your great-aunt Margaret."

"I did," Natalie admitted. "She wouldn't tell me. She'd rather have an ax murderer in the family than a Socialist."

"Not to worry, it's a recessive gene."

On the tape, Wallace was saying, *"They married, and had two children, James and Gregory. Rachel was naïve in her way and proceeded to fill the young banker's head with the Socialist doctrine of the age, which entertained the belief that war between the tottering corrupt regimes in Europe was inevitable—capitalism's last gasp, from which would be forged international revolution.*

"Here James Stuart proved to be less the twit than his family supposed. If European war was inevitable, he reasoned, the United States would inevitably supply weapons and matériel. With an ocean between them, great profits lay in shipping. So while his wife prattled on about the new order, young James invested in ships. The world war Rachel promised commenced in 1914. In the two years before most Americans grasped its implications, young James turned a small fortune into a very large one, and the Stuart family, whose illustrious generations had frittered away an inheritance won in the China trade, was back in the pink.

"Rachel was appalled by his war profiteering, and begged him to stop. A true SR would have loved the delicious irony: by supplying England, France, and Russia against Germany, Rachel's capitalist husband was helping prolong a war that was destroying the czar. But Rachel could not see it that coldly. She was, in the end, a romantic Socialist. And it was a terrible war.

"James refused to abandon the shipping business, pleading that it was for the good of his family. They fought and drifted apart, Rachel into the figurative arms of the SR movement, which used her as a

courier. Securely ensconced as a New York matron, she returned to Russia under the auspices of a ladies' war nursing association.

"She arrived in Petrograd just as the Russian Revolution broke out."

The Radio Shack telephone whistled.

Natalie scrambled for the desk drawer. She had it halfway open before she realized that she had heard the phone on Wallace's recording.

"Hang on," said Wallace.

Natalie heard a click on the tape when Wallace switched off the recorder. She had no way of knowing how long he spoke on the telephone, or who had called, because the tape clicked again immediately, signaling where Wallace had turned it back on.

"Where was I, kids? Right, Petrograd." She thought his voice had changed. He sounded distracted.

"The czar abdicated. Workers' soviets seized control of the country and six months later the Bolsheviks seized control of the soviets.

"Heady times for a bold young woman, in the midst of a revolution she'd been part of half her life. Wealthy, attractive by all accounts, on her own, and holding some very impressive Social Revolutionary credentials, not to mention a precious American passport. The world in Petrograd that winter must have been her oyster. And the pearl she chose was a dashing Cossack officer, a hero of the revolution, who had charged the czar's police at a crucial moment on the Nevsky Boulevard, and had turned up again in October outside the Winter Palace with sufficient armored cars to unnerve the provisional government. The Bolsheviks had no love of Cossacks in general, but they knew who they needed. The Germans still threatened, White armies were gathering, and civil war loomed. Rachel's young Cossack rose quickly in Red Army ranks, until Rachel became pregnant.

"This should have been cause for celebration—a new life in a new society. But something terrible had gone wrong in Russia. And a relatively bloodless revolution was turning gruesome. Lenin, who had taken charge, had begun shooting entire classes of people purely for who they were. Ironically, the first group to taste this new 'justice' were the violent Social Revolutionaries.

"Pregnant with me, Rachel Klimovitzsky Stuart had to flee Russia, again. My father's future lay with the Red Army. It must have been heartbreaking, for they stalled until conditions had deteriorated so badly that Rachel barely found passage on a freighter. I was born in a Baltic storm and named Wallace after the Scots sea captain who

delivered me. So you can see, can't you, that slipping across Russian borders is in my genes.

"*Rachel made her way home to New York. Her husband had moved his capital out of war shipping into the stock market just in time for the twenties' financial boom. James took Rachel back, even though she insisted that he adopt me, which he did, reluctantly. I am quite sure I am the only Jewish Cossack ever baptized in St. Thomas' Episcopal.*"

Natalie laughed.

"*He hated me,*" Wallace continued soberly. "*I symbolized his wife's indiscretion, shall we say. He said he forgave her, but he lied. He was a prisoner of that peculiarly American unwillingness to share his bedmate.*"

Natalie pressed Stop and Rewind, and played it again. "*He was a prisoner of that peculiarly American unwillingness to share his bedmate.*" Stop. Rewind. "*. . . unwillingness to share—*" Stop. Natalie sat still, the word *bastard* forming on her lips, but oddly, not in her heart. Too soon, she thought, and wondered if she was being cynical. Play.

"*. . . bedmate. He shipped me off to boarding school when I was five. There I languished with other abandoned children, sopping up the tastes, if not the sensibilities, of upper-class Americans until the stock market crash of 1929. Rachel had predicted it, of course— what Socialist hadn't?—but this time James hadn't listened and I was suddenly shipped home for lack of funds.*

"*Home was hell. My stepfather was ruined, a cuckold and a failure. Mother, financed by the Comintern, was busy with Soviet causes and maintaining a long-distance affair with my real father, who was still rising in the ranks of the Red Army and had adopted the* nom de revolution *Aleksandr Nevsky, after an old Russian patriot. Lenin was dead and Mother's social station made her valuable to the Soviets, who were desperate to trade for American machinery. The U.S. hadn't yet recognized the Communist regime, but my mother served on friendship commissions, provided introductions, and generally made herself useful, traveling tirelessly. Russians admire strength, especially in a woman, and she was a very strong woman.*

"*I turned to the one person who both loved me and had time for me, my mother's father, the furrier on Delancey Street. Grandfather was grouchy. He smelled funny. And though it was twenty-five years since he had fled Russia, he still could not launch an English sentence without the phrase 'De idea is dat.'*

"*We spoke Russian. He taught me the trade, from marking pelts to dressing, letting out, sewing, blocking, nailing. To this day I can build a coat from raw skins.*

"*My early teens were a schizophrenic time, tanning wolverine skins one weekend, whacking polo balls the next with my old chums from boarding school. But as I grew older, and matured, I embraced my mother's politics, fought for the furriers' union. I changed my name to Nevsky, and, at fifteen, enlisted in the Abraham Lincoln Battalion to fight the fascists in Spain.*

"*Mother and I crossed on the* Normandie *and parted at Le Havre. She was off to Russia, where, outspoken as usual, she informed Stalin that the show trials of the old Bolsheviks ought to be stopped. Stalin thanked her warmly for her opinion. She was arrested the next day. . . .*"

His effort to sound casual came out brittle, though Natalie knew that only she could hear the failure.

"*After we lost in Spain, I drifted to Paris. Through Russians I had met in the International Brigades, I tried to make contact with my father. But by then, Stalin had turned his purges against the Red Army and the Cossack, too, had vanished.*

"*In Paris I did a little freelance spying—a sort of industrial espionage directed against the Nazis—then fell in with a group who were spiriting Jews out of Germany. I'm half Jewish, of course. What I knew of being a Jew, I knew from my grandfather. My mother was political. The fur trade being international, the Jews I contacted in Germany were furriers, too.*

"*When Stalin signed the nonaggression pact with the Nazis, I lost my taste for the Soviet regime. Stalin had taken my mother and my father; as I had seen the Nazis' work close up in Spain and again on the Jews, I enlisted with the British, who honed my spy craft, such as it was, and sent me back to Europe. When America finally entered the war, I switched over to the OSS, the new American intelligence outfit. OSS, God bless 'em, sent me to liaise with Russian intelligence.*

"*In Moscow, I learned that Stalin had rehabilitated my father.*"

Natalie stopped the recorder. Wallace had never told her about his real father. She had asked him at dinner on their first date, but the most he would say was, "That's another story," as he picked up the wine list and signaled the waiter. "Very romantic, and one with which I have not yet made my peace. I don't like California whites, do you?"

He never told her that his father had been released from prison. It was the first clue that Wallace might have had a reason to disguise the tape cassette. She pressed Play, with a gut feeling that she was about to hear the truth.

"The Red Army had discovered that Cossack cavalry had a place in the modern war fighting German tanks. Under the right conditions, they were devastatingly effective as mobile guerrillas, and my father at age fifty-two was a hero once again.

"We had a magnificent reunion, if you can call the first meeting between father and son a reunion. Somehow we stole some days from the war, went hunting, rode horses, and drank vodka. It was the happiest time in my life.

"In the spring of 1945, days before Berlin fell, my father was captured by the Germans while leading an advance light horse squadron. Happily, he was freed by American troops. By then we knew Russia well enough to know that the purges were only temporarily suspended until the war was over and I persuaded him to come to America.

"But President Roosevelt and Prime Minister Churchill had promised Stalin they would repatriate captured Russian soldiers. It seemed little to ask, because they had no idea that concentration camps awaited Russian prisoners of war.

"The Cossack knew he would be killed or imprisoned. I knew some powerful people by then and I pleaded my father's case. But the Allies had agreed, and I couldn't engineer an exception.

"I watched the prison trains steam back to Russia. The man beside my father broke the window and slashed his own throat with the glass. My father was too brave for that, but he had been wounded and it was unlikely he would survive the winter. . . ."

Natalie listened to Wallace's voice echo silently. The hissing tape ran a long minute. Then Wallace said, in still, clear tones, *"Ordinary revenge is for fools who can't see the future for the past. Change is the best revenge, the only revenge. Thwart the monsters by changing the world. Ignorance had caused my father's death—ignorance in the West of what was evil in the East, Roosevelt and Churchill's ignorance of the monster Stalin."*

The telephone whistled again.

"Sorry, kids. Grand Central Station in here today."

The tape clicked off and on and he was back. His voice had changed again. He was brisk, hurried, but more than that, distant.

"Speaking of change, kids. The master calls. The serf tugs his forelock, but he'll be back soon, and he'll tell you the rest of the story, including how he met the two most important people in his life—President Harry Truman and the beautiful woman who became your mother. . . . Wish the old man luck." Before the switch clicked he muttered to himself, *"He's bloody well going to need it."*

Natalie stopped the machine, climbed out of Wallace's chair, and stared out the window, remembering another conversation on their first date. Despite the attraction she had felt, she had been put off by his reputation as a womanizer, and had kept things strictly business-like. They had been working together for months launching Cotillion, and she had thought at first he meant just another working dinner, until he suggested the Russian Tea Room, where, according to the gossip columnists, he pursued his conquests, including Diana.

She had protested that she would like someplace else. Undaunted, Wallace chose the Jockey Club on Central Park South, which Natalie assumed was another glitzy showoff place. She was disconcerted to discover a romantic, candlelit back room decorated with exquisite flowers. The couples dining looked as though they had booked nearby hotel rooms for coffee and dessert.

"You look lovely," Wallace greeted her, rising until she was seated. She braced for a hand kiss, but he merely asked, "Champagne?"

"Scotch."

"That's a pretty dress."

"I borrowed it from my mother." Everything she had tried on at her own apartment had looked too young. Ambivalent, to say the least, about going out with him, she didn't want to look like his granddaughter.

"Don't let her see you in it, she might not wear it again."

Natalie had tried to shift the subject back to business and Wallace had obliged, after a fashion, explaining that V. O. Sojuzpushnina—the Soviet fur monopoly—was merely a modern extension of the czar's old monopoly on sable. Suddenly his eyes were burning. "Nothing changes in Russia. Czar–Stalin. Siberia–gulag. *Okhranka*–KGB. The spy in the tavern–the tapped telephone, including pay phones near your hotel. The Crimean conquest–Afghanistan."

"You really love Russia, don't you?"

Wallace's laughter had been deep and bittersweet. "Like all Russians, I'm in love with what Russia could be."

And from that moment on, Natalie had been in love with what Wallace Nevsky could be.

She rewound the tape and pressed the Play button to bring back his voice.

8

The morning came soft, windless, and remarkably mild for November. By noon it was warm enough for the Hopkins Inn to serve lunch outdoors on a stone terrace. From her table under tall bare trees, Natalie could see the road in front of the white clapboard building and beyond it Lake Waramaug, small, gray-blue, and surrounded by low brown hills. She watched the road, where people were arriving for lunch, toyed with a Perrier, and wondered what to expect.

Car after car parked and decanted older men and women dressed in tweeds. The woman on the telephone had sounded young, but it suddenly occurred to Natalie that Wallace could have been involved with a woman any age.

She beckoned a waitress. "I'm expecting another woman. I already told the maître d', but could you please check in the bar?" The waitress looked harassed. "She may have slipped past him," Natalie explained, annoyed with herself for allowing a tentative note to creep into her voice.

"What does she look like?"

"Probably very attractive."

"Another Perrier?"

"I think I'll have a CC and water—change that—on the rocks. Water on the side."

Be something, she thought. Be a reason. Don't be a girlfriend.

Last night Natalie had played Wallace's last words over and over until his voice grew muddy as the power ebbed from the batteries. God knew, or cared, what he meant about Harry Truman; she was hunting for proof that she was to be the mother of those unborn children to whom he had addressed his life story. But all she had found were questions that ranged from why he had recorded on that clunky old tape player instead of his prized pocket Panasonic, to what could be so secret about an oral history for his children? That answer had been lost when the second telephone call cut his story short.

So, after Luba explained who she was and who the "millionaire" was, and what Valentine's Day meant, Natalie intended to ask if it was Luba's call that had dragged Wallace to Russia, early. She had not thought anything of it at the time, but he had left, suddenly, on a Sunday, that October Sunday, instead of the Tuesday he had originally planned. If Luba had been the one who called, perhaps she knew why he had been killed, hours after he returned from that trip.

A red Ford Escort appeared on the road bearing New York plates with a rental Z. It passed the inn, and she saw that the driver was alone. The car turned around and came back and parked. A woman got out and hurried up the front walk. Through the shrubbery Natalie caught a glimpse of a pale peach suit and heard high heels clicking. The woman went inside and moments later followed the maître d' onto the terrace.

Natalie's stomach clenched. Her hair was golden in the dappled sunlight. She was very young, twenty-five at most, and terrifyingly beautiful. She had a wide sensual mouth and Natalie died a small death when she imagined it on Wallace's skin. Her suit was Chanel, her legs slim, her breasts a little full, and while she was not as angular as Natalie, she still fit the tall, rangy type that drew Wallace's attention at a party.

The maître d' headed directly for Natalie's table, but Luba scrutinized the terrace before following. Her bag and shoes looked Italian and matched perfectly the peach-colored wool suit. She arrived smiling, with a cheery, "Sorry, darling. I'm late again."

Natalie stared at her extended hand. She wore no gloves; gold rings flashed in the sunlight. No wedding ring.

Luba twice brushed a perfumed cheek to hers, first the left, then, when Natalie recoiled, the right. She had a tabloid newspaper tucked incongruously under her arm. She sat down and laid it on the table, facing Natalie. It was *The Village Voice,* open to the "Personals" columns in the back.

Luba asked for black coffee. Her voice was thin and musical. The cheery greeting, Natalie finally realized, was an act. Luba's cool, gray eyes were wary, and miles from her smile. Who, Natalie wondered, was she trying to fool?

They sat silently a moment, looking each other over, until the waitress interrupted them with Natalie's drink. "You found your friend."

"Yes."

"Do you want to see the specials?"

"No. She's having a black coffee."

Again, they waited silently. Finally the coffee arrived. Luba stirred in two sugars and placed the empty packets on her newspaper. She said, "It's good of you to see me."

"You made it sound vital."

"It is," Luba said, toying with her pearls.

"Why?"

"Because it was vital to Wallace Nevsky." She spoke so low that no one could have heard a yard away. Nonetheless, she shot quick glances at the tables around them.

"I don't want to fence. And I don't want to play games."

"I realize this is hard for you."

"What was my husband to you?"

Luba looked down at her newspaper and back at Natalie. She seemed exhausted. Awed by her beauty, Natalie hadn't noticed at first that her eyes were like pinpricks, as if she hadn't slept in days or was running on pills. She pulled a cigarette case from her handbag. Her index finger was tinged yellow from smoke. Her perfume failed to disguise the cigarette smoke in her clothes, and a second odor, familiar and vaguely industrial. It took a moment, then she got it. Kerosene. Jet fuel. A smell that clung when you traveled for days.

"Did you have a good flight?" she asked, as Luba got the cigarette lighted with a shaking hand.

"Interminable."

"From where?"

"Natalie, what did Wallace tell you about me?"

"Nothing."

Luba tapped the sugar packs with a chipped polished nail. "Please tell me."

"I never heard of you until you called. Did you use that phone often?"

Luba was silent. Her eyes darted about the terrace. They were gray in shadow, silver in the light.

"My husband went to Russia before he was killed. Right after someone called him on that telephone. Was it you?"

"Yes," whispered Luba.

"Did you see him in Russia?"

"Yes."

Natalie could not ask what she had to ask so she said, instead, "Why did he go early?"

"As you say, because I called him."

"Why?"

"He had business in Russia."

"It was early for the fur auction."

"He knew people. He had to see them." She grew suddenly animated, as if she were proud of Wallace. "He knew everyone, you see. He knew the *Nomenklatura*. All who counted. He had *blat*."

"Influence?"

"Oh yes. He could talk to anyone. Even a Politburo member."

"Which one?"

"Many."

Many? Natalie was mystified. In America that would be like knowing the White House chief of staff, the leaders of the House and Senate, and Lee Iacocca.

"He knew—how do you say?—to go *na lyeva*."

"On the left?"

"Yes, you know, around things. He knew how to get things, legally or . . . the other way. You don't know this?"

"What kind of business did he come for when you called? Why did you call?"

Luba's face closed up again. The gray eyes went blank like clouded mirrors. "Did he bring you anything?" she asked.

"Like what?"

The Russian woman's hands flew impatiently. "A souvenir. Anything—from Russia."

"No. We both traveled too often for souvenirs. What did he do on that trip?"

"Something. He must have brought you something."

"Airplane tickets. We were going back to Russia for Christmas."

Luba looked astonished. "Vassily would bring *you* to Russia? He thought it safe?"

"What do you mean, safe?" Natalie asked sharply.

"Nothing." She fell silent, her eyes dull, and Natalie suspected that whatever she was running on was running down. Dragging deep on her cigarette, she held the smoke a long time, then exhaled it in a slow, dreamy trickle. Quietly, hesitantly, shooting looks about her, Luba asked, "Did he ever speak of millionaires?"

"Millionaires? No. The first I heard of millionaires was when you said it on the phone. What millionaires?"

"*Vozhd?*" Luba asked. "The Boss?"

"What boss?"

Luba shook her head.

"What did you mean by Valentine's Day?" Natalie asked.

"The Western love day. It's February fourteenth, isn't it?"

"I know what date it is," Natalie snapped.

She thought Luba mumbled, "He was a fool," but she might have said, "He was fooled." Before she could ask, Luba's eyes, which had continued to scan the luncheon terrace, the road, and the front walk, froze on a well-dressed couple who had driven up in a black Mercedes and were entering the hotel by the front door.

"Where," she asked, rising abruptly, "is the lavatory?"

Without waiting for Natalie's answer, the tall blonde strode across the stone terrace, turning male heads, and went inside the hotel. Natalie took a large, reckless swallow of her Canadian Club. Definitely Wallace's type: elegant and beautiful. And young. Even younger than Natalie when she had met him. Around the age Diana had started with him.

How could she have missed his affair? He had had the opportunity, of course, countless times apart, but when they were together they had been so close. How could he have fooled her? And why would he have wanted to? Had he lied when he told her how she excited him, how happy she made him? Had she been alone in her own excitement?

More than that, she had never doubted, and still did not, how much he cherished her. It was on that rock of appreciation that she had built her trust in him. To this moment, she could not believe that she had been so stupid and insensitive not to have noticed that Wallace found so much lacking in their lovemaking. As for the paperback *The Pearl*, the porn book was baffling.

She forced her mind to easier thoughts, no less strange. She had known Wallace moved comfortably in Russia, but Luba had made him sound like a very important man, and from what she knew of the Russians it wasn't their way to court outsiders. Then again, Luba could be exaggerating with lovesick pride.

The waitress came over with her pad. "Are you going to order?"

"I'll wait for the other woman."

"The blonde lady?"

"Yes."

"She left."

"What?"

"She lit out the kitchen door."

The red rental lurched off the grass shoulder and raced away. Natalie stared down the road. She still didn't know why Wallace had gone early to Russia or what Luba meant to him. The waitress cleared Luba's coffee and picked up the empty sugar packets. "You want her paper?"

"No—*wait!* Yes, leave it."

Grains of sugar marked the spot where Luba had dropped the empty packets. Sandwiched between "SWM Fitness Walker Seeks Swift SWF Partner" and "GJM Seeks Same" was a personal advertisement that began: "Have You Cast THE PEARL Before Swine? Join the Club."

She reached for her drink, thinking, This can't be a coincidence. And the longer she studied the wording of the personal ad in the context of *The Pearl,* the pornography, and Luba's erotic good looks, the more the "club" sounded like a sex club. I'm losing my mind, she thought. There has to be more to this. There has to be. She felt sick, debased by evidence of conclusions she could neither bear, nor refute. The whiskey clung in her throat, thick and oily. Nauseated, she fumbled in her bag, found her wallet, dropped money on the table and fled the terrace. In the lobby, she saw the couple Luba had fixed on, talking to the desk clerk. Natalie said, "Excuse me, did you recognize the tall blonde at my table?"

They looked at her, then at each other.

"I beg your pardon," said the man.

"The woman I was with recognized you, I think. We were on the terrace, and. . . ."

Wait, thought Natalie. What am I doing? She didn't know these people and she didn't really know the full extent of Luba's connection to Wallace. What if the Russian woman had had good reason to run? They were staring openly now, their conversation with the clerk apparently forgotten.

"Sorry," she mumbled, backing away with a flustered smile. "I thought I knew you." That excuse made no sense at all, but it gave her time to push out the door and hurry down the granite walk, her mind roaring with Wallace's secrets.

If they follow me it means something, she told herself. But as she struggled to turn Wallace's big Cadillac around on the narrow road, the only person who approached the black Mercedes was a bellboy, who hefted their luggage out of the trunk.

9

She fled to New York, so agitated by the Russian woman and the advertisement in the *Voice* that she was halfway there before she remembered to turn on Wallace's fore and aft radar detectors. Within seconds they shrilled and she got under sixty in the nick of time. Passing the trooper, she suddenly recalled that Leo Margulies had occasionally traveled with Wallace to Russia.

She telephoned his workroom on the car phone. "Just touching base. How are we doing?"

Leo hated the telephone. It made him belligerent, as if he suspected that his caller had somehow devised a way to rob him through the wire. "How are we doing?" he echoed. "We're doing fine. I'll tell you if there's problems."

"Well, don't wait too long, please. I'd rather have a disaster I can deal with than one that's out of control."

Leo sighed. "How are we doing! I got some furriers who promise they'll supply Cotillion coats like always. Half are lying. And a third are exaggerating. Then I got furriers who say they're going to work for somebody else 'cause Cotillion looks a little rocky and maybe they won't get paid. Then I got furriers who are dying to make you coats."

"So it's not all bad."

"They're people Wallace wouldn'ta asked for rope if he was drowning. But don't worry, I'm keeping at it."

"I appreciate the time you're putting in."

"Hey, I'm enjoying myself. I never got ulcers for somebody else. They don't hurt so much."

"Leo, did Wallace give you anything when he came back from his last trip?"

"Give? You mean on the boat?"

"Or when he picked up the coat?"

"Picked up the coat?"

"By the way, it's gorgeous. I never told you."

"I liked it on you at the board meeting. You should let me make you a hat."

"But did he bring you anything? From Russia."

"Like what?"

"A present, maybe."

"A *present*? Like those *meshuggana* dolls? No. Wallace never brought me presents. Broads he brought presents. Not Leo. Only a big fat note. Speaking of which, Natalie, I'm going to the auction in January."

"I guess you'll have to mark your own, now."

"Yes, but that's not what I mean when I say I'm going to the auction."

"I don't understand."

"Natalie, there's a six-month turnover in the sable business. If I spend two million dollars for skins in Leningrad in January, I'll be lucky to see it back in August."

"Are you saying Wallace lent you the money?"

"Thank you."

"Can I expect other furriers to tell me they're going to the auction?"

"Count on it."

"Will you help me sort them out?"

"Will you give me a break on the interest?"

"You've got it. Tell me, do you know the people Wallace knew in Russia?"

"Wallace saw them for me. That's how he earned his commission."

"I meant Russians other than Sojuzpushnina."

"In case you don't recall, Natalie, I sell lynx coats. I see Texas millionaires and Arabs and *gonifs* in the stock market. What's a Russian going to buy from me?"

"I don't know. I just meant people you might have met when you traveled with Wallace."

"Yeah! I met one, once. This crazy general had a mink farm."

"A Soviet general owned a mink farm?"

"Nobody *owns* anything over there, that's what's wrong with the place. This was like a research laboratory farm. Outside Moscow. He and Wallace were old buddies, from the war."

"What was his name?"

"Hell, I don't remember. Lap—something. Didn't sound that Russian. Hang on, I'm going through my book." Leo laughed aloud. "Hey, Natalie, you shoulda seen Leo the Jew drinking vodka at this table full of Red Army officers. We're watching the army gymnastic team perform. All girls. Maybe the oldest is twenty. Bodies you wouldn't believe."

"When was this?"

"Before you. Sorry, I don't have the name. You should have seen me, getting *schockered,* not knowing whose girlie not to stare at and just waiting for them to yell, 'Beat the Jew.' Wallace had some strange friends."

"You look like a ghost," her father greeted her uneasily.

"I'm not sleeping," she explained.

Richard Stuart was drinking at the Harvard Club, dressed in his day-off costume of blazer and bow tie. The martini before him was his second, she guessed, judging by the pinkness of his long, patrician face. He was several years younger than Wallace.

Natalie ducked a dinner invitation, accepted a drink, and asked him to intervene with certain family stockholders. It was vital to the business, but her mind was still on Luba and *The Village Voice* advertisement.

Her father echoed her aunt's complaint at the board meeting, "Don't you think it's a bit soon to be running around New York conducting business?"

"Too soon," she agreed docilely, struggling to swallow a weird laugh that started bubbling in her throat.

She had lost six pounds. The circles under her eyes resembled a linebacker's glare smudges. Her cheeks, ordinarily hollowed by a high bone structure, were, despite her best makeup efforts, gaunt. Most worrisome, however, was a peculiar feverish glow in her eyes. She had just enough of her wits about her to know she couldn't make deals looking crazy.

Richard Stuart leaned over the backgammon table that separated them and said, "As usual, it falls to my generation to inform your generation that the conventions you love to ignore are grounded in reason."

Natalie moved closer. What might have sounded cold to ears at the next table made her feel safer. Despite her many differences with her father, she was used to his finding words to explain the unexplainable. He was, by nature, a teacher. "What convention?"

"A decent period of mourning is more than seemly. It's not just 'nice.' It serves a purpose, gives you time to accept what has happened, to adjust to the consequences, to complete the past, and face the future."

"But I'm trying to save my future."

"You can't ignore reality forever."

"Why not?"

"Because reality moves on, even when you stand still."

"But I have an immediate reality I have to deal with first. Daddy, please. I've never asked your help in business."

"Wisely so," he agreed, cocking his glass at the waiter for another round. "As I know nothing about business."

"Well, I do. And I know this can't wait. I need your help now. The family shareholders all respect you and trust you."

"I can't understand why. They're the ones with money to invest. I'm just a washed-up diplomat who never learned how to get along with fools." Last year he had been finally forced out of his stormy foreign service career. Teaching Soviet bloc politics part-time at Columbia while he wrote his book had done nothing to assuage his bitterness, and a clever tongue was turning sharp.

"What I'm asking," she coaxed, "is more like diplomacy."

"Or war."

"Same thing, different means."

He liked that, and laughed appreciatively. Natalie pressed her advantage. "Dad, I'll lose everything if the family sells out. Some corporation will buy my company and break it up."

"Would that be the worst thing in the world?"

Compared to what, Natalie thought bleakly as the "reality" she could not discuss with him or anyone crashed back into the moment. Compared to your husband joining a sex club that advertised in *The Village Voice*? "Join the Club," the ad had read. "Have You Cast THE PEARL Before Swine? Join the Club." There was even a box number. What did the members do, enact a different pornographic chapter each evening?

Stop, she thought. Luba had bracketed the ad with the sugar packs deliberately to identify herself. No, to identify Natalie. To see if she knew. Knew what? The woman had telephoned from Europe. She had flown thousands of miles. She was a wreck. It had to be more than sex.

Why not put an ad in the *Voice* for Luba? "Dear PEARL, Let's Finish Lunch." How would Luba find her? Wallace's secret phone. Put an answering machine on it. "Dear PEARL. You've Got My Number. Lunch Is Getting Cold." The idea cheered her in a perverse way. How about, "Let's Do It On Valentine's Day."

"The worst thing in the world?" She smiled for her father. "Compared to nuclear holocaust, no."

"Sounds to me like you're gaining perspective," he said, smiling back. "Are you sure you won't have dinner?"

"Can't. I've set up a meeting with The Comedy Club."

He pulled a face at the mention of his daughter's network. "And how are the acquisitive airheads? Ready to buy the world? Or sell it?"

"My friends are taking time out to help me."

"That's nice— But, seriously, could not your tragedy be your opportunity to start over?"

"Start over?" she asked warily, fearing what was coming.

"A chance to do something better with your life."

"Wallace was my life," she protested, her words echoing hollowly in his cavern of secrets. "I've lost him, my best thing in the world. I don't want to lose the second best too, the business we made together."

"Listen, Natalie. This is your chance—"

"Oh, God. Not now, please."

"Yes, now! Listen, the Soviet thaw is genuine. With your business background and the language, I can still pull a few strings, get you posted to the Moscow embassy. Or at least Leningrad, to start."

"It doesn't take us long to get back to that old story, does it?" she asked, but he was too excited to hear. "Dad, you beat your head against the State Department bureaucracy for forty years. Why do you insist I do it?"

"Service is what our people do," he said with simple conviction. His brother Ronald was a deputy director of the Ford Foundation, his brother Jeffrey, curator of the Chinese section at the Metropolitan. He and his father had given their lives to the State Department under nine presidents. "The government is only as good as those who serve. Particularly with the yo-yos we elect."

"Please, Daddy, I hurt so much. I'm not twenty-two and off to foreign service school. I'm a widow. And I'm in a fight for my life."

"Your life?" he asked incredulously. "I can't believe that selling fur coats is my daughter's life."

Stunned by the onslaught, she heard herself protest like a twelve-year-old. "Why me? What about Mike trading bonds? He was playing computer games on Wall Street. Now he's just tried to organize shareholders against me as if he were some business genius. Send *him* to Russia."

"I've given up on your brother," her father said bluntly. "He's a fool."

In the midst of all her pain and confusion, and in spite of Michael's betrayal at the board meeting, she found herself rising on a sort of atavistic sibling tide to try to defend her little brother as she always had. "He's not a fool. He just doesn't—"

Richard Stuart cut her off before she could speak. "But you are special. And you were born to a tradition of public service."

"Let's say it aloud: Why do I prefer to hang around a bunch of low-class Jews?"

"Being Jewish has nothing to do with it. You've told me yourself, there are Greeks and God-knows-what."

"But all certifiably low class."

"Natalie, please."

"Do you know why I prefer the people Wallace and I work with to the smug salaried men in this club? Look at these John Wayne imitators, brave on somebody else's courage. The furriers are exciting people. They have real strength. They take real risks. If they don't get up in the morning and cut their deals and take their chances and spin their stories, they don't eat. They're adventurous. They have passion about what they do. Their blood is pumping. A vampire would starve in this room."

To her amazement, her father gave her a look of puzzled respect. Then he drained his glass and waved for another and Natalie had an awful feeling he had turned to drink to kill himself.

"Couldn't you see how happy I was? Didn't you care?"

"I didn't credit the coat trade. I presumed that Wallace was good to you."

"He was," she said quickly. But the truth was that Cotillion Furs, Limited had begun to look like the only part of their life that wasn't a lie.

"Did Wallace ever talk to you about Russia?" she asked.

"No."

"Did you know he had *blat*?"

"No."

"Did you ever hear that he knew members of the Politburo?"

"A Jewish furrier? Sounds like a Wallace exaggeration."

Between phone calls, late that afternoon, she contrived a way to use Kenny Wilson without drawing attention. She went down the hall to his office and found him getting ready to go home. He was a pink-cheeked Irishman in his fifties, unfailingly polite. He jumped to his feet when she entered.

"Didn't expect to see you so soon. How are you today?"

"Pretty flaky. It's been the longest week of my life."

"I'll bet. Can I do anything for you?"

"Yes. I need a favor."

"Name it."

She handed him the number on Wallace's telephone. "Some time at the funeral, I wrote this number down, but I forgot to write the person's name. It's probably just for a thank-you, but I simply can't remember. Can you find out whose phone this is?"

"Sure. No problem." He glanced at his watch. "I'll give it a shot right now."

The Comedy Club was her creation.

Nearly ten years ago, as an investment banking trainee fresh out of business school, Natalie had founded the young women's lunch group to share career news and lend a sympathetic ear to the trials and frustrations of running deals with the big boys. Rhonda, the banker, wanted to name their fledgling network The Luncheonettes, but something stiff and unyielding in Natalie recoiled from the too-cute. Rhonda speculated that if Natalie Stuart could loosen up a little she might dance with abandon and laugh loudly in restaurants, or at least learn to enjoy one-night stands like any normal person. While Rhonda was making jokes, Natalie had trumped her with The Comedy Club and the name had stuck.

Most of the members had flourished. Lynn Brown was already a name partner in her law firm. Rita Dabney had opened her own commercial real estate brokerage. Rhonda Rosenfeld headed a huge Citicorp commando unit poised to raid Fairfield County as soon as the bank's lobbyists had their way with Congress. Daphne, the currency trader, had dropped out for a baby, but they had found a star replacement in Laura Drake, a former fashion model who had opened her own advertising agency at age twenty-six and now numbered Cotillion Furs as her top client.

At its best, The Comedy Club had grown from a hand-holding operation to a savvy forum whose members could shout their options and listen for the echo.

Her father had dubbed them "acquisitive airheads," indulging his penchant for catchphrases gleaned from *The New Republic*, "with all the social awareness of snakes and snapping turtles." What he could never know was that a woman in business had to talk to someone who had no stake in using her.

Thus, years ago, it had been natural to present The Comedy Club with her Cotillion Furs idea at its inception. A few days after meeting Wallace, fear of risk had been setting in, and a vice-presidency at her investment firm had taken on the allure of stability. In her heart she wanted to get out and fly, but her banker's brain said, Don't rush, think it through.

The Comedy Club had met at its usual big round table in the garden of Barbetta a week after Bill Malcolm, her boss and former lover, had presented SM&H's vice-presidency offer, and two days after a follow-up lunch with Wallace Nevsky.

She sat between the exotic-looking, raven-haired Rhonda and stocky little Lynn. Across from her were Rita, the realtor, and Laura Drake, whose glamorous beauty concealed an ambition surpassed only by Natalie's. The expensive theater district restaurant was packed with suburban women in for the matinees, yet The Comedy Club stood out. They were younger, dressed for business, and they laughed less. Their waiters were particularly attentive, as they were known as tippers.

Natalie popped her promotion news first, over salad. Rita and Laura, the entrepreneurs, were most impressed because her responsibilities would include opening a new office in Anaheim. "Your own shop, Nat. Fantastic."

Lynn wanted to know precisely what an associate partnership vice-presidency really meant, but she was a lawyer and, besides, sometimes a little envious of her friends getting rich in business. However, she raised a good point. "Your whole five years of connections are in New York."

"Not necessarily. I'm always traveling to the institutions." Thanks to traveling half her life, road-showing investment opportunities to SM&H clients, her connections were more national than an office in New York might suggest.

"It's the management experience that's important," said Laura. "You'll be much broader."

"What guarantees are they offering?" asked Lynn.

They broke into smaller groups over coffee. Natalie found herself head to head with Rhonda, who said quietly, "There's another thing. Anaheim is too close to LA." The recently dropped Bill Malcolm was living in Los Angeles that year.

"If I go to Anaheim," Natalie joked, "I'll get a guy in New York."

"You probably would."

"Why not? I don't need that in my life."

Rhonda gazed contemplatively at the ailanthus trees overhanging the garden fence. "There are long-range things to consider," she mused.

"Forget my love life."

"What's to forget? I meant things you care about."

"Like what?"

"At my bank, we're seeing some interesting moves by the insurance companies. You're probably seeing them, too. Down on Wall Street."

Natalie had lowered her brandy and stared at her friend, who just kept looking at the garden. "Oh, my God."

The rules on insider information were as strict as they were unenforceable. Rhonda had hinted clearly that she had heard that Natalie's investment firm was talking merger. Yet, were SEC investigators to ask, Natalie could testify, truthfully, if not accurately, that Rhonda never said that an insurance company was trying to take over Stuart, Malcolm and Hardy.

In that moment, she made up her mind about the fur trade. For if Rhonda was right, if the firm's partners were angling secretly to sell SM&H, at an enormous profit to themselves, they would doom her to be an employee for the rest of her career, never a partner. A highly paid employee, to be sure. The new management would pay huge bonuses to keep key young people like herself, and they would offer fast promotion, too. But she'd never be a partner, never control a piece of it.

"The hell with them. They can keep their VP. I'm going into business on my own."

"Doing what?"

"Listen, everyone," she said, and blurted out her idea to sell quality mink coats to young career women like themselves.

"Furs? Natalie, you're leaving investment banking for the *fur trade*? Are you crazy?"

"Fur sales have grown every year since 1971. They've doubled since '74. They've hit a billion a year. They can go to ten billion."

"But Stuart, Malcolm and Hardy is giving you your own office."

"The fur market is ten percent tapped. Max. I want a piece of it on the ground floor."

"In the garment center? Yecch. They'll eat you alive. You don't know. You work in a nice orderly world of SEC regs. Tell her, Laura, you modeled down there."

"Believe it," said Laura. "When I was ten, I had furriers offering to take me to Florida. Mother had to explain they didn't mean Disney World. Granted, I looked twelve, but Nat, these were not nice people."

"I want to do something real. I want to own something."

"Fur's a fantasy."

"It *is!*" she said excitedly. "That's why it'll be fun to sell. But it's real, too. Listen! I went into a factory. It's an old-fashioned skilled craft. They call the people making the coats mechanics. Isn't that beautiful? *Mechanics.* They actually *make* stuff."

"*Make* stuff? Nobody making stuff makes money anymore."

"And mechanics belong to unions."

"It's an obsolete, maxed-out industry," said Rita Dabney. "Christ, you might as well go into wagon wheels."

"I read the Koreans are taking over," Lynn agreed.

The Greeks and Hong Kong were the real threat to American furriers, Wallace had told her. The Koreans were moving up, too. "The *market* is not maxed out. It's barely tapped."

"Natalie, don't do this to yourself. You're just a little weirded out because you're projecting turning thirty in a few years."

"I know what I'm talking about. I met this guy. He's a furrier and—"

"Ohhhhhh."

Her friends turned to her with a subdued clinking of simultaneously lowered glasses and cake forks. As Natalie was the founder of The Comedy Club and, her friends believed, the most driven, she had always been the first among equals. They were slightly awed by her reserve and her polish. She was the least likely to go through sudden changes, and even less likely to talk about it. Rhonda was still the only Comedy Clubber who knew she had dumped Bill Malcolm.

"Who?"

"Not a guy guy. A relative."

"Oh."

"Sort of."

"Sort of?"

"Wait," said Rhonda. "Something doesn't compute. Would you please explain how 'The Stuarts of New York' get a furrier for a relative?"

"As a matter of fact, my family started in the fur trade."

"Two hundred years ago with John Jacob Astor doesn't count," said Rhonda. "Natalie, you know I don't mean this as a criticism, but a Jew in your family is like a Nazi in mine."

"He's an adopted stepson of my great-great-uncle. And he's only half-Jewish."

"Top or bottom?"

"So you met this guy? This nonrelative."

"Wallace Nevsky. He's a skin broker."

"Sounds like a peep show distributor."

"He buys pelts at auction. Anyway, he was very knowledgeable. Showed me what to look for. Where the business is going. And I pitched an idea and he liked it."

"What's Uncle Wallace like?"

"He's very knowledgeable."

"Is he married?"

"Widowed."

"What's he like?"

"He's a lot of different things. He's very elegant, very easy. He walks into the Russian Tea Room, and they treat him like a czar. But at the same time he's kind of hip and fast, considering his age."

"Which is?"

"I don't know," Natalie replied casually. "Maybe sixty."

"Speaking of maxed out."

"Well, that eliminates one problem," said Rita, and the others agreed, all but Rhonda, who knew her best and gave Natalie a private smile that Natalie didn't feel like returning.

"He doesn't look any older than fifty, I guess, except his hair is this incredible silver white."

"Handsome, elegant, hip, and old," Laura mused. "Anything else? Would he happen to be rich?"

"I think he's a little lonely."

Lynn and Rhonda exchanged looks and Rita said, "You should not be allowed out after dark."

"What did I say? He seems lonely. He's very outgoing, but there's an empty space inside. I mean he was widowed. He's had a lot of girlfriends. Diana Darbee came up to him in the restaurant—forget this, I'm trying to talk business."

"Diana Darbee? What's she like?"

"A real charmer. Throwing her body all over him and dumping on me."

"Is she gorgeous?"

"I kept hoping the ceiling would fall on her."

"How old does she look close up?"

"Younger than anyone at this table."

"Bimbo."

"Actually, she's not a bimbo. I'm going to invite her to have lunch with us. She's made a fortune franchising her name. And she did it all herself. Wallace says she has a UNIVAC for a brain."

"What's a UNIVAC?" asked Lynn.

"An older person's expression for a computer."

"Did old Uncle Wallace come on to you?"

"He was sort of paternal."

"I mean after Diana Darbee left."

"A little, maybe. But I think mainly to be polite. Men that age feel they have to. Like tipping their hats."

"Earth to Natalie, earth to Natalie: Is it remotely possible he thought you were cute?"

Natalie shrugged. "He's funny, sometimes. Sometimes a little aloof. You know, you're right. I think he seems to like me."

" 'I *think* he *seems* to like me.' " Rhonda opened her purse. "Twenty bucks says Nat marries this turkey."

"No way," said Natalie.

"Takers?"

They pulled money from their bags. "You're covered. Natalie would never make it with a business partner."

"I said *marry*. Not make."

"Same thing with Natalie. Nat, you hold the money."

"Same thing? What am I, a nun?"

"Control, baby. Control. You'll never give it up."

"What if I do?"

"Then you can keep the money."

"When are you going to see him again?"

"I've made up my mind. We're forming a company."

"Who're your customers?"

"Successful, driven, busy, insecure women."

"Here's your first four sales."

"Twelve."

"Twelve?"

"I'm creating repeat customers. I'm going to sell you a good basic mink for the office and traveling. Then a little jacket for the weekends. And something really wild for going out. Later, you'll come back for a leather and fur thing for your fella."

"The fella we met going out in something really wild."

"You'll come back again and again because we're going to pitch quality at a good price. I'll give you a label you can trust."

"Give me a label that guarantees I look good," said Lynn, pressing her palms to her temples. "I don't have time to *think* about shopping, much less do it. If I can walk in, write a reasonable check, and walk out feeling good, I'll be back."

Natalie had adopted Lynn's plea as Cotillion's credo and for five years it had worked. But Wallace had been the key that made quality possible at a price her young customers could afford. And Wallace was gone.

Five and a half years ago she had brought them a dream. Tonight, a nightmare.

"We still don't know who's trying to buy Natalie's stock," Lynn said, opening the meeting at Cotillion's office. "But Rhonda told me in the cab the Street says they're raising the ante a buck a share."

"Two bucks," said Natalie, who had been on the telephone since she left her father. It was seven-thirty and her friends looked tired. Joannie had set up a bar and wine on ice, but no one was drinking, though the smoked salmon was going fast.

Lynn launched into an analysis of the company. Lynn, if not the most ambitious of the group, definitely possessed the sharpest mind. She was the person you tried ideas on. "Cotillion Furs is like a circus. A juggler here, a clown there, the high wire, the elephant. When I got done analyzing what Natalie and Wallace created, all I could imagine were two circus trains colliding in the night. She's got animals all over the place. In my opinion it's time to consolidate. Get some of them back in their cages and let the rest run into the jungle."

"It's getting late for screwed up metaphors," said Rita. "Could we—"

"Here's what Natalie's got to play with: A dynamite franchise retail fur business that's about to run into trouble with higher coat prices as skin costs rise. If higher prices cause the fur industry to falter, Natalie won't be able to sell any new franchises for a while, which could be a problem because her income from franchise sales tends to cover a lot of marginal operations, the worst of which is Cotillion's wholly owned suburban store chain. The third piece of the business is Wallace Nevsky's fur brokerage, in which Wallace bought furskins on the world auction circuit, especially in Russia, and sold or brokered them to various New York and Canadian furriers. Wallace also had a money-lending operation, which came within an SEC cat's whisker of falling under merchant and investment bank regulations. Finally, Cotillion holds varying degrees of ownership in a variety of New York fur factories.

"To hang on to all this, Natalie needs money to buy back investors' shares before they sell to someone else. So what does she do? Keeping in mind she's carrying enough debt to pave the Hudson River with promissory notes."

"Sell the chain in the 'burbs," Rita answered. "I've got a client, a software retail chain, who'd kill for those mall locations. Look at this." She unfurled blueprints onto Natalie's desk, anchoring them with wooden dolls Wallace had bought in Russia on his first trip after they had met. "I had my design guys sketch an idea—we'd hang neon lights over the existing mirrors in your showroom. High tech in a can! My computer clients oughta go for it. They're cheap sons-of-bitches and this'll cost zip. They'll buy your leases and cover most of the cost of your fixtures."

"All *right*," said Rhonda. "Cut your losses and get your cash."

"No," said Natalie.

"What no?"

"Wallace loved those stores. The mall chain was Wallace's baby. I think you've got an interesting idea there, Rita. But I don't want to rush into it."

"I only brought it up because you were always bitching about what a turkey the chain turned out to be. Your real customers are in the city."

"I can't sell it."

"What's going on with the fur brokerage?" Lynn smoothly changed the subject.

"The Leningrad auction is in three months, early February. Then Denmark and Leipzig."

"Are you going?"

"I can bid, of course, but I can't mark the skins. I mean, Wallace graded skins for fifty years."

"Why waste the time traveling, with all this going on?"

"I ought to show the Cotillion flag on the auction circuit. The shareholders fall into three groups: family, money men, and furriers. My father's helping persuade the family to hang in a while. But I've probably lost the money guys; they'll want their money out by spring. So the furriers swing the power, and right now they're against me. Also, Wallace's good will won't last forever, so I have to convince our suppliers I still belong in their business. Maybe I can prove myself by buying good skins at auction."

"How can you—"

"I'll hire brokers and spend money."

"You don't have to be there personally to spend money," Lynn protested.

"I *want* to be there," she said, almost fiercely. Lynn gave her an odd look and Natalie suddenly realized the larger truth behind her trip to the Soviet Union. She wanted to be in Russia, where Wallace would have been. And she wanted to meet the people he would have met.

Kenny Wilson passed by the open door with a one-minute finger raised. "Excuse me," Natalie said. "I'll be right back."

In the hall, Kenny handed her a memo sheet with two names and several addresses, including ones on the East Side of Manhattan; Greenwich, Connecticut; Princeton, New Jersey; and Washington, DC. "The number's unlisted. The bills go to a corporation that belongs to this lawyer who runs errands for this guy."

"Jeff Jervis. The takeover man?"

"You don't know him? I thought he gave you his number."

She had forgotten the story she'd told Kenny; she stammered another lie. "It must have been his wife. I was so out of it. Thanks, Kenny. Thanks a lot." Stop talking, she told herself. He's an ex-FBI agent. He can hear that I'm babbling. "I'll drop her a note."

She was astonished that Wallace had even known Jefferson Jervis. Not only had he never mentioned him, he had despised corporate takeover artists on principle, for abandoning productive American industry for paper profits.

Back in the early eighties Jefferson Jervis had been the darling of *New York* magazine: a self-made billionaire, art collector, party giver and pursuer of gorgeous women, at the pinnacle of Manhattan success. He had largely invented the paper-moving games used to spook corporate management into spending money to defend themselves and was already a legend when Natalie had started at Stuart, Malcolm and Hardy.

The insider trading prosecutions ravaging the investment banking business in the withering days of the Reagan era had never touched him. Jervis had long since shifted his ambition to Washington—about the time Natalie had started Cotillion Furs—where, as one of the President's closest friends, he had served as assistant secretary of the army, then with the National Security Council, bailing out before the Irangate disaster and starting a conservative think tank; many men of power, he had discovered, would give almost anything for advice from a billionaire.

Now, it seemed Wallace had known him well enough to install his secret telephone. An ugly phrase plowed through her mind, a rough remark that a macho furrier might pass in the steamroom: one whoremaster covering for another.

She returned to the meeting, her head spinning with Kenny's information. How had Wallace Nevsky ever gotten mixed up with a megaslime like Jefferson Jervis?

"Sorry. Listen, guys, I've got to cut this short."

They looked surprised.

"I left the dog in the house," she explained hurriedly, so confused by this latest revelation that she spun the flimsiest of excuses. "I've got to get back to the country."

"What dog? You don't own a dog."

Kicking herself for being so clumsy, she realized she was stuck with the lie and had to play it through. Otherwise they would keep her here for hours and she could not stand to stay another minute.

"My neighbor's dog. The red setter from the farm. It visited me. I borrowed it."

"What?"

"I called them up and asked if it could stay at my house and they said yes. It makes me feel good. But I forgot. I have to feed it and walk it. I'm sorry."

"Natalie, call your cleaning lady or the guy who cuts the grass and tell him to go feed your dog."

"No. She doesn't know them."

"Natalie." Lynn put her arm around her. "Come on. They'll introduce themselves. Get a grip."

"Listen, we've got to discuss Diana Darbee," Laura Drake said. "She's going to walk."

Diana made Natalie recall the sun in Luba's hair. The woman was so beautiful. She felt the warning fullness in her throat again as the crazy laugh began to escape. "I'll call you soon. Hey, bear with me, guys. I've never been widowed before."

She drove across town on her way to the country and stopped at Jervis's East Sixty-fourth Street address. It was a broad graystone house, the mullioned bay windows dark. She headed north on the FDR and decided to swing out of her way, through Greenwich.

There was something else about Jefferson Jervis, she recalled. Jervis had begun to do a lot of business with the Soviet Union. While trying to negotiate a compromise on the Soviet gas pipeline embargo fiasco, he had made good contacts with the Russians and had spun them into so many trade arrangements that he was becoming a sort of latter-day Armand Hammer. Like Hammer—like Wallace, for that matter—he was that rarest of birds, one who moved relatively freely between the United States and the Soviet Union.

Jervis's estate was near Greg's wife's place, although it made that lavish setup look puny. She saw the main house, floodlit, in the distance through bare trees. It looked like a replica of the White House. A broad driveway was guarded by massive iron gates. Shortly after she parked, a car came down the driveway, through the gates, which opened electrically, and pulled up alongside. It had a seal on the door. A uniformed guard climbed out. He shone a light in her face. "Help you?"

The scary laugh had died in her. She felt bold and angry. "No, thank you."

"Then I'll have to ask you to move on."

"Are you a cop?"

"Yes."

"Then you're aware this is a public road."

At that moment a second car appeared around the bend in the driveway and the gates swung open again. A huge Mercedes-Benz turned onto the road and rocketed into the night. Natalie caught a glimpse of Jervis's much-photographed face—the hawk nose, sunken cheeks, and a long narrow brow. "Don't let me catch you hanging around here again," the cop said, returned to his car, and drove up to the house.

Natalie backed and filled, intending to follow the Mercedes, but by the time she got Wallace's Cadillac turned around, Jervis had vanished. She headed north, for the country, wishing she had someone to talk to.

She woke up suddenly that night, heart pounding, ears fine-tuned to the dark. Frightened, acutely aware that she was alone at the end of a quarter-mile dirt road, she listened for the second clunk of the ice maker down in the kitchen. It usually calved in twos, but it was silent. The furnace might have awakened her when it rumbled off, but the hot air fans weren't humming and the house felt cold. She cocked her ear for the hiss of the water softener recharging in the cellar, but the pipes were quiet. The clock said three.

Fully awake now, she tried to listen but her brain had already clicked back in gear. Wallace. Luba. The woman. His secrets. His secrets raced in her mind, the secret lease on the boat, the secret telephone, the secret caller, the secret message in the *Voice*. How did Wallace's secrets connect to the woman who had killed him?

She heard a noise downstairs, like a magazine falling on the floor. Her imagination was wild now. But beside her, the old dog stirred awake, neck stiffening. A low growl vibrated in its throat. Natalie closed her fingers around the dog's muzzle to keep it from barking. There was silence again, and in it she recalled that anyone breaking into the house should have set off the alarms wired to every door and window. It was nothing. Then she heard someone moving about the living room.

10

She felt in the dark for the telephone—911 for the town police, 888 for the burglar alarm company. The dialing pad, ordinarily lighted, was dark, the telephone silent when she pressed it to her ear. She remained propped rigidly on one elbow, fighting panic.

Wallace had been something of a nut about home security, but now she blessed him for it. In the night table was a second dialer, a direct line to the burglar alarm company. She eased the drawer open. The pulls rattled like horseshoes. But inside, the panic button that was supposed to emit a faint green glow was as dark as the phone. She pressed it anyway, knowing in her heart that the wires were cut. If a thief cut them, the alarm brochures had promised, the alarms were programmed to go off automatically. But that had not happened tonight.

Natalie leaned over the side of the bed and felt underneath. The rustling sheets sounded like thunder. Groping on the carpet, she found Wallace's Mag light. The powerful halogen flashlight was cold and reassuringly heavy. She drew it under the blankets, turning the knurled metal in her hands until she found the rubber push switch. She lay still, listening, hoping the sounds would go away. Maybe they would take the silver and leave. Maybe there was no one. Then a board she knew well groaned in the front hall, just below the stairs.

She forced herself out of the squeaking bed and crossed the carpet.

113

Silently opening her closet, she fished in the back for her muskrat gun, a scope-sight .22 target rifle Wallace had bought for her when the muskrats attacked her flower beds and undermined the dam. The gun was leaning where she had left it a year ago. She crawled into the closet, feeling for the cleaning kit in its plastic bag, a box of shells, and finally, the magazine. She found the front, squeezed down on the top bullet to make sure it was full, and inserted it clumsily in the slot under the rifle. A stair tread creaked.

Natalie faced the bedroom door. She held the heavy light in one hand, the rifle in the other. She remembered the safety, but fumbling for it, found the whole combination too awkward. Another tread creaked. She felt her way back to bed and sat down, feeling for her robe. It was partly under the dog, which had stayed where it was, stiff and alert. Keeping the gun pointed at the door, she pulled the belt from her robe, placed the light beside the long gun barrel on her lap, and wrapped the two together with several turns of the belt. She tied the loose ends, put one finger on the flashlight switch and the other on the trigger and aimed again at the door.

But even as the top stair groaned, she felt leaden with doubt. If the thief had a gun, he would see exactly where to shoot when she turned on her light. She had to shoot first, but she feared she couldn't. The muskrat shooting had left her a trembling wreck and it had been hours before she could don a thick fireplace glove to pick up the huddled body.

A heavy tread in the hall sent fear through her stomach. The dog growled. Natalie grabbed her muzzle again, but had to let go to hold the gun. She saw light, a pale yellow line oscillating under the door. A flashlight, she guessed, as the intruder proceeded down the hall. It faded, reappeared, and faded again. She guessed he was searching each bedroom. He would look at the bed first. She stood up, pulled the comforter up over the sheets and pillows and dragged the dog to the corner nearest the door. There she crouched, back wedged between the walls, gun leveled at the door.

The doorknob scratched, clicked. The door swung open and the yellow beam half blinded her as it skipped across the carpet. It brushed the bed, then began to probe the room.

Natalie pressed the Mag light switch. Brilliant white glazed her bedroom like an exploding sun. A figure crouched in the doorway. It loomed erect with a gasp. Natalie tried to force herself to pull the trigger. The figure whirled and through the flying folds of cloth she saw a flashlight and a gun.

He was gone. She heard him scrambling along the hall, pounding, crashing down the stairs. Natalie jumped up from her corner and she did something she knew was crazy even as she did it.

"Get him!" she screamed at the dog. "Get him!"

The dog erupted from the room, barking wildly. Natalie charged after the animal with the light and the gun. The dog went howling down the stairs, nails clattering on the smooth wood. Natalie bounded after it, too fast to think to be afraid. The front door was open. She ran onto the granite front steps, heard a scream, and zeroed in on it with the Mag light.

The dog was barking and snapping at the fleeing housebreaker, who ran into the low ilex hedge that separated the lawn from the driveway and tore through it, shedding the dog long enough to sprint down the driveway. Natalie heard a car door bang. She went around the hedge, saw lights, heard an engine race, and brought the heavy gun to her shoulder.

Roaring tires flung long rooster tails of gravel. The dog bashed through the hedge, barking. The car swerved into the gunsights, bright blue in the brilliant glare of the halogen Mag light. A head filled the sight. Natalie dipped the rifle. The moment was gone, the heat was dissipating, and she could not pull the trigger.

She dropped to one knee, breathing hard. The narrow light beam seemed locked to the license plate. "ZIU three-six-nine," she gasped to the dog as the car raced away. "Remember that. ZIU three-six-nine. New York plates."

The dog fell at her feet, flanks heaving as if she would burst. Natalie stroked her ribs. "Thanks, pal. Oh Christ, look at this. I forgot to close the bolt." She worked it shut, then opened it again and made sure the safety was on.

They started back to the house, Natalie saying, "And another thing, pal. Z means rental in New York. Connecticut housebreakers don't rent cars in New York."

A large, clean, white unmarked van was parked outside Ralph Lauren's on Madison Avenue. Ahead of it were two small clean cars and behind it two more. Two men emerged from each car and watched the van as its driver and his helper unlocked it and began wheeling covered coat racks across the sidewalk and through a heavy door in the side of the clothing store.

The men watching wore little earpieces like secret service agents. Occasionally a man in a fifth car spoke and one or more of them moved. The man in the fifth car was Kenny Wilson, and he looked surprised when Natalie Stuart Nevsky knocked on the window. He loosed the lock and let her in.

"Hello there."

"Mind if I watch?"

"Course not. Excuse me one second." He muttered in his hand-held mike, "Pete, tell that new guy to talk on his own time. He's supposed to be watching the corner." He grinned at Natalie. "Tough to find good help these days. Nice to see you. Out shopping?"

"Kenny, are you happy at Cotillion?"

"Sure." He looked wary, however.

"Any plans to move on?"

"Not unless you know something I don't."

"Tell you why I ask. This is something Wallace and I were talking about before he was killed. You really have set up some effective programs. We're not losing coats like we used to. And I'm also pleased the way you're protecting our labels."

Kenny Wilson ducked his head, clearly uncomfortable with praise.

"We were thinking—and now I'm thinking—we've developed a security service here we could lease to other furriers. Smaller outfits that can't afford your kind of treatment. What do you think?"

"Means hiring more people."

"Of course. We don't intend to give anything up. If you're interested, why don't you type up a proposal? Just a page with your ideas."

"Okay."

"Now I've got a problem."

Kenny Wilson gave her a shrewd smile. "Another phone number?"

"What if it were?"

"There's a lot I can do for you, Mrs. Nevsky. But nothing illegal."

Natalie let a speculative silence gather between them before she asked, "Legally, Kenny, what exactly can your old friends do for you?"

Kenny shrugged. "Anything, almost. Phone numbers, licenses, addresses, phone records, credit info."

"I'll cover expenses, of course. I imagine you'll need cash."

"Not much. Probably never. Nobody's *giving* me anything, but they're not selling it either. It's just that cops and agents know I'm a guy who hires. One of these days they'll be retiring."

"Excellent. Here's a license number. I want to know who was driving this car yesterday."

"Looks like a rental. If this has to do with what happened to Mr. Nevsky, you really ought to talk to the cops." He gave her a hard, no-nonsense stare. Natalie's chin came up and she stared back. This was one issue she had already settled in her mind.

"Kenny, you know what's going on. I'm fighting for my investors' support. If the media learn I've gone to the police, Cotillion will be front page news again and I will not look like someone in control of the situation."

Kenny nodded, reluctantly. "I don't like it, but I get it."

"Thanks, Kenny. And do me that proposal. It could be a real money-maker."

Kenny Wilson was better than his word. Natalie received his memo that afternoon: Blue Ford Escort ZIU 369 New York. Avis rented to Margot Klein. Flat 13. Barbazon Estate. London, SE 1. Telephone 248-3548. Car returned this morning. No problem.

A woman. Natalie's heart started pumping. She thought, of course, of the woman who had shot Wallace. She had never seen the intruder's face, not even a profile, just swirls of a heavy coat. It could have been a woman.

It was ten o'clock in London. "Three-five-four-eight," a woman answered.

"Margot Klein, please."

"She's still in New York."

"Still?"

"Oh, you haven't heard. The poor thing is in hospital."

"What happened?"

"Apparently, she slipped on some stairs."

"I'll visit her. What hospital?"

"Doctors'."

Natalie knew Doctors' Hospital from the days when her Uncle Norbert used to check in periodically to dry out. The hospital nestled placidly on East End Avenue, across from Gracie Mansion. The emergency entrance was tucked on the side street and inside, the halls were quiet, the staff deferential. The answers she received at the nursing station on Margot Klein's floor seemed to confirm that Natalie had tracked down her housebreaker, but her first thought upon entering the semiprivate room was that Kenny Wilson had made a mistake.

A seventy-year-old woman was dozing before a silent television. She appeared compact and rugged, but it was hard to imagine her prowling a dark house with a gun. Natalie checked the bed chart. Margot Klein. The woman sleeping in the next bed was even older, and frail as a bundle of twigs.

Margot Klein awakened with a start. An expression of bewildered innocence settled in the lines of her face, but not before Natalie thought she had recognized her. "Yes? . . . Is it time for the pills?"

Natalie held a piece of paper over the bed.

"What is that, dear? I can't see without my specs." Her accent sounded both European and upper-crust British, as if she had learned English as a second language at Oxford.

"This is a copy of the rental receipt for the car you drove to Connecticut last night to break into my country house."

"I beg your pardon?"

"You checked into the hospital this morning with bruises and two cracked ribs, which you got falling down my stairs."

The English accent got sharper. "I'm afraid I haven't the foggiest notion of what you're talking about, dear. I say, Nurse! Nurse!"

"And I'm really glad to hear you've got a dog bite on your bum."

Margot Klein betrayed herself with an anxious glance at the sleeping woman in the next bed.

"I haven't reported you to the police, yet. You're not what I expected. But I will if you don't tell me what you were doing in my house."

The old woman sighed. "I'm Mrs. Nevsky, Mrs. Nevsky."

BOOK TWO

GLASNOST

11

I'm Wallace's first wife."

"You are not! Wallace's wife died in the London blitz."

"Who told you that?"

"Wallace."

"Well, you know how Wallace exaggerated."

Natalie gaped, utterly bewildered. "What?"

Margot returned a smug smile. "I am his first wife. I am not dead."

Natalie's anger, which seemed to dance a minuet with a scary laugh, erupted in a peevish wail that she hated, but couldn't stop. "You broke into my house."

"You left your BMW in New York. How was I to know you were there?"

"You cut the burglar wires. You had a gun."

Margot glanced again at the old woman fast asleep in the next bed. "Lower your voice."

"You cut the wires," Natalie accused again. Knowing how, without tripping the alarm, was dark knowledge, more frightening than the gun.

"I'll mend them."

"Don't joke with me, Margot. I'm one inch from calling the cops." But wouldn't the newspapers love this story? "Why did you break into my house?"

"I was wondering what Wallace had smuggled out of Russia."

"*Smuggled?* Are you kidding? Smuggling would jeopardize our business."

"*Your* business might not have been all that Wallace was doing."

Natalie gaped again. Surfing across the sea of questions that rolled and tumbled in her mind came the memory of something similar Luba had said at the Hopkins Inn. Hadn't the Russian woman implied that Wallace had business in the Soviet Union other than the fur auction? Other business and unusual influence. She braced herself to ask the only thing that mattered.

"Do you know who shot my husband?"

"I can't tell you that."

"You'll tell me, or I'll take you to the police."

Margot reacted fearfully. "I mean I can't tell you precisely who the woman was. But I'm reasonably sure it wasn't for love."

Natalie felt relief seep through her in warm, soft waves, like soaking tired muscles in a hot tub. For the first time since Wallace had been killed someone had finally suggested he hadn't been cheating on her.

Margot dashed her hope with a malicious smile. "Of course, with Wallace, one can never be sure on that score, can one?"

Angry, Natalie snapped, "Frankly, Margot, you don't look like Wallace's type."

"Don't remind me," the old woman said wearily. "He preferred taller, angular women like yourself."

"Or Luba?"

"Who?"

She looked innocent, but Natalie didn't trust her. "Go on, Margot. Tell me. How did you know my husband?"

"I met Wallace Nevsky in Germany, in 1939, a month before the war. He was one of the young men negotiating with the Nazis to allow a boat train of Jewish children to go to England. I was nineteen, in charge of my little sisters. Something went wrong.

"They stopped our train at the border. We waited hours in terror. Finally a German staff car pulled up with a general, waving us on. As we pulled away, I saw Wallace, smiling, sitting in the open car between the general and his aide-de-camp while the Germans waved good-bye.

"He turned up weeks later in London, talked me into bed in less time than it takes to tell it, and as a thank you for my virginity, explained what had happened at the border."

"What?" asked Natalie, who found even that fifty-year-old conquest hard to hear.

"In the car, he held a gun to the aide-de-camp's ribs. He had already shot the general."

"But the general was waving."

"Wallace waved his arm for him."

Natalie shivered and her throat began to fill. "It's hard to fit that story to the man I married."

"It fit our times."

"He never told me."

The old lady shrugged. "Ancient history."

Natalie sensed something else untold. "What about you?"

Margot shrugged again, but looked pleased with herself. "I volunteered, too. Back into Germany for a while."

Natalie nodded. That explained the burglar alarms, she supposed. The gun and the smug pride.

"Lost my nerve, finally, and settled into London as a finisher, sewing linings. I'd learned in my father's factory in Leipzig. I studied English to make sense of my new life, and history to try to understand the old. And I married Wallace."

"Wallace said you were killed in the blitz."

Pain annihilated Margot's superior smile. "I heard you earlier. There was another girl on the train. She was killed in The Strand, in 1940, by a bomb."

"Tall, slim, and blonde? Right?"

"Actually, her hair was colored like yours. . . . Wallace took what he wanted. Always . . ."

"How did Wallace meet President Truman?"

"Excellent! He's told you."

"Almost nothing."

Margot eyed her shrewdly. "Did he tell you about his father?"

"In a way."

"Being shipped back to Stalin."

"Yes. And his mother."

"He was enraged by the ignorance that allowed it to happen. Then an opportunity arose. He was presented to President Truman with a group of clandestine operators, to receive a secret medal. . . . Well, I don't have to tell you how persuasive he was. He spirited Truman into a corner and told him what had happened to the Russian prisoners, and why, that the West was dangerously naïve about Stalin and the Soviet gangster regime.

" 'Nothing in Russia is simple,' he told President Truman. 'Little is obvious. Yet you have few reliable sources of information.' The established intelligence services like British MI-6 and the American OSS were fighting units, wedded to operations. Worse, they were more than likely infiltrated by the Soviets. Worse still, Wallace warned him, the bigger those agencies grew, the more deeply layered their bureaucracies, the more they would try to manipulate Truman.

"Truman turned increasing shades of purple, as Wallace knew he would. It was common knowledge the President hated spies in general and the 'oh so social' OSS in particular. And he was angry at himself that he was about to approve a new group, the Central Intelligence Agency, because the future of the postwar generation was quite clear: for years to come, two great empires would contend for the planet—I'm sure you know all this from your own father."

"What do you know about me?"

Margot smiled. "Bits and pieces. Wallace knew that Truman knew he was trapped. He needed the very spy services that he hated and distrusted. Wallace offered him a way out. He proposed establishing a private Russian information network that would report directly to Truman and *only* to Truman—a presidential intelligence service."

"Truman loved it."

"I don't believe you. From what my grandfather told me about Truman, he would have tossed Wallace down the front steps of Blair House. You're describing the kind of private army I'd expect to hear about today, not forty years ago."

Margot gave her a long, steady look. "I would be surprised if your grandfather knew President Truman one tenth as well as Wallace Nevsky.... Don't misunderstand, Truman laid down strict rules. Absolutely no operations were allowed. No sabotage. No Harvard cowboys, as he called them, tunneling into the Kremlin to dynamite Stalin's chamber pot. He was too honest, too smart, and too patriotic to covet a vest pocket CIA.

"All he wanted was unbiased, inside information about Soviet Russia, which was precisely what Wallace had proposed, don't you see? Wallace had been in the spy game since Spain. He knew he'd lose his objectivity if he tried to run operations. It was a marriage made in heaven. Likely his only such."

She greeted Natalie's angry glare with another smile.

"Seeking only the best, and proceeding with great caution, Wallace

assembled a network inside Russia—soliders he'd fought beside, partners in the fur trade, Party functionaries, engineers, all those trying to
rebuild Russia after the war. Only Wallace knew the extent of the
operation. And only Wallace knew he reported to Truman."

"How do *you* know?"

"We were still married. I organized the London office. And continued to after we divorced."

"Who paid for it?"

"Truman channeled funds from the Secret Service, I believe. But it
cost very little. Wallace established a profitable business brokering
furskins."

"Somebody had to pay for it. How many people were involved?
Twenty? Thirty?"

"Hundreds."

"It cost."

Margot shrugged, clearly uninterested. "Wallace's trips to Russia
were all on legitimate business, the perfect cover, and paid for out of
the fur business. Many of the connections inside Russia served selflessly,
believing, like Wallace, that accurate information could prevent un-
necessary tragedies and keep the peace between the Russian and
American empires. Those he paid he didn't have to pay much. Others
traded information for favors Wallace could arrange. He ran it like
any network, with cells and cutouts and drops, though unusually
securely. What was not typical was that Wallace's information went
directly, personally, from his mouth to the ear of the President."

"That's a lot of raw data for a busy man."

"Filtered through Wallace's unusually broad experience," Margot
countered. "It worked admirably. As time went on and Wallace's
contacts rose in the Soviet hierarchy, his information grew more and
more important. And the favors he could perform grew bigger as he
became a sort of middleman between his increasingly powerful Russian contacts."

"*Blat,*" Natalie murmured.

Margot nodded. "He had *blat* coming out his ears."

"I can't believe that President Truman would have risked it."

"You mean, what if SMERSH wired electrodes to Wallace's geni-
tals and Wallace screamed 'Truman!' "

"Well, yes, I guess that's exactly what I mean."

"Truman's answer would have been a perfectly innocent, 'Who?' It
was private. No one knew but Wallace and Truman."

"How long did it go on?"

"Well," Margot said with another of her smug smiles, "Eisenhower liked the arrangement."

Silence gathered. Natalie grew aware of the hospital noises beyond the door, soft phones, the whisper of a rubber-wheeled gurney, slippers shuffling, and in the room, the almost imperceptible breathing of the old woman dying in the next bed.

"Each retiring President offered Wallace to his successor. At some moment the 'transition teams' would retire and the President-elect would find himself alone with the outgoing President. In would come Wallace, and he would explain the ground rules: if the new President told anyone of his existence—chief of staff, wife, anyone—Wallace would quit. He was the one risking his life behind the iron curtain. If the President didn't want his service, fine. He was happy to continue full time in the fur trade."

"Who finally turned him down? Carter?"

"I think you can guess the answer to that."

"Tell me," she demanded, hope and dread mingling curiously in her heart. "Say it. Please."

"Would you have turned Wallace down if you were President? Would you refuse your own private window into Soviet Russia? Eyes and ears inside the Kremlin? The Party? The *dachas* of the leadership? Would you turn down information you would already have when some self-satisfied CIA director minced into the Oval Office dangling his favors? Information that gave you another side of an argument the NSA was coaxing you to accept? Would you be as awed by your defense secretary's DIA Soviet rocket analysis when you already *knew* that the strategic rocket force commander-in-chief has confided to his mistress—who happens to be the granddaughter of another marshal of the Soviet Union and whom Wallace, perhaps, enjoyed in Paris during her year abroad with the Soviet Trade Mission—that his new missiles require twice the launch time the designers had promised?"

"Enjoyed?" Natalie flared. "What are you saying? My husband was a spy who seduced Russian women for their secrets?"

"Your husband was a spy*master*," Margot said soberly. "And a bloody good one. It's been years since he had to do his own fucking."

Natalie fell silent. She got up, walked to the window, and watched a sailboat beating toward Hell Gate. It looked cold out there on the water. Finally, she whispered, "You're asking me to believe that the sixty-five-year-old furrier I was married to was shot for spying on Russia?"

"There are worse ways to die."

"I can't believe this."

"And worse ways to be widowed."

"Am I supposed to be grateful?"

"But you are."

"Shut up."

"I know jealousy. I was married to him too. Of course you're grateful. Hope is burning in your eyes. You'd much prefer for him to have been killed by the enemy than by his lover."

"Now who is Luba?" Margot went on sternly. A nurse had come and gone, changing the IV bottle on the sleeping woman, and closing the door at Margot's request. Natalie had stayed at the window, staring at the East River. One lie answered had raised a dozen more.

"You said earlier, like Luba."

"Wallace had a private telephone I hadn't known about. A Russian woman named Luba called, thinking he was still alive. We met. She asked what Wallace had told me about her. Nothing, of course. She was beautiful. I got her to admit she had seen Wallace in Russia. She said he had business beyond the fur trade. He was very important. He had *blat*. And he was good at going *na lyeva*. Do you know—"

"Yes, yes. Go on."

"She asked if he had mentioned millionaires."

"Millionaires?"

"He hadn't. She said something like, he was a fool. Or he had been fooled. She seemed surprised when I said Wallace was taking me to Russia. Who do you think she is?"

"An agent in Wallace's net, if you're lucky. KGB out fishing, if you're not, checking your role."

"Me?"

"Answering that telephone would have aroused interest and if the KGB is rolling up Wallace's network, then . . ."

Natalie ignored the heavy implication. She simply didn't care. Nor did she believe it. "Luba was not checking like that. She was terrified. As if she were fleeing. She saw a couple come in and got scared and ran out the kitchen door."

"Good. I wonder who scared her?"

"Luba left a newspaper open to the personals. After she ran I realized she was trying to direct my attention to a certain ad. It contained the title *The Pearl*."

"So?"

"Well, it's a porn book. I found a copy with Wallace's phone."

"Randy bastard," Margot laughed. "Leave it to Wallace to choose a dirty book for his book code."

"I figured it had to be some kind of message. What is a book code?"

"It's a secure way to communicate. You write your message with a set of numbers representing page, line, and word. Simple and foolproof until they discover what book you're using. The only trick is to use a book that contains the words you need. *Madame Bovary* would present difficulties in passing information about Soviet tank parts."

"There were no numbers."

"What you saw was a general alert. Luba was hoping you'd accept it as a password—testing whether you knew, which of course you didn't."

"She kept asking if Wallace had brought me anything. Just like you. Now you show up. What are you looking for?"

Margot stopped smiling. "Something small enough to smuggle and important enough to get him killed."

"Like what?"

"Knowing Wallace, it could be a recording. A message that had to be personal."

"There was a blank tape in his Panasonic. The police played it over and over."

"I don't think he'd carry it on his body."

"I just realized, you're the one who ransacked my apartment."

"*What!*"

"You broke into my apartment. You searched it."

Margot scrambled off the bed. She cried out, clutching her ribs. Mewing with pain, she hauled a rough tweed traveling suit from the closet. "Help me dress."

"What are you doing?"

"I most certainly did not search your apartment," she said through gritted teeth. "Don't you understand? It means I'm not the only one hunting whatever the hell Wallace took out of the Soviet Union."

"You're hurt."

"Better hurt than dead, young lady."

12

At daybreak, Natalie stood at her kitchen window in Connecticut, watching her reflection disappear. Outside, the light formed tangibly on a translucent mist that the cold had drawn from the ground. The mist lay thin where there was stone and heaviest on the ponds. Through it, the distant tree line looked as dense and orderly as prison bars.

Wallace had asked her to drive him to the airport, the Sunday he left hurriedly on his last trip. They had talked business in the car, last minute details for the winter collection, but now she recalled how intently he had stared at her, as if he were deliberately searing her image into his brain. A picture to cling to, she realized belatedly, an icon for a safe return. Or a vision for the grave. Ironically, he thought he had made it; he had returned triumphant to the showing.

Natalie shuddered. She had to summon the courage to explore her thoughts, which were beginning to range past the hope that the old woman had claimed to see in her eyes.

Margot removed a cold teacup from Natalie's hands and replaced it with one that burned her fingers. "You look angry."

She had persuaded Natalie that they must search the country house. Natalie had agreed largely because in times of stress, it was the place she preferred to be. And indeed, as night withdrew and she could see the land, she felt better equipped to deal with Margot's story. Margot had popped a Valium for the pain as soon as they got in the car. The drug and her cracked ribs had knocked her cold and Natalie had had to carry her to the guest room. She herself had dozed intermittently on the settee before the kitchen fire. Now Margot was up, rested, feisty, and making friends with the red setter, which was sitting shamelessly with its head on the old lady's lap. Margot also had her gun, in her handbag on the banquette table.

"I *am* angry," Natalie admitted. "My husband risked his life without telling me."

"He was risking it before you were born."

"But he kept doing it."

"So does a policeman."

"A policeman doesn't tell his wife he works for the post office."

"Perhaps that depends on the wife," Margot said tartly. "Frankly, if you're an example of this new woman I'm hearing so much about, I'm not impressed. You've made a virtue of petulance."

"I can get sarcastic criticism from my father, any time I want, thank you."

Margot shrugged impatiently, which made her wince. "Let's get looking."

"You're only guessing Wallace hid something."

Exuding superiority, Margot replied, "In my experience, the KGB and the GRU kill either as an example to instill fear, or to halt events they can't stop any other way. An attack before two hundred people suggests they were desperate to stop him."

"But you said Wallace didn't *do* things. He just gathered information."

"Then they feared his information. It's obvious the clock was running. And as they don't seem to have found it, it's still running."

"You're making them smarter than they are. It was just luck that woman got away."

"Cheek and skill's more like it. She'd have killed herself if she'd been captured. And you can be sure they had a second agent poised to kill her if she lost heart."

Natalie sank to the settee. "I still can't believe we're talking about my husband."

"In this respect"—Margot smiled unpleasantly—"we're talking about *my* husband."

"No! My husband. Not yours."

"Call him what you will, he smuggled—"

"I don't need this in my life. I've got a business to run. I want you out of my house. I'll drive you to the bus. Get on your broom and leave. Go."

Margot said, "You'll have to throw me out."

"No, I don't. I pay taxes for police. And we have a perfectly good mental institution in the next town. Tell them your story." She went to the wall phone.

"For forty years," Margot said, "your husband ran his net. Last week he found something they killed him for. It must have been very important."

"To you."

"And perhaps the world."

"I don't care."

"Wallace cared."

"Oh really? Well, he didn't care to tell me, did he? What makes you think he'd want you to tell me? You're the one who cares. He's dead. He didn't want me involved before. What makes you think he wants me involved now?"

Margot dipped into her bag and Natalie got frightened. One reason she didn't like the old woman was that Margot seemed quite capable of hurting her. Quickly, she picked up the phone.

Margot yanked an envelope from her bag and sailed it across the kitchen. It hit the half wooden bowl that held dry flowers on the wall and fell to the counter. "Read that, you silly bitch. Then tell me what Wallace wanted."

Natalie stared at Wallace's handwriting on the envelope. "What does it say?"

"I don't know."

"Your name is on it, Margot."

"It's still sealed. Look at the postmark. Wallace mailed it on your wedding day."

A secret that day?

Natalie snatched a parer from the knife rack. Inside the envelope was another, addressed, "N." She slit the flap.

"Everything she tells you is true," Wallace had written. "She's a pain in the ass, but loyal. What you do with it is up to you. I love you."

She felt suddenly bitter. A secret he wouldn't share in life was her responsibility in death? What you do with it is up to you. Thanks,

Wallace. All I want to do is save Cotillion and see if it's possible to live without you, and now you've given me a job.

Natalie walked to the fireplace and let it burn.

"What did he say?"

"Why didn't you show me this earlier?"

"I wanted to see who you were, first. He sometimes became besotted by youth and beauty."

"I passed your test?"

"Barely. . . . What did he say?"

"He said to ask you about what he was working on."

"I've told you all I know. Wallace played strictly by the security book. His net was celled. No one knew whom else he knew. I know more than most, because in the early days the London office was so important, but he didn't confide in me. What if I turned?"

"He didn't think that would happen."

The old woman puffed up at the compliment. But Natalie wondered, could Margot have become Wallace's enemy? Was this how he thought? she asked herself. Always afraid?

"So you're only guessing that he smuggled something out."

"Surmising."

"Wallace didn't have time to come here from the airport, hide something, and get back to New York. He went from the plane to the apartment to the yacht. We shouldn't be here. We should be searching the apartment."

"You're assuming he was on the flight he told you he was on."

Natalie blinked, suddenly teary again; the simplest moment between them might often have contained a lie. Wallace always knew something she didn't. Her half of his life was always smaller than his. Then she recalled he had agreed to meet her at Greg's party because she spoke Russian.

"But what if all he carried out of Russia was in his head?"

"It's possible," Margot admitted, regaining her smug smile. "In which case there's nothing left to find. It's also possible that the burglar in your New York apartment was just a burglar. And the woman who shot Wallace was just a disappointed lover."

"Stop."

They divided the property. Margot took the house, contending that a stranger would spot things a resident wouldn't. Natalie went to the barn. She did not want Margot poking through the office where she had found Wallace's phone; it seemed more intimate.

On her way to the barn she came across a mole track and began tapping it down with her foot as she walked; it went on a long ways, heading toward the barn. Suddenly she broke into a run, racing the track. She tore into the barn, into Wallace's office, and yanked the drawer. The telephone was gone. The wire was gone from the desk, the staples were gone. In the cellar, the wire was gone and when she went outside again she confirmed that the cable, strung underground, had been ripped out of the lawn from the barn, past the house, all the way to the nearest telephone pole.

"The phone's gone," she cried to Margot.

Margot shrugged. "It was a balls-up they left it so long."

She went up to her bedroom and made two telephone calls, came down, and found Margot inspecting the electrical outlets with the Mag light.

"Forget it. I checked his passport. He came into Kennedy on the flight he said he did. The day he was shot."

Margot crawled to the next outlet, trailed by the dog.

"Did you hear? He didn't have time to hide anything in this house."

"Wallace was quite capable of fixing the date stamp."

"I figured that much myself," said Natalie. "I had my security man check with a friend in Customs. Wallace arrived the day he was shot."

Margot looked up with an almost friendly smile. "Very good. And did Customs also confirm that Wallace didn't come and go out again earlier on a different passport?"

Natalie stared.

Margot said, "Your husband didn't survive forty years being predictable."

"I don't think that way."

"Another thing, be careful about asking questions. They have a way of coming back as somebody else's answer."

In the guest room, Margot discovered scratches in the paint on a wall receptacle. She unscrewed the plate. Inside there appeared to be a new fixture, recently installed. Nonetheless, she asked Natalie to remove the proper fuse. She loosened the fixture and pulled out the slack cable. There was nothing hidden in the outlet box.

She played Wallace's Mag light along moldings, door frames, and wooden joints until the power cell went flat. While it recharged, she opened every book in the library and poked through closets and cabinets. Then she started on the cellar.

In the barn, Natalie played all of Wallace's music tapes, carrying the player with her as she unstacked woodpiles, poured through the swimming pool machinery, and searched the loft. She doubted he would hide anything outside where the mice could get it. She uncovered nests everywhere, many lined with Muffin's black fluff. As the old poodle had grown frail, Natalie would clip her herself to save her the misery of a day with the groomer.

I'm a wreck, she thought. I'm losing everything.

Returning to the house, she found Margot collapsed on a couch. She covered her and started on the attic. When she came down in an hour, Margot was brewing tea. "This would be bloody impossible if you'd lived here long enough to collect more junk." She concluded the search at nightfall and announced they would do the same to the New York apartment.

Natalie lowered the heat, shut the flues, locked the doors, and drove the red setter home to its farm. Margot popped another Valium. Before they reached the main road, she had fallen fast asleep, leaving Natalie deep in solitude and second thoughts. The old woman could be crazy. Or exaggerating the past, harboring a fixation on Wallace that went back to the Second World War. Had Wallace died peacefully in their bed, she would have laughed Margot out of her house.

Margot's bag was open beside her. Natalie reached in, past the cold gun, and carefully extracted her thick wallet. Opening it on her lap, while watching the road, she withdrew several credit cards, which she read in the light of the dashboard. Then she found her passport. It too bore the name Margot Klein. She doubted whether a woman who ran the London office of a spy network would break into people's houses under her own name.

Natalie switched on the car phone. She felt a sudden, desperate need for a dose of reality and knew exactly where to get it. It was six o'clock and Lynn Brown was still in her office. "Who's calling?" asked her secretary.

"Tell her the merry widow."

Lynn was on in a flash. "Are you okay?"

"Much better. Listen, I'm sorry about running out the other day. Can you set up a conference call with The Comedy Club? I'd like to finish our discussion about Cotillion."

"The merry widow? Are you *sure* you're okay?"

"Fine. I've just got to do something real, for a change."

She was touched by their response. By the time she entered Route 684, Lynn, Rita, Rhonda, and Laura had all joined the conference call. "I really appreciate this."

"You better."

"Where were we?"

"Why don't we talk about Wallace's money lending."

Natalie said, "I don't have the time to get to know the borrowers, like he did."

"For twenty-one percent," replied Rhonda Rosenfeld, "I'd get to know my mother."

"But I don't have the *chutzpah* to collect. Wallace used a Hasidic collection agency that stands in the street screaming, 'Pay us.' "

"Sounds good to me," said Rhonda. "I would give very careful thought to maintaining that operation."

"Natalie's right," Lynn countered. "Simplification has to be your theme of reorganization. Get this company down to two functions: acquire fur coats and sell them."

"Speaking of which," said Rita, her voice accompanied by a sharp crackling noise.

"Sounds like you're unrolling another blueprint, Rita."

"A loft–office conversion. Those fur factories you own lock, stock, and overhead are worth a ton in lease value. The landlords will pay you to move. Shut 'em down."

Natalie tried with little success to explain that Wallace's old Nevsky Russian Furs factories set the standards by which Cotillion acquired coats from outside manufacturers. Nor was The Comedy Club moved by her arguments against ending silent partnerships with Wallace's old friends, and pulling out of the new Long Island City fur center.

"I see he believed in unions, too," Rhonda noted acidly. "When's the last time you stood your labor costs, in house or out, beside Korea and Hong Kong?"

"Cotillion sells American quality."

"So did International Harvester. Once upon a time."

"Nat," Lynn pleaded, "make believe the last five years never happened. Make believe you're still an investment banker. Look at this like you would for a client in trouble. What would you advise?"

As they hammered at her, Natalie heard again the same arguments she used to have with Wallace. Now she was defending him. What had her father said? Reality moves on, but I'm standing still. She grew aware of a silence in the car, punctuated by Margot's snoring. They were waiting for her to answer, but she had run out of arguments. Laura Drake finally spoke.

"Advertising. We've got an ad campaign on self-destruct if Diana Darbee bows out."

"Bimbo," Lynn snarled.

"Bimbo or not, Natalie won't sell many coats without ads. I can buy space, but what's to make our ads special if we lose Diana?"

Alarms started buzzing in Natalie's head.

What's to make our ads special? What the hell was wrong with Laura Drake? Why wasn't her agency working up ideas for an alternative campaign? Was she getting complacent? Natalie was angry enough to take away the account right this minute, but the timing was wrong. She was still struggling to conserve, to hold things together. If she couldn't line up a new ad agency, though, she could at least light a fire under Laura.

"Let's get somebody else in the wings, Laura—like right now. We're shipping coats for Christmas. I don't want to change in midstream, but let's get prepared. All right? As for Diana, Wallace often said—"

"Wallace is gone," Rita said sharply. "Sorry, Natalie, but—"

"Wallace," Natalie repeated, "often said that we wasted Diana."

"Wasted?" Laura, who had written the smart woman campaign, asked coldly. "What do you mean, *wasted?*"

"Diana is an actress," Natalie explained. "All we've really done, Laura, is parade her around like a model. We've used her famous face, but not her talent."

"A debatable asset."

"She was committed to Wallace. I want her committed to Cotillion Furs. Let's offer her something she doesn't have yet."

"Like what? Her own nation?"

"Let me finish," Natalie said, in a voice that invited no further interruption. "We can kill two birds with one stone by using her talents more fully: a better ad to sell more coats and such a deep commitment to Cotillion that no matter how bad the publicity about Wallace gets, Diana will never leave. Laura, that's what I want you to do. Write a campaign for Diana Darbee the actress. And just in case ... go have a talk with Donna Mills."

"Hey, Natalie?" Rita called.

"What?"

"Welcome back. But go easy, okay?"

Margot awakened when Natalie slowed the car to pay the Upper Manhattan Bridge toll. Before Natalie could mention the passport, Margot asked, "Did he bring you a present?"

"I told you no."

"No present? Not even those silly little dolls?"

"No. He went to Russia all the time. He didn't have to bring me dolls."

"He always brought me presents."

"He gave me a beautiful lynx coat," Natalie snapped back.

"What?"

"Russian lynx. Leo Margulies made it for him here."

"Yes, of course," Margot agreed. "No point paying duty on a finished coat when you can have it made better in New York."

At the apartment, Margot searched the master bedroom while Natalie showered. When she finished drying her hair she could still hear the old woman banging around like an invading army. Suddenly she couldn't stand the idea of her rummaging through the quiet, elegant room she had shared with Wallace.

"Margot? How come you're traveling on your own passport and using your own credit cards? I found you so easily through that license plate."

Margot backed out of Wallace's closet, exploring the pockets of an old suit he hadn't worn in years. "Searched my bag, did you?"

"I'm not sure I believe your story."

"In that case, thanks for letting me look anyhow."

"Who answered your telephone?"

"A lady taking care of my plants."

"But—"

Margot looked embarrassed. "Wallace retired me a few years ago. I can't afford to buy a forged passport."

"*Retired?* What are you doing here?"

"I don't like the way he died. Any more questions?"

*   *   *

Natalie got into bed. "I'll help you in the morning. I'm so knocked out."

She slept deeply until Margot shook her awake at seven in the morning, handing her a cup of tea and demanding, "The coat."

"What?"

"Where is the coat? The lynx coat he brought you."

"Locked in Cotillion's vault. It's probably worth more than the apartment."

"Get it."

"What for? Leo Margulies made it. Wallace didn't bring it from Russia."

"How do you know Leo made it?"

"His label. His box."

"You ninny! Did it ever occur to you that Wallace could sew a Leo Margulies label in a Russian coat and wrap it in a Leo Margulies box?"

"Why?"

"To slip it out of the Soviet Union. Get the coat."

"I'll call Leo."

"Leave others out of this! Get the coat."

Natalie caught Joannie Frye at the office at eight o'clock and asked her to messenger the coat. Margot waited impatiently, pacing the living room, pausing with each turn for a quick look at the street below the windows.

"I don't understand," said Natalie. "The Soviets don't make fur coats."

"That is correct. The furriers left with their customers, after the Revolution."

"So why—"

"They send their pelts to Europe. Russian women of means have their coats made in Italy. So if your coat was made in America, fine, it is a Leo Margulies as his box and label would suggest. But if it was made in Italy or Germany or France and purchased in the Soviet Union, we may find something that Wallace hid inside it."

When it arrived, Natalie took it out of the carry bag and showed it to Margot, who frowned. "Dammit, it's a good piece of work. Let's see the inside. Pull the lining away."

"It's not a French bottom," Natalie said. "Leo tacked the lining."

"Oh did he now?" Margot smiled. "That's rather unusual in such a fine garment."

"It's a tricky hem."

"Let's just have a little look, shall we?" Margot replied, dragging the coat into the light from a window and attacking it with a razor.

"What are you doing?"

"Opening the lining. I doubt he'd stash it in the pocket."

It was soon obvious that Margot was the expert finisher she claimed to be. Her razor flashed as she demolished the tiny stitches that secured the outer and inner silk linings. She flayed open an entire corner, peeling the liners and exposing the myriad whipstitches that connected the skins and closed the letting-out slices.

Her eyes glittered like the blade and her cheeks grew flushed. Her breath came short and hard in excited gasps. Then, as her fingers slowed, her breathing returned to normal and the excitement seemed to abate.

"What's wrong?"

Margot dropped the razor and ran her blunt, work-hardened fingers over the whipstitching. "Look at this reinforcing tape."

Natalie peered at the tape sewn over a seam in the skins. "What am I looking for?"

"Even the best European furrier, who might be able to let out like this, wouldn't spend the time on that tape. He'd bond it on to save money. . . . Bloody hell!" She hurled the coat to the carpet. "American work. . . . Dammit, I thought I was on to something. . . . I don't presume you have a sewing kit."

"I have Wallace's."

"Get it. I'll fix your coat."

Natalie was awed by the precision of her handwork and said so. Margot snorted. "In my day, we finished one coat a day. Now they dash through twenty."

When Margot was done, she said she was tired. Natalie invited her to use the guest room, but was relieved that Margot said she had places to go. "I'll see you tonight, Natalie. We'll finish up here. Don't talk to strangers." With that she was gone.

Natalie shrugged into the coat and stood in the window. Below, Margot dashed onto Central Park West, waving for a taxi. She was swift and dogged, like the short, stocky tennis player who dominated the net with sheer energy. Natalie smiled in spite of herself. A couple of men on either side of the avenue were already waiting for cabs, and one of them made the mistake of pointing this out to Margot, who replied by stepping into the traffic as if to stop a cab with her body.

Both men moved up the avenue, closer to Margot. And in the next block, just at the edge of Natalie's vision, a car began pulling out of a parking space. A red light stopped traffic. Margot glared at her competition, as they moved even closer. Natalie sensed a connection between them and the car, a nod, a look, she wasn't sure. She ran out her door, hit the elevator button, and then, knowing its glacial progress at rush hour, bolted down six flights of fire stairs. She burst into the lobby and out the front door.

The car, a gypsy cab, had stopped for Margot. One of the men opened the door, but she beat him to it, sliding under him into the seat. The second man opened the opposite door and both men entered the cab. From where Natalie observed, half a block away, Margot appeared to struggle with them. She ran to help.

She heard a shrill whistle and the next thing she knew she was flat on her face with a sharp pain in her leg, her hands stinging on the pavement, and a brief vision of a bicycle messenger, wobbling, recovering, and speeding away. Then her doorman was kneeling beside her.

"Are you okay, Mrs. Nevsky? Did you see that son of a bitch?"

"I'm okay. I'm okay." She sat up. The gypsy cab was gone, as were Margot and both men.

"Goddamned bikes. They oughta ban every one of them. You sure you're okay?"

"I'm okay." She limped a little into the building.

Upstairs she put ice on her leg, which was going to have a beautiful bruise the length of her thigh, and wondered what had happened that did not happen any day in New York. A woman not watching where she's going gets knocked down by a bike. The bike keeps going. Normal. Unless the bicycle had been protecting two men kidnapping Margot? Three people fight for a cab. But do all three then get in?

Twice she reached for the telephone. And what would she report? She *thought* maybe two men had kidnapped a little old lady in a gypsy cab on Central Park West. There were at least ten thousand gypsy cabs in New York, she reminded herself. And the little old lady carried a gun.

It suddenly occurred to her that Margot could have found what she was looking for in the lynx coat and stolen it when she sent Natalie for the sewing kit. Those men could have been her men, waiting for her to trick Wallace's dumb widow into giving up what he had died for.

Natalie dialed the telephone.

"It's Mrs. Nevsky, Kenny. . . . Yes, your information was good. The thing is, Margot Klein is here in New York. I want you to find her for me. . . . Seventy. About five feet one inch. One hundred and twenty pounds. Short, stocky, gray hair, blue eyes. Round face. British accent."

Margot didn't return that night. The middle of the next morning, Kenny Wilson telephoned the apartment. He sounded very serious. "Again, I have to say to you, if this has anything to do with your husband's death, you've got to tell the cops."

"What have you found?"

"She's a Jane Doe in the city morgue."

"What?"

"An unidentified body. An apparent mugging victim."

"Dead?"

"Yes, Mrs. Nevsky. Dead."

"A mugging?"

"It looks like a mugging got out of hand. They grabbed her bag. She fought back. Hit on the head. Dead."

"She was very feisty," Natalie whispered.

"Sometimes feisty works, sometimes it gets you killed. It sounds like you met her."

"Yes."

"I have to ask you what you know about this."

"Nothing."

Kenny was silent. Natalie listened to him light a cigarette. She waited him out, her mind racing.

Had Margot lied? Had she been mugged? Had she lied and been mugged? Had she told the truth and been killed by the ones who killed Wallace? Or had her husband's first wife found and stolen whatever it was he had smuggled out of the Soviet Union, if he had smuggled anything at all?

She felt a sudden sadness for the old woman. Margot had said one thing that had touched her deeply. Margot had said she did not like the way Wallace died.

"Do you have a problem with this, Kenny?"

"My immediate problem is how do I tell my friends at the morgue who Margot Klein is without having to answer some embarrassing questions."

"That's easy. Call her apartment in London. Tell whoever answers the phone to report her missing to the New York Police Department."

"I'll do that, Mrs. Nevsky. But I would appreciate it if you'd do a little thinking about your next few steps."

"I already have, thank you, Kenny."

Kenny grew more solemn. "We're talking about people getting killed here. I'm talking about going to the police."

She thought he sounded a breath away from doing just that.

"Kenny, I can't afford crazy publicity with the police."

Two days ago she had bullied Laura Drake into looking at the bright side. Today, she had to point Kenny at the dark. "The Laura Drake Advertising Agency," she said solemnly, "informs me that we will lose Diana Darbee as Cotillion's spokesperson if one more word of adverse publicity gets into the media. I don't suppose I have to tell you that six weeks before Christmas is the worst possible time to ditch a costly and very successful ad campaign. If Diana quits, you and I will very likely both be looking for a job." She hung up and immediately dialed Greg Stuart in Washington.

"Something's come up. I'd like to see you."

"I'll be home this weekend."

"The homicide detectives are asking strange questions about Russia."

"Why don't we have dinner tonight?"

"I thought you'd say that," Natalie whispered after he had hung up. It was hardly surprising. Everything kept pointing at the Soviet Union.

13

A heavyset man in a jacket and turtleneck kept watching her, so when the Metroliner stopped at Trenton, New Jersey, where she was meeting Greg Stuart, Natalie waited for the last second to alight suddenly from the club car. Racing up the escalator, plunging through the harshly lit, grimy, and oddly empty corridor, she sensed him behind her, and when she emerged from the terminal and looked back through the glass doors, there he was, shrugging into his raincoat as he hurried in pursuit.

Natalie brushed past some cabs and station wagons, looking around to orient herself. There was a busy intersection to her left, a couple of big brick buildings beyond it. Immediately ahead was the busy four-lane road that Greg had instructed her to cross. She saw signs for the restaurant, Pete Lorenzo's Cafe. Glancing back again, she saw the man push through the doors and dodge the cabs as she had. Natalie broke into a run, got blocked by cars waiting for the light, found a way between them, and crossed the road. At the cafe door, she looked back again, breathing hard. The man was climbing into a station wagon. A woman greeted him with a perfunctory kiss and they drove away.

"Get a grip," Natalie murmured to herself, and turned gratefully into the warm and noisy restaurant.

Greg waved from the end of the dark, crowded wood-paneled bar.

People were lined up four deep and in the moment it took her cousin to negotiate the distance, she had drawn some interested glances and at least one invitation. She was surprised how glad she was to see him.

Greg looked splendid—young, vital, and prosperous. His suit and shoes were English; his shirt, tie, and handkerchief Italian. He had once told her that the best thing about marrying Sally was that public servants with wealthy wives were treated seriously. Smiling, Greg took her hands, drew her close, and nuzzled her cheek.

"You're shaking."

"I got lost in the station."

"My fault. I should have met you on the platform." He stood back, surveying her face and revealing nothing on his own but warmth and concern. "You look lovely."

"I feel like Camille in the rain."

"All Camille needed was a CC on the rocks. They're on the way to our table." He took her arm and guided her into a small, dark wood dining room to a quiet table. "You really do look lovely, a little thin, maybe, and I don't think you're sleeping enough, but the gleam is back. What is it, the business? Or are you eyeing me assessingly?"

"Is this where you would meet Wallace?"

"Sometimes. He'd take the train down. I'd take it up. Just like you and me tonight. He loved this place."

"He never mentioned it."

"I'm surprised. The State House is in Trenton and these well-fed gentlemen with the full-bosomed consorts are Jersey politicians. Wallace called that roar you hear money masticating democracy. He was such a provincial New Yorker, he used to say these guys are no more or less greedy than any other politicos, but being out here in the sticks makes it seem so marvelously innocent."

"That sounds more like something you would say."

He smiled. "Maybe I did."

"Something very strange happened."

"That's why I gave you my card. What did the police say?"

"Not the police."

"You mentioned the police this morning."

"Did I?"

Greg gave her a look. "Are we fencing?"

Natalie took her first sip of the icy Canadian Club as a reward, and a second for courage. "A woman turned up claiming to be Wallace's first wife."

"I thought she was dead."

"So did I. But she knew details about his life I didn't. She said he was OSS in the war."

Greg nodded noncommittally. "Not the only one in the family. Uncle Norbert, to name the most obvious, went on with the CIA through Kennedy. I always thought Joan Didion used him as a model for one of her characters."

"She said that after the war Wallace set up a private Russian spy ring for President Truman and went on to serve Eisenhower and Kennedy and on and on. That's why he was killed. She thinks Wallace smuggled something out of Russia that the KGB killed him for."

"Like what?"

"We looked everywhere. Nothing."

Greg grinned. "I'd give Joan Didion a ring."

"I had my doubts, too, naturally. But a weird thing happened. I *think* I saw two men grab her in a cab. I could be wrong. Maybe she could have been meeting them—she said she had appointments—but that was yesterday. This morning she was found dead."

"Dead? What do the cops say?"

"Maybe a mugging."

Greg sipped his drink. "The lady vanishes. Sounds like case closed."

"We're talking about a woman *dead*, Greg."

"It's still case closed."

"Except for one thing."

"What's that?"

Natalie had been speaking at the tablecloth and fidgeting with her drink. Now she watched his fathomless eyes. "If it's true that Wallace led a private president's spy service, he could not just pick up the telephone and say, 'Hi, Mr. President, thought you'd like to know Gorbachev's won another round in the Politburo.' Do you know what I mean, Greg? He would need a contact man, Greg. Someone to arrange these supersecret meetings. Someone who works in the White House, Greg. Get my drift, Greg?"

Greg signaled a waiter, then asked Natalie as casually as if they were discussing the next election, "Shall we order?"

"Greg."

"Your 'drift' is about as subtle as the Gulf Stream. But I don't understand your purpose."

"Tell me it's true! Don't you see, if Wallace had a secret life as a spy, he had a secret death. He wasn't 'shot by a blonde.' He was killed . . . lost in action."

"He's still dead."

"But at least for a reason I can live with. Then I can be proud of him again—of us. Proud of our marriage."

Greg took her hand. "I sympathize with your logic. I wish we had some facts to support it."

The waiter approached, flourishing menus. Natalie stopped him with a cold glance and said to Greg, "I think the police will get me some facts."

Greg tried to look his sardonic best, but his expression was less opaque than complex. She detected grudging admiration and even fear. "Check, please," he called to the waiter.

She had been storing secrets like capital, keeping from Greg *The Pearl* book code, the call from Luba, Wallace's telephone, his tape recording, and Valentine's Day. Now, as a strange-looking, stretched BMW limousine approached the restaurant canopy, she made a quick decision to invest.

"Is that for us?" she asked. The chauffeur jumped out and stood ready to open the passenger door.

"Someone I want you to meet," Greg answered.

"Jeff Jervis?"

Greg's smile peeled from his face like blistering paint. "How—?"

"What are you doing to me, Greg?"

"Hey, I'm just the guy in the middle. How'd you know it's Jervis?"

The chauffeur was the cop she had seen stationed outside Jervis's Greenwich estate, but she was not about to explain. "What does he have to do with Wallace?"

"Everything."

The cop-chauffeur was gazing at a point above Natalie's head. He opened the door. "Shall we?" asked Greg.

"You first."

She stepped after him into a well-lit cabin that smelled of new leather and furniture polish. Paired bucket seats faced each other fore and aft. Greg patted the seat beside him. Natalie took the one diagonally opposite instead. The cop steered into traffic and west at the intersection. Greg shut the driver partition.

"Quite a car."

"What?"

"The car. Jervis's car. Something, isn't it?"

Natalie shrugged. All she had noticed was that the limousine rode silently and the windows were so dark they might have been alone on a mountain.

"She's bulletproof." Greg smiled, shaking his head in mock astonishment. "Bombproof, too. Ramming bumpers. Night vision. Jervis can cruise at a hundred and twenty with the lights off."

"That will be nice when the SEC cracks down."

Greg laughed. "Wait 'til you see his house."

"Are we driving to Connecticut?"

"Nope. Just outside Princeton."

"What does he have to do with Wallace?"

"I'll let him explain."

After half an hour they turned off a road and continued in darkness. Natalie lowered the partition so she could see out the windshield. They were on a driveway lined with pristine white fences. "What is this, a horse farm?"

"He's got about two hundred thoroughbreds. Fifty out at tracks around the country and a hundred mares with foal. Big money."

She was surprised by how impressed Greg sounded. But when she looked at him askance, he smiled back and she could not tell whether he was mocking himself, Jefferson Jervis, or her.

The headlights fell on orderly red barns with Dutch roofs, men loading horse vans, outbuildings, and then a sprawling modern ranch house with many wings and sheet glass walls. As they drove past it she saw a tiny, frail-looking woman alone in a huge room playing a grand piano.

"Who's that?"

"Mrs. J."

The limousine skirted the house and pulled into a jam-packed parking lot beside another big barn. When they got out, Natalie could hear a party and amplified country–western music. Greg led her inside, where the barn had been converted into a party room with a mahogany bar running the width of the back wall. Six musicians were playing on a bandstand—three guitars, bass, drums, and a mournful fiddle. A hundred people in flannel and blue jeans were drinking and dancing. Guests were manning the beer taps, while aproned waiters delivered chicken wings and ribs to the tables set around the dance floor.

Natalie saw Jervis weaving toward them through the crowds, shaking hands as he asked, over and over, "Having a good time?"

He too was dressed in jeans, with a suede vest over a cowboy shirt and elaborate tooled boots. His sharp nose, sunken cheeks, and long, narrow brow gathered in an engaging smile, even as his unblinking gaze settled firmly on her face. Natalie braced herself. She had practiced banking long enough to recognize raw power when she was in its presence.

"Hello, Greg. You forgot to tell me she was beautiful."

He had a vague sort of Groton–English accent that sounded put on and an irritating glint of assumed ownership in his eyes as he looked her up and down. When he got to her legs, she closed her coat.

"Jeff Jervis," he said, smiling. His thinning, pale ginger hair was combed economically to spread it evenly across his scalp.

"How are you?" Natalie answered, ignoring his hand.

"Perplexed," Jervis answered.

"That makes two of us."

"Yes." The English accent got strong. "I suppose it does. What can I tell you?"

"It's your house, Mr. Jervis. Your meeting. Is there someplace quieter we could talk?"

"Sure."

He led them through a door, up a flight of stairs, and into an office with a window overlooking the party room. When he shut the door it was quiet, except for the muted thump of the bass and drums. "Sit down," he said.

Natalie took the couch. Greg sat by the window. Jervis moved behind his desk. He had a wall covered with plaques and awards from civic, religious, and law enforcement groups. An overhead shelf circling the room held a vast collection of baseball hats bearing the insignia of Army units, the Secret Service, fire departments of New York and Los Angeles, SWAT teams from innumerable police departments, and naval ships and submarines.

"So?"

"What's going on, Mr. Jervis? How did you know my husband?"

"I like to think we became friends."

"Don't jerk me around!" She flared, too keyed up to handle herself well. "He despised manipulators. He was more than enough of an old socialist to call you a bloodsucker."

Jervis returned a mild, even, sympathetic smile. "Actually, we got on famously—spoke the same language. A couple of hardheaded, opportunistic realists, he and I. We rather liked each other, wouldn't you say, Greg?"

Greg nodded noncommittally without shifting his gaze from the window over the dance floor. He was tapping the beat lightly on his chair. His handsome face was a mask.

"We played some tennis. Could he hit! That long, lanky frame, wow! I forgot his age the second we got on the court. He told me you were the only one he couldn't beat. I sort of expected an Amazon, not a sylph."

"You played here?" she asked.

"Here, Greenwich, Washington, wherever we ran into each other. He told me you always got him on his backhand. He said he learned to play in Big Bill Tilden's time, when the backhand was treated as a problem, but that you're a Chrissie Evert player and see the backhand as an opportunity."

Natalie smiled in spite of herself. She could see where Wallace and Jervis might have gotten on pretty well. "That was his favorite excuse. The fact is, I did not beat him all the time. How did you meet Wallace?"

"The President lateral-passed him to me in 1981."

"I don't understand."

"The President, you may recall, entered office with a kitchen cabinet consisting of, shall we say, 'accomplished' men like myself." Jervis flashed a self-deprecating smile. "With my background in military intelligence in Vietnam, it fell to me to liaise informally with the intelligence services. Among the nuggets to drop in my lap was a bright young careerist—Greg, here—representing a New York furrier who claimed to run a Russian-intelligence-gathering network and who insisted on reporting only to the President.

"That was a no-no. Those of us who run the President have a rule—"

Natalie stiffened. "*Run* the President."

"Got a problem with that?"

"I grew up in a family where the people who worked for the President were run by him."

"Times change. Our rule is: Never, ever, leave him alone in a room with one person because as sure as one and one makes two, he will come out of that room believing that person. I persuaded the President to order Wallace Nevsky to report to me, instead."

"Wallace would never do that."

"Of course he wouldn't. He quit."

"Quit?"

"Retired. He was certainly old enough. The President awarded him this." Jervis pulled a box from his vest and tossed it to Natalie. It fell in her lap. She hinged it open and found a gold medal shining on a velvet field. "The highest civilian decoration he could give Wallace without an act of Congress. Big joke, of course. Wallace got to hold it a moment before he had to hand it back."

Natalie removed the medal and closed it in her hand. She looked at her cousin. "Greg?"

"You heard the man, Natalie. Wallace's first wife told the truth, up to that point. Maybe his death set her off. A little weird trying to get back in action, but figure old and alone, it might be hard to give up the excitement. Cloak and dagger, book codes, assignations, drops, all that stuff. Spies are like criminals, you know. They feel a notch above the rest of us, wolves among the sheep. Jeff, what is it the terrorists call citizens?"

"Donkeys, I think."

"What are you, Greg?" Natalie asked.

He smiled. "I ain't no wolf. Just a bureaucrat knitting wool."

"And you, Mr. Jervis."

"An old elephant with a memory."

"Well, you forgot something."

"What's that, Natalie? Do you mind if I call you Natalie?"

"Both of you forgot something. You're lying to me, but you screwed up."

"How so?"

"Wallace kept a secret telephone."

"So?"

"Someone called him right after he was killed. She didn't know he was dead."

"A woman?"

"Yes."

"Well . . . I don't know a delicate way to put this, Mrs. Nevsky. But Wallace . . . a woman . . . I mean, you know."

"She's Russian. And she's scared."

"I still don't know what to say."

"You'll be relieved to know she didn't call collect."

"I beg your pardon?"

"The telephone was billed to a company you own."

Jervis shot Greg an annoyed look and her cousin looked uncomfortable. "We've had that removed, Mrs. Nevsky."

"I know. You ripped up my lawn."

"Whatever expense—"

"This is your last chance, both of you, to level with me. My husband was shot to death. There's an open police investigation. I will tell them everything I know and it's more than I've told you so far."

"Let's just calm down."

"And I'll admit I'd be afraid to threaten you if Greg weren't here, because I don't know who you are or where you are coming from."

"All right. All right."

"Don't patronize me. Just tell me the truth."

"I've told you the truth, though not all of it. . . . Your husband retired, just as I said. But two years later, he tried to pull an end run, suborning Greg, here, to take him to the President. Naturally, I slapped them both down."

Natalie looked at Greg. His blue eyes had turned cold at the insult. "Jeff," he said, "you're out of line."

"No! *You* stepped out of line."

Greg rose from the couch. He moved with startling swiftness and Natalie realized that she had never seen him angry before. Everything she knew of Greg—his sardonic grins, his mocking smiles, his warm eye for his children—had vanished. His face was a hard mask with white points at his cheekbones. He took a step toward Jefferson Jervis, and she saw, within the soft drape of his flannel suit, his body set in fierce angles.

But as suddenly as he had risen, Greg sank back on the couch and turned his face, still a mask, toward the party below. Natalie released the breath that had caught in her throat. She felt strangely disappointed.

Jefferson Jervis picked up his story and continued smoothly as if nothing had happened. "So, anyway, Wallace claimed he had discovered some sort of Soviet conspiracy. He said he was still traveling in and out of the Soviet Union, buying furs, and had kept up his clandestine contacts. He demanded to see the President. I told him that the rules hadn't changed. Wallace pleaded that he was accumulating information so explosive that only the President could hear it. If it leaked back to the Soviets through the CIA, for instance, there would be disaster.

"Well, we just didn't run the President that way. Wallace was beside himself. Later, I learned that he had already tried several end runs. But they all had failed. The wall around the President held."

Again Natalie glanced at Greg, but her cousin was gazing gloomily at the dance floor.

"What kind of conspiracy?"

"He wouldn't say. He said if word of it leaked it would blow Russia apart. I made some crack that that wouldn't be the worst thing in the world, which I meant. He said it would. He said millions would suffer. He said we'd suffer too, since a country that owns half the nuclear weapons in the world shouldn't have a civil war. It seemed a good point."

"So why didn't you help him?"

"Because, underneath it all, there was no goddamned conspiracy. Still, I felt bad for him. And maybe, just maybe, he was right. So, against my better judgment, I allowed him to persuade me to support him financially, at least until he could discover something, some evidence so conclusive, so demonstrably vital, that I would in good conscience allow him to report to the President."

Jefferson Jervis was not the type of man to spend his own money on what he regarded as another's wrong idea. Sadly, she knew now how Wallace had lost *Panache*.

"So you bought his yacht."

Jervis laughed. "Greg. You've got a busy cousin, here."

"Next time maybe you'll listen."

The look on Jervis's face made clear he did not like to be corrected. He glared at Greg, who returned a look that said he didn't care what Jervis liked, then turned back to Natalie. "Your husband suggested a buy–lease deal. It was a neat way to finance what he was doing with real money no one had to lie about."

"What sort of a conspiracy was he investigating?"

"God knows. Wallace wouldn't give me even a hint."

"What do you *think* he was investigating?"

"Nothing. Listen. I've got my own connections in the Soviet Union. I know some bureaucrats. I know some army men. I'm also friendly with various groups, including *Pamyat*, the supernationalists. As friendly as they'll get with any foreigner. The point is, I've sniffed around and come up zero."

"*Pamyat?*"

"*Pamyat* means memory. You speak Russian, don't you? It's a sort of back-to-the-good-old-days, roots-of-Russia movement. Russia for the Russians. Getting to be quite a force, actually. Gorby's going to have his hands full."

Natalie nodded. "Yes, Wallace mentioned them." On his tape recording, she recalled. *For every good and honest Gorbachev espousing perestroika . . . every ardent reformer . . . an anti-Semitic reactionary member of* Pamyat.

"Who's the Boss?"

"Where'd you hear that?" Jervis asked sharply.

"Around. Who is he?"

"It's the old name for Stalin is all I know."

Certain that he knew more, she decided not to mention Luba's Millionaire.

Jervis said, "Don't you get it, Mrs. Nevsky? There was nothing. I couldn't bear to cut him off, but the fact was the old gent was just spinning his wheels. He just refused to give it up."

"If it was nothing, who killed him?"

Jervis sighed. Greg started to speak, but the financier cut him off with a gesture. "No one of consequence, I assure you."

"How do you assure me?"

"On two levels. First, Mrs. Nevsky, an old operative is shot? Think about it. We immediately put the question in every corner of the globe. Nothing."

"But they didn't know he was a spy."

"Trust me, Mrs. Nevsky, we asked the right questions of the right people."

"What's the second level?"

"In all those years he kept digging, he found nothing. Nor did anything unfold in Moscow that fit his grandiose suspicions. The CIA found nothing. The Brits found nothing. *He accomplished nothing. . . .* I did not have the heart to tell him to stop. I mean, he was a fine old veteran who was at it nearly fifty years."

"That woman was not his girlfriend."

"Mrs. Nevsky, I am willing to assume that the blonde in question was not a blonde in the sense of what we mean by a blonde."

"If you're willing to assume that, you have to ask who killed him and why."

"My best guess—backed up by vague rumor—is that Wallace got sloppy."

"What do you mean?"

"He made a mistake. The KGB finally tumbled to him. When they rolled up his net and discovered all the secret sharp sticks he had poked in their eyes over the years, they decided to even up a lot of old scores at once. A public lesson to anyone else who entertains the notion of spying on the Soviet Union, with a dash of revenge. They're human, you know."

"Maybe *you* got sloppy. Maybe you were telling stories about him in your kitchen cabinet."

Jervis's eyes flashed. "Hold on, Mrs. Nevsky! You're treating me like a lightweight, which is the sort of mistake certain career diplomats have made, to their regret. Just because I made my pile in business doesn't mean I'm not qualified to operate in the government."

"Who elected you?"

"The President of the United States—I've been dealing with the Soviets for ten years. I know what makes them tick and I know what they want. And I'm telling you, I checked out your husband's story and it wasn't true. Got that?"

"What I'm 'getting,' " Natalie shot back, "is that your checking Wallace out might have tipped the Soviets to his work. Maybe your questions gave them an answer."

"Goddammit, you're doing it again. I was an intelligence officer in Southeast Asia. I'm not a dummy. I didn't blow your husband's cover."

"Then why was he killed?"

"Greg, will you talk to this woman?"

"Don't patronize me, Mr. Jervis."

"I can understand your bitterness, but I assure you I don't tell stories. He wasn't getting any younger, Mrs. Nevsky. I'm sure this is little comfort, but it's better you know the truth than go careening to the cops with strange stories. And don't forget you'd put his old friends in Russia at risk."

Natalie looked at Greg.

"He just didn't know when to stop," Greg murmured sadly.

Jervis said, "It would be wrong to blame him for trying to get back into harness. He was dedicated."

"Wallace was not an old fool," Natalie whispered.

"Beg your pardon?"

"You've left me with a terrible choice: my husband was shot by a girlfriend or shot because he was an old fool."

Silence stretched. Natalie closed her eyes, her mind empty of hope. It ends here, she thought, on some nickel billionaire's tax shelter horse farm. But she wished more for her husband.

"There is something I would like to do for you," Jervis said after a while. "For Wallace."

"I'll keep his medal."

"That's not a good idea."

She closed it tighter in her fist. "Don't try to take it from me."

Greg intervened. "It's yours. Don't worry."

"I'm not worried," she snapped back.

"That's not a good idea," Jervis repeated. He locked eyes with Greg and Natalie had a feeling that, despite their conflicts, which appeared to run deep, when it came to the issue of Wallace's medal they had merely gotten their signals crossed.

"Keep it," Greg told her. "It's yours."

"I intend to."

"There are security considerations," Jervis persisted.

"Fuck security," Greg shot back. "Give her a break."

Jervis shrugged and changed the subject. "I don't know if you're aware how precarious your position is at Cotillion Furs."

"I've been learning a lot I don't know."

"Somebody's making an effort to buy control. Do you know Stevie Weintraub?"

"He's a *schlock* importer."

"Did Wallace know him?"

"Couldn't stand him."

"Well, he's working a takeover."

"Thanks for the warning."

"Want help?"

Natalie looked up, cut the distance with a level gaze. "No, thanks."

"I'd do it for Wallace."

"You've done plenty for Wallace, already. And I wouldn't be surprised if you were underwriting Stevie Weintraub to shill for you."

Greg said, "Natalie, don't be foolish. Jeff can save you."

"Don't talk to me, Greg."

She felt her cousin had betrayed her by siding against Wallace. Right or wrong, Greg should have drawn a line. If that wasn't logical, she hurt too much to reason clearly. Her hopes for the past were a shambles, and the void ahead loomed as cold as a winter night.

BOOK THREE

PERESTROIKA

14

I can't believe he's been gone two months," said Diana Darbee. "It seems less."

Two months, a week and three days, but Natalie let it go. She felt as if she had come indoors from a blizzard, and her skin still burned from the pelting snow, but the snow itself was no longer blinding. He lay heavily in her heart, but he was not quite every second in her mind. Work had helped, at least during the day.

"Christmas was a bitch," said Diana. "I couldn't get him out of my head. My sleepover finally went home without his present."

Natalie nodded politely, tuning her out.

"And New Year's," Diana moaned. "Forget New Year's. What did you do New Year's?"

"Got through it," Natalie replied, drawing strength from that week-old memory. "Asleep at ten."

"Goddamned holidays." Then, social amenities apparently concluded, Diana shook her blonde hair impatiently. The actress was wearing a metal-studded, skintight, black lizard jump suit, zipped open to the navel, exposing ferocious cleavage, which had reduced briskly efficient Joannie Frye to a state of dewy-eyed paralysis. She glanced significantly at the big, bright chrome man's Rolex on her lizard-swathed wrist and said, "Okay, buddy. What do we got?"

This visit was the culmination of weeks of negotiation between Laura Drake and Diana's agent, Natalie and Diana's business manager, and everyone's lawyers. With publicity dying down, at last, Diana might stay with Cotillion. But she was playing hard to get and talking openly with Furrari and Revillon, and had only reluctantly agreed to view an informal presentation of Natalie's new campaign. Thus, this casual meeting at Cotillion, instead of at the Drake Agency's extravagant offices in the Flatiron Building.

It had been a crazy morning, even before Joannie announced that Diana had arrived early. Natalie's neck ached from holding the telephone and the huge partners' desk she used to share with Wallace was buried under paper. Before she had her coat off, her Binghamton, New York, salon owner had called in panic: his mink shipment was lost. Natalie ran it down in three calls and reassured the salon owner, as Joannie routed an angry complaint from a Canadian manufacturer demanding his check. Four calls later she got the Canadian back and explained that Barclays and Citicorp had somehow conspired to send his check to London. Joannie hustled in with invoices to sign, trailed by a lawyer with court documents pertaining to one of her New York supplier's Chapter 11 proceedings. Then Pete Kastoria, the factory foreman, reported that the Brooklyn tannery was sitting on mink pelts that had been promised for a month. Natalie telephoned and yelled until she had exacted a promise her skins would be aboard a truck by noon. She told Pete to get back to her if he didn't have them by two. Then, already in a solid yelling mood, she had a long, acrimonious and ultimately halfway satisfying conversation with a liar on Thirtieth Street who owed her a thousand fox jackets. Her bookkeeper reported that certain invoices she was holding for collateral were incorrect; Natalie told another lawyer, who looked after Wallace's money lending, to draft a stern warning. A designer she liked called to quit; Natalie hung on the phone until she realized the issue was money and hired him back, while Joannie stood at her side, passing letters to be read and signed.

She had been dictating answers to more letters into Wallace's pocket Panasonic while waiting on hold for one of her bankers, when Joannie reported that Diana had arrived early. Diana had given Natalie's desk a hard look, nodded knowingly at her coat on the chair, her untouched cold coffee, and the piles of paperwork.

"You too can work in a glamour industry. How the hell are you?"

"Pretty good. I really appreciate your coming."

Diana introduced her secretary, publicist, hairdresser, and two lawyers. Natalie presented Joannie, and snared Leo Margulies, who happened to be in the hall, and an old furrier she had hired out of retirement to lean on suppliers. Everyone had coffee and finally when coffee, assistants, and entourage had been cleared, Natalie found herself alone with Diana for the first time since the funeral.

She went to an easel opposite the couch. "We decided two things. One, 'The Smart Woman's Furrier' is as good a slogan as we'll ever get. So we're keeping it. Two, Wallace always said we wasted your talents."

"Which talents?" Diana grinned.

"We've relied on your famous face and voice and your smart woman rep. But we used you as a clotheshorse, not an actress."

Diana's expression turned feline—intrigued and wary in equal parts. "Yeah?"

"Laura sent over these roughs," said Natalie, flipping the top sheet off the first four-color ink sketch. A twenties flapper in bobbed hair and a slinky fur coat was reading a ticker tape. "Keep in mind that Cotillion Furs is an old name in the fur trade. I chose it for its classic sound from the bankrupt labels Wallace had bought up over the years."

"Too old," Diana interrupted. "Cotillion sounds old-fashioned. You ought to goose it up."

"My customers," Natalie replied evenly, "are conservative high-achievers who like to fantasize that their Puritan families arrived on the *Mayflower*."

"Like yours?" Diana asked with a sulky smile.

"We're Scots Presbyterians. We had our own boat. I'll read the voice-over, the narration by Granddaughter. Ready?"

"Wait a minute." Diana gave the easel a suspicious nearsighted squint. "Who's the flapper who looks very much like me?"

" 'Grandmother,' " Natalie read, " 'had her own seat on the Stock Exchange. She sold short before the Crash, and bought her furs at Cotillion.' Segue to present." Natalie flipped the sheet. The next sketch showed Diana Darbee in a modern fur scanning an overhead computer tape. "Granddaughter addresses the camera: 'Cotillion, The Smart Woman's Furrier.' "

She glanced at Diana, who looked as impassive as a sphinx in lizard. "Here's another that's kind of fun."

Diana was pictured mushing a dog sled through a blizzard. " 'Dashing to the Pole, Grandmother stayed warm in furs by Cotillion.' " In the next sketch she strode down Park Avenue in modern mink with a husky tugging a leash. " 'Cotillion, The Smart Woman's Furrier.' "

"And . . ." The last sketch showed Diana in a substantial Eleanor Roosevelt fur coat as she smashed a champagne bottle on a flag-draped warship. " 'Grandmother represented our district in Congress,' " read Natalie.

"Elected in furs by Cotillion," Diana finished for her. "Well, you've certainly put your down time to good use. Let me think about it over the weekend." She glanced again at her watch, walked to the easel, and flipped speculatively through the drawings.

"Do you have time for lunch?" Natalie asked. "I booked a table at The Russian Tea Room."

"Is Sables still around the corner?"

Natalie hesitated. "It's called The Garden, now."

"Same food?"

"I think so."

"I want a pastrami sandwich. I want pickles. I want mustard. Let's go. You're buying—hey, what's wrong?"

"I feel funny going in. All the furriers eat there and they—I think they're staring because of Wallace and everything."

"What?"

"I'm embarrassed. I don't go there anymore."

"Fuck them!" said Diana, flinging a jet black Cotillion mink over her studs and lizard skin. "You're going there with me."

Silence washed over the big delicatessen like an East Hampton breaker as the dapper old manager led Natalie to an empty table dead center in the high-ceilinged room. Diana pranced in her wake. "Tell me something," she asked him, loudly enough to make Natalie wish again she hadn't come. "A hundred furriers just lost their voice. What's the matter with those two talking in the corner?"

"They're from the People's Republic of China. Very nice to see you again, Mrs. Nevsky," he said, patting Natalie's arm. "As for you, Miss Bigshot"—he pinched Diana's cheek—"eight years you don't have time for a sandwich?"

"I sent you my picture. I don't see it on the wall."

"It got stolen."

"You shoulda asked for another."

"It was attracting the wrong element. Menus?"

"Pastrami. And a round of celery tonic, diet for me. And more pickles."

The manager went off calling, "Pickles for the movie star," conversations resumed, and Diana said, "That wasn't so bad, was it?"

"It's a scene I'm not part of. It's such a club."

"Bullshit. You know what your problem is?"

"I know, I take things too seriously."

"No. You take the wrong things seriously. Must have driven Wallace nuts."

Natalie bristled.

"Lighten up. Hey, I hear you're selling your shopping mall stores."

"Rita Dabney found me a buyer for the whole chain, but they're cash poor, so I'm trying to do a deal to get them with the right people."

"My business manager said the dentist had to check his gold fillings after your last phone call. Sounds like you're putting things back together."

"Day by day. Work helps. I'm grateful to have something else to concentrate on."

"How's business?"

"We're getting killed on furskin prices. Mink's gone crazy."

"Who's holding your hand?"

"Joannie's good at the office. Leo Margulies helps. Old Irving does most of my yelling for me. Joannie calls him my one-man *gonif* squad. You should hear him." She tried an imitation of Irving on the telephone, " 'Retired? What kind of a man stays in Florida when his friend's widow is *raped* by a manufacturer like you?' "

"That's Wallace's act!" Diana applauded. "Not bad."

"I wish. The act is the hardest part. I'm a one-on-one person. I could sell you the Brooklyn Bridge, face to face. Wallace could sell it to a crowd." Memory washed over her like a sullen gray wave. "Sometimes," she said, "I want to die."

"Except it's 'rrrlaped.' " Diana backtracked to correct Natalie's pronunciation, clearly choosing to ignore any confession of weakness. "The old Jews say, 'Rrrlaped,' with a long *r* and a little bit of *l*."

"Right," said Natalie. "But old Irving is so old he falls asleep between phone calls. At least he's a beginning. I'm setting up systems, trying to turn this one-man, one-woman show into a modern business. Wallace and I were always promising to delegate authority. Now I have no choice. It's either get organized or swallowed up."

"Who's holding your hand at home?"

"Me, mostly. I prefer it that way. And I've got my friends at The Comedy Club when I need them. They still want you to address a lunch, by the way."

Diana waved the invitation aside. "Father any help?"

"Not really."

"Mom?"

Natalie shook her head. In fact, both parents were lobbying her to quit the fur trade.

"And how about cool and cute cousin Gregory?" Diana asked with an inquiring smile.

"We haven't spoken since the funeral. He's in Washington, mostly." The truth was Greg telephoned weekly, but she refused to talk to him. She needed an enemy—someone to blame for losing Wallace to death and innuendo—and her cousin, who had lied to her and conspired with him, was perfect for the role.

"Diana," she whispered suddenly. "Sometimes I feel him inside me."

"Who?"

"Wallace."

She had not told a soul, barely admitted it to herself. Diana regarded her nervously.

Natalie hugged herself. "It's so real, it's weird. I swear I can *feel* his body inside mine."

Diana grinned. "Where, exactly, do you have this feeling?"

Natalie blinked. But Diana's grin was like an oar in the water to climb back into the boat. "Pretty crazy, isn't it? So. What do you think about Laura's campaign?"

"Hokey, but on target," Diana said noncommittally. "My question still is, does it fit my needs?"

But Diana's real concern, Natalie knew, was whether the police would arrest the woman who had shot Wallace. She would commit to nothing that bound her hard-earned and very valuable name to a murder trial.

Their conversation faltered there and they sat silent, while the babble around them was punctuated by the manager's shouts to his waiters and the greetings and backslaps traded by old friends. The sandwiches arrived and Diana tore into hers. "Eat," she ordered. "You're skin and bones. And another thing, I want you walking to work. Get rid of those bags."

"They're from not sleeping."

"Get the blood moving in the morning and they'll go away. Walking's the second best way to do that." She watched the room as she talked, taking it in greedily, reminding Natalie of how Wallace devoured sights and scenes he enjoyed. "Wallace told me how to tell the millionaires from the hustlers. The millionaires wear the shiny off-the-rack suits. The hustlers wear gold."

"Diana, why did Wallace call you the day he left for his last Russian trip?"

Diana looked mildly surprised that Natalie knew about the call. "He called to say good-bye."

"Just good-bye?"

Diana started to smile, thought better of it, and replied, seriously, "I thought he sounded a little weird."

"What do you mean?"

"Like he was saying good-bye forever. Like he might not come back. He was more emotional than usual."

Natalie picked up her sandwich. Afraid to hear what was "usual," she changed the subject. "Diana? Did Wallace give you anything that last day?"

"What last day?"

"On the boat. When he was shot."

"Oh." Diana looked blank, as if her public relations people who had whisked her off the yacht ahead of the reporters had also erased the moment from her brain. "What do you mean?"

"Like a present from Russia?"

"You mean those stupid little dolls?"

"Anything."

"No. He didn't bring me anything." She grinned mischievously and licked mustard from her hand. "What did he bring you?"

"A full-length Russian lynx coat."

"Alllll right!" Diana shot a greasy high-five across the table and held it there until Natalie had to return it.

"It's not exactly me, of course, but it's gorgeous."

"I want to see it."

"Really?"

"Yes! Pay. Pay. Let's get out of here."

They raced across the street to 333.

Natalie went into the Cotillion vault and came out wearing the sleek white fur.

"Oh my God," Diana whispered. "It looks like a fucking blizzard."

"Try it on."

"You may not get it back," Diana warned, sliding into it with practiced ease. "A *warm* blizzard. I feel like Scrooge McDuck diving into his money."

She closed the big wing collar up to her nose and peered through the silky guard hairs. "You and me, we gotta talk."

"Monday," Natalie answered, reluctant to reopen discussion on the campaign.

"No, not that," said Diana, staring with sincere and puzzled admiration. "How do you do it?"

"Do what?"

"I mean—Christ, Natalie. You must be a pistol in the sack."

Early the next morning on the corner of Broadway and Forty-fourth while walking to work as Diana had suggested, she laughed out loud. People stared and so she pretended she was reading the news sign circling the tower at Times Square. The dollar was still falling against the yen, which meant even higher mink prices at the upcoming Seattle fur auction. She had a gut feeling that some opportunity lay in that problem, but "pistol in the sack" kept scrambling her thoughts and she laughed again, wondering what Diana would have made of her first time with Wallace.

It happened the night they opened their first Cotillion salon, the test store in a cheap, temporary lease Rita had found in a building slated for demolition on Madison Avenue. Their smart woman's furrier ads had worked, and lines of affluent working women had practically looted the place. An evening press party had turned into a caviar-and-champagne celebration. Finally, everyone left. A sexy pile of mink and fox and fisher, heaped decadently in the shadows as the building heat died, made a warm and cozy nest while they finished the caviar. Natalie's glass was empty. Wallace touched his cold champagne to her lips. Some spilled.

"The fox! I promised it."

"Promises in the fur trade are made to be broken," Wallace whispered, brushing idly at the golden droplets.

She found herself staring at his long, beautifully formed hands.

When she looked up, it was into his eyes. Wallace leaned close and kissed the drops on her chin away. This is not happening, she thought.

He's sixty-something. By then his lips were closing lightly upon hers, and six months' hard work day and night, the celebrations and the fights, seemed, at last, a reason to kiss him back.

After a while he got up to turn out the lights. She lay still, listening to her heart in the silence. "I have to tell you something," she murmured. "I'm not so good at this."

"Not to worry. The old gent recalls a trick or two."

"I don't let go easily."

"I never would have guessed." A shaft of light from the street caught his smile. "Why not explore?" he said. "Ask me things. Tell me things."

"You would lie here all night talking to me if I wanted," she marveled.

"Hardly my first choice, but—"

"You're not always this patient. You push the hell out of me."

"That's business. Try treating love like a vacation."

"Vacations are for amateurs."

"You've already admitted that."

"Hey, I'm twenty-seven. I'm not really an amateur."

"So we're both amateurs with each other."

She was acutely aware of his body beside her, though he was not pushing. Nor was he detached. He wanted her, but more than that, he wanted her to want him. She knew his reputation, had seen his girlfriends. But with her he seemed uncharacteristically serious, and that frightened her. "Wallace, what's wrong with me?"

"I'll deliver a complete diagnosis in the morning."

"What time is it?"

"Time for the truth."

"You first."

"I am much happier tonight than I was before we met. Now it's your turn. Tell me something true."

Despite the dark, she hid her face against his shoulder. "The truth is I'm afraid of getting caught between sex and work. What if you *devastate* me in bed? We're business partners. You're already much older and more experienced. How am I going to stand up against you in the morning?"

"That's really a question for a lawyer. Why don't we invite cousin Greg to draft a contract indicating you're boss and I'm minority partner. Devastation in bed could be keyed to stock options."

"I'm serious."

"That's a serious offer."

"Just to sleep with me?" Natalie teased, snuggling deeper under a silver fox cape.

"Cheap at twice the price. Deal?"

"No. Let's stay partners."

"Done," he said, stroking her cheek with one light finger and kissing the path it made. "Now it's your turn to make me an offer."

"What do you want?"

"An invitation."

Natalie closed her eyes. "I invite you to my side of the heap."

In the dark, his first kiss landed in an apparently innocuous, yet wildly sensitive hollow that her last lover had taken a year to stumble across. He tugged the fox from her body and his second kiss fell like a rocket.

Giving away Wallace's clothes, Natalie's mother suggested several times, would be good therapy. Natalie was in no rush, but her mother persisted until Natalie finally gave in and invited her to come over and help on a Saturday morning. Martha Stuart took one look at Wallace's walk-in closet and stiffened like a wire coat hanger. "Good Lord, it looks as if he went shopping with Mrs. Marcos."

"Wallace was in the business, Mother. He felt it was important to dress the part."

"Your father was a diplomat," her mother replied frostily. "I rather doubt he ever owned more than four suits at once. Natalie, there must be thirty pairs of shoes here."

Natalie, who didn't like having her mother in her bedroom, much less Wallace's closet, showed her a tasseled calfskin loafer. "Wallace had this made in London forty years ago. He respected things people made with their hands and took care of them. Anyway, some tall, skinny actor is going to find a bonanza at the Goodwill—no, not that one, Mother. It stays."

She plucked a white linen suit from her mother's hands and laid it on the bed. "It's his auction suit. He wore it like a uniform to every furskin auction in the world. Always with a red tie and handkerchief. So the auctioneer could see him."

"What are you going to do with it?"

"I don't know."

"Well, you can't just keep it. And what about all those neckties?"

Natalie was still waking up at six and she had started on his neckties hours before her mother came, putting aside those she liked. "I told you, I'm keeping some."

"Natalie, you've covered the bed."

There were scores of silk neckties, in the reds and blues that Wallace favored. "I gave him so many."

"What are you going to do with them?"

"You know, you gave me a good idea, Mother. I'll have them sewn into a bedspread."

Her mother stared. "You're going to *sleep* under a blanket of Wallace's ties?"

"Why not? They're beautiful silk. Look, spread the colors around." She swirled them with her hands, like finger painting.

"Well. I mean. Not right away of course. But. Well, you know. Don't be dense, Natalie. You know what I mean."

"No. I don't know anything." She put on Wallace's linen jacket and studied herself in the mirror. It was long, but she had the shoulders for it. Not bad. Her eyes, she noticed, were responding nicely to Diana Darbee's walking therapy.

"Natalie. One does not mourn forever. It's not natural."

A smile made her mouth grow wider. "Mother, I promise. I won't do anything unnatural under Wallace's neckties."

She could joke, and there were days when she did not cry, but there were dark days, too, when she refused to believe what everyone else presumed was true and asked herself what Wallace had been investigating when he made a "mistake," as Jervis had put it. What had Wallace thought was so important? Had he discovered a spy within the American government? Or a plot against the President? Or a military incursion into Europe? Or a new Soviet weapon? Or a plot in the Middle East? Or a push to the Persian Gulf? A rapprochement with China? Ideas popped into her head from novels, movies, history, and the daily news. For in a world where two empires had contended head to head for more than forty years, any secret was possible—anything, or nothing, as Jervis claimed. Which was why, once a week or so, when Natalie had a dark day, she hid her hair under a flat cap, donned a battered suede jacket she had had since college, faded jeans, and big sunglasses, and made the rounds of the *Voice*, the *Times*, and *New York* magazine.

Her personals mailboxes were always empty. Neither "Pearl, Let's Do Lunch," nor "Pearl, Be My Valentine," drew any replies. "Nothing yet," the clerk at the *Voice* began to answer with wary regard for a potential nut case. In January, Natalie placed an ad in the *International Herald Tribune*.

She had made a bargain with herself. For her sanity, and to get through the days, and with no evidence to the contrary, she decided to believe Greg and Jervis's claim that Wallace had retired. But at the same time, she kept hoping it wasn't true, and waiting for some sign that Wallace had been killed for a better reason than it seemed. But Luba never answered.

Hope took other forms. She imagined she was being followed when a face would repeat in the cityscape of moving faces. She imagined clicks on the telephone lines. And speculative glances from people who had known Wallace. Yet she had normal days, more than not, busy, work-filled days when she never cried at all, and when logic suggested that hoping was so much easier than trying to rediscover who Natalie Stuart had been before she married Wallace Nevsky.

She made a flying trip to the Seattle Fur Exchange and sat through a mink auction, watching Wallace's former colleagues and competitors operate. Four caught her attention. A man who wore a red satin jump suit. A man who wore a checked flannel trapper's shirt and leather vest. And two elderly fur markers who worked in old-fashioned baseball caps, a legacy of the days when bright lights glared on the pelts. She found them clannish and unresponsive. She could hire them on commission, like anyone else, but she knew that Cotillion would be only one of their many clients, which would never replicate the tight control Wallace had exerted over their acquisition of furs. On the other hand, the old broker in the Yukon trappings offered an intriguing point.

"You can hire any kid to mark mink," he declared, swigging a bottle of ale in the hospitality suite where Natalie had cornered him. "Who needs the old skills when ninety-five percent of the skins are ranched?"

Wallace had intimated this numerous times: the old men of the auction circuit had learned their trade when most skins were trapped wild; their clients had depended on their ability to distinguish quality, variations in color, and skillfully concealed repairs stitched by the trappers.

"Anyone can mark mink," the broker grumped. "All they need is an idea of what they want and ready cash."

Natalie signaled a waitress in a fur miniskirt to bring the broker another ale. "What do you think of Russian mink?"

"*Norka?* Not much."

"Why?"

"Honey, mink is rich countries' fur. The mink you see here, they ate like kings. Delicious turkey scraps. Rich fish guts. It makes them big and strong with thick coats. In poor countries like Russia, the people make soup out of turkey scraps and fish guts. The minks suffer. No, no matter how finely they breed, and they breed from the best American stock—I suppose Wallace must have told you."

"Refresh me."

"After the Second World War, American mink ranchers sold breeders to the Scandinavians and the Russians, even the Chinese. Back then, we sold three million mink a year. Today the Russians sell ten million and the Scandinavians seven million and the Chinese more than you'd want to think about. And we still sell three million. Brilliant American enterprise. Anyway, since the Russians don't feed their mink as well, *Norka* mink is, on the average, second rate."

"But Wallace bought hundreds of thousands of Russian mink for the Canadians."

"Don't remind me. Even before you came along he could make the market with the money he spent for Canadians."

"But the Canadians demand quality."

The broker, whom Natalie had heard people refer to as Yukon Jack, scratched under his vest, emptied his bottle, and reached for the new bottle Natalie had ordered. "I said, on the average. Out of those ten million, there's some pretty good pelts, and damned good at the price. The trick is finding that two or three percent that are really top-notch. The Cossack knew the right people when it came to buying Russian mink."

"Come on, Sojuzpushnina would never favor one buyer at an auction."

"Of course not. But the Cossack always knew, months ahead, when the best lots were going to be offered, so he was positioned to buy."

"I'm not sure I follow," Natalie said slowly.

"What I'm saying, as clearly as I know how, Mrs. Nevsky, is that if

I saw the Cossack marking mink, I'd take a closer look. It was his turf."

She asked for a breakfast meeting with Bill Malcolm, her old boss and one-time lover at Stuart, Malcolm and Hardy. They met over smoked salmon and shirred eggs in the firm's sumptuous partners' dining room. She had eaten there three times before, once with Aunt Margaret when she was a little girl, again when the investment banking house had recruited her from Harvard, and finally with Bill Malcolm to celebrate closing a deal. Their affair had dated from that lunch, making it her last, because SM&H gentlemen did not entertain their mistresses in the partners' dining room. Her goal had been to dine here every day as SM&H's first female partner. Then she met Wallace.

The acquisition of SM&H by a cash-rich Hartford insurance company had not cramped the habits of the partners, who had sold their independence for employment as managing directors. The room was wood-paneled, with a high-coffered mahogany ceiling and leather chairs. A Whistler portrait of the firm's founder, a great-uncle of the man who had adopted Wallace so reluctantly, graced the wall above the fireplace. Nineteenth-century silver, Limoges china, and fresh flowers were laid on linen tablecloths whiter than the purest cocaine snorted in the traders' bathrooms.

"You look great," said Bill Malcolm, flourishing his napkin as he finished his eggs. "At risk of repeating myself, you look really fine. Now I've been talking to some of the directors and the answer is yes, one way or another, we'll find a place for you."

He had put on a little weight in the years since she had worked for him, which rounded his smile with the dubious effect of making him look a little more self-satisfied. He had lost some hair, heightening his brow to advantage. A smart man, now he looked it, quick, capable, and shrewd. He had been a good teacher. And a pleasant enough occasional lover, conveniently married, when, fresh from business school, all her energies were focused on her career. If his old wedding ring was a guide, he had stayed with his wife, after all, which did not surprise her.

"Bill, no. I'm not here for a job."

"Nat, you're not going to Shearson. This is your home."

"I have a job. I'm president of Cotillion Furs."

"Oh, I was afraid you would say that."

"Why?"

"I hope you're not here trying to raise money, because I'll tell you right now, darling, we can't help unless you install seasoned management. Professional retailers and a bunch of old Jews buying the coats."

"Don't worry. I won't embarrass you when I'm ready to discuss money. No, what's happening is, I'm selling my entire suburban setup, all the stores I own and lease in shopping malls. It'll raise a ton and cut losses at the same time."

"Any luck finding a buyer?"

"I found them, already. Rita Dabney found them. We've put together a beautiful deal and Cotillion comes out smelling like a rose."

"Congratulations. You're doing grand. I'm not sure why we're sharing breakfast. Not that it isn't a pleasure. It's wonderful seeing—"

"I convinced them they need an investment banker. A solid, old-line outfit that will help them set up management and raise capital."

"What do they need capital for?"

"To buy my stores."

Malcolm laughed, a trifle anxiously. "Very cute. You bring them to me to raise money to buy your stores. Are these the sorts of clients SM&H usually underwrites?"

"They're more like a new opportunity. Two insane Israeli brothers, maybe twenty-five years old. They own a huge mail order computer software business and a chain of computer stores. Their gimmick is they guarantee to replace, not repair, broken computers. They sell like crazy. They want my stores because the locations are dynamite and Rita showed them how to cover the mirrors with neon, for almost no money, and turn them ultra-tech."

"Israelis?" Bill asked.

"It took me three meetings to convince them to talk to you. They're very primitive. When they sent out for coffee they pulled bills out of a filing cabinet heaped with cash. On the other hand, they've doubled their gross every year for the last five years."

"What is that gross?"

Natalie told him.

Bill pursed his lips, stroked his chin, and glanced suspiciously at the other tables as if noticing belatedly that, unlike the old days of cozy partnership, now he might possibly be overheard by a stranger. He motioned to one of the waiters who was delivering cigars in an ornately carved wooden humidor.

"Pick one for me, too," said Natalie. "I'll give it to my foreman."

Bill handed it over and she stashed it in her bag. He touched her hand. "Listen, dear. If you ever get lonely, you know who to come to."

Every time she thought she had her emotions under control, something untied them. She was already on edge, waiting for his answer on the Israelis. Instead, he was coming on to her. "Lonely?" she asked sharply.

A pink flush crept up his brow. "Well, you know, we're old friends and all, and there are normal needs that women—people—get. Sorry. What I'm trying to say is . . . you always brought the worst out in me."

She forced a steadying breath. "Well, put it back." She gave him a smile. She supposed she owed him that much, but mostly she needed him on her side.

Bill nodded. "I think we could arrange a meeting with your Israelites. Have a look at them, at least."

"I'd say thank you, but I think you're going to end up thanking me. These guys are hot."

"Maybe. . . . What would you do with the money?"

"Buy skins."

"That's a lot of skins."

"A lot," she agreed. "Skins are getting expensive, but no skins, no coats."

"But you shouldn't use that money to buy supplies. That's investment capital."

"No kidding. But I don't have a choice. I've used my investment capital buying up loose shares."

Bill lit his cigar and gazed speculatively into the smoke. "Ever think of taking Cotillion public?"

"Not while Wallace was alive."

"And now?"

"I'd rather not."

"Well, if you're harboring any plans to raise more cash—and I gather in the fur trade that's a given, particularly with the takeover rumors I've heard that have your name attached—keep us in mind to take you public."

"I don't want to go public. I'd rather hunt up individual investors."

"Then you'd better come up with some terrific idea to sell. And I don't mean ten new franchises."

"I started with single investors."

"You were a pioneer. If you want more capital you better pioneer something new and noteworthy, again."

"Like what?"

"An idea we can sell. Something as hot today as your franchising scheme was six years ago."

She was eating a quick lunch alone at The Garden Restaurant when Stevie Weintraub cast a shadow on her reading. "Hey, Natalie. How are you doing?"

Her stomach clenched and her neck went tight with the effort to hide her anger. Like Greg, Stevie was a convenient target, someone to blame, a businessman she had befriended who had turned on her when Wallace died. Now, seeing him rattling his gold bracelet and preening his mustache, she knew she wanted to get back at him, somehow, beat him at his own game. Her lawyers had unearthed no connection yet between the Hong Kong importer and Jefferson Jervis, but she still had a feeling one existed.

She conjured a smile. "Sit down, Stevie."

Stevie sat. "Whacha reading?"

"A new market report I commissioned," she said, folding it. "How are you?"

"Fine. You look pretty good for a lady who's been through what you've been through." When her face clouded, despite her best efforts, he added hastily, "Wallace was a hell of a guy."

"Thank you, Stevie. It's nice to see you. I had the impression you were avoiding me in Seattle."

"We should talk."

"You were going to sell me fur jackets," she replied innocently. "Then I never heard from you. What happened?"

"Well, I—I thought Wallace was against imports."

"It's my decision, now."

"And I figured with you losing the Diana line, you didn't need them."

"I haven't lost the Diana line."

"I heard she was quitting, because of the way Wallace—you know."

"Got shot by a blonde?" Natalie finished for him, her anger flaring before she could stop it. "You heard wrong. Diana Darbee is one hundred percent committed to Cotillion Furs. We're building a whole new ad campaign around her. We'll have room for your jackets, but only if you can supply quality."

Stevie was no pushover and he proved it now, recovering swiftly and conjuring his own innocent smile to say, "That makes Cotillion even more valuable than ever, doesn't it?"

"Worth its weight in mink. It makes me very happy to own it. How many of those jackets do you have left?"

"Maybe half."

"Half?" she echoed, disappointed. "Who bought them?"

"I think Northern Lights got some and Furrari, and we sold a ton to Revillon."

Natalie cut down the lie in Wallace Nevsky's best Garment-Centerese: "*Puh-leez,* Stevie. Revillon wouldn't touch your imports with a rake."

"I meant the Fur Vault."

"Those jackets were *too* good for The Fur Vault. That's why you came to me. Did you say you have half left?"

"Maybe a little more than half."

"Shall we say ten thousand jackets?"

"About."

At this point Wallace would have mocked him hard for his lies, but Natalie switched to her own negotiating tactics. "If you could see your way clear to knocking fifteen percent off your last price, I'll take all ten thousand."

"Ten percent off's the best I can do."

"Twelve percent off. And an exclusive on that line."

"Natalie! You want my leg, too."

"You've been sitting on those jackets four months. Deal?"

"Yeah. Sure."

"Thanks." They shook hands across the table. Natalie asked, "Do you know Alex Moschos?"

"Mr. Perfection. The biggest *kvetch* in the fur trade. Alex Moschos drove my father nuts and now he drives me nuts. The man buys five coats and sends back four for repairs."

"So you know him?"

"His name is etched on my ulcers."

"Well, just so we don't waste your money shipping returns, Mr. Moschos works for me now."

Stevie Weintraub buried his face in his hands. "I can't believe you would do this to me. . . . Listen, Natalie, it may be more like eight thousand jackets."

"I understand. By the way, I ran into a friend of yours. He said to say hello."

"Who?"

"Jefferson Jervis."

Stevie kept his expression intact, but his noncommittal, "Oh," was too studied to be real.

"I didn't realize you moved in such high circles."

"Yeah, well, you know."

"Is he an investor?"

"No! No. We just met at a . . . fundraiser. UJA thing for Israel, I think it was."

"Say hello when you see him again." Natalie smiled back.

That Stevie had not flatly denied knowing the financier confirmed what Natalie still suspected on dark nights. Jervis was backing Stevie—certainly not for the money, because Cotillion was very small potatoes by his lights—but because he wanted leverage over her, to scare her off if she ever resumed asking questions about Wallace. She knew it was a deviously convoluted line of reasoning that circled back on itself like a snake swallowing its tail, but she could not let it go.

"Will I see you in Leningrad?" she asked Stevie.

"You're going to the auction?"

"Of course."

"I can't make Leningrad. One of my Hong Kong partners is running a fat cat deal with the PRC, so I've got to go there."

"*What* is a fat cat deal with the PRC?"

"The People's Republic of China underwrites a factory on their territory. My partner will supply the technology, run the factory, and train the Red Chinese to be furriers."

"That is very interesting."

"I thought you didn't like imports."

"I like when business crosses borders. It kind of erases them. I love that idea. Fat cat?"

"Listen, would you do me a favor?"

"Sure, Stevie."

"Would you deliver a letter to some friends of mine?"

"Who?"

"Jews. You know, Refuseniks. Waiting forever for permission to emigrate. No job, no cash, they're kind of hard up, so I bring them money."

Natalie couldn't conceal her surprise. And even Stevie seemed embarrassed to be caught doing good without the benefit of a tax deduction.

"I'd be happy to. . . . Stevie, can I offer you some advice?"

"What?"

"Jefferson Jervis could buy and sell the entire New York fur trade if he felt like it. He's not the kind of investor I would count on for the long run."

"What investor? He's not my investor."

"Stevie."

"Why are you saying this to me?"

"You're a better furrier than Wallace would admit."

"How do you know?"

"You sat on those jackets. Right? The good ones. You can't help yourself, Stevie, down deep inside you appreciate quality."

"So?" he asked belligerently.

"I used to be a banker. I know how guys like Jervis operate. He'll pull out on a whim, or whip around and take you over in a flash."

"Listen, Natalie. Between you and me, maybe I'm a little overextended. So Jervis throws me a rope. Am I complaining?"

Natalie smiled. She had brought Jervis's stalking horse to the brink of a complete confession. Now to capture him. "What do you do when that rope turns into a snake?"

"Get off it! I won't turn down this shot just to save your ass. Sorry. Jervis found out I needed the money."

"You're attacking me, with no guarantee that you won't get hurt yourself. Right?"

"Right. I don't have a choice."

"Let me find you a banker."

"I wish you could, but I'm tapped out." He glanced about the restaurant, confirmed no one was close enough to hear, and said, simply, "Nobody's lending me any more money this year."

"Maybe I can persuade Eddie Mayall to talk to you."

"Who's he?"

"Do you remember the Knits! deal last year?"

"I still don't know how it worked. You got this Seventh Avenue *schlocker*—a guy who has to hondle the travel agent for the cheapest economy class ticket to Hong Kong—he writes the word *Knits,* diagonally, his eight-year-old daughter sticks an exclamation mark on the end, and *pow,* he's in every store in the country."

"Promotion and distribution. Eddie Mayall reorganized his company, paid off his creditors, bought out his shareholders, and took him public, which raised the money to promote and distribute."

"What did the *schlocker* have to pay for it?"

"Mayall takes a straight percentage fee off the top of the money he raises. It won't cost you a penny. Shall I give him a call?"

"Sure, I'll talk to anybody," Stevie said casually, but the gleam in his eye would have melted mascara.

"I'll set it up."

"Hey, Nat. This Mayall sounds like somebody for you, too."

"No, thank you. Cotillion Furs is not going public."

In fact, she thought on the way back to her office, going public was no longer an option under present conditions, as Bill Malcolm had pointed out. Neither he nor Eddie was a magician. They needed something to sell. The Seventh Avenue *schlocker* had had a hot idea. Stevie Weintraub was hot, too, with exclusive access to the new Hong Kong furriers he had helped establish. Whereas all she was doing at Cotillion was treading water and getting tired.

"Good to hear your voice, darlin'," Eddie Mayall growled over the telephone. "How are you doing?"

"I'm doing well. There's someone I think you might want to meet."

"How old is he?"

"Thirtyish."

"Straight player?"

"By furrier standards."

Eddie laughed. "Fair warning." Then he asked, "Is he worth it, or is this a favor, which, of course, is yours for the asking?"

"He's grown very big, very fast, importing Hong Kong coats. He's worth it."

"Okay. Tell him to call me. If he's a *young* thirtyish, if he's willing to hustle, I'll go with him."

"I appreciate that." They had never done business before, and she was impressed by Eddie's decisiveness.

"Frankly, I thought you were calling about yourself. I understand you've still got some nervous shareholders—I know, I know. You've got them in hand. May I offer a piece of advice?"

"Surely."

"Unless you're prepared to leave the fur trade and take up clam farming—from the bottom—you've got to get ahold of your financial situation. You're going to need independence, darlin'. You're going to need an investment banker who's a nonfur guy."

"Thank you, Eddie," she said coolly. "But I already have Bill Malcolm at SM&H."

"Solid man, if a little laid back, shall we say?"

"He understands my needs. He realizes that Wallace and I were committed to retaining a privately held company."

Eddie's silence spoke volumes.

"I used to work for Bill," she explained, repeating, "he knows my needs."

Eddie said, "I'll give you one more piece of advice, gratis, and then I'll hang up and we'll both go back to work. Remember this: Nobody ever sees you any older or better than the day they met you."

Riding down in the elevator from the lawyer's office where they had closed the fox jacket deal a week later, Stevie Weintraub remarked casually that Edward R. Mayall Capital had agreed to manage the financing of his imports.

"You're welcome," said Natalie. Neither mentioned Jefferson Jervis as they parted on the sidewalk, but she felt reasonably satisfied that if Jervis still wanted to raid her shareholders, he would have to find himself another shill. She headed for the office, where she was scheduled to present her January interim report to the board.

The streets of the fur district, West Twenty-sixth to West Thirtieth between Sixth and Eighth Avenues, seemed narrower than other midtown streets, an illusion that Natalie attributed to the tall loft buildings erected sheer to the lot lines, the old-fashioned, ill-lit store windows, unchanged, as far as she could tell from fifty-year-old photographs, from the days of Wallace's apprenticeship, and the ever present rows of double-parked trucks.

She was walking east on Twenty-ninth, her street antennae automatically scanning individuals who might rob or molest her, aggressive taxis in crosswalks, and speeding pushcarts. Like some of her age and means she had taken to carrying a pocketful of dollar bills to pass to the homeless, which she was doing automatically, and making herself smile when it appeared a smile or eye contact might help.

Yet she was distracted, rehearsing in her mind her speech to the board, in which she intended to announce long-range plans to appeal to new customers in the teeth of rising mink prices. A truck started backing over the sidewalk and she stopped to let it pass.

While not unduly worried about outpricing her current clientele, she knew her younger customers could not afford the new mink coats, which were going to jump at least fifty percent this year alone. One answer was to offer less expensive furs, like Stevie's fox jackets, but without giving up Cotillion's hard-earned exclusivity. She had just coined the phrase, Give Her That Cotillion Feeling, when the driver of the truck, a bulky, slab-sided step van, motioned her to pass. She walked behind it and was astonished to see the truck, which she had thought was standing still, suddenly lunge at her.

15

It seemed impossible to make such a mistake. She had been walking these streets for five years. But somehow she had stepped into the blind spot between the driver's side view mirrors. She heard the first beep of the reverse alarm and the harsh screech of tires and then he was roaring back, about to crush her against the loading dock, a raised opening in the building rimmed with splintered wood.

Natalie had no time to yell, no time to run forward, no time to stop and jump back, no time to think. And yet, without thinking, she was already trying to escape, alerted, despite her distraction, by some new sense born in the weeks after Wallace's death when she still half-expected another Luba to appear, or a Margot, or the men she had seen in Margot's cab.

The loading dock stood nearly four feet high. Were she not as tall, or even not wearing high-heeled boots, she could not have tried to roll onto it. She turned on her shoulder, frantically tucking her arms and legs after her. Her right arm was last. She felt the splintered wood rim scrape the back of her hand. Her briefcase, slung from her left shoulder, was already with her, but her pocketbook, a sturdy Coach bag, caught on the splinters and held. She felt the truck push an ugly breath of air. Then it slammed into the dock with a bang that shook the cement under her. Where her pocketbook had been was a vivid smear spurting up between the bumper and the wood. She smelled a

182

sickly explosion of perfumes and makeup and held up her hand, counting four unblemished fingers and a thumb with a broken nail.

"Are you okay?" a man yelled.

"I think so."

"Lady, he almost killed you."

Natalie lay still, counting her fingers repeatedly. The man, a burly black warehouseman, leaned over her, his face a mask of horror. "You don't know how close you came."

"I'm okay. I think."

He exploded around the side of the truck, which was pulling forward, as if shouting would release the fear he had felt for her. *"You dumb fuck, you almost killed this lady."* He pounded the truck with his hand. "You almost killed her. Get out of that cab!"

Natalie sat up in time to see a knife flash from the driver's window.

"Oh yeah?" yelled her benefactor, scooping up a large piece of broken crate. The truck roared into the street, with the warehouseman beating its sides until it sped out of reach. Natalie stood up very slowly, brushing off her skirt, deflecting the offers of passersby to call an ambulance or a cop.

She drifted through the board report, far more frightened in retrospect than she had been at the time. A little vagueness actually seemed to help; the board appeared to misinterpret her detachment as self-confidence. They approved the moves she had made since Wallace had died, especially selling off the suburban chain and persuading Diana to hang on. She worried a little about Aunt Margaret's absence, but her mind kept returning to the space between the truck and the loading platform. Had she been that out of it, or had the driver really tried to kill her?

Why? She had stopped asking questions. She had let Wallace's past, whatever it was, lie undisturbed since her meeting with Greg and Jervis, except for her ads in the paper. But no one could trace "Pearl" to her. The simpler explanation was more logical. Accidents happened on crowded streets. Some people stopped to apologize. Others didn't, out of fear, or anger, or just from being high. She blamed herself as much as the driver. She should have had her eyes open.

Twice she caught herself staring at her right hand. The third time, she noticed her brother eyeing her curiously.

"Are you okay?" he asked when they broke for coffee.

"No. I almost got hit by a truck. It scared me."

"Jesus." He threw an arm around her shoulders. "You're shaking."

"Just reaction."

"You're apologizing for blood in your veins?"

"No. I'm fine. Really."

"Sis, you look ready to cry."

"Just my style," she retorted. She was holding on tightly, these days, and if she did cry it would be for Wallace, not a near miss.

"It wouldn't hurt to let go a little," her brother coaxed, annoying her because she just wanted to get through this alone and be done with it.

"Thank you, Doctor. How sensitive we've become."

Mike shrugged and answered her seriously and she realized he had been looking for an excuse to tell her. "I'm in therapy. They're teaching me to think differently."

"*Therapy?*" she blurted in shocked astonishment. "You're kidding."

"What's so strange about therapy?"

"What for?"

"What do you mean, what for? Cocaine. Annie said she'd leave if I didn't get treatment. That woke me up. Nothing like the scorn of a good woman to clear the mind. Hey, don't look so horrified. My therapy is not a personal attack on your tightly wrapped sensibilities."

"I know, I know. People do it all the time. It's just when it's your own family ..." She trailed off, genuinely puzzled by her strong reaction. In fact, Michael was a prime candidate for therapy, after all the misery he'd suffered with their father.

"Uncle Norbert did it," Mike reminded her.

"He's in the loony bin."

Mike grinned. "It's really helping. I'm much, much better already. You know, it wouldn't hurt you to talk to somebody, considering what you've been through."

Natalie told herself that she was staying on top of the situation and fully aware of her feelings and reactions. As for Mike, she had promised him a job when he was straight. "Can you look me in the eye and say you haven't touched coke in two months?"

"Five weeks," he said with a steady smile. She waited, but he asked no favors, which impressed her deeply. For the first time in years, she believed he might survive.

"Are you working?"

"I'm thinking of going back to school."

"Law?"

"No. I don't want to be somebody's servant."

"Then what?"

"I don't know. Any suggestions?"

"Sure. Management."

"I had two years of that before law school."

"And you were great at it. You would have been wonderful if you hadn't let Dad talk you into switching into law."

"We are born to serve," Mike intoned.

"Serve yourself," Natalie snapped.

Mike shrugged his meaty shoulders and stood in embarrassed silence until Natalie asked, "How do you think I did in there?"

"Not bad. But where's Aunt Margaret?"

Natalie telephoned her great-aunt from the privacy of her office. Aunt Margaret invited her to the Berkshires for the weekend. And Natalie said yes, because it sounded like a command.

She awakened Saturday morning in a narrow bed in a cold guest room where she had slept a night or two every year of her life. The wallpaper was flowered with pink dahlias on a gray–green field. A vast tree loomed outside the curtains, its black bark rimmed with snow. The furniture was ancient pine bought at house sales in the previous century, or fashioned on the estate.

Aunt Margaret brought her tea. "Breakfast in twenty minutes." She had dodged all of Natalie's attempts to talk business the night before and retired early, and when Natalie came down for breakfast, she found the old woman just as remote as she fried eggs and ladled out oatmeal.

"I don't usually eat breakfast, Aunt Margaret."

"We're going skiing. You'll wish you had."

"Right."

Battered cross-country skis of various dimensions were propped along the walls of the covered porch. A wicker basket held the boots. By the time Natalie sorted them out, found poles, and locked in the old-fashioned three-point bindings, Aunt Margaret was disappearing over the rise above the house. Natalie mushed after her, skating up the slope, slowing to a herringbone walk where it was steep. Margaret waited for her beside an apple tree on the crest.

Catching her breath, Natalie looked back at the house, which stood splendidly isolated in the snowy meadows, and sheltered from the north by a crescent of towering pines. Three stories tall, clad in weathered shingles, draped with porches and buttressed by fieldstone foundations, it commanded long views of the Berkshire hills to the south and west.

"Who's going to maintain that barn when I'm gone?" Aunt Margaret asked.

"That depends on who you leave it to."

"I won't leave it to any one person. It belongs to the family."

"There's a hundred of us. We'll figure a way."

"Don't be coy. Someone has to take responsibility."

"You've got ten grandchildren who love it."

"Not one with the brains of a bluejay."

"If you're asking my advice, Aunt Margaret, I would find a local family to live in the cottage as caretakers and I would require each person named in my will to chip in a small yearly amount to pay for it. Everyone's having children now. They'll love it and use it."

"Would you mind if I put the house in your name?"

"What?"

"The house and two hundred acres. . . . What the *devil* are you sniffling about?"

Natalie, brushing her eyes with the backs of her gloves, suddenly burst into loud sobs. Crying would still leap on her like an animal from the dark.

"What is wrong with you?" Margaret demanded.

"Nothing. I'm overwhelmed. You make me feel as if I belong."

"Of course, you belong, you ninny. Now do you want the house or don't you?"

Perversely, Natalie turned away. "It's wonderful of you, but I already have a house. I can't manage this place. I'd hardly ever have the time to come up here and there are so many people you're more closely related to." For the briefest instant she heard herself babbling. All her life she had roved the edges of the Stuarts, but there was something terribly frightening about the prospect of being in their midst. She felt perverse and obstinate. She longed to accept, but somehow couldn't. As was her way, she negotiated.

"You're a responsible person," said Margaret.

"Why not leave it to my father?"

"Your father is not a responsible person in the way I mean responsible. He's morally responsible, but he wouldn't know a termite from a cockroach."

"Then leave it to my mother. She is totally practical."

"I'm not leaving my house to the daughter of a missionary. She'd fill it with nuns."

"She would not," Natalie countered fiercely, thrilled with the hope of her mother actually owning a beautiful house. "She would care for it and cherish it. And she'd be like you, always welcoming anyone in the family. Oh, Margaret, it's a wonderful idea. She'd be perfect."

Aunt Margaret's mouth tightened and her jaw worked. "I suppose that's true enough. But your mother is not a Stuart."

"She would leave it to me, when the time came, and I *am* a Stuart."

"I won't have it go to that pinhead brother of yours."

"Mother would honor your wishes. Put a covenant in the will."

"I'll think about it." The old lady pushed off on her skis and swooped down the slope, telemarking into a graceful turn that took her away from the house.

Natalie suspected her great-aunt had more to say and followed. She screwed up the telemark and fell. When she finally caught her again, Margaret was waiting atop the final ridge of the meadow range.

"By the way," she gasped. "My pinhead brother is making a real effort to straighten himself out."

"He got hooked on cocaine in that brokerage house."

"You knew?"

"Of course I knew. He tried to borrow money from me."

"Well, I think he's taking hold."

"Bloody well hope so. He's too old for that nonsense." Margaret braced her skis and extended a pole for Natalie to grab.

"Look!" she commanded, sweeping her other pole over the view as Natalie cleared the crest. Rolling hills, dense pine forest, and vast meadows stretched for miles.

"I'd forgotten how beautiful this is."

"Five thousand acres," Margaret replied, her voice suddenly hard. "Untouched. I've camped in there. There are stretches without a single stone wall. Never been farmed. Just wood lots and hunting preserves. It's unique."

"You're so lucky to live next to it."

"The family that owns it has fallen apart. A developer is angling to buy it for home sites. Two thousand five hundred plots, roads, country club, and sewage plant."

"Can he do it?"

"Nothing to stop him. . . . Well, almost nothing."

"What do you mean?"

Margaret turned to her. "I'm sorry, dear. But I had to show you why I'm doing what I have to do."

"What do you mean?"

"I'm selling my shares of Cotillion Furs."

"*What?*"

"They're all I have of real value. I'm buying this land. I'm establishing a trust."

Natalie shook her head in disbelief.

"Needless to say," said Margaret, "it will be very expensive."

"Does it have to be now?"

"I'm eighty-seven years old. I could die tonight. I must protect this before I die. . . . Don't look so sad, dear."

"I'm terrifically disappointed. I mean the timing is awful. I'm leaving for Russia. . . . I'm against the wall."

Margaret cut her off, firmly, though not unkindly.

"Natalie," she said, gazing happily over the snow-covered land, "when I am dead, when you are dead, when your children, God bless them, are dead and their children dead too, and their children's children are enjoying their moment, no one will remember or care about Cotillion Furs. But this habitat will be here, just as it is today, only richer in the bones of a million creatures that lived and died their lives in peace."

"How much time do I have?" Natalie asked numbly.

"I'm afraid I'm against the wall, too, as you say."

Natalie was seized by an unusual burst of panic that drove every clear thought from her mind. The money she would realize from the sale of the suburban stores was earmarked to reduce debt and buy skins. She was tapped out at the bank. Nor would Stuart, Malcolm and Hardy help her raise money without some new project that promised a major return, and even then SM&H would demand she go public. Wallace, where are you when I need you?

Gradually, she became aware that Aunt Margaret was staring with displeasure and realized she had forgotten her manners. "I understand," she said mechanically, and then manufacturing enthusiasm, added, "you're absolutely right. This is a wonderful legacy."

"It's not a legacy, dear. It is simply the only thing to do."

"Would you like to discuss the details?" she asked. Though she had no means of raising the money to buy her great-aunt's shares, she ought to try to establish a price and a payout and commit Margaret to selling to her. But Margaret only said, "My lawyers will handle that. They're waiting for your call."

Natalie turned her face to hide a grim smile. As she had suspected, Aunt Margaret was too smart by far to negotiate with a pro.

When she visited Leo Margulies to persuade him to accompany her to Leningrad, he greeted her with a lynx hat to match the coat Wallace had given her. She put it on, with a gasp of pleasure at its silky lightness, and straightened it in a mirror. Leo reached up to tilt it over one eye.

"I'm not sure I'm the woman to wear this outfit."

"Let me tell you something, sweetheart. All auctions, but especially that one, are theater. If you want to wave the Cotillion flag, you better have a flag they'll see. Wear the coat and wear the hat. And stand in the light."

"Will you come with me?"

"I gotta bring my sons, too. My wife won't let me travel alone with you."

"Leo." Natalie was shocked.

"Hey. Sylvia's my second wife. How do you think we met? By the way, congratulations on buying your aunt's stock. Pretty cute. Dump the malls and buy control. So now you're almost your own boss."

"Leo, it took every penny I raised. I am so broke and so in debt that if I tried to pay for this coffee, the banks would shut me down."

"That bad?"

"Worse than you could imagine. I've got to put together some wonderful deal so I can get more credit. Otherwise, come late spring when the cash stops flowing, I'll be out of business."

"So you're broke, you're in debt, and you got nowhere to turn."

"That's about it."

"Congratulations! You're a furrier."

"It's a good joke, Leo, but I don't have Wallace to fall back on. Besides, buying Margaret's stock doesn't give me total control. If anybody else sells, I'm still in trouble."

Leo shrugged. "What are you gonna do?"

"I wake up in a cold sweat. I've never been so financially out of control."

"Take a pill."

"It wouldn't help."

"Hey, you can always be a banker."

"That's not funny."

"I'm not joking."

Just in case Luba had seen any of her ads and tried to make contact in Russia, she decided to bring Wallace's paperback copy of *The Pearl* with her. But despite the much proclaimed reforms sweeping the Soviet Union—the new openness, the release of political prisoners, the party elections, and the hope—Communist border guards were known to seize Bibles and pornography with equal zeal.

That meant smuggling *The Pearl* into Russia, which frightened her until she came up with a plausible story for why she had concealed the book if they found it. The lie came easily out of truth. She would indeed be embarrassed to be caught at the airport with pornographic bedtime reading.

16

The morning she was to leave for Russia, Joannie Frye marched into her office and dumped a shopping bag full of condoms on her desk.

"If this is a hint, I'm not ready."

"Wallace always took them. You can use them to tip waiters and get theater tickets and all kinds of favors."

"What's in the other bag?"

"Floppy disks. They love computers but they never have enough disks. And tampons. They don't take very good care of women."

Joannie came in again an hour before she was to pick up her father for a crash course in current Soviet politics on the ride to the airport.

"There's a model wants to see you. He knew Wallace."

"Come on, Joannie. I don't hire models. Give him a note to Laura Drake."

"He's been hanging around all day."

"The cute blond when I came in this morning?"

"Stefan. He's one of the top guys. He says it's personal. Should I get rid of him?"

"Oh, God. . . . No, I'll see him."

The boy looked about twenty-two, with a handsome, chiseled face and a fine mouth. His haircut was perfect and Natalie estimated he was wearing about a thousand dollars' worth of crewneck sweater, cashmere slacks, and Italian shoes. He had a gold crucifix earring and soft eyes that made him look like a very nice and not particularly bright kid.

"Hi, Stefan, what can I do for you?"

"I really appreciate your seeing me, Mrs. Nevsky."

"It's okay, but I'm really busy and . . . what's up?"

"I don't know how else to say this, so I'm just going to say I need your help."

"What kind of help?"

"Well, it's sort of a long story and I have to ask you to promise to keep it to yourself."

"Stefan, I'm right against the wall. Couldn't Joannie help you? Or how about the Laura Drake Agency? I'll be glad to call for you."

"No, it has to be you. It's something Mr. Nevsky, Wallace, did for me."

"What?"

Joannie buzzed, checking to see if Natalie needed rescue. "Give me five minutes," Natalie said. "Hold my calls. Okay, Stefan. Tell me the long story, briefly. Sit down, sit down."

He sat on the edge of the chair beside her desk. "Two years ago I did a shoot for Ben Kahn in Russia. I met a girl in Leningrad, an actress. We really clicked."

Natalie was surprised. Stefan was so beautiful to look at that she had just assumed he was gay. His face grew animated.

"Her name's Vera. She is so beautiful I couldn't believe she would ever talk to me. I went to the theater every night and saw this Russian play over and over and over. I don't speak Russian, but I just had to see her. She's this great actress. I could tell, and the audience went crazy. I gave her everything I had with me—my tapes, my Walkman, my running suit for her brother, my jeans. I would have given her my life. Russian women will blow you away.

"Finally, she agreed to go out with me. We walked around Leningrad holding hands in the dark. She was afraid to be seen with me."

"Why?"

"I'm an actor, too, sort of. So I know the life. Here, you run into the occasional bastard who'll try to screw you out of a part or mess up your audition. In Russia, they all work in a company. They don't have to wait tables to keep going, but the company politics are real cutthroat. If some actress wants Vera's parts bad enough, she'll report Vera's dating an American and wants to emigrate. Vera would get fired, or demoted. I couldn't believe it at first, but it's true. . . . Anyhow, I finally had to leave."

"That's the last time you saw her?"

"We write back and forth, but we can't say anything because they open mail. So it's like pen pals."

"Where's this going, Stefan?"

"I want to marry her. And she wants to marry me. But when she applies for permission, she'll be fired."

"How'd you get to marriage if you can't communicate?"

"Wallace—Mr. Nevsky—carried messages for us. The last I sent her, I told her I was ready. And she said she's ready to chance it. Then Wallace couldn't find her. I haven't heard a thing, not a word or a letter."

"Wallace carried your messages?" Another secret.

"Verbally. He wouldn't carry letters. He was going to try again his last trip, but I didn't see him when he came back because . . ."

"Yes, I know."

"I'm so sorry to trouble you, but I have to find out about Vera. Could you contact her?"

"How?" Natalie asked cautiously.

"Telephone her. Get her to meet you. Tell her I'm worried and I need to know what I can do to help her emigrate. I've got money saved up. If she wants, I'll even go to Russia. Tell her I can't wait any longer."

Natalie stood up and Stefan shot to his feet.

"Stefan, I'm going to be so busy at the auction. It's new territory for me. I really won't have time and frankly, I'd be very nervous meeting anyone clandestinely to pass secrets."

"It's not secrets," Stefan protested. "I love her."

"Not this trip. Wallace was an old Russian hand. I'm not. Maybe after I've become more comfortable traveling in Russia and get used to the auction, but it's something I don't want to get involved in now. I'm going through a pretty heavy time myself."

"Of course. I wouldn't ask, but—"

"I've already agreed to a similar request to help a Jewish dissident. I just don't want to get involved at this point in time. Do you understand?" She herself did not fully understand. She vehemently did not want to be involved; part of it was that Wallace kept it secret, part was simple fear. She had vital business in the Soviet Union as well as her own hopes. She could not antagonize the KGB.

Blinking like a little boy who'd caught a baseball in the face, Stefan settled slowly into the chair. "Sure, I understand." He bowed his head and Natalie, who was preparing to steer him to the door, was horrified to see big tears splash on the model's expensive slacks. "It's okay, it's okay," he stammered. "You have your own problems."

"I really wish I could help. Next time."

"I know, I know. It's just that I'm so worried. I don't know what happened to her." He began to sob in earnest and Natalie moved to comfort him. She patted his shoulder, praying Joannie would burst in with an emergency. She could see where his sweater puckered open that he was powerfully built, but the sobbing made him seem small and in need. She touched his hair. It was like gold silk.

She cradled his head in her hands, stroked his wet cheeks and the smooth skin on the muscles that rippled in his neck. Like a wind in the woods heard in the treetops before it was felt, she sensed her body stirring to him. She was stunned, sexually aroused for the first time since she and Wallace had made love on *Panache*. It had to happen sometime, she thought guiltily, trying to retreat by analyzing the moment. The boy was safe; there were no complications since he was desperate for another woman. She kept stroking his hair with trembling hands. The tenderest pressure would turn his face against her thighs. She could feel his heat through her skirt.

Suddenly, tears burned her own eyes. She didn't want this beautiful boy. She wanted her husband.

"Okay. Stop crying. Stop. . . . Tell me how to find her."

"You'll do it?" He jumped up, relief blazing on his eager face, and she realized that Stefan hadn't even felt her hands, much less her desire.

"I'm scared, but I'll do it. I'll do it for my husband. What do I do?"

"I'll give you her telephone number. She lives with her parents. But only call from a pay phone. Never from the hotel. Never. And never from a pay phone near the hotel. She speaks English, but her parents don't."

"I speak Russian."

"Don't tell them about me. They'd be frightened. Just say you're a friend of Vera's from the theater and when can you call back."

"All right." She was thinking, This is crazy, and imagining already that every pay phone was tapped.

"You must promise to be very careful. If anyone in her company finds out, they'll use it against her."

"What do you want me to tell her?"

"Tell her I love her. First make sure she's all right. Hang up if anyone but her or her parents answers. Tell her we'll have a better chance of permission to emigrate under the new government. Tell her I love her."

"Do you want me to bring her anything?"

"No!"

"A letter. I'll be careful."

"Too dangerous."

"The dissident's friend I told you about said he'd type his. It would be safe with no name."

"That's very dangerous for you, Mrs. Nevsky. Your husband would only talk to Vera, never deliver anything. They set traps, you see."

"Traps."

"Anyone who asks you to smuggle something could be KGB."

"You're making this even scarier."

"I learned from Wallace. One thing you can give her, if she's lost her job, is money. Only in rubles. I'll give you cash."

He flourished a money clip, but Natalie stopped him. "We'll settle up later."

"Mrs. Nevsky, you have no idea how happy you've made me."

"What does she look like?"

"Beautiful. Tall and dark with stunning blue eyes."

"Would you have a picture?"

"Sure," Stefan laughed. "Sorry. Here."

It was a professional studio shot. Subtly lighted, skillfully made up, and dramatically posed, Vera was pretty, though hardly a knockout. But there was no mistaking the pride on Stefan's face as he said, "She's even prettier than this."

"You'll make a great-looking couple."

"I can't wait."

When he left, Natalie tore up Stevie's letter.

Natalie's heart soared when she saw her father striding out of Columbia's gates with his open coat flapping about his long legs. Taken by surprise at her response, she had to admit to herself that querying him about the current Soviet situation had been an excuse. She had craved the comfort of his clear, analytical thinking. And now she was doubly glad because the encounter with Stefan had drained her emotionally. She felt lonely and a little apprehensive about the risks she might have to take in Russia to uncover Wallace's past.

Richard Stuart broke his brisk stride for a moment when a student hailed him. Inclining his head, he listened thoughtfully, said something that made the boy smile, and hurried on. He was taking well to teaching, she thought. He had what he had always wanted, a captive audience for his quick mind and fierce opinions. She noticed a flush in his cheek, which she attributed to his downing a quick one after his lecture. When he climbed into the car service sedan, she smelled the liquor on his breath.

"What, no stretch limo? Has ostentation lost its sting?"

"I thought we'd settle for pomposity. Close the door. I'm late."

The car pulled onto Broadway, gunning for the lights. Her father surveyed her with a cold grin.

"You've got your feist back, I see."

"Just enough to conquer Russia."

"That's what Napoleon thought."

"But Napoleon's father wasn't a brilliant Sovietologist. I'll be better prepared."

"Retired State Department drudge, if you please."

The last thing she wanted was another diatribe on State, and she steered him from it. "Fill me in, Professor. Give me *glasnost* in forty-five minutes."

"Take an hour," the driver flung over his shoulder. "They're doing something to the Van Wyck."

Richard Stuart glanced about as if wishing the sedan were a limousine with a bar. "It's a pleasure to pass the ride with you, of course, but the goings-on in Russia don't concern you."

"I'm trying to do business. I have to know the territory."

He shook his head. "A wealthy *Americanskaya biznizmin* on a state-sanctioned fur-buying trip? You'll be as cosseted as a Victorian duchess touring Saint Petersburg—drivers, porters, guides, obsequious clerks, and clever concierges, providing all the trappings the Revolution abolished. So what if they're KGB informers on the side?"

"That doesn't make me feel very cosseted."

"*Everyone* reports to the KGB on the side. Do you think your mother and I had any secrets in Moscow? Remember your beloved Nini? They probably knew your birthday before we did. But these days they don't bother legitimate business people—other than clumsy entrapments of an amorous sort, which I can't see being a problem for you. They want your dollars, not your democratic soul."

"What if they got the wrong impression?"

"What kind of a silly question is that, Natalie? Good God, you're a foreign service brat. You certainly know better than to leave a totalitarian official with the wrong impression. At least I *hope* you do."

"Of course I do," she said contritely.

"So, what can I tell you that Wallace hadn't already told you? I'm not entirely sure what you want from me."

What she wanted was to be safe in this car with someone who would tell her that everything would be all right. She said, "Wallace was almost a native. I'll be operating like you did, as a foreigner. What's that like?"

Her father thought a moment, stroking his chin and casting a private smile into the middle distance. "In a sentence," he said, "the Soviet Union was a place where I always believed the rumors."

"Do you think Wallace exaggerated about being followed in the streets?"

"No."

"Even under *glasnost*?"

"People, whether they are furriers or policemen, continue to do their jobs. Do you think because Mr. Gorbachev shouts *glasnost* the KGB opens up yogurt factories? What is this obsession you have with the KGB?"

"I don't. I—I just thought some background would help me deal with the Soviets."

He looked at her quizzically.

Natalie returned a confused smile. "Just some history."

"Good, because I don't know much about the KGB. I was a diplomat, not a spook. Okay, I'll give you background until we reach the airport, and then you can buy me a drink. I can tell you that the 'KGB impulse,' shall we say, is historically Russian. These people have been invaded for a thousand years. In the past seventy years alone, the comrades have suffered four great waves of violence." He ticked them off on his long, graceful fingers. "Brutal civil war. An inhuman land clearance. Stalin's purge of the Communist party. And a horrific German invasion that laid waste to half the motherland. Of Europe's seventy million violent deaths in the twentieth century, Russia can claim the biggest share."

As the car crept across Manhattan he wove a rich tapestry of

Russian-Soviet history embossed with tales and observations gleaned from his diplomatic days in Moscow, Leningrad, and Eastern Europe.

Natalie clung to the sound of his voice, trying to stave off a numbing dread.

"... The civil war between Reds and Whites destroyed the old czarist upper middle class. Twenty years later Stalin slaughtered the new Communist party upper middle class that had replaced it. When these most Westernized classes were gone, some say, there was nothing left to bridle the ancient Muscovite Russian tradition of expansionism." He uttered this last with a cocked eyebrow. Natalie responded in kind.

"The sinister Orient theory?"

"Tentacles of the East." He smiled back. "A more optimistic theory states that Russia is reformable, thanks to the rise of yet another new upper middle class—educated, broadly based in government and the professions, and eager to taste the pleasures it sees enjoyed by our Western upper middle classes—Gorbachev's contemporaries. They're aware that internal reforms like freedom of expression and economic experimentation are vital if the Soviet Union is to compete in the modern, postindustrial world."

"The 'they-want-to-be-like-us' theory?" Natalie asked.

"But an unlikely one, according to the yo-yos in this present administration who are convinced that our two societies are locked forever in historical rivalry because communism's goal is to eliminate private ownership of the means of production and replace the free world's system with an internal republic of soviets controlled by Moscow. Believe it or not, there are still people at State who talk like that."

Jeff Jervis, Natalie thought, would have applauded. "Maybe things will get better after the election."

"I don't mean that the Russians aren't potentially very dangerous. Their history suggests why they are insatiably defensive. They fear war and chaos. To wit: the logic behind their stupid incursions into Afghanistan and Poland is that they prefer to fight on the other side of their borders. That kind of aggressive defense is damned costly, particularly when your economic system is hobbled by bureaucracy, muzzled by ideology, and calcified by fear.

"Enter Mikhail S. Gorbachev—a man with a gift for believing in Russian success."

"Success?"

"The Russian people and the Russian leadership have a real inferiority complex about failure and screwing up in general. But they *did* go to the moon, they *did* beat Hitler, they *did* electrify a gigantic backward country. They have become self-sufficient in countless areas. Gorbachev understands that they can accomplish whatever they're allowed to concentrate on. Look where Reagan's pipeline technology embargo got us."

"Daddy, I'm scared."

But she only whispered it at the window. And only when she knew that he was aboard his favorite hobbyhorse—his fall from State—and spurring to full gallop, so he could not hear her. His voice was rising, strident and bitter.

"I warned them. I flew home from Moscow to warn them personally. I told them that if we refused to sell the Soviets the gas compressors, Russian engineers would be forced to learn to build their own. You know the outcome."

Natalie nodded. He had told her countless times.

"The Russians designed and built their own. Then they completed the line, without our help. And worse—just as I predicted—they now sell that technology around the world. Outselling our manufacturers. And what did I get for being right? Early retirement."

He stared moodily out the window. The car was creeping into the Triboro toll gates, where young blacks in thin jackets were hawking the *New York Post*. Gorbachev's upcoming UN visit was headlined.

Richard Stuart snorted. "At least I never lied."

Natalie returned a sympathetic smile, but the embargo controversy wasn't the only fight he had waged too abrasively, merely the last. She thought privately that if she had learned one thing from her father's example it was that telling the truth was not enough. You had to sell the truth, too. To persuade, you had to help people believe. Ironically, that went double for a diplomat. He was not a stupid man, far from it. But she saw with sudden, new clarity that there was part of him that sometimes went out of control, a part that wanted to fight to the death—his death. She knew, too, that she didn't want to be that way. She shivered. Maybe Mike had inherited that death wish. But not her. No way.

He surprised her then, asking, "Did I hear you say you were scared?"

"A little."

"Of what?"

She hovered on the verge of telling him all about Wallace, her suspicions, his past, and what she intended to do. But even as she formed the words in her mind they sounded foolish, and she knew he would tell her to forget the whole thing. Or had she become so wary that she trusted no one? "I guess I'm afraid of going alone. . . . Tell me, do I run any risks contacting Wallace's old friends?"

Her father looked at her sharply.

"Wallace had many friends, dear."

Dear? She couldn't remember the last time he had called her *dear* or spoken so affectionately. She found the concern in his voice frightening in this context. *He knows,* she thought suddenly. *He already knows. For God's sake, he served in the Soviet Union for years.* Of course he knew about Wallace. Or, at least, suspected. She glanced at the driver, who appeared to be absorbed in merging onto the bridge approach.

"What do you mean?" she breathed.

"You are in no position to assess risk. How could you distinguish a 'safe friend,' shall we say, from an 'unsafe' friend?"

"What do you mean by unsafe?"

"I mean buy your furs and come home."

"That sounds rather melodramatic."

"Not at all," he demurred, "I'm only suggesting caution. The Soviet Union is not a theme park, despite what breakfast-time television coverage might lead you to think. It is a totalitarian state on the other side of the world, and it is crawling with secret police."

"Well," she said with forced lightness, "being a foreign service brat, as you're so fond of reminding me, I can always make a run for the back door of our embassy."

"If you can get past the KGB *dvornik*. . . . Seriously, though, I've written David Finny, he's *chargé* in Moscow at the moment. He can help you with legitimate problems."

Natalie looked at him for some additional meaning to "legitimate." He smiled back mildly, his patrician features a mask of innocence. As self-destructively blunt as he could become when roused, when caution prevailed her father was the consummate diplomat—maddeningly oblique, as he demonstrated now with a smooth change of subject. "Bringing our little history up to date, did I mention that last month I invited a Russian *emigré* to lecture my seminar? A defrocked Soviet intellectual. Do you know what he said?"

Natalie shook her head impatiently, straining to read his expression for more about Wallace. It was hopeless. He was in full retreat from possible revelations, and there was nothing she could do to stop him.

"The intellectual told my students, 'The peasants hate us.' The *muzhik*. *Nadar*. Russia's conservative, angry, frightened, cynical, brutal masses. 'They hate us,' he said. It got me thinking. I've chosen my theme for next semester. Would you like to hear it?"

Defeated, she said, "Yes."

"Is the Soviet Union a powder keg?"

Natalie nodded. "I suppose if real reform is taking place, the big question is, who has the most to lose?"

"Exactly! Will those conservative, frightened, angry, cynical, brutal Russians crucify this reformer as they did Nikita Khrushchev? . . . I might even write a paper on it, if I'm not too late." He smiled vaguely, then startled her again by taking her hand in his and squeezing it hard. "Be careful, dear. Remember the Russian saying: Before going into the room, make sure you can get out again."

17

The Air France stewardess brought her coat as the plane descended into the Soviet Union, and it struck Natalie that the woman cradled the lynx in her arms like a lover. She seized the image for a television ad: pretty cabin attendant wafts a Cotillion mink dreamily down the aisle, revels in the sensual cool caress on her bare arms, longs to sink her face into the fur, but settles, with Gallic reserve, for a touch against her cheek. Excellent ad, Natalie thought, smiling to herself—especially if Diana didn't shape up. She took it as a good omen, a sign that she could keep Cotillion hers—if she made her mark in Russia.

"Leningrad," said Leo.

Natalie leaned over him for a look. Golden domes and needle spires gleamed in the dying light. Barely midafternoon, the winter sun had set, trailing a mauve tint over palaces, snow, and ice. The broad river Neva, frozen from bank to bank, entered like a fat snake, only to split into tendrilous canals that laced the delta city like Gorgon hair.

In a dark section of the terminal Natalie was forced to place her passport and visa on a high counter above her line of sight where a frighteningly young and hard-eyed soldier scrutinized her documents, then compared her photographs to her face with meticulous care. Expressionless, he picked up a telephone and whispered. Then he waited, staring at her impassively.

In the next line Leo Margulies said, "I thought they were loosening up. This is just to get in. Wait'll we try to get out." His son David laughed nervously. Natalie wanted to ask if something was wrong, but she stuck to Wallace's first rule in dealing with functionaries, which was, Ask nothing.

An officer entered the glass booth. The soldier presented Natalie's papers, which the officer studied. He looked at Natalie, looked at the photographs, then stared again. He brushed impatiently at his cheeks, pantomiming that Natalie should do the same, and it dawned on her that her hair was slightly longer than in her passport and visa photos. She pulled it back from her cheeks and stood still, feeling almost naked as his eyes raked her again. Then, with no hint of humor or irony at the absurdity of rules and regulations, he left the booth. The soldier stamped her visa and attached it to her passport.

Shaken, Natalie dragged her luggage to the customs examination, worrying now about the condoms, tampons, and floppy disks she had brought on Joannie's advice, and wishing she had left *The Pearl* at home.

Leo's son had forged ahead. His bags were open, his clothes scattered on a table. A soldier demanded Natalie's customs form, on which she had carefully listed everything of value she was bringing into Russia, starting with the lynx coat; Wallace had once had to pay duty on his own camera as he left Russia, having neglected to list it on the way in.

The soldier plunged into her garment bags, then began peering into hair curlers, drier, transformer, and makeup. He opened jars and pawed suspiciously through a couple of Donald E. Westlake and Lawrence Block paperbacks. An officer came by and placed her shoulder bag on an X-ray conveyor belt.

Leo's son suddenly flushed red as a soldier plucked a video cassette from his socks and underwear. "No pornography," the Soviet lectured loudly.

"You dummy," said Leo.

Natalie struggled to control her expression as the soldier inspecting her books hefted a thick Robert Ludlum novel. At that moment, the officer who had sent her bag through the X-ray upended it, dumping out an enormous heap of condoms.

"Personal use?" he asked with a broad smile.

"Gratuities," she stammered.

He smiled again. "I have no doubt you will receive the service you're accustomed to, Mrs. Nevsky."

She was stuffing them back into her bag when it occurred to her that he had not seen her declaration, or her visa. Oddly, at that moment, her hands stopped shaking, even as a distinct chill settled in her spine, because the customs officer had known her name.

Nerves, she thought. They must have lists. And indeed, waiting at the final barrier were smiling Sojuzpushnina escorts, greeting the fur buyers in English by name and shepherding them toward an Intourist bus. The welcome by the Soviet fur monopoly was as warm as the entry procedures had been cold. At the door to the bus, however, Natalie was stopped by a small, nervously smiling Russian in a fine Italian suit.

"Mrs. Nevsky." He bowed, greeting her in English. "I am Fyodor Shelpin." While not entirely obsequious, Shelpin's anxious demeanor and wary stance suggested to Natalie a small mongrel unsure of its welcome.

"Oh, I'm so happy to meet you. Wallace spoke of you fondly."

Shelpin beamed. "I have taken the liberty of booking a suite for you at the Astoria Hotel."

"I thought all the fur buyers stayed at the Pribaltiskaya."

"That's right," said Leo. "She's with us, Freddy."

"Ah, my friend Leo. Greetings, after so many years. It is just that Mr. Nevsky always stayed at the Astoria and I thought Mrs. Nevsky might prefer it, too."

"It's an old dump," Leo said. "Come with us, kid. The Finns built the Pribaltiskaya. They give good hotel."

"Why did Wallace prefer the Astoria?"

"Said it reminded him of the czar."

"If I stay there, Mr. Shelpin, can I hire a car to the Pribaltiskaya?"

"No problem."

"We've got a party before dinner," Leo warned.

"Tonight I am driving Mrs. Nevsky myself," Shelpin promised.

He carried her bags to a small black car.

"Times *have* changed," Leo whispered. "He used to be one of Sojuzpushnina's first-class pricks."

But Wallace had liked Shelpin, she thought. And the little man was going out of his way to be kind to her.

Shelpin sat beside the driver, Natalie in back. They raced out of the Leningrad airport ahead of the bus. "This is very nice of you."

"Your husband was my special friend for many years. Is least I can do."

How special? Natalie wondered, acutely aware that hers was not to ask, but to wait for some signal. She touched her pearl earrings.

"Is first visit to Soviet Union?" Shelpin asked.

"My first since I was born. My parents were in the foreign service, in Moscow." She would have expected Wallace to have told him that, if they were friends. Or was this conversation for the benefit of Shelpin's driver?

"Do you speak Russian?"

"Da," she answered. "But I'll need time to get my ear back. I missed a lot in the airport."

"Is good to make friends in Russia," Shelpin replied. "We prefer foreign people who speak our language. A little, anyway. We're not a stranger-loving people."

"You're being very hospitable."

"We are hospitable, to our friends."

Was he trying to tell her something or was her imagination jumping into overdrive? She reminded herself that Fyodor Shelpin was first and foremost an official of a Soviet government agency whose job it was to sell furs to foreigners for hard currency. She had flown six thousand miles to be here. The next move was his.

At first glance the drive into Leningrad reminded Natalie of many cities with the typical broad highway and new construction, but the comparison quickly paled. The slab-sided housing projects were too massive, the spaces between the buildings too broad. And when they entered the city itself, Natalie, who had traveled most of her life, suddenly felt farther from home than ever before.

It was old, but not ancient, eighteenth-century European in flavor, with incongruous flashes of the twentieth century and equally incongruous Third World apparitions. Old women swept the streets with twig brooms, dodging brightly colored trams and buses. She saw more cars than she had expected. Palaces, churches, and old buildings looked remarkably well-kept, but shops appeared dingy, their ill-lit entrances a mystery in the darkening afternoon.

They crossed countless low bridges spanning canals and narrow rivers—six hundred and thirty-seven bridges, Shelpin told her. She compared it to the old section of Amsterdam, but Shelpin said Leningrad was ten times bigger. The broad Nevsky Prospekt, the main shopping street since czarist times, glittered. Near the bottom of the

Nevsky, they turned off. Shelpin spoke, and the driver slowed the car in front of a columned, neoclassic building with a huge neon Sojuzpushnina sign above the portico. "The auction," he said. "You can walk from hotel."

The car went up a narrow street, crossed another frozen canal, and entered a square commanded by an enormous domed cathedral Natalie had seen from the distance.

"St. Isaac's," Shelpin answered. "And here is hotel."

The Astoria Hotel crouched on one side of the square, a dignified six-story building with cabs and tour buses parked helter-skelter on the cobblestones. A brass plaque beside the door seemed particularly welcoming as it was written in Western letters, and she saw immediately why Wallace liked the place. It could have been a grand old apartment building on Manhattan's West Side, a homey link with New York.

Shelpin escorted her to the desk where a smiling manager shook her hand warmly. "Mr. Nevsky was our favorite American and we are honored to greet his daughter."

"Wife," she corrected sharply, stung by the reminder of how separate a life Wallace had lived on the auction circuit.

"Forgive me," the manager stammered. To Shelpin he muttered, "Yolki-Palki. How do I say, 'So young,' without offending?"

"I'm not offended," Natalie answered in Russian. "I'm grateful for your kind welcome. I was used to the mistake. Is there a wire room where I can send a cable to New York?" She wanted to send her stewardess-and-coat idea to Laura Drake.

But the manager looked far from soothed. To her surprise, his face had turned bright red. Then he went white and a thick rime of sweat formed on his brow. "Don't worry about it," she said. Then she realized he was staring past her. Shelpin edged her firmly from the desk.

Three young men in dark suits strode across the lobby. A fourth man—lean, almost cadaverous, with thinning hair, a high brow, and dark piercing eyes—watched from the door. The manager backed up a step, eyes darting sightlessly, like a trapped animal that had given up. Shelpin moved her further away. The men stopped at the desk and spoke quietly to the manager, whose whole body seemed to melt inside his clothes.

"What's going on?" Natalie whispered.

"Nothing," Shelpin hissed. "We'll go upstairs as soon as we can get a key."

"Who are those men?"

"Nobody."

"Who are they?" she repeated firmly and a little less quietly.

"KGB."

"They look like accountants." They were even carrying attaché cases.

"They *are* accountants," Shelpin muttered through his teeth. "It's the fraud squad."

Natalie almost laughed. But the fear on the manager's face was terrible. Head bowed, he lurched from behind the desk and led the three KGB agents into his office. When the door was closed behind them, Natalie glanced at the thin man who had not moved from his position at the entrance. He was staring at her.

A clerk appeared at the desk. Shelpin sidled up nervously for Natalie's key. The KGB man's eyes stayed on Natalie. She returned the level gaze, while a comforting mantra repeated in her head, "I'm an American. I'm an American."

"Who is that?" Natalie murmured as they started toward the elevator.

"I don't know," Shelpin answered quickly. She looked up, suddenly, as the elevator door closed, and the man was still watching.

"Was he with the others?"

Shelpin handed her some messages and mail that had been waiting at the desk. "I don't know, Mrs. Nevsky. It doesn't matter."

"But he acted like he knows me."

"Impossible!" Shelpin snapped. "Whatever that manager's crime, it has nothing to do with the furskin auction.... This elevator, you may be interested to know, was the finest elevator in Russia when it was installed in 1913."

She glanced at the messages. Joannie had called from New York, and there were several party invitations related to the fur auction and an engraved invitation to an American embassy reception in Moscow, thanks, she presumed, to her father leaning on the few friends he had left at State.

On the third floor, the grim-looking hall attendant, the *dezhurnaya*, rose, beaming, when Shelpin introduced Natalie. Wreathed in smiles, she personally escorted Natalie to her door, announcing, "Mr. Nevsky's regular suite."

Very Wallace, Natalie thought with a sudden rush of loneliness. It was big, with a grand piano in the living room and views of St. Isaac's across the square. The plush furniture was a trifle shabby, as in the lobby, and the decor ancient—pre-Revolutionary imported copies of eighteenth-century French designs—but the effect was warm and cozy and a welcome change from the careful blandness of business hotels. An old white refrigerator, humming in a corner, served as a bar. For a startling second in the tile bathroom she thought she smelled Wallace's old-fashioned lavender cologne.

The shower was hopeless, so she filled the deep tub, intending to soak and doze to gather the strength for tonight's party. As she stepped in, the telephone rang. She ran for it, wrapped in a towel. It was Joannie Frye, with the worst news since Wallace had died.

"The bank has shut us down."

"What do you mean?" Joannie, while brilliant, was only twenty-three and could be forgiven the occasional exaggeration. "What have they done?"

"No more credit."

"You mean they won't renew?" Cotillion had a fifty-million-dollar credit line, renewable yearly, when they cleared the books. She had intended to nudge them to fifty-five in the spring to relieve some of the pressure from the Aunt Margaret buyout.

"They said we need sixty-five million credit," Joannie replied, "and they'll only go fifty. We have to get the rest from other sources."

"I don't need sixty-five. All I need is another five."

"They say if we don't get the additional fifteen million in three weeks, they'll block our notes."

"Three weeks?" Natalie sank to the bed. Blocking Cotillion's notes meant they wouldn't pay invoices, which meant no one would sell her a coat or a skin.

"Actually, they're already sending notices out to our creditors."

"*What?* They never do that right away."

Joannie said, "I've got that son-of-a-bitch vice president who handles our account on the conference phone. Do you want to talk to him?"

Her head was spinning. She was exhausted from the flight. She had to think. "First, call Rhonda Rosenfeld. Call Lynn Brown. Call my brother. Call Bill Malcolm. Ask them to find out everything they can and I'll talk to all of them tomorrow. . . ."

Think.

"I have to find out what kind of position Jefferson Jervis holds in our bank. Ask Bill—" No, she thought, Mike. Her hail-fellow-well-met brother was the better choice to ferret out information like that. It cost club men like Bill Malcolm too many favors, which always left a trail. "Ask Michael to check it out."

"Anything else?"

Natalie wracked her brain. She had come to Russia to buy furskins and wave Cotillion's flag, not fight New York banks. "There must be, but I can't think what— Okay, give me this guy."

The banker managed to sound grim and unctuous in the same breath. "Natalie, you can't imagine how sorry we are about this."

"Wallace banked with you for forty years," she reminded him. Bad start. She had meant to sound outraged, but her voice betrayed her fear.

"Of course, which is really why I thought it best to talk to you."

"Oh?" She grew alert. He was up to something more than an apology.

"We're a commercial bank, so of course we're enjoined by the law from promoting deals. I can only lend you money or not lend you money."

"I know this," said Natalie.

"But occasionally I feel comfortable suggesting to one good customer they talk to another."

So that was it. A raid.

"Let me guess. Hyndo."

"As a matter of fact, yes. Hyndo is a fine Korean furrier with real assets. I had lunch with their comptroller the other day and got the impression Hyndo might be interested in covering your debts."

"And what do they want back, eighty-five percent of my company?"

"With their production and your retail outlets, it could—"

"Their production is sweatshop garbage that will never be sold in my stores. Cotillion stands for quality and it always will."

"Well, it's a way out."

"What if I raise the additional fifteen million? Will you renew my fifty?"

His silence said more clearly than words that he would contrive some reason to demand she find *twenty* million. And if she managed that, then twenty-five. "Tell me something," she said. "How big is Hyndo's account in your bank?"

"Well, I can hardly—"

"Don't bother," she said angrily. "You're allowing them to pull a leveraged buyout of Cotillion using your bank's money. I think it's disgraceful."

"Now, Natalie—"

"Don't now Natalie me. I'm not some furrier, hat in hand. I'm a banker and don't forget it. I'll fight you! And I know how."

Bold words, though somewhat hollow. In her banking days she and Bill Malcolm had spearheaded many more takeover attacks than defenses. But in her heart-pounding rage she was determined to fight the bank and Hyndo Furs and anyone else who dared to steal her and Wallace's creation. "Cotillion is ours—is mine! It's—"

The telephone line went dead, suddenly. She thought at first that the banker had hung up on her; then a sharp metallic click made her think someone was listening in on her call. "Hello? Joannie, are you back?"

Two clicks.

"Excuse please, front desk," said a Russian speaking English. "Is waiting Comrade Shelpin."

"What!" Her anger at the banker exploded at this unexpected target. "You cut me off. I was talking to New York."

"Is waiting long," came the unrepentant retort.

Natalie banged the phone down hard. Panic fragmented her thoughts. There was too much going on at once. She was going to lose it. She stormed to the window, tore aside the curtains, and stared blindly at the square. She had to do something. She had to call back the banker. But no, there was nothing more to say to him. She was late. She had to calm down and get dressed. Now, more than ever, thanks to this new disaster, she had to get to the Sojuzpushnina reception in good shape and make something work. Slowly, she forced air into her lungs. That was what she had come to Leningrad for. Save Cotillion. One step at a time. *Get dressed.*

Face, hair, stockings, slip; she threw on a dark Italian wool sheath dress, two strands of pearls and her pearl drop earrings, grabbed the speckled white lynx, and raced down the broad stairs to the lobby. Shelpin was glancing nervously at his watch. His driver was scowling by the door.

Carafes of flavored vodka stood in the center of the Pribaltiskaya's *zakuska* table, encircled by miniature glasses Shelpin called *ryumochki.*

Natalie recognized lemon peel in some carafes, buffalo grass and saffron strands in others, but the pale blue cornflower vodka was new to her, as were the mauve-colored lichen and the cedar-flavored *kedrovka*.

Natalie, Leo, and Shelpin joined the fur brokers heaping their plates with hot and cold *zakuski*—"little bites" of smoked sturgeon, salmon, eel layered in lemon, sardines in sauces, herring, sliced meats, Russian sausages, pickled vegetables, and gray caviar. Information, rumor, and innuendo spewed across the table in nine languages, a dizzying torrent of English, French, Russian, German, Italian, Greek, Korean, and Japanese. The occasional confusion was cleared up in Yiddish.

Looks cast her way suggested that one of tonight's hot topics was Hyndo's move on Cotillion. Even if the KGB was not tapping her phone calls, there were no secrets in the fur trade and few opportunities to bluff. But bluff she did, steadying her best party smile, as if Cotillion Furs had all sorts of options in its arsenal and her near-hysterical conversation with her treacherous banker had been nothing more than a minor dispute.

The auction, however, was the main subject. This party was the first gathering before the marking began, and the tension was palpable. No one had seen the Russian pelts, yet, but the advancing mink prices and the falling dollar, which had shaken the international furskin market this season, were expected to instigate rises in all skins, both domestic and wild. The Japanese owned the most valuable money, while the Russians, it was expected, would take advantage of the situation by offering their biggest and finest quality collection in many years. As a buyer, even without this latest disaster, Natalie worried how far her money would go, but as a manufacturer and retailer, she had to wonder how the consumer would react to higher finished coat prices. It was very possible to spend money she could not afford on mink she could not sell.

She was reminded of the Seattle auction, but on a bigger, more international scale, private preserve where everyone knew everyone else and she knew almost no one. When she saw that the old broker she had met in Seattle was already wearing his plaid trapper's vest, she realized she had made a mistake saving her new auction costume for the actual bidding. The play had already begun and she should have started with a bang.

The important brokers took little notice of her until Shelpin or Leo made an introduction. Then it was, "Nice to meet you, Mrs. Nevsky. Wallace always talked about you." Clearly the old guard had liked her husband, and just as clearly they did not miss the competition. Occasionally an elderly European, a legend to whom Wallace had introduced her at a fur show, would seize her hands and draw her close for a kiss, followed by anecdotes of great moments he had shared with Wallace. When she tried to steer these conversations to the present auction, however, she received deep shrugs and empty smiles and more than one grandfatherly pat on the behind.

Back at the caviar she met a petite Englishwoman with a friendly smile. Dripping in jewels and wearing a Dior original that made Natalie feel dressed for beer and hamburgers, she seemed much more than the wife of a fur buyer. Natalie asked what she was doing at the auction. Between greetings to others in French and German, she explained she had come to lend money and that her great-grand-mother had been the first female Imperial Master-Guild Furrier in the Austro-Hungarian Empire.

"Pity about your husband, you know. It's an old man's business. He'd have had decades more of this."

"I know." Saddened and lonely, Natalie wandered. She suddenly realized that this was her first party by herself. She felt her anger rising, but it kept crashing into helplessness. Maybe tomorrow. Maybe something—God knew what.

"Hey there, Yukon Jack." She had noticed him ruminating alone in a corner. Blearily, the fur broker looked up from contemplating the checks on his vest. If his eyes and the empty *ryumochki* on the table beside him were any clue, he was deeply pickled in several flavors of vodka.

"Why, if it ain't the widder woman," he said grumpily. "Welcome to Mother Russia, widder woman."

Hurt, she jibed back at him, "Off your turf, aren't you, Jack?"

"Not as far off as you."

Natalie whirled away, then felt silly about it, and went back. "Did I say something wrong?"

"Name's not Yukon Jack."

"It's Harvey. I'm sorry. And my name's not widder woman."

"I know who you are, Mrs. Nevsky."

"Natalie."

Harvey belched. "Natalie, if I were you I'd step aside, 'cause old Harvey's about to fall on his face."

"Can I get you some *zakuski?*"

Harvey gazed at his reflection in the black window that looked over the Gulf of Finland and contemplated her offer.

"Yeah. Caviar. And maybe one more shot of the blue stuff."

"Hang in there, I'll be right back."

Small plates and silver were arranged at either end of the table. She spread thin slices of *kalach* with sweet butter and mounded each with gray beluga that she spooned from a deep crystal bowl floating in ice. The sight of the neatly arranged plate cheered Harvey almost as much as the cornflower vodka. She stood by uncertainly as he wolfed it down.

"So how do things look, Harvey?"

"Gonna be a massacre." He contemplated the vodka a moment, then tossed it straight back in the Russian style. His eyes turned fluorescent. "I've never seen it so crazy. Half the manufacturers have panicked and overbought. The other half are slitting their wrists because they didn't buy enough. When *they* buy, the first half are going to think they have to buy more, driving the bids through the roof."

At that moment an American mink farmer on a junket came by, smiling broadly. "After six years getting stomped on, it's the ranchers' turn."

"Enjoy it while it lasts, fella."

The rancher lurched off and Harvey said, "There's going to be blood in the streets."

"That's when the money's made."

The old broker conjured a smile. "There's a hoary old sentiment. Sit down, young lady, let's see what else that son of a bitch taught you."

"Like what?"

"If, here—in Leningrad—then next month in Copenhagen, Leipzig, and Hudson's Bay, London—you could corner a pelt market, what would you go for? Mink? Sable?"

Natalie leaned closer. "Don't tell anybody."

"Mum's the word."

She took a chance and whispered, "Fox."

Harvey grinned. "Got any money?"

"Yup. Only thing is I need mink, too. My customers won't buy tip-dyed coats."

"Understood," said Harvey. "Let's you and me talk next time I'm sober."

Natalie agreed, though a glint in Harvey's eye suggested he was more sober already than he appeared. In fact, he had very cleverly moved in on a fat brokerage fee to supply skins to Cotillion Furs. She still resisted the thought that she couldn't depend on Leo forever. Nor could she mark skins herself. The hard part was that hiring an outsider was yet another acceptance, a big admission, that Wallace was gone forever. She hated to lose the control of supply that Wallace had given her. And yet, there were things she could do, and things she couldn't do. Delegate, said Wallace. Perhaps she would. She looked around the party, still felt a stranger, and wondered what was here for her.

From the *zakuska* table the Sojuzpushnina hosts led the fur buyers to a sitdown dinner. Fyodor Shelpin graciously invited Natalie to sit with him, but she was disappointed to land far from the A table. Or so it seemed, at first.

The four top brokers and their wives were seated with Sojuzpushnina's director. That would have been Wallace's table. The English financier and the prominent European furriers were at his deputy's table, and a crowd of younger sable designers had gathered with the director's personal staff.

By contrast, the elderly man to Natalie's left appeared to be a rumpled academic. He was a statistician, it seemed, a statistician with a theory into which he launched before the soup arrived. "It is called," he explained earnestly, "The Elite Decline."

He stared at her through thick glasses, blinking rapidly as if he feared she would suddenly stand up and walk away. She took pity and repeated, dutifully, "Really, Mr. uh—"

"Starkov," he said. "Ivan Starkov. I am director of Amerika Institut. My organization collects production figures. American production. German production. British production. Japanese production. When I was a student, many years ago, they laughed when I predicted that one day New York City would buy subway cars from the Japanese."

"Subway cars?" she echoed, aching for Wallace, whose knee she could have nudged to provoke an ebullient and totally unstoppable intervention.

"It was the year Stalin died. My superiors laughed. Japan? Comrade Starkov, Japan can barely assemble bicycle parts."

A cold smile made him look ten years younger, and revealed an underlying toughness that prompted Natalie to reassess her seemingly chance dinner partner.

"Japan destroyed two of the czar's navies, I reminded them. I was naïve. I thought I could sway them with facts and logic. The czar was corrupt, they sneered. Why would an American city buy subway cars from a foreign country? This was before you were born, my dear, but in those days American heavy industry led the world in productivity, quality, and innovation. I explained my theory of elite decline. They transferred me to Gorky, cut my pay, and denied me permission to marry. . . . When my prediction that the Germans would resume building Volkswagens came true, they brought me back, but she had married a soldier by then." Starkov smiled his icy smile again. And he had stopped blinking, Natalie noticed.

"It was in the history, you see. You've been buying Japanese subway cars for some time now. The United States is careening down the same steep slope as England, the Romans, and the Greeks. And do you know why?"

"Tell me."

"Because the elite decline responsibility."

"That's a favorite phrase of my father's."

"Your father is a wise man, young woman. He understands history. But you are a glitch."

"Me? Me personally? What makes me a glitch?"

"At a time when American business atrophies due to misappropriated talent and imagination, an upstart success like Cotillion Furs makes a shambles of my theory."

"You know who I am?"

"I make study of your company in *Fur Age Weekly, The International Fur Fashion Review, Women's Wear Daily, Advertising Age, Crain's New York Business.* Every year I look for your bankruptcy, but every year you disappoint me. You're an anomaly, and for that matter, so is the entire American fur trade."

"You must have known my husband, Wallace Nevsky."

"Only by reputation," Starkov replied enigmatically.

"Then I don't understand. Why do you study Cotillion Furs?"

Starkov smiled. "Sometimes I study what is interesting. Sometimes I study what I am asked to study."

"Were you asked to study me?"

"It has been suggested," Starkov replied in Russian officialese, "that the Soviet Union, which produces millions and millions of fur skins, ought perhaps to manufacture fur coats." He picked up his spoon at last, and tasted his soup.

Now it was Natalie who wanted to talk, to learn how he had happened to single out *her* company. "You've studied my company. What do you know about us?"

Starkov warmed to his subject. "Cotillion Furs was rather late in joining the American trend toward national franchising, Davey Tree Surgery being one of the oldest examples. And certainly national retailing is hardly new either with K-Mart at one end of the spectrum and Neiman-Marcus at the other. Nonetheless, you were the first in the fur trade. I am hoping you will be the exception that proves the rule of my theory of elite decline. Interestingly, you, as a woman who left banking to enter the fur trade, have broken the pattern."

"Excuse me. How did you know I was a banker?"

Starkov gave her a hard look. "My theory is grounded in a thousand specifics, Mrs. Nevsky. I do not speculate about gossip. I investigate my subjects."

"Do you understand that this makes me feel uncomfortable? As if you've invaded my privacy?"

"I hardly expected to meet you face to face," Starkov replied irritably.

"Did you arrange for us to sit together this evening?"

"I am fascinated by the facts of your life," Starkov answered obliquely. "You quit banking for the rough-and-tumble fur trade. That is most unusual. Generally speaking, the citizens of mature empires do not abandon nonproductive elite positions."

I'm getting paranoid, thought Natalie. She tried to mollify him. "Is the Soviet Union on that same English, Roman, Greek slope, Mr. Starkov?"

"My specialty is the West," Starkov demurred. "I'm afraid I put more study into your country than mine."

"But you'd agree that the Soviet Union is a maturing empire?"

"We have our problems, competing in a youthful world. But if the new Gen Sec inspires our young people and shows them ways to use their energy, then the Soviet Union will bury you sooner than Premier Khrushchev promised."

"Race will do you in," an auctioneer called drunkenly across the table. "America is catapulting toward an explosion due to racial exploitation."

The other Russians looked horrified at the breach of manners, and timid Fyodor Shelpin surprised Natalie by criticizing him sternly. "You're being very Soviet, Comrade."

Starkov, however, spoke to his point. "If I might correct you, young man, Americans do not exploit their minorities. They ignore them."

"But clearly the denial of civil rights angers the poor and— "

Starkov removed his glasses and stared. The auctioneer stopped with a nervous swallow. Again Starkov explained, but now his voice conveyed quiet menace. "American civil rights are guaranteed to those who can afford them. Even the poor believe that rights are yet another purchase to strive for, like microwave ovens."

Turning back to Natalie and putting his glasses on again, he said, "Forgive me, Mrs. Nevsky. I exaggerate to make a point to a dunderhead—"

Starkov's voice trailed off abruptly.

Natalie tracked his gaze across the dining room, where it had fixed on a well-dressed man in his early fifties who appeared to be heading for their table. He was quite handsome, in the Russian mode, with a high, shiny pompadour riding a broad brow, and if the conversations dying in his wake were any indication, he was a man of consequence. When Fyodor Shelpin saw him, he leaped from his chair like a frightened puppy. "Please sit here, Comrade Rostov."

"He'll sit where he pleases, Fyodor Ivanovich," Starkov growled.

"Who is that?" Natalie asked.

"Rostov. The new foreign trade minister."

Rostov paused to shake hands with the director of Sojuzpushnina, who had risen with obsequious haste. He declined with an urbane smile an offer to join the director's party and continued on toward Natalie's table.

"A plutocrat," Starkov joked. "Russia's first *perestroika* plutocrat." But, Natalie noticed, he lowered his voice so only she could hear.

"Take my chair," little Shelpin repeated.

Rostov looked Natalie up and down and said, "Delighted."

"Mrs. Nevsky, may I present Foreign Trade Minister Vladimir Rostov, an old friend of your husband?"

Rostov bowed over her hand.

Seating was rearranged, with Shelpin moving over and the drunken auctioneer surrendering his place without a word. Old Starkov, who traded nods with Rostov, stayed where he was on Natalie's left. Rostov flashed a showy gold Rolex and repeated that he and Wallace had been the best of friends for many years. Natalie wondered why Wallace had never mentioned him.

"We were all so happy when you married," Rostov joked. "It gave the rest of us—how you call it, a shot—at the womens. Do you remember, Fyodor Ivanovich?"

"I remember," Shelpin mumbled warily, "that Vassily was the happiest of all."

"I don't quite understand, Mr. Rostov. Do you represent Sojuzpushnina abroad?"

"Sojuzpushnina is one of my, what you would call, clients." Rostov smiled easily. "My ministry guides the efforts of various Soviet enterprises overseas. I'm in Washington quite often. Sometimes New York. Perhaps sometime I might call on you there."

Through the long meal he regaled her with tales of doing business with Wallace, most of which involved drinking bouts and chance meetings with attractive women. Judging solely by his manner, Natalie would have written him off as a slick salesman, but every time Rostov looked up, the other men in the room got busy pretending they were not trying to eavesdrop. Suddenly, as Natalie downed what had to be her fifth toast, Rostov asked bluntly, "And now you are here on Wallace's business?"

"Cotillion Furs still needs skins."

"But surely a businesswoman like yourself is not going to mark pelts."

"I have excellent brokers. But I wanted to be personally in charge."

"I wish you luck," he said, and then in an apparent non sequitur, added, "Most of the women come shopping."

"Not me, this time."

"If you have a moment, I'd be delighted to take you around. You can buy excellent diamonds this year. And pearls. Though I see you've brought your own pearls. They're very lovely, don't you think, Fyodor Ivanovich?"

"Lovely pearls," Shelpin agreed with a nervous, head-bobbing smile that seemed designed to stampede her imagination. "Lovely pearls for a pearl of a lady."

Natalie glanced from one Russian to the other. She had worn pearls innocently, part of what she had belatedly realized at the *zakuska* table was an ill-chosen business outfit. Was she being tested with the code? Or had it been a simple compliment? Or some not so simple flirting. Or an out-and-out come-on from a horny Soviet official. Rostov was certainly sitting closer than he had to.

"Wallace gave them to me."

Rostov caught Shelpin's eye, she thought. He might have signaled. He might not, but Shelpin rose immediately. "I'm obliged to visit hospitality suites in the hotel tonight. Would you mind, Mrs. Nevsky, if Vladimir Rostov drove you home?"

"I'll be fine in a taxi."

"Absolutely not," said Rostov. "It will be my pleasure to drive you."

He owned an elderly Mercedes-Benz with cracked-leather seats, and he seemed as proud of it as of his watch. Natalie noticed him patting the wheel when it responded as he wanted. Thick snow was blowing in from the Gulf of Finland, pelting the windshield and storming darkly about the street lamps. They went slowly over a humpback bridge. Natalie caught a glimpse of black iron lion heads adorning the rails.

Glancing back, she saw that their escort was still behind them and she wondered whether the men in the black cars were guarding Rostov or watching him. Her father had warned her that few Soviet officials were allowed to spend time unaccompanied with a foreigner. That they were alone in his own car confirmed that Rostov was a very important man. Shelpin, by contrast, was always accompanied by his driver.

Rostov chattered volubly, gesturing with his hands, shooting his cuff when it covered his Rolex. She supposed the wristwatch had been a bribe in a foreign business deal. The so-called Texas Seikos were standard currency for international kickbacks, and at the table, he had boasted that his contacts with foreign businessmen extended far beyond the fur trade.

"What car do you drive?" he asked suddenly.

"I have a little BMW, but lately I've been driving Wallace's Cadillac."

"How do they compare?"

"Apples and oranges."

Rostov was puzzled by the English expression. They were speaking English at his insistence, and Natalie was grateful for the rest from struggling with her neglected Russian, although Rostov's Russianized

Americanisms took some getting used to. He claimed to be a "hard-driving *rabotagolik*," which she figured out, finally, was a Soviet workaholic. Then he started in on the *Mafiya* and the automobile parts *rekket*.

"The car has changed us. Now that we have cars we must keep them running. But fixing them is beyond the state. So we fix our own. Black market for parts. Black market *rekket* is corruption. But more than *rekket*. Also, new way to get things done. Now we *expect* to get things done. People like me, who are used to getting things done, don't settle for less. *Perestroika*, you see, is real. Not just *imedzh*."

"But the new leadership fights corruption?" Natalie asked.

"The new Gen Sec?" Rostov asked, referring to Mikhail Gorbachev, general secretary of the Communist Party. "He's our guy."

"Your 'guy'?"

"He's like us. Of course he can't come out and just say it, so he proceeds cautiously, announcing programs, putting in new guys to run things. He wants it to work like all of us new guys."

"Why can't he just come out and say it?"

In answer, Rostov turned on the high beams, which illuminated swirling clouds of snow. He waved at the blackness past the headlights. "Because out there, in Russia, are two hundred and fifty million peasants who would dearly love to cut our throats. . . . And now I am asking you for date."

"What?"

"Come to *dacha* for weekend. Iceboating. Sauna. Very relaxing."

Was that all this private moment would yield? "Uh, I don't date. I mean, I'm just widowed."

"In New York, you are widow, Mrs. Nevsky. Here. . . ."

"You told me you're married."

"In Leningrad, I am not married."

"In Leningrad, I am working. I don't date when I'm working. And especially not a 'sleepover' date," she added, with a not-too-friendly smile.

"Then maybe we talk one night next week . . . about things."

Wondering what "things," she asked bluntly, "How did you happen to end up at my table tonight?"

"The Gen Sec tour and the new trade law make this a propitious time for Soviet–foreign commerce. I'm traveling every day to welcome foreign businessmen. I'm practically a conventioneer," he laughed. "The fur auction is one of many stops." He smiled and patted her knee. "As to the actual table I chose? A privilege of rank. If you were a man, would you sit with a group of eighty-year-old furriers or a pretty young woman?"

Natalie brushed his hand away. "That English merchant banker was gorgeous."

"I prefer tall women."

"Tell me about the new trade law."

"I'm sure you already know, but anything to make conversation. The new trade law permits joint enterprises with foreign investors."

"And who does the foreign investor sue if there's a breach?"

"The Soviet government always honors contracts. Ever since your husband's mother negotiated machinery purchases in the 1920s."

This, Natalie knew, was true. Lie, cheat, and fudge as the Soviet Union might on political treaties, the Russians always paid their bills.

"But who does the foreign investor sue if there is a legitimate disagreement?"

"Is now possible to sue government company, under certain conditions. Is major change."

"Major," Natalie agreed, scrunching down in her seat to see back in the sideview mirror. The lights of the escorts still hung in the glass. Pairs of yellow dots, like eyes in a forest.

"We should have lunch," she mused.

Rostov turned his attention from the road. In the backglow reflected by the swirling snow, she could see a vein pulsing in his broad forehead. He said, "When an American says lunch she means business."

"I do mean business," Natalie replied. "At dinner Mr. Starkov reminded me of something I hadn't thought much about before. The Soviet Union produces millions of furskins, but doesn't make fur coats."

"Hats. We make hats. And trimmings."

"Yet you raise ten million minks, alone. God knows how many fox, not to mention the luxury furs. But if you want a fur coat, you have to buy from the Europeans."

"Do you suggest the Soviet Union buy American fur coats instead?" Rostov smiled.

"You'd get a much better made coat."

"But importing American coats would not be in our interest."

"I suppose not," Natalie agreed reluctantly. "You have to save hard currency to import computers and lasers."

"Is not one-way road," Rostov retorted heatedly. "We *export* technology, too. Metallurgy, welding, casting, chemistry. Thanks to

Soviet flash-butt welding machines that my ministry sold Washington Metro, even your Pentagon generals ride to work on Soviet technology."

Natalie refrained from mentioning that American generals did not ride the subway, saying instead, "While your poor wife shivers in an Italian-made fur coat?"

"*Touché*," Rostov laughed. "*Touché. Touché.* But only the highest of the high can get permission to import an American coat."

"Ideally she would wear a Russian fur coat."

Rostov swung onto the Lieutenant Schmidt Bridge and crossed the Neva before replying. "Vassily and I held similar discussion."

When he did not volunteer the nature of that discussion, Natalie said, "Mr. Starkov implied that he had been asked to research the American fur trade."

Again, Rostov paused. Finally he said, "That is true. As matter of fact, I was one who requested that report. About America, Ivan Starkov is the man to ask. His research is impeccable."

"Did he tell you that Russia made fur coats before the Revolution?"

"Czarist Russia manufactured many luxuries before the Revolution. From the tiniest Fabergé egg to the greatest palace. But, as your people say, that market has dwindled."

"It's my understanding that Fabergé's factories exported most of his products," Natalie replied. She had no idea whether that was true, and hoped Rostov did not either. "As for palaces, from the restorations I see in Leningrad, palace building is hardly a lost art in the Soviet Union."

"Lenin said respect the work of Russian hands."

"Then I think the work of Russian hands would make a perfect agenda for a business lunch."

Rostov shot his cuff for another look at his Rolex. "Lunch would be my pleasure. Monday?"

"Tuesday would be better for me. And I hope you'll bring along any of your colleagues who might lend expertise."

"In what areas?"

"Joint ventures."

"*Dzhoint venchur?*"

Rostov raised an inquiring eyebrow, but Natalie did not respond. She sat back, pleased with herself. She could never shake the sense of being an outsider among the furriers. But putting together a deal, even an embryonic deal that was still as shapeless and ephemeral as steam rising from a grate, made her feel at home and in charge. Six thousand miles from New York with a horny Russian in a car in a blizzard, she felt as if she belonged.

"What is the name of Mr. Starkov's institute?" she asked.

Rostov laughed.

"What's funny?"

"Nothing."

"No, tell me. Did I miss something?"

"Starkov is a character."

"You know him well?"

"Don't be alarmed. I'm just repeating stories, but the story is . . ." He glanced at the night and the snow blowing in the headlights, and lowered his voice. "The story is that Starkov is KGB."

"That little old man?" Natalie asked with innocent-sounding surprise, but she felt cold as ice inside. "No."

"Who knows? But it is said that the Institute for Amerika Studies, or whatever Starkov calls it this year, is a KGB operation."

"Wait a minute," Natalie said carefully. "That doesn't mean he's a spy or a secret agent. Aren't there many KGB organizations? I've heard the KGB called an elite within the elite. You could be KGB."

"Many organizations," Rostov said, smiling. He laughed again. "Do you know what they say that old man did?"

"What?" Natalie prompted. "Tell me."

"He bought a credit bureau. Do you know what credit bureau is?"

"In Russia?"

"No, no, no. America. He bought a credit bureau in America that investigates people's creditworthiness. In Washington, D.C. With computer records of citizens' debts. Credit cards, mortgages, loans. Starkov's agency owned it. If a senator or an Army general borrowed money, Starkov had his records. Don't you see?"

"I see. . . . Do you think it's true?"

"Vassily roared when I told him."

"Is it widely known?"

"No. I shouldn't tell you, except it is old history now. They say he's retired."

"What happened to the credit bureau?"

"Probably sold it to the Bulgarians," Rostov chortled.

St. Isaac's Cathedral suddenly loomed through the snow and the car slid to a stop in front of the Astoria. "Do you invite me for nightcap?"

"Jet lag," Natalie pleaded. "I'm reeling. Tuesday lunch?"

"Perhaps we drive to *dacha* for business lunch."

"If we have the time. Good night."

She stood in the snow, breathing the cold damp air, and watched the swirling darkness swallow up Vladimir Rostov and his escorts. She felt utterly baffled. Running the evening through her mind— the *zakuski* party, dinner, Fyodor Shelpin's nervousness, Rostov's tales about Wallace, their references to pearls, Ivan Starkov's knowledge about Cotillion and herself, the rumor that the old statistician was KGB—Natalie tried to recall a single word that would have sounded different if she did not know that Wallace had been a spy.

Why had both Ivan Starkov and Vladimir Rostov sat at her table, when they were probably the two most important Soviet officials at the party? But, of course, her imagination was already inflated to bursting by the tall KGB officer's inquisitive stare.

There was one consolation, she thought as she turned from the night into the warm lobby, and it almost made her laugh. In the real world—the so-called aboveboard business arena where her own bank was helping a foreign competitor steal Cotillion Furs—her first night in Russia had suggested a fascinating, albeit vague, opportunity to save herself by doing a deal with the Soviets. *Dzhoint venchur.*

Leningrad's thin winter sunrise, which gleamed on gilt roofs and blue ice, found Natalie awake for hours in a state of high tension. She had to wait until afternoon to telephone her people in New York. Breakfast from room service proved impossible. She was too anxious to stomach more than tea.

She busied herself adding personal notes to a hundred postcards that she had addressed to Cotillion franchise owners before she left New York.

"Weather cold, furskins hot. Love from Leningrad, Natalie."

It was the best she could do on most of them. Although she knew each and every owner personally, having sold them their franchises, her mind kept locking on the scary possibility that by the time her cards arrived in the mail she might not own Cotillion.

At last, it was morning in New York. She telephoned Joannie, who had been up half the night gathering information and hounding their accountants to produce firm numbers on everything from inventory to billings. Next she spoke with Rhonda at Citicorp, Lynn Brown, and her brother, who had done a very creditable job of ferreting out what lay behind the attack. As the winter sun commenced its early slide into evening, the picture became clearer, if no less bleak.

Jefferson Jervis had indeed leaned on her bank—a bank, Natalie recalled bitterly, that she had tried and failed to convince Wallace to leave, precisely because it was small and vulnerable to pressure. Wallace was loyal; now she was paying the price. Mike had also discovered that Jefferson Jervis had bought into Hyndo Industries, which stunned Natalie. The financier was going to a lot of trouble to cause her trouble. But Mike, who knew nothing about Wallace's secret life, had a more innocent explanation:

"There's a lot of money to be made ripping you off, Sis."

Lynn Brown had conferred with Hyndo's attorneys. Hyndo demanded, as Natalie had predicted, eighty-five percent of Cotillion in return for assuming Natalie's debts. Her creditors, who had the legal right to approve any payoff plan, were meeting today to try to agree on a settlement. Joannie Frye had sampled their mood and reported that all that prevented an immediate takeover by the Korean fur manufacturer was greed and confusion.

Natalie's creditors were sharply divided into two camps. Those from whom Cotillion had borrowed actual cash—the merchant banks, factors, and moneylenders—insisted on full payment. One-hundred-cents-on-the-dollar. Her trade creditors—suppliers to whom she owed payment for goods—were willing to settle for less. This apparent generosity could be traced, Joannie noted in her most scornful Queens accent, to the suppliers' willingness to forgo part of their usual two-hundred-percent markup.

Remembering Wallace's many misadventures with the Soviet telephone system, Natalie had booked her international lines hours ahead, and had Joannie patch her into conference calls, but the Russian phones still drove her crazy. Three times she was cut off in mid-sentence. She used the intervals to talk to Leo and Harvey in Leningrad and once managed by a miracle to reach Stevie Weintraub in Hong Kong for a few words about Red Chinese joint ventures. It was eerie to know that every word she uttered, every tactic discussed, every decision made, was being recorded, but what the KGB telephone tappers made of their references to the People's Republic brought the only smile of the day to Natalie's lips.

Finally she got through to Bill Malcolm of Stuart, Malcolm and Hardy, who promised, "Come hell or high water, I personally guarantee that SM&H will not permit this to happen to you, Natalie."

The hollow ring of bravado in Bill's voice made her flinch. Wallace used to warn her, "Look out for men in business who talk tough and talk rich. At the first whiff of cordite, they're hugging the floor in the fetal position."

She knew at that moment that Bill and SM&H's enormous clout could not save her. It was an awful shock. She had been counting on him as her last resort.

Covering her distress, she eased out of their conversation, with a promise to speak on Monday, hung up the telephone, and sat quietly for a while, gazing out the window at St. Isaac's Square, where fresh snow began to settle on the parked cars. Night had fallen. The great cathedral rose like a domed mountain in its spotlights. Wallace once told her that every building in Leningrad stood on wooden pilings, thousands of tree trunks driven into the swamp the city covered.

She drew a bath and let her thoughts drift while she soaked. Slowly, the flip side of Wallace's warning flickered back at her like a candle in a mirror. If her friends were frightened, there must be frightened men among her enemies, too. Fear was the handmaiden of greed. Her creditors were fighting. Could she sow more dissension in their ranks? Buy some time? If Jefferson Jervis could infiltrate Hyndo, why couldn't she infiltrate Cotillion's creditors?

She telephoned her brother.

In whatever heaven Communists ruled, Nikolai Lenin must have smiled, for she got through immediately with a clear connection. "I was just thinking how clever you were finding out about Jervis and Hyndo," she greeted him.

"Now that I'm off the coke my friends return my calls. They're happy to talk, particularly when I'm not asking for a job."

"How would you like to work with Bill Malcolm?"

"You know I don't have a track record. Guys like Bill Malcolm aren't interested in a twenty-nine-year-old Jack-of-all-trades."

"I said *with* him, not for him. Organize a syndicate to raise money to pay my creditors. Hit your best contacts. Hit the richest Cotillion franchise holders. Joannie's got a special list. It's yours with my blessing."

"Thank you," he said sincerely. "I appreciate the trust. But what do I sell them? Cotillion is not a great investment this week."

"Just start talking. Tell them I'm working something here that'll blow their socks off. You don't need commitments. But you do need to invite Bill Malcolm into the syndicate."

"Bill? Doesn't he represent some of your creditors?"

"He can persuade the other creditors to accept our payout offer."

Mike laughed. "You want me to make Bill Malcolm your spy in the creditors?"

"He will thank you for the chance to cover himself. I'm not worth much to him bankrupt."

"Your spy in the creditors," Mike repeated. "I love it. You'll know what they're thinking—Christ, he could even goose 'em into fighting with each other."

"The longer they fight, the longer I have to run a deal here that will help you raise money in New York."

Mike laughed again. "How'd you get so devious?"

"I think I inherited it from my hus—"

Suddenly, she noticed a buff-colored envelope on the bed. Propped against the pillow, it had not been there when she undressed for her bath.

"Hey, Princess Machiavelli, you still there? What do we do next? . . . Hello?"

Natalie stared at the envelope, her passions stretched between Cotillion and Wallace's secret life.

"I'll get back to you," she said, and hung up.

BOOK FOUR

MOSCOW MILLIONAIRES

18

Natalie circled the envelope warily. She ran to the front door. She hadn't thought to lock it from the inside. She wouldn't have heard them while she was running the tub. Returning to the bedroom, she picked up the envelope and inspected both sides. Blank. She slit it open with her nail.

She found a single folded page from *Vechernaya Moska,* a Moscow evening newspaper. There was no note, only an interior page of the newspaper dated two days ago. Puzzled, she skimmed it for a clue.

Glasnost had transformed Soviet journalism. Even in Cyrillic letters, the headlines spoke with a breathless, hysterical outrage reminiscent of the tabloid *New York Post.* Corruption was everywhere and *Vechernaya Moska* was determined to root it out:

Mechanics at a state-run garage had been cannibalizing customers' cars for working parts; no wonder, *Vechernaya Moska* thundered, citizens preferred that moonlighters fix their cars, although the source of the moonlighting mechanics' spare parts constituted yet another scandal. Elsewhere in the city, policemen had been caught commandeering taxis for free rides home, while young working mothers were protesting inadequate day care in the new housing projects, and the *luberi,* teenage gangs from the suburbs, had again attacked heavy metal fans at a Gorky Park concert.

Mystified, Natalie turned it over. This side listed classified ads and public announcements. Her eye froze on four lines of numbers penciled lightly in the margin.

379-33-01
250-36-04
382-14-01
278-18-02

The three-digit, two-digit, two-digit combinations looked like Russian telephone numbers and, indeed, could have been scribbled innocently in her newspaper by someone meeting new friends. Moscow was notorious for hostile information operators and a dearth of telephone books, but these numbers were book code—page, line, and word.

She locked her door and brought the newspaper page and her shoulder bag to the writing desk by the window. On the dimly lit square, hunched figures in black cloth coats plodded over a sea of cobblestones. Seated at the desk, she could not see the Intourist buses and modern taxis parked at the hotel entrance, only the pedestrians huddled in an ancient, suffering pose, and she suddenly felt a century from home.

The suite was too big and open. She drew the curtains, but it didn't help dispel all the old stories about KGB entrapment and bugged hotel rooms. She had hoped, of course, that someone would send the numbers. Now, she was almost paralyzed by her fear. Every lamp could hide a microphone, every mirror a camera. The crystal chandelier—

She took her bag into the bathroom, locked that door too, and studied the light fixture. Sinking below the mirrors to the floor, she sorted through her paperbacks with shaking hands. The Westlake novels and the Blocks had been too thin for her purpose. The new David Morrell novel had been almost fat enough, as had the latest Christopher Newman. The Ludlum had been just right. She could not say she had done it on impulse because it had been too tedious and she had muffed the first try, but shortly before she left New York she had stripped the entire cover off the Ludlum and glued it around Wallace's copy of *The Pearl*.

The threat level had seemed low in the privacy of her own bedroom, markedly higher when the puritanical Russian customs inspectors had nailed Leo's son's X-rated video, but now, seated on the cold tile floor on a heap of thin towels, she felt the risk curve was rocketing off the screen. The smart move would be to flush the page down the toilet and concentrate on the auction. But she had to know.

She tore off the margin with the numbers, a thin strip she could jettison in a second. Then she opened *The Pearl*.

379-33-01.

Page 379, line 33, read, "Three fingers entered easily. The soft warm folds . . ." 01. The first word was *Three. Three.*

She turned to page 250, and traced down the page to line 36: "slightly gaping open, from . . ." *From.*

Page 382, line 14, word 01, yielded *right,* which gave her, so far, *Three from right,* with one word to go. Three from right what? Muttering, "Who reads this stuff?" she thumbed her way toward page 278. *Wallace,* for one. Line 18: "her bottom as she was riding . . ." *Bottom.* The second word was bottom.

Three from right bottom.

"That's it?"

Three from right bottom made no sense. But it was the whole message. With a sinking feeling she wondered whether there might be a kicker number in the code that altered each number by a given amount. If there was, she didn't know it.

Three from right bottom. She picked up the newspaper page. Classifieds and announcements. Right column. Bottom. Third from bottom. The third announcement from the bottom read: "Gladishev Warehouse. Kitai-Gorod district. Carpenters, stonemasons, and labor."

All that Natalie understood of the cryptic announcement was that the Kitai-Gorod was an ancient Moscow neighborhood near the Kremlin. But a paragraph heading the column explained that weekend volunteers were welcome to join in the restoration of the buildings listed. Skills were valued, but if you had none, you could haul bricks or make lunch. Gentrification, it seemed, had hit even Moscow.

It seemed a safe place to meet. She could always say she had wanted to experience something off the beaten tourist track. That was a story she could defend, she thought. She could say that, if someone asked. She could not quite form a picture in her mind of who might ask. But she persuaded herself that volunteering at a Moscow restoration site sounded plausible.

The telephone shrilled in the living room.

Natalie jumped, flushed the margin down the toilet, and ran to answer the phone. She recognized Foreign Trade Minister Rostov's hearty voice. "Good evening. I am in hotel. Perhaps we might have dinner."

A "jump" on Tuesday's lunch, he called it. It sounded as much an official summons as an invitation.

When Rostov's knee sought hers under the table he had procured in the darkest, quietest corner of the Astoria's bar, Natalie prayed that the Soviet official was truly just coming on to her. But the coincidence of his call and the book code summons to Moscow could not be ignored. Had she passed some sort of test last night at the Sojuzpushnina party? Or did he really mean it when he cooed, "You must tell me what can I do to persuade you to join me for the weekend." He shot his cuff, read his Rolex, and said, "It's early. My car awaits. The *dacha* is only one hour ride."

"I'm sorry, Comrade Rostov."

"Vladimir."

"I'm sorry, Vladimir. But I really am committed to a Moscow visit. My father would be heartbroken if I didn't call on his old friends at the embassy."

"You made no mention of this visit last night."

"I hadn't firmed up my schedule yet," she explained. "In fact, I just booked my tickets, right after you called."

"Where are you staying?"

"The National."

"Vassily's favorite."

"That's why. He was going to take me there last Christmas."

"Of course."

"Tuesday," she said brightly. "We're still on for lunch Tuesday?"

"You raised an interesting point about fur coats, I thought. My staff tells me you were essentially correct."

"Vladimir, just between you and me and the vodka, we're talking about the possibility of some kind of partnership, aren't we?"

Rostov delivered a variation on a joke he obviously resorted to on many occasions. "To the extent that a lovely woman could be *part-nyori* with a monolithic, totalitarian, evil empire."

"I'm willing to try."

Rostov pulled a folder from his briefcase. "Read this. New rules and regulations to make doing Soviet business easier." He dangled it like bait. She took it from his hand.

"Thank you very much."

Rostov raised a cautioning finger. "Keep in mind, Mrs. Nevsky. This is not New York. You do not deal one on one with a Soviet official. I am just one man. We have different ways, and many officials. Now, if you'll spend the weekend with me, I'll introduce you to others."

"I'm afraid I can't."

"Don't think you can operate here without knowledgeable friends," Rostov relented testily. "Permit me to demonstrate."

He placed a folded ten-ruble note beside his empty glass, covered it with his hand, and beckoned a waiter.

"More vodka."

"You have consumed the state-authorized limit, Comrade."

Rostov removed his hand. "Then bring us two Perrier," he said, laying strong emphasis on the *a* sound in Perrier. The waiter scooped up the money and returned quickly with two glasses of clear liquid. One bubbled, one didn't. Rostov offered a glass to Natalie. "Drink."

She raised it to her lips. Pure vodka.

"Friends, Mrs. Nevsky. You need them, badly."

19

Wallace had joked that being followed in Russia was as common as getting mugged by the disaffected in New York, but more fun. Natalie was not sure about the fun part. The guy was scary.

He had pushed into the taxi behind hers when she left the Astoria Hotel for the airport early in the morning. Heavyset, he wore a dirty raincoat and an exceptionally tall fur hat. She had given that first sighting little notice because while Leningrad was dark at seven o'clock—the winter dawn was still hours away—the city was lively. Trams, buses, taxis, and private cars plied the streets, which had already been cleared of snow.

Dozing on the ride to the airport, she recovered slightly from a painful amalgam of hangover and jet lag. Tea accelerated the process, and with a few minutes to spare after checking in at the foreigners' section, she searched out a pay telephone and called Stefan's Russian girlfriend. The actress was sleeping, her father said. Natalie left a message that she was a friend from the theater, wondering if Vera was free for lunch on Monday.

The tall hat caught her eye, silhouetted against the high ceiling. He was gazing down from a second-level overhang, watching so intently that if the terminal had not been busy, she would have been afraid he meant to hurt her. She hurried back to the safety of the Intourist lounge, feeling his eyes tracking her.

She glanced up from the door. He had gone. The Moscow flight was called. She boarded without incident and found her narrow seat. It was a tight fit, six abreast, and the upholstery was redolent of pungent cigarettes. Seated on the aisle, she was able to watch the door until it thunked shut. When the engines began to whine, she decided that she had imagined being followed. She fastened her seat belt and opened the folder Minister Rostov had provided at dinner.

A commotion ten rows astern turned heads. The flight attendants were ordering a woman to surrender her seat. Dragging a huge jar of pickles in a string bag, she disembarked, angry but silent, and now the passengers craned their necks to see who rated.

Natalie already knew. He put his hat on his lap, closed his eyes, and appeared to sleep throughout the one-hour flight, while Natalie stared blankly at the new *glasnost*-inspired foreign trade regulations and tried to think. This had gone way past coincidence, far beyond imagination. But she was still wrestling with the who and why when it dawned on her that whoever he was and whyever he was following her, she had to duck him before she entered the Kitai-Gorod.

The sky was still black when the plane set down at Sheremetyevo Airport. He stayed in his seat while the other passengers crowded into the aisle, looked Natalie up and down as she passed, but avoided her eye. He did not appear at the luggage pickup, nor at the taxi stand. On the ride through morning darkness into Moscow, she began to hope again that he was just one of those creeps who stared at women alone.

Somehow, he beat her to the hotel. The implications of his knowing which hotel she was using were unsettling on their own, but he had also switched tactics, changing into a dark overcoat and a less conspicuous fur hat. He looked like half the men walking on Gorky Street. She could not place what had given him away, but something, if only heightened imagination, had drawn her attention to a post rack in a gift shop across the lobby from the reception desk and there he was, pretending interest in a newspaper.

Her room had a view of the Kremlin towers etched against a faintly graying sky. She changed her clothes, pulling faded blue jeans over her Damart long underwear and adding rubber-soled boots and a thick cashmere turtleneck sweater. Then, stealing a leaf from the

Russian's book, she tucked her hair under a doubleknit watch cap, pulled a scarf around her mouth and nose as she had seen Russians do on the street, and exchanged her reversible sheared-beaver traveling coat for a fur-lined leather bomber jacket.

But in the mirror she still saw Natalie Stuart Nevsky in a short jacket and knit hat. With her hair off her face, her dark eyebrows were the most prominent feature on her pale skin. She dabbed them with light-colored foundation. The result was magic. A Nordic stranger smiled back, with a pulse point fluttering wildly in her temple.

There was a foreign currency bar on her floor, near the elevator. She ordered an orange juice and waited until a group of four people rang for the elevator. She joined them and followed them off the elevator and across the lobby, alert for the man who had trailed her from Leningrad.

The National's front door faced the Kremlin. Her group turned left, straight at the man. He was leaning against a parked taxi, reading his newspaper by the street light, despite the cold, which turned his breath white and puffy. They swept past, Natalie hugging the inside, and turned up Gorky Street, away from the Kremlin. She moved with them, past the Intourist Hotel. A couple of them looked at her, but she kept going, head down, wrapping her scarf across her mouth and nose like the other Muscovites on the street.

A cafeteria appeared on the left and she dropped away, pausing in the doorway to glance back. She had done it. He was still guarding the corner, eyeing the front door of the National over his newspaper. Natalie stood on line for tea and sat near the door, waiting for another group to cover her exit. It was a busy spot, full of people coming and going singly. A group of three women were finishing their breakfast. Natalie prepared to follow, then dropped back in her chair, exhilaration fading. Something was wrong. She sensed someone was playing games with her and she was losing. She had missed something. No, worse, she had done something they had wanted her to do. What was the point in the guy changing clothes, shifting from the obvious to the subtle? Why not just bring in another person to follow her? Which of course, she realized with leaden finality, was exactly what they had done. A new face while she was congratulating herself on spotting the old. A dozen people had come in the cafeteria after her. One of them had come for her.

A woman at the next table was staring. Natalie looked at her and she turned away. The jacket. Of course, the leather jacket lined with warm, silky opossum was a Cotillion best seller. Women often stopped her on the street to ask where she had found it. She felt eyes somewhere in the silent throng and had to force herself not to swivel madly in every direction.

An older woman was watching from a standup counter, a stockily built woman with round, ruddy cheeks, chewing a pastry and staring at Natalie's feet. Natalie dismissed her too. Everyone knew Muscovites stared at good boots in winter. *Fine Italian leather boots:* she could almost hear Wallace savor the phrase.

A college kid took a table nearby and eyed her over a book he had propped beside his breakfast. He *looked* like a student in patched jeans, and even had a badly stenciled copy of a Princeton sweatshirt under his coat. And his book was a physics text. Natalie smiled at him. He ducked his head, embarrassed. All right, with her dark hair tucked under the wool cap, maybe she did look a little like Cybill Shepherd.

A gray uniform sleeve intruded on her view and her heart jumped. Two soldiers sat in the empty chairs at her table, grinning at the girl alone. She returned a smile she hoped looked shy and prayed they were too young and inexperienced to put serious thought to why she had light makeup on her eyebrows.

The cafeteria was hot, the air smoky and heavy with food smells. People continued to pour in and she despaired. It could be anyone here. Anyone waiting outside on the sidewalk. Frustrated, trapped, she felt, suddenly, that all she wanted to do was go back to the hotel and sleep.

She was a danger to whoever was waiting in the Kitai-Gorod. Even if Wallace's friends were clever enough to see she was followed, they would ignore her and the whole effort would be for nothing. But if they were not clever, who knew what would happen to them? She was a fool, she berated herself. She had smuggled *The Pearl* in hopes of this one last chance to believe in Wallace. His friends had responded. But she had blown it.

A workman in felt boots and a thick, quilted jacket brought his breakfast tray to the cashier, who totaled up the cost on an abacus. He paid and took his change. Coins went in his pocket, ruble notes in his billfold, which he then tried to slip inside the quilted jacket. Fumbling, he quickly reversed his action and shoved the billfold into his back pants pocket.

Natalie hid a triumphant grin. The "workman" was used to wearing a suit and had groped, carelessly, for the inside breast pocket where a man in a suit carried his wallet. Pulse rising, she watched him take a seat, three tables from hers. She smiled at the soldiers, glancing past them out the window, where trolleybuses headed up and down Gorky Street. The soldiers beamed. She saw the tail end of a line of people at the trolleybus stop up the street.

She stirred more sugar into her cup. A trolleybus approached. She held the spoon until the man in the quilted jacket had raised his cup to his lips. She moved quickly for the door.

A waddling babushka blocked the way. She went around the grandmother and pushed through the door, practically into the arms of a pair of gray-coated militiamen patrolling the sideway. Circling the police, she bolted into the broad street, weaving through the cars, and ignoring a shout. Reaching the westbound lanes, she ran with the flow of traffic, drawing ahead of the trolleybus to cross in front of it so the driver would see her and hold the door.

She lucked out. The driver was a woman and she waited, probably to get a look at her jacket. Working her way to the coin box to drop in a five-kopeck piece, Natalie looked back on her trail. She had made it. The "workman" had been trapped between the traffic and the militiamen, who were beckoning sternly from the sidewalk.

Her smile of triumph turned speculative; she had made it, but barely, for at that moment the red-faced woman who had stared at her "fine Italian boots" marched up to the militiamen, flashed something in her hand, and ordered the police away. Natalie nodded with satisfaction. She had learned something, and that made her escape even better.

A midmorning dawn had finally broken when Natalie rounded a turn in a narrow, twisting lane, a short walk from GUM, and sighted the restoration project. Dirty mustard-yellow paint flaked from the four-story warehouse, and here and there stucco had broken away, revealing the underlying wood and stone. A ramshackle wooden debris chute ran down the front.

Next door shone an example of what it would one day become—a beautifully renovated old building painted soft shades of rose with gleaming white embellishments trimming the window frames.

Through the open windows of the current project she saw men and women of various ages dismantling partitions and dropping the scraps down the chute. The pieces banged and rattled into a dump truck waiting at the bottom. In the truck, two men, dodging and laughing at near misses, spread the debris to keep the chute clear.

Natalie shook her dark hair from her hat and attached herself to a group that was following a sprightly little man who appeared to be explaining what was going on to volunteers.

"I'm Andrei," he said. "I'm the architect. And what we have here is the Gladishev Warehouse, built in the eighteenth century and greatly expanded in the nineteenth. Comrade Gladishev—or Monsieur Gladishev, as he was known before the Revolution—inherited a bakery business, which he parlayed into a vast empire of flour mills. He was one of the richest of the Moscow Millionaires, with huge estates across Russia and a grand mansion in Leningrad—St. Petersburg— where he maintained a salon for liberal-bourgeois political debate. He belonged to the Kadet Party and served in the Duma. The czar thought him a revolutionary and the revolutionaries thought him a czarist."

Andrei grinned at the group, a few of whom smiled at his casually irreverent reference to the Revolution. "So why do we restore it? Well, aside from its intrinsic value as a centrally located, sound old building, it has a delicious history. It was appropriated for the people's use after the Revolution and it is said that Lenin himself slept here—while hiding from reactionary assassins—in the very bed in the penthouse apartment where M. Gladishev used to entertain his mistress, the Countess . . ."

Natalie scanned the demolition crews for men or women likely to have sent her the message in the *Moscow Evening News*. She got looks back, but mostly from women intrigued by her jacket and jeans and men interested in a new face.

". . . The cellar and first floor will become a restaurant and the wagon yard within will be an outdoor cafe. What you'll do this morning is expose the cobblestones in the wagon yard. Follow me."

Andrei had already assigned the huskier men to demolishing partitions on the fourth floor. Now he led Natalie and several others through the building by a covered alley. The wagon yard was a surprisingly large space, enclosed by the warehouse on three sides and a wall on the fourth, and sheltering an old black-barked tree in the center.

Natalie joined the volunteers who were chipping at the frozen mud with picks and shoveling the broken chunks into wheelbarrows. Ten minutes passed slowly. Her fingers were getting cold through her

gloves. She waited another twenty minutes, then went out to the
street in case whoever had summoned her was watching the front.
When no one approached, she went back into the wagon yard. After
another half hour she tried again.

A gleaming red two-door Jaguar was rounding the corner, as incongruous a sight in the dirty, narrow lane as the moon drifting to a soft
landing in Central Park. It was the V-12 model Natalie had once
test-driven before settling, reluctantly, on the more practical BMW,
and probably burned as much expensive gasoline as a Soviet locomo-
tive. Its cost in rubles, not to mention the *blat* necessary to import it,
staggered the imagination.

Out of it, to her astonishment, stepped Luba.

The Russian beauty was bundled like the other volunteers in a
quilted jacket. Her golden hair was concealed by a thick, woolen
babushka, and she was adjusting a second scarf over her mouth and
nose. But there was no hiding her long-legged stance, and Natalie
recognized her instantly. Fuming, she waited until Luba saw her, then
stalked back into the wagon yard.

Luba joined her with a shovel.

"That was a pretty splashy arrival," Natalie snapped angrily. "Why'd
you bother with the code? Why didn't you just fax me at my hotel?"

"I always drive a Jag," Luba replied in Russian. "Not to would
arouse suspicion. Could you manage to speak Russian? This is
dangerous."

Natalie looked at her, saw genuine fear, and apologized hastily.
"Sorry. I just didn't expect you—"

"I am who I am. For now, I hope, I'm safer this way. Careful! Here
comes Andrei. He's not ours." Raising her voice as the architect
neared, she said, "You've dug down to the cobbles already."

"Where do we put it?" Natalie contributed to the charade, thinking
she would feel silly if earlier she had not been followed.

"Andrei," Luba called. "Where do we wheel the muck?"

"Out to the street. On the truck."

"Excuse me," said Natalie. "You said you're going to plant flowers. This is beautiful soil."

"City dirt?"

Luba shot her a frightened glance, but Natalie persisted, grasping
this unexpected link to the simpler, safer world of her Connecticut
gardens. "It's been under this tree for years. It's rich compost."

"*Yolki-Palki.* I'm a city boy. Spare me your peasantries." Looking her up and down, he asked, "Where are you from, dear? I don't recognize your accent. Is it Baltic?"

Natalie froze. She felt like a fool for starting the conversation and looked in desperation to Luba, who stammered, "She's from Petropavlovsky."

"*Where?*"

"Near Omsk. Beyond the Urals. Don't you travel?"

Surely, Natalie thought, the architect could hear the almost hysterical edge in Luba's voice, but all he said was, "I travel between Moscow and Leningrad, preferably by air. So, if the soil is good, put it there. We'll work around it."

"Andrei!" someone called. "The ceiling moved." The architect bolted into the building. Natalie closed shaking hands around the wheelbarrow handles and concentrated on the homey sound of the iron wheel grating on the hard ground. She trundled a load of frozen mud to the corner Andrei had indicated. Luba dropped all pretense and stood waiting with her shovel and shifting nervously from one foot to the other. Her face was twitching and her eyes rounded like a deer's. She was a wreck, Natalie thought. Hard to believe Wallace could have trusted his life to her.

Natalie positioned the wheelbarrow and resumed chipping the mud. "Why did you contact me?" she whispered.

"I found your advertisement in the *International Herald Tribune*. Why did you do that?"

"I wanted to know more about Vassily."

"Is that why you met the woman from London? Did she tell you what Vassily did?"

"How did my husband recruit you?"

"I loved him."

Natalie felt as if she had been hit in the face. Flesh on flesh; Wallace's body and Luba's. Mouths—

"I loved him," Luba repeated, defiantly. "I loved him more than you did."

"That is not true," she told the girl.

"I would not have let him come here alone."

"I don't have to defend that."

Luba's reply was a superior shrug. Natalie blinked hot tears. She tried to make herself ask, Did you sleep with him? but she was speechless, her body churning.

"It was exciting, at first, the spying," Luba explained, skating back to the brink of hysteria. "We had grand times. But it's gotten out of hand. They're trying to kill us."

Natalie whispered. "I don't believe you. My husband retired several years ago."

Something harsh and bitter flashed like heat lightning in Luba's eyes. "Permit me to guess," she sneered. "You were told he retired by the man he reported to."

"I didn't say it was a man."

"It doesn't matter. How would I know who he served? But Vassily did not retire. He was active to the last. He reported the day he died. Do you understand what that means? *The day he died.*"

"How do you know?"

"He *told* me he was going to report. That's why he gave me the message for the Millionaire."

"Wait." The NYPD homicide detective had said that Wallace had had his driver stop the car at a pay phone. She had wondered why he had not used the phone in their apartment or in the car. Now she realized he could not risk it. "Vassily telephoned you from New York?"

"No, no, no. I was *in* New York."

Natalie shook her head, trying to collect her thoughts. She was sure she was missing something. From the warehouse came a shout for a tea break. The other volunteers hurried inside. Natalie stood alone with Luba. Above the yard the sky was clearing, showing blue, and a silent bird had settled into the tree. Luba sniffled, rubbed her nose, and nervously patted the pockets of her quilted jacket.

"Wait! You said you didn't know Vassily was dead."

"I had immediately flown back to Soviet Union."

"It seems to me you travel very freely for a Soviet citizen. Five days later you came back to the States."

"My father is very highly placed," the Russian woman replied airily. "I go where I please."

Oh my God, thought Natalie, suddenly understanding Luba. She was like a space cadet from Bard or Sarah Lawrence, some corporate CEO's daughter playing at revolution. Her father's position explained Luba's extraordinary freedom to travel in and out of the Soviet Union. And there was the source of her stylish makeup, the expensive clothes she had worn in Connecticut, the haughty attitude, her Jag, even the chemical haze in her eyes. She was one of Moscow's fabled

"Gilded Youth," the *zolotaya molodyozh* who had flowered in the autumn of the Brezhnev era.

Natalie shook her head in sheer admiration. Who better to serve Wallace's information network with a special insiders' view than the pampered daughters of the *Nomenklatura*, the class that ran the Soviet Union?

"Why do you smile?" Luba demanded.

"I think I'm proud of him. . . . So Vassily gave you a message to carry back to Russia. The message you gave the Millionaire . . . the message about Valentine's Day," Natalie prompted.

"He laughed," Luba said bitterly.

"Who was he?"

"I don't know."

"You *called* him!"

"Vassily only gave me the telephone number, not his name. He always broke information into small pieces. The man laughed because he already knew that Vassily was dead. Vassily was betrayed."

"By whom?"

"The Millionaires."

"Who are the Millionaires?"

Luba had finally located a pack of Marlboros. Extracting a cigarette clumsily with her gloves on, she put it in her mouth. Natalie noticed charred wool where her cigarettes had burned the fingers.

"Who are the Millionaires? Answer me!" Losing patience, she grabbed Luba's arm. In that instant she felt someone rush up behind them.

"There you are, Luba. We've been looking everywhere."

Natalie turned to see a beautiful young girl, younger than Luba, with silky black hair that fanned from a knit hat and framed her pale cheeks like lace. What she thought at first was a bruise, a faint darkness on her cheek, was a birthmark that made her look both mysterious and vulnerable, and Natalie knew immediately that this was another of Wallace's tall, lean goddesses.

"Elena, this is her," Luba whispered. "The American. Vassily's American."

Elena spoke soothingly, as if to a child. "We've been looking everywhere. Nikita is waiting outside."

Luba's eyes skipped hungrily toward the alley.

"Go see Nikita," Elena coaxed. "I'll talk to your friend."

"Wait," said Natalie, but Luba was already springing into the alley. "Where's she going?"

"Nikita sells her drugs. Now you must go."

Behind her fixed smile, Elena looked terrified, as afraid as Luba herself had been the day Natalie had first met her six thousand miles from Moscow. An artery beat hard in her throat and she had the same wild look in her eye, a heartbeat from panic. Natalie warred with her own terror; it was dangerous enough, talking to Luba, but a stranger.... Yet she trusted in the girl's fear. No one could pretend such terror.

"Luba should not have contacted you. Go home, while you can. It's too dangerous."

"But Luba—"

"You're putting yourself—and us—at risk."

"But Luba asked for my help."

"Luba was too attached to Vassily," Elena replied. Natalie flinched, but the Russian girl didn't notice. "It was Luba's insane idea to see you in America and her idea to approach you in Leningrad. We begged her not to, but she has no discipline. You saw her, running to her pusher like a starving beggar. Would you trust her?"

But Wallace had trusted her. Or had he, too, been "too attached"? Elena turned to go.

"Just answer one question," Natalie pleaded. "Who are the Millionaires?"

"Go back to Leningrad, Mrs. Nevsky. Buy your furs and go home."

Elena hurried toward the alley. Natalie stared helplessly after her, while inside her a voice screamed a futile What would Wallace have done?

Just then Andrei appeared, balancing a tray of steaming glasses of tea. Elena started to edge past him and Natalie saw her chance.

"Elena!" she called loudly. "Here's Andrei. Andrei, my friend Elena has come to volunteer. Can she work with me?"

For one second the Russian girl could have kept going, but surprise or fear caused her to hesitate. Natalie darted across the yard, grabbed two of the tea glasses and shoved one into Elena's gloves. "Tea! You must be frozen. I am. Andrei, is it all right?"

The architect cast an appraising eye over Elena's dark beauty. "No problem. Where's Luba?"

"She had to go to the doctor."

Andrei's gaze fell on the single pile of earth Natalie had dumped in

THE WIDOW OF DESIRE 247

the corner. "How long does it take to move some dirt? I thought you peasants were hard workers. Are you another peasant, Elena?"

Natalie said, "The earth is very hard. We'll do better."

"Tell me," he asked. "What do you do when you're not playing peasant?"

Elena stared mutely into her glass.

"I work for Sojuzpushnina," Natalie answered, gulping the hot brew quickly to get rid of him. "In Leningrad."

"What are you doing in Moscow?"

"Visiting my boyfriend. But he's working today."

"You look a little old for a boyfriend. I thought you'd be married."

Natalie turned to Elena. "Are Moscow men always so tactful?"

Elena ignored her, but Andrei blithely replied, "I'm nicer in Leningrad. May I visit you there?"

"In Leningrad, my husband would object."

Andrei returned a slow smile. "Perhaps I'll undertake a restoration in Novgorod. You could meet me halfway."

Natalie returned the glass. "I think I have a full plate, already. Drink up, Elena. We'll get warm working." Elena returned her glass with murmured thanks. Andrei walked away, shaking his head, and Natalie handed Elena a shovel.

"You think you're very clever."

Natalie shook her head. "I feel like a bull in a china shop. All I want to know is why my husband was killed and who did it. Who are the Millionaires?"

"I can't help you."

Natalie played her best card. She was, after all, their only link to Wallace in America. "But I can help you."

"Oh?"

"I know who my husband reported to. I can relay a message."

"No," Elena cried. "Do not do that."

"Why not?"

"Don't. You mustn't. Please."

Natalie did not know how she had done it, but she had unwittingly turned the tables. Now it was Elena who pleaded. "Do not do that. Tell no one. No one."

Natalie felt a cold certainty as she deliberately worked the wedge of the young woman's fear. "I'm obliged to report to my husband's superior, what I've seen and heard so far."

Elena turned white and looked suddenly older, and Natalie had an eerie feeling she feared for more than her personal safety. "You don't know what you're saying."

"Enlighten me."

Elena hesitated. "You don't understand what is at stake."

Instinct born of a thousand negotiations told Natalie it was time to shift to gentler tactics. "I'm on your side," she assured Elena. "Vassily's side. I would never hurt his friends."

"You ask too much."

"I've already given my husband. Tell me why."

Elena looked to the sky as if for deliverance, but there was none, only another young woman, muffled in scarves, who seemed to be standing watch on the roof. Sober, weary, and resigned, Elena capitulated.

"All right. I'll tell you the little I know from Vassily, and Luba, and what I've learned since Vassily died. . . . God help all of us if you don't have the intelligence to understand the danger.

"Your husband code-named the Millionaires after the so-called Moscow Millionaires. He said they were merchants who grew richer than the aristocracy and demanded that the czar make Russia a modern country."

"But who are they now?"

"They are a group of generals and technocrats who conspire to make change. They're in the highest echelons of the *Nomenklatura*. Some are on the Central Committee even, some in the Politburo, and some in the Army. Especially the Army, Vassily thought."

"Is this going on *now*?"

"Yes."

Natalie's heart filled. Wallace Nevsky had neither been the victim of his mistress, nor an old fool who did not know when to quit. "And this 'boss,'" she asked eagerly, "is their leader?"

"'The Boss' was an old name for Comrade Stalin, the General Secretary who led the Soviet Union through the Great Patriotic War. Vassily apparently did not like this Stalin at all. I think perhaps he knew more about him than we learned in school. The leader of the Millionaires adopted the old name. They say that Russia needs Stalinesque leadership—discipline—to reform the economy."

"But Gorbachev is a reformer."

"The Millionaires say Gorbachev has failed."

"Failed? He's just getting started."

Elena shrugged. "They blame him for the Azerbaijan riots. They blame him for the bootleg vodka. They blame him for the economy, for resistance in the Warsaw nations, and especially for the debacle in Afghanistan."

"Do you think he's failed?"

"What I think does not matter. It is what the Millionaires think that matters. They accuse him of promising much and delivering little. But remember this: the Millionaires know that if the General Secretary succeeds with his reforms, many will lose their privileges. So you see, there are some elements with whom he cannot win."

"Did Wallace know who the Boss is?"

"I don't know."

"Can you guess?"

"Only that he is likely someone who lost out to Gorbachev in the Politburo. So along with everything else, his quarrel could be personal."

Natalie nodded. For a people who had endured rule by Catherine the Great, Peter, Nikolai Lenin, and Joseph Stalin, the personal was rarely absent from Russian history.

"Did Vassily—did my husband support the Millionaires?"

"Never!"

"Are you sure?"

"He said they would destroy Russia."

Traitor! the woman with the gun had accused. She had been angry—Natalie knew at last—because Wallace had infiltrated the conspiracy.

But he had failed to stop it.

"What is Valentine's Day?"

"It can only be," Elena answered bleakly, "the day of the coup d'état."

20

coup?" Natalie echoed. "In *Russia?*"

Vladimir Rostov flew to mind—the *perestroika* plutocrat—and she imagined the jolly spokesman of *glasnost* shuffling into a gray prison yard, smart suit filthy, face blank with fear of those who had seized control in the name of discipline. Impossible?

"The KGB will stop it. They're everywhere."

"That was Vassily's greatest fear. If the KGB catches wind of the plot, there will be a purge, maybe even a civil war."

"But you say there are Millionaires in the Central Committee, the Politburo, and the Army. A plot that big can't be kept secret. The KGB must be aware."

"Probably they're investigating. But the Millionaires also have supporters in the KGB. And Valentine's Day is only one week from today."

"They know *something*," Natalie insisted. "A KGB officer was watching in the lobby when I checked into my hotel. I was followed to the airport, on the plane, and again on Gorky Street."

Fear flared anew in Elena's eyes. "Vassily said the Millionaires would make Russia a slaughterhouse. He said we were the only ones who could stop them."

"How?"

"Quiet as mice. No one could know or the KGB would tear Russia

250

to pieces. That's why I speak to you. I warn you. You can't just report willy-nilly. It will get back to the KGB."

High above Natalie, through the tree's black branches, the pale, liquid sky seemed to circle as if the courtyard were spinning and she were at the vortex. "How many are you?" she asked.

"Everyone's hiding. The Millionaires are hunting us."

The entire Moscow apparatus had gone underground, Elena explained. Fighting to survive had taken precedence over carrying on Wallace's commitment to stop the Millionaires.

Natalie said, "Luba said Vassily was betrayed."

"Yes. We managed to trace the telephone number Vassily gave her. The man who laughed, who knew Vassily was dead, was a Captain Nestorov."

"Is he the Boss?"

"Just a functionary on the staff of Marshal Lapshin."

"Lapshin?"

"Do you know this man?"

Lap. Lap-something, Leo Margulies had said, trying to recall the name of Wallace's old Red Army friend. "Who is he?"

"Viktor Lapshin is on the Chief Military Council. Only the Defense Council is higher."

"How do you know?"

"My father is a general," said Elena, and again Natalie had an image of Wallace raiding Moscow's better girls' academies for his little spies.

"I want to meet Marshal Lapshin."

The girl looked at Natalie as if she were insane. Big eyes opened wide and her mouth formed an incredulous pout. Natalie took her arm. "If I can get close enough to introduce myself as Vassily's widow, Marshal Lapshin might talk to me."

"If I could get close enough to God," Elena muttered, "he'd make me a saint."

"Is Viktor Lapshin in Moscow?"

"Possibly," said Elena. "There's an army reception at the Kremlin tonight."

"Get me invited."

"My own father isn't invited. It's terribly top drawer—general staff, Central Committee, Politburo, and perhaps a few ambassadors."

Natalie's gaze flickered about the cold, empty wagon yard. "Do you think Luba is still functioning?"

"Stay away from her."

Natalie tossed her shovel in the wheelbarrow and ran through the covered alley into the street. Luba was leaning against the dump truck, cracking jokes with a couple of dazzled young men clearing the chute. Whatever she had inhaled or swallowed had left her bright-eyed and jovial. She listened amiably to Natalie's request.

"No problem," she said, hurrying down the street. "Back soon."

Elena had disappeared, Natalie discovered when she returned to the wagon yard. Andrei spotted Natalie and told her to work on the fourth floor where the volunteers were carrying pieces of broken partitions. Luba found her there, half an hour later, and they spoke against a noise curtain of plaster banging down the walls of the chute.

"The reception is to honor a Politburo candidate who's been appointed deputy defense minister. It's in the Kremlin."

"Will Marshal Lapshin be there?"

"Almost certainly," Luba assured her. But she admitted, when Natalie pressed her, that she had had no luck procuring an invitation. Natalie began stuffing her hair into her hat again. "Will you meet me here tomorrow?"

"Where are you going?"

"I'm going to meet this guy."

She ran down the stairs, ducked past Andrei, who was helping clear the jammed debris chute, and hurried away from the warehouse, pausing as she rounded street corners to see if she was being followed. Certain at last she was not, she passed between the remnants of the old city walls and emerged from the tangled lanes of the Kitai-Gorod district. The sky spread open over Revolution Square. Diagonally across from her was the National Hotel.

Pacing her room, with her eyes fixed on the thick Kremlin Walls across the Marx Prospekt, she telephoned Fyodor Shelpin in Leningrad, and asked the Sojuzpushnina official if he could get her an invitation to the reception.

"What a bore," said Shelpin. "You'd be so much happier at the Bolshoi. Now, as luck would have it, I have a dear friend in Moscow who is a grand balletomane. That is the right word? An aficionado.

He'll take you backstage afterwards, and perhaps to supper with the performers. I'll call him now and get right back to you."

"Mr. Shelpin, I appreciate that and ordinarily would love the opportunity, but it is very important to me to go to that reception."

"You have no idea what a bore such an event is. Why would you even want to go?"

"I'm hoping to run into some old friends of Vassily."

"Ah. Well, I'll see what I can do."

She waited an anxious half hour, but Shelpin did not call back. Finally, she called him.

"I was just about to telephone. It's impossible. They simply do not invite foreigners, other than a few ambassadors. Still, I have good news."

"What?" she asked eagerly.

"The ballet—"

"No, I don't think so, Mr. Shelpin."

"Let me finish. There is a man very important in Sojuzpushnina—a man who might help your business, I am sure—who wishes you might join him and his wife at the ballet."

"Was he a friend of Wallace?" she asked, wondering whether he was part of Wallace's net. Shelpin dashed her hopes.

"No. They never met. This man, quite young, is recently moved to Sojuzpushnina from Foreign Trade Ministry."

Natalie stared across the square. She was in a quandary. The fur monopoly official with foreign trade ties sounded exactly like the sort of Soviet bureaucrat she should cultivate.

"From what I understand of your discussion with Comrade Rostov," Shelpin prompted, "I think this man could be very useful to your cause."

She was caught again between her fight to save Cotillion and her passion to make sense of Wallace's death. Passion won, again.

"Thank you, Mr. Shelpin, but I'm committed now to attending the reception. Thank you very much. I'll see you in Leningrad on Monday."

Shelpin did not take her refusal graciously, and continued to mutter about disappointments. She told herself she had already made the necessary connection with Rostov, but it was a lie. Rostov was hardly in the bag. At this point Cotillion needed every break that came along, and she had just turned another down.

Natalie telephoned the American embassy. The chargé d'affaires, she was told, was off for the weekend. No, the duty officer could not help. She persuaded the operator to call the chargé at home and ask him to return her call at the National. He did, in ten minutes, but he sounded brusque, like a man who did not want to conduct business on a Saturday.

Natalie reminded him who she was. "My father mentioned you served together in Prague."

"I was under him, in Prague, for a while. I got a note someplace on my desk, now that you mention it. He said you'd be in Leningrad. Enjoying yourself?"

"Very much, thank you. I came down to Moscow to see some of my husband's friends."

"That's nice. I think we sent you an invitation to a party here next week. We're receiving some hockey team. Might be fun if you can make it down this way again."

"Actually, the reason I called is that Cotillion Furs is expanding our Russian pelt purchases for our Canadian suppliers and I'm trying to solidify some of the contacts my husband maintained so long in the Soviet Union."

"We have a trade guy you ought to talk to Monday."

"There's a reception tonight at the Kremlin. I imagine some of his army friends will be there. I'd love to go."

The chargé d'affaires laughed. "So would half of Moscow. That's a hot ticket. The only reason my wife and I are going is that the ambassador is tied up escorting some Jewish émigrés through immigration."

"Could you possibly slip a second woman on your dance card?"

"Sorry, Mrs. Nevsky. Hope to see you at the hockey reception. We'll have a drink. 'Bye now."

Natalie hung up, seething. Maybe it was too big a favor to ask, but he could have been a lot more respectful in the way he ignored her father's request to extend courtesies. So it was with a certain malicious pleasure that she asked the hotel operator to dial Greg Stuart's anytime number in Washington, D.C.

It took an hour to get through. It was early morning there and Greg was not in his office. Worried, she left her number. Greg was her last shot and it was getting late. The sky was darkening over the Kremlin. Watching the ruby red stars above the towers grow brighter and brighter, she waited another hour, ordering tea and cakes from room service, but afraid to shower and miss the telephone. Finally it rang.

The connection was awful, but it was Greg's voice, asking, "Are you all right?"

"It's wonderful to hear you," she said, startled by the intensity of her reaction.

"Good to hear you too. It's been a while." They had not spoken since the night she met Jefferson Jervis.

"I mean to speak English to you, so far away." The man who had followed her was not at the hotel when she returned, but she assumed the telephone was tapped.

"You okay?"

"Sure. Fine. Fine. Listen, I need a very big favor. There's a party I want to go to at the Kremlin, tonight. A lot of Wallace's friends are going to be there. My father's friend Finny at the embassy has invitations, but he says he can't take me. Could you rattle his chain?"

"It sounds important," Greg said, as if he too were trying to talk around a tap.

"It would have made Wallace happy, I think."

"Anything for the fur trade," Greg answered.

Natalie took a shower, soaked the cold out of her bones, and laid out a finely knit wool Perry Ellis sheath that she hoped her gold jewelry would dress up enough for what had to be a formal affair.

Finny called at six o'clock, his voice flat as an ironing board.

"Natalie, how are you, dear? The damnedest thing just happened. Poor Carolyn caught a horrible bug."

"Ohhh."

"Moscow swamp flu, probably. It'll jump you faster than a New York minute. Anyway, she's buried under quilts and hot water bottles. If you're still free, by any chance, could you please accompany me to that party we were talking about?"

"Sure, if you need me."

"You're a brick, Natalie. Carolyn would hate for me to go alone. Pick you up in an hour."

Mollifying Finny was top priority. Getting into the party was one thing; she needed a guide, better yet, an ally. But the chargé d'affaires was livid. He looked a lot like a balding Harry Truman, with a perfect little mustache and dapper evening clothes. He was short, his shiny dome coming up to her shoulder, and as he helped her into the car, an embassy limousine flying American flags, no less, he muttered icily, out of earshot of his Russian driver, "Let's just stretch the truth a little further and say you're my goddamned goddaughter."

Natalie kissed his cheek. "Thank you, very much. And my father thanks you, too."

"Well, he seems to have raised a splinter off the old block, I'll give him that."

GAI traffic police controlled the Marx Prospekt along the Kremlin Wall, stopping traffic to let long lines of Zil, Mercedes, and Cadillac limousines turn into the gate in the Borovitsky Tower at the western corner. "Most of the license plates are black," Natalie commented, in a desperate gambit to start a conversation. "Ours is red. What does that mean?"

"It means you're crashing a party for the cream of the *vlasti*."

"Red means diplomat?"

"Right. This do is Russian only, except for us, the Brits, the French, and maybe the Japs. The Red Army has a lot in common with the Japs—both have an interest in stealing American computers."

"I am evermore grateful, Mr. Finny."

"Better call me Uncle David."

At the gate, military guards in full dress regalia inspected their invitations and peered into the car before allowing them into the tunnellike gateway. Emerging from the wall, the car labored up a steep road. On the left were an armory museum and the Grand Kremlin Palace. On the right, Natalie saw the tops of massive fir trees looming up from a park in the hollow below the road, and she had the feeling they had left the world, as well as the city of Moscow, behind them at the gate.

They entered the Square of Cathedrals, a grouping of onion-domed churches and cathedrals, some solemn, others lively with gilt shining in the lights. Natalie asked about the octagonal tower rising in their midst, but Finny had fallen as silent as the great iron Czar Cannon at its base. The car stopped in a line of vehicles at a canopy where soldiers opened the doors and held umbrellas against a misty snow that had just begun to fall.

In the foyer, cadets took their coats and showed Natalie where she could exchange her boots for heels. Her mother had reminded her of the Russian custom.

Finny steered her toward a reception line. Beyond it, Natalie saw a gilt ballroom lit by gigantic crystal chandeliers. There was music and long *zakuska* tables. Liveried waiters passed champagne on silver trays.

"Don't tell anybody, but the Czar's back."

Finny had already remarked favorably upon her conservative dress. Now his mustache twitched in what might have been a smile. "The Red Army is not afraid to flaunt it, even under the new regime."

"This room is breathtaking."

"The Soviets are the most elegant revolutionaries on the planet."

"But things look so seedy in the streets."

"They're better at big display, like the subways, the war monuments. If you want shop windows you go to the French; of course, Versailles looks as if Sotheby's has looted the furniture. Here, thanks to Lenin, they kept the mob outside the palace. That throne over there's been sitting in that corner for five hundred years."

Natalie was wondering how she would pick out Marshal Lapshin or even Captain Nestorov from the sea of uniforms undulating across the ballroom floor when Finny said, "That's Politburo candidate Khodinko manning the receiving line with his wife. Couple of army marshals behind him, Aksyonov and Kapiusky, I think."

"Khodinko's wife is gorgeous."

"That's how you tell the new regime from the old. The Gorbachev wives are svelte. The old Brezhnev crowd married bears.... Of course, *they* could afford mistresses."

The Politburo candidate and his wife conducted the reception line with the practiced ease of a pair of Upper East Side Manhattan fundraisers, accepting the American ambassador's regrets, welcoming Finny in English, conveying sympathy to his ailing wife, and greeting Natalie warmly. An aide murmured in Mrs. Khodinko's ear and her smile broadened. "Cotillion Furs, of course. I bought one of your coats when last in New York. A gorgeous ranch mink. Gregori, Mrs. Nevsky manufactured my coat from America."

"Customs was not amused," her husband replied with a suave smile. "Coals to Newcastle, they said. We finally persuaded them we were bringing it home to copy."

"I'm flattered," Natalie replied in Russian. "Please come and see me the next time you're in New York."

They moved along the reception line, but neither of the military men blinked an eye at the name Nevsky.

"Didn't realize you spoke Russian," Finny said admiringly.

"My father wanted me to be a diplomat."

"What happened?"

"I wanted to be rich."

Waiters brought champagne and they strolled through the ball-room, with Finny introducing Natalie to Russians and Europeans, who dutifully expressed sympathy for the chargé's wife, while eyeing Natalie curiously. He was a find, she thought. He seemed to know everyone and had a story about many.

"Tell me something. Could you call this a pro- or anti-Gorbachev crowd?"

Finny chuckled. "That depends on who's listening."

"Seriously."

"The Red Army's conservative, of course, but Gorby's been careful not to offend it too much, though he did get a little ham-handed when the German kid dropped in."

"What about the civilians?" There were more guests out of uniform than she had expected at a military reception.

"The young hotshots are his people, and I don't see too many old mossbacks from the old days here tonight. I'd call this a new wave crowd. The opposition is pretty amorphous and not very organized."

"What does the opposition want?"

"Like the song says, they want to do it their way. Sure, they pay lip service to discipline, but not at the expense of their own privilege. It's the same old story here for years. Socialism works as long as you have an elite running it. They just want to exchange elites."

"Could you imagine an actual coup?"

Finny chuckled at the absurdity of such a thought. "Yeah, led by a deprived alcoholic. If anything pisses them off it's the crackdown on vodka."

"Of which I see no shortage here."

"I told you, the man's a clever politician," Finny answered, leading Natalie to yet another officer for an introduction.

It was a big party and obviously she couldn't count on bumping into Lapshin. Finny, of course, knew she had some reason to want to be here and finally asked, "Anyone special you want to meet?"

Natalie said, "My husband spoke of so many people. There was a Marshal Lapshin. Is he here by any chance?"

Finny had the diplomat's gift for surveying a room without appearing to. "I just saw him . . ." Natalie thought again of her mother as she moved slowly with him, so neither appeared obvious. "There! Heavyset bald gent, through that doorway. Built like a tank." Finny indicated a doorway that led into one of the picture galleries that ringed the ballroom. "That's him, the one with more battle ribbons than Goliath."

She spotted him. He was as broad as Eddie Mayall, with a fringe of cropped white hair circling his massive head.

"Why isn't Lapshin on the reception line?"

"Good question. Back at the embassy, five sovietologists are working on that as we speak. We know he's on the Stavka, the Chief Military Council, and he was commander-in-chief of Soviet Group Forces in Germany, which is a sure road to the top. But the word around is the Gen Sec canned him, so he won't make it to the Defense Council, which sits with the Politburo. My guess is Lapshin's slipping down the pole, but that's just a guess. You could spend your life— and guys do—trying to figure out who runs the Red Army. Want to meet him?"

Natalie touched his arm with a smile. "I'm monopolizing you. I'll wander. I'm sure you've got people you have to see."

"Appreciate that," Finny said. "I'll look for you at dinner." He departed, hailing a Russian naval officer who greeted him like an old friend.

Natalie worked her way across the crowded ballroom, exchanged her empty glass for a fresh one, and approached the picture gallery. Lapshin was plodding from painting to painting, planting himself in front of each with a belligerent scowl. Heels clicking on the gleaming parquet, Natalie entered the gallery and strode to a magnificent Levitan landscape that hung in Lapshin's path.

Another couple completed the circuit and left them alone, the Red Army marshal standing several paintings down the wall from the American widow. Natalie knew when he moved closer because the medals that blanketed half his chest made a muted ringing sound, like the tinkle of candle-driven brass angels spinning above the flames. It was a pretty noise and the third time she heard it, Marshal Lapshin was standing beside her, glowering at the Levitan while inspecting her sidelong.

"Good trees," he remarked of the mossy birches.

"They remind me of home," Natalie answered. "The light."

"America?"

Leave it to a ranking soldier to recognize an American accent.

"Connecticut."

"You must be rich."

Natalie turned to face him. He looked like a fat old poodle—amiable, fuzzy, content, and infinitely wise. She made a conscious decision not to underestimate him, and extended her hand. "Good evening, sir, I am Natalie Stuart Nevsky."

"Viktor Lapshin." He shook her hand, looked at her ring and asked, "And your husband?"

"I am widowed."

"So young! Wait! Mrs. *Nevsky*. *Bozhe Moy*, Vassily's bride!"

21

Marshal Lapshin seized Natalie's shoulders and kissed her hard on the cheeks. "So young, so young," he cried. Tears poured from his eyes. "I served with Vassily's father in the war. Horse soldiers. *Cavalry,* can you imagine?" He bellowed laughter at the thought, even while he wept. "The Cossack! Then, in forty-two, came the little American Cossack. But he was not little for long. What a man you had."

Natalie tried to read the old marshal and failed abysmally, unable to bridge the gulf of years, miles, history, and culture that sabotaged her instincts, unable to judge whether Lapshin's tears were anything less than a genuine demonstration of the famous Russian emotionalism. But it did seem strange how long he had taken to recognize her name.

"Now, poor Vassily, even younger than me, to die."

"Well, Wallace didn't exactly die in that sense, Marshal Lapshin. He was shot."

"Is this true? We heard, but it sounded so . . . insane. Have they arrested the killer?"

"Not yet."

"Ah. You hear about American violence, but you don't think of it happening to someone you know. Crazy world we live in. I'm delighted to meet you. I wish it were happier times."

"Did you know my husband well?"

"He would visit, time to time. More so in recent years, when he helped me with a mink breeding project."

"Were you close?"

"What is close? You see a man once or twice a year for forty years. One day he dies and you say to yourself, *Bozhe Moy*, he was my friend. And how are you, Mrs. Nevsky? What are you doing in Russia?"

"I came for the Leningrad auction," she answered, imagining an edge to his question.

"What a lovely coincidence you should end up in Moscow at this party."

"I took the weekend off. The party was a bonus. An old friend of my parents is chargé d'affaires at our embassy."

"Ah," said Lapshin, his expression opaque.

I am the dead man's wife, Natalie reminded herself of her position. The widow. His friend will treat me as if I know nothing. But he has to answer a widow's questions. "When did you last see Wallace?"

Lapshin hesitated and she thought he was going to lie. Instead of answering he snapped his fingers. An aide who was hovering near the door gestured and two waiters in army uniforms marched into the picture gallery, one bearing iced vodka, the other golden champagne in a crystal-clear bottle.

"We will drink to Vassily," said Lapshin. "He liked champagne. Is that your taste, too?"

"Yes, please. *Zolotoye*, isn't it? I've never had it."

The vodka waiter was dismissed and the Russian champagne opened and poured. Lapshin seized the bottle and unwrapped the towel. "You see the glass is clear?"

"Yes."

"It is said Louis Roederer designed this bottle for Alexander the third so the czar could see if assassins had put poison in his wine. And see here." Marshal Lapshin showed her that the bottle had a flat bottom. "No punt."

"No room to hide a bomb?"

"How did you know?"

"Vassily told me."

Crestfallen, Lapshin moaned, "He spoiled my story."

"Vassily could not tell me why you still use the bottle. The czars are gone."

"Inertia, perhaps," Lapshin replied with a sly smile for the opulent palace. "Or, perhaps, the czars live on. . . ."

"Perhaps," said Natalie, "assassins do, too."

Lapshin looked at her. If she lived to be a hundred, she thought, she would never know whether she had seen or imagined a cold shadow in his eye. "When did you last see Vassily?" she asked again.

In that instant, Lapshin's round face brightened with warmth and pride as he waved to someone coming up behind her. "Come here, come here. I've captured a beautiful American."

Natalie turned to see a youthful Russian general with a line of medals on his chest. He was short and compact, with a full, well-formed, sensual mouth. A slight stiffness in his right cheek suggested plastic surgery, and the hand he extended had a lattice of fine white scar tissue. His eyes were small, steady, and hazel-colored, she thought. It was hard to tell in the light from the paintings.

"My son," Marshal Lapshin announced proudly. "General Aleksandr Lapshin. This is Mrs. Nevsky, Aleksandr. She was married to our friend Vassily, the American furrier."

"Of course." Aleksandr Lapshin smiled, and Natalie smiled back, intrigued. If his father was a wise old poodle, Aleksandr Lapshin possessed the careless grace—and the controlled violence—of a hunting bird. Keyed up, as he probably always was, he looked a little dangerous. Had she met him in New York she might have guessed he was one of those rare corporation men who manage to streak skyward by breaking the rules.

"Welcome to Moscow," he said, and surprised her by taking her hand with a courtly half-bow. "My father knew your husband many years. I met him several times."

"Recently?"

"What do you think of her, boy?" Marshal Lapshin demanded. "Vassily did all right for himself, didn't he?"

"Forgive my father." Lapshin smiled, switching easily from Russian to English. "He abuses the privileges of old age. What are you doing here?"

"As I just told your father, I'm buying furs," Natalie replied in Russian, anxious to keep them both in the conversation.

"Not in Moscow."

"In Moscow I'm a tourist."

"Don't tell me Intourist put this reception on the package tour."

"I sort of stumbled in the last moment. The chargé d'affaires is an old family friend."

"The last American I met by chance sent me to the hospital for six months."

Natalie glanced uncertainly at Lapshin, senior, who looked perplexed. "I'm afraid I don't follow."

"Her name was Stinger. We met in Afghanistan."

"Aleksandr," cautioned his father, but Aleksandr ignored him.

"She slid up my gunship's engine exhaust like an old friend. There was a hell of a fire when we hit ground." He offered Natalie a stiff grin, challenging her to answer. Russians, Wallace—who loved them—always insisted, respected strength, and doubly so in a woman.

"It sounds as if you weren't liked in Afghanistan."

"They learned to hate from the Vietnamese," Lapshin parried. "They're awfully good at it. I'm not complaining, mind you. I went into the Hindu Kush a colonel; I came out a general."

"Be careful," said his father, nodding toward the door. A group of men and women were entering, chattering and laughing. Behind them, staring over their heads, was the tall KGB officer Natalie had seen at the Astoria Hotel.

"What is he doing here?" Marshal Lapshin murmured.

Aleksandr shrugged. "Kirichenko! Over here. We caught an American. Maybe she's a spy. . . . Or is it us you're after?"

"Don't antagonize him," his father ordered.

Kirichenko approached, parting the group between them like a blade, greeted the marshal with a younger man's deference, and traded stiff nods with Aleksandr.

"Valery Kirichenko, meet Mrs. Nevsky. Did you know her husband Vassily?"

Kirichenko extended a bony hand and said coolly, "I have met your husband. I understand he was shot. I offer my condolences."

Natalie nodded her thanks and pressed her hand to her side to stop it shaking. The younger Lapshin noticed.

"We were just saying what a wonderful war we've had in Afghanistan, Kirichenko. It's a hundred times more effective than training exercises. Officers and noncoms blooded, tens of thousands of troops rotated through the action. . . ."

His father looked concerned, if not afraid, that his son was openly baiting the KGB officer, whose face remained expressionless. But if

Natalie doubted whether Lapshin's remarks were unusual, she only had to look at the people nearby who were hanging on every bold word the young general uttered: "We are not a peacetime army anymore."

Natalie asked, "Are you trying to shock me again, or is this more of the *glasnost* I've been hearing so much about?"

General Lapshin grinned. "If you prefer I treat you like a fool, let me say, instead, we are fighting the good fight against counterrevolutionary elements perfidiously establishing a hostile regime along our exposed southern flank. The future of communism hangs in the balance."

He glanced about the party, his eyes quick and amused, daring the tall KGB man to contradict him. "But something tells me you're not a fool, Mrs. Nevsky, so I won't lie. Nor will I apologize. No one knows better than an American that great powers need great armies. And great armies are honed in blood. Don't you agree, Kirichenko?"

"Foreign blood, preferably."

As if determined to provoke the KGB officer at any cost, Lapshin said, "Just as policemen strengthen their eyesight peeping through keyholes."

"Protecting the homes of those brave soldiers at the front."

The two men locked eyes and hatred shimmered between them like heat rising from sun-baked sand. Natalie chose the moment to goad them in another direction. "Americans have the impression that Russia is in the midst of a new revolution."

"It's as much hope as truth," General Lapshin replied bleakly.

Kirichenko, however, seemed eager to answer. "We do have a revolution, guided by General Secretary Gorbachev. It is happening exactly as Lenin explained it must when he said a revolutionary situation exists when the top layers can no longer rule in the old way and the bottom layers can no longer live in the old way. While Brezhnev slept and the Soviet people healed the wounds of the Great Patriotic War, our new and educated generation took a place among the leadership."

Animated, he nodded about the picture gallery and the ballroom beyond. "Yuri, there, head of his department at Moscow University; his wife, a surgeon. There, Aleksandr, editor; Mikhail, physicist; Ivan, gas plasma engineer."

"At least two of whom are sponsored by the KGB," Lapshin interrupted. "In a fine tradition of recruiting the best young minds in the Motherland—or should I say subverting?" He turned to Natalie, who had begun to suspect that the Soviet general was a little drunker than he looked. "Few Westerners are aware, Mrs. Nevsky, that Comrade Kirichenko's KGB has hundreds of departments, research institutes, and think tanks that employ battalions of enlightened sophisticates. An elite within the elite, protectors of the party and centurions of the ideology. Baffling, isn't it, Kirichenko, this persistent image of a gang of spies, policemen, and jailers?"

Kirichenko ignored him. "A new generation, Mrs. Nevsky. Can you imagine what the new Gen Sec means to men and women like these?"

Kirichenko's enthusiasm seemed ingenuous, but several of the men and women he had looked at appeared discomfited at having drawn his attention.

"A gentleman in Leningrad told me, 'He's our guy.' "

"That's it!" Something like a smile moved on the KGB officer's lips.

"Camelot on ice?" the younger Lapshin asked with heavy sarcasm.

Kirichenko's face closed up, but Natalie had to agree that a lively energy emanated from the well-dressed men and women in their forties who shone like jewels among the military uniforms. With all the trim bodies and good tailoring and stylish coifs and handsome neckties and gold earrings, the Kremlin reception resembled a gathering of competitive, accomplished professionals at a Georgetown cocktail party.

Kirichenko turned his cold gaze on Natalie. "Gorbachev lived fine, and I lived fine, under the old system, but we're smashing it up anyway because it doesn't work for the country."

"You reformers conveniently ignore who you are dealing with," said General Lapshin. "The Russian people are not necessarily fodder for the new order. *Perestroika* and *glasnost* and economic reforms and the right to go into business lead to what? In Moscow last summer, every third citizen opened a lemonade stand. I've never seen anything like it, except in America, where on the first hot day, lemonade stands spring up on every street, operated by little children."

"Which is why leadership is so important," said his father.

"We'll end up like the czars," young Lapshin countered, "convinced that the only way to lead the Russian *muzhik* is to beat him soundly. You've got the same situation in your country, Mrs. Nevsky. Who listens to your eastern establishment anymore? While Brezhnev slept we created our own eastern establishment, but the *Nomenklatura* is resented and ultimately will be ignored. Meanwhile, we stagnate, betwixt and between. We've built arsenals, mastered heavy industry, but the world changed and we missed it. We boast of pig iron production, the world makes plastic. We scrabble in the dirt for more oil, the world invents engines that use less oil. We struggle to build VCRs, the world's infants have computers in their cribs. Sometimes I wonder, so what? What value has the West lost in these changes? What do you hold sacred anymore with your plastic and computers?"

"Philosophy's a luxury," Kirichenko said. "We'll philosophize after we catch up."

"You'll be running alone, Comrade Leader. The *muzhik* doesn't cross himself until it thunders. A slow drift toward chaos doesn't frighten the Russian people. It takes thunder. . . ."

Natalie said, "That sounds as if one of you should step forward and take action."

"To inspire them?" Lapshin mocked. "Or terrify—"

"The days of one-man rule are over in Russia," his father interrupted smoothly. "Wouldn't you agree, Kirichenko? It's committees now. What do you call it in America, Mrs. Nevsky? Corporation men?"

"I mean a strongman," Natalie persisted, arriving at last at Luba's *vozhd*. "A boss."

The three Russians exchanged studiedly neutral looks. "Stalin?"

"Stalin," Kirichenko repeated. "They called Stalin *vozhd*."

Natalie pretended innocence. "I don't mean a *Stalin*," she said hastily. "I'm sure people remember the price of *that* boss."

"They remember results. Discipline. Efficiency. Can you blame them?" Marshal Lapshin smiled.

"But doesn't the new leadership also call for discipline and efficiency?"

"Calls get boring," his son replied. "The Boss shot people. Shootings retain a certain breath of excitement. Focus the mind."

"You and Mr. Kirichenko and your friends just don't look like the types to allow shootings."

"We may not be asked."

"What do you mean?"

They shrugged.

"A revolt?" Natalie persisted. "A coup?"

"Ask Kirichenko. He's already leading a purge."

"I am not!" Kirichenko snapped vehemently, his taut face reddening.

"Oh really? And what is the effect of the KGB's fraud squad?"

"The honest man starves in a corrupt society. Our people have dodged a decadent government for so many years that it's become a habit. It is our duty, therefore, to arrest the corrupt to make it possible to be honest."

"Perhaps," Lapshin replied heavily, "the tricks they learned in the black market can be turned to accelerating productivity."

Minister Rostov's point the other night, Natalie recalled. It was difficult to discern who inhabited whose camp.

"Our best hope is to extend this example of discipline to our youth," said Kirichenko. "The young make change permanent."

"Excuse me." Lapshin spread his hands. "You see, Mrs. Nevsky, a *nice* purge. A high-minded purge, to be sure. But a purge nonetheless."

The KGB man turned white. "I protect the revolution," he said loudly.

Heads turned. General Lapshin grinned, triumphant that he had goaded Kirichenko into embarrassing himself. To Natalie he observed in mild, conversational tones, "There are two problems with watchdogs. First they eat too much. Then they run wild and turn into wolves. If they were human, we would not call watchdogs revolutionaries, but anarchists."

Before Kirichenko could answer, old Marshal Lapshin seized his arm. "Kirichenko, could the Soviet Army prevail upon the Committee for State Security to lead an old warhorse to a drink?" He turned him forcibly toward the door, with a black look at his son, and Kirichenko allowed himself to be steered away.

Natalie stared into her glass, pretending the embarrassment she would have felt if she weren't desperately probing for a connection to Wallace.

When she looked up, General Lapshin was watching her. She smiled uncertainly, determined to milk him for what, if anything, he knew. "Comrade Kirichenko seemed terribly upset. I thought you two were kidding."

"He's a cop with muddy shoes. A peasant who knows he's out of place."

"What's wrong with being a peasant in the Soviet Union?"

Lapshin gave her a sharp look and Natalie concluded it was dangerous to play dumb around him. "Nothing," he said. "Unless one resents it."

"I'm surprised how blunt you were around Kirichenko. Aren't you afraid?"

"Afraid? Of what?"

"Kirichenko seems high up in the KGB."

"Near the top, as a matter of fact. The youngest on the Central Committee and heading straight for candidate membership in the Politburo. Snaring petty thieves is a sure road to success these days. As I am not corrupt, I have nothing to fear from Kirichenko."

Natalie glanced through the door, across the ballroom in the direction that Kirichenko had disappeared with Lapshin's father. If the KGB officer was in fact "near the top," what was he doing arresting an assistant manager of the Astoria Hotel? The frightening answer was inescapable: Kirichenko had attended both the arrest and tonight's reception to observe Wallace Nevsky's widow.

When she turned her attention back to General Lapshin, she found him eyeing her speculatively. She said, "Your father doesn't seem to agree. He seemed concerned you were going too far."

"Fathers worry. It's in their nature."

"I'd worry that Kirichenko might trump up charges if he was angry enough."

"That's because you don't know Kirichenko. He's incorruptible. If I steal, I'm dead. But I don't steal. It's not in my makeup. Nor do I have to. I have everything I want, already."

"Everything?"

"Would you like to see?"

"What do you mean?"

"Join me for dinner."

"Aren't we eating here?"

"I know a better place."

22

I'd like that," Natalie smiled. "Very much. But I already have a date."

General Lapshin's return smile was content and easy and edged with a mocking grin that reminded her of Greg Stuart. He was built like Greg, too, but the resemblance stopped at his broad Slavic face and his strange hazel eyes, which just now seemed to turn black as ink.

"Give me his name. I'll post him to Kabul."

"That's a wonderful idea, but unfortunately he's with my embassy."

"No problem. I've American friends. We'll ship him to Nicaragua. Or, failing that, you and I will whisper to Valery Kirichenko that your date is a spy and let the KGB do something terrible to him."

"I think I can handle it. Give me a few minutes."

Lapshin relieved her of her empty glass. "My hopes ride with you. I'll meet you at the door."

She hurried across the crowded ballroom, hunting Finny, who intercepted her at a *zakuska* table that happened to offer a view of the picture gallery. "How are you making out?"

Natalie explained the situation, and apologized. "Would you forgive me if I skipped dinner?"

The *chargé d'affaires* was delighted. "Breakfast eight o'clock. Your hotel. I want to hear everything that General Lapshin says and does."

"Everything?"

"Everything." Finny grinned. "I would love to send Washington a confidential cable about him. You owe me, so be there."

"Yes, Uncle David. Tell me, what's the word on him? My husband only mentioned his father."

"A rarity. A real oddball."

"How?"

"In this society, the sons and daughters of successful men do not fight their father's battles. The reward for success is that your kid doesn't have to struggle like you did. The son of a major military figure like Marshal Lapshin does not become a soldier. He works for a think tank and travels abroad or maybe is *attaché* in Paris or London. Which works beautifully, by the way. Because the top slots are always open to new blood. But Lapshin's a soldier, just like Dad. The real McCoy. Major war hero in Afghanistan. The guy's a legend. The *Pamyat* love him—traditional Russian manhood at its bravest and patriotic best. Defender of the Motherland."

"He's really outspoken. I was surprised by things he said in front of everybody."

"He's a rich kid. A 'godden,' they call them, brought up with privilege. The fact that he never hid behind it gives him even greater license—or so he thinks. He'll go too far, one of these days. This is not a society that encourages mavericks."

"I wonder what he wants with me."

"Probably the same thing I'd want if I weren't married."

Natalie shook hands good-night. "By the way, what's the word on Kirichenko?"

"Who?"

"Valery Kirichenko, the KGB officer."

"Never heard of him."

"Lapshin says he's very important. . . ."

"The important ones don't advertise."

General Lapshin was waiting with her coat and boots. "Allow me," he said, taking her high heels and offering his arm, which she declined. They went out the front door, but instead of continuing under the canopy to the cars, ducked into a path that skirted the building and led toward three towers looming above the Kremlin Wall. The path was subtly lit and swept of snow even though wet snow was blowing. Where the tower lights shone, snow was caking into the red brick on the bias, etching kaleidoscopic patterns of red and white.

Natalie stopped. She felt compelled to whisper, "That is so beautiful."

"Those bricks were laid the year Columbus discovered the New World."

They passed another church. It was like walking through a village, and again Natalie found it hard to believe that just beyond the high thick walls lay modern Moscow. They rounded a copse of trees and found a small field freshly layered in snow. In the middle of the field was a landing pad, which a soldier was sweeping with a twig broom. On the pad was a dark helicopter.

"What's this?"

"Transport."

General Lapshin led Natalie to the machine. Uniformed airmen jumped down, saluted smartly, and helped them up to a passenger cabin behind the pilots. The rotors started turning, wound up swiftly. Snow billowed, the helicopter lurched, and suddenly they were airborne, above the blowing snow, over the tree tops, clearing the Kremlin Walls between two towers, and thundering over the city.

"How can you do this?" Natalie laughed, high on the power and the noise. "I'm a civilian. I'm a *foreigner*."

General Lapshin laughed back, happy with her excitement. "It's an Army helicopter," he explained, drawing a purloined bottle of *Zolotoye* champagne from his coat. "I'm the Army."

"But I'm the *enemy*."

"Then you're my prisoner," came the sobering reply, and Natalie hoped that the pang of alarm she felt in her stomach had not shown on her face in the moment she needed to hear the joke. Lapshin popped the cork.

"Do you mind no glass?"

"This is perfect."

Moscow spread below the helicopter like a dimly lit Queens. They crossed row upon row of housing blocks separated by broad thoroughfares. There were no suburbs sprawling in the American sense and the massed lights ended rather abruptly at a final wall of apartment high-rises. Twenty minutes after they rose from the Kremlin, they were flying over darkness, pocked here and there by what Natalie guessed were farms and villages. Those lights grew sparse and finally vanished altogether. On they flew, over a land that spread as endlessly as the sea, a dark carpet that occasionally glowed blue from starlight when the clouds grew ragged. Astern, on the right, Natalie glimpsed Orion's belt rising. Orienting herself by the stars she knew in Connecticut, she concluded General Lapshin was taking her north.

"It's so empty," she marveled, "to be so close to Moscow."

"Emptier every year," he replied. "We're abandoning our villages, cramming people like penned cattle into soulless flats. Imagine what it does to their spirit."

"It's the history of the world," Natalie said. "Everywhere." Broad generalities, she had noticed, spurred him to open up. Lapshin obliged, pausing only to finish off the bottle.

"It's a sorry history. And in military terms, it's a disaster. Where do we recruit? Given a choice between a feral street tough or a boy bred strong on the farm, I'll take the peasant's son. He's got strength, loyalty, and stamina. And a memory of his land to fight for."

"*Pamyat*," she repeated, the Russian word for "memory." "David Finny—the *chargé d'affaires*—mentioned that the *Pamyat* movement likes you very much."

Lapshin considered that with a self-deprecating smile. "Russians who long for the old values have a limited choice of heroes in a modern world."

"Still, you sound pleased. What are they like, the *Pamyat*?"

"They're traditionalists, which means they embody the best and worst of Russia."

"What's the worst?"

"When we were a Christian nation we had a rationale for despising the unconverted Jews. Now that we are a godless people, we still use the fear of international Zionism as an excuse for our own shortcomings. But the Soviet Union cannot survive on excuses. You look disappointed. Do you want me to take a moral stand?"

"My husband was Jewish."

"I will take a moral stand to please a beautiful woman and say, It is wrong to kill Jews. But as a soldier I can tell you that the best defense the Jews have ever had has been when they made it *impractical* to kill Jews, just as we have made it impractical to kill Russians."

"I don't understand."

"It has been more than forty years since a German dared cross our border with a gun."

Ahead, a yellow-gold pinpoint brightened on the horizon, a lonely outpost toward which the helicopter descended. Lapshin picked up a mike and ordered, "*Nizhe*." Lower.

The pilot skimmed the snowy fields, dodging the occasional tree and once a barn that loomed suddenly out of the dark. Natalie strained to see ahead.

"Look down," said Lapshin. Then, suddenly, to the pilot, "*Svet!*"

The landing lights blazed on all at once, burning a big, white, moving circle on the snow. "My God," Natalie gasped.

In a circle, twisting their heads over their shoulders, glaring back at the offending sky, enormous wolves ran like demons.

"How did you know they were there?"

Lapshin smiled. "They're predictable."

The helicopter swooped high to clear the dense treeline the wolves were running for, crossed a deep thicket and a swift river that was tearing a jagged black line through the ice, circled a field filled with long rows of low sheds, and set down two hundred yards from a very large country mansion. Soldiers raced to the lighted landing pad and helped them out. The air was bitterly cold.

"Where are we?" Natalie asked as Lapshin took her hand and they ran from the icy prop wash.

"A *dacha*." He led her toward the house on lighted paths that reminded Natalie of Greg's wife's or Jeff Jervis's Greenwich estates. The difference was the isolation. Surrounded by the woods and thicket, the *dacha* was the first light they had seen in many miles. The sky was pitch black, filled with stars she had never seen.

They entered through double French doors into a beautiful library, where a fire was crackling in the hearth.

"Let me take your coat."

She warmed her hands by the fire.

"Vodka?"

"*Da!*"

He brought it in Venetian crystal stemware, touched his glass to hers. "*Na Zdorov'y*," he toasted, and tossed his back, *zalpon*.

"And your health, too." Natalie chugged the icy vodka, too, savoring the fire in her throat, and hoping Wallace had been right to claim that drinking *zalpon* eliminated the spirit fumes that made one drunk. She extended her glass when Lapshin offered a refill.

Beside the vodka decanter was a plate of *buterbrod* and a dish of golden caviar, which Lapshin said came from the Volga sterlet, a rare fish bred in the estate fish ponds.

"When I prepped for this trip I was told that the new Gen Sec frowned on luxury."

"This is not luxury. This is an experimental agricultural station maintained by the Defense Ministry. One of many. As the Defense

Ministry supplies much of the armed forces' own food, we experiment to do better. Here we have vegetable greenhouses, hydroponic gardens, flowers, battery chickens and geese, and thoroughbred troika horses. But you'll be most interested in our mink farm."

Mink explained the long sheds in the field. "Mink and troika horses? Not luxury?"

"You think I'm sarcastic, but I'm not entirely. I don't deny we have comfort here, but comfort is a rightful reward for jobs well done. That's our problem—we're like Puritans, denying, denouncing any sign of pleasure. How the hell are we to reward people who shoulder responsibility? Personally, I couldn't care less, but many people do, and we lose them because we don't allow them to accumulate the benefits of hard work. When we need something done right in Russia, we assign the Army. Perhaps that's because the Army has ways to reward excellence. I'll demonstrate."

He tossed an ash tray on the Kazakh carpet. "Excuse me." He returned dragging a heavy vacuum cleaner, plugged it in, and ran the head over the mess. "Good Hoover? All gone, yes?"

Natalie looked at him dubiously. "Seems to be."

"Army product, built in a rocket factory. Ask any housewife, she'll buy an Army vacuum."

"Are you serious?"

"I certainly am. Whatever we turn our hand to we do efficiently, in a modern manner. Because when the consumer controls production, production improves. The next step will be to provide permanent rewards. At present all we really do is bestow privilege, privilege that can be taken away. We need to give tangible rewards—property— that a man can work for, can set goals for, and know that once it's his, it's his to keep."

"That doesn't sound like communism."

"First, we are Russians."

"By any chance, are you considering defecting?"

General Lapshin gave a mirthless laugh. "One does not leave the center of the world, one improves it."

"Are you personally involved with production?"

"They consult me on tanks. Are you hungry?"

"I thought you were shot down in a helicopter."

"A helicopter is a tank that flies. You pay close attention, don't you? . . ."

*   *   *

Natalie tried to meet his puzzled stare. She was taller than he, but he didn't seem to notice as he gazed up at her inquisitively.

"I do a lot of work at parties," she explained. "It's a habit to listen."

"What work?"

"Selling, mostly."

"Furs?"

"Franchises, to sell furs. Before I met Vassily I was a banker, so I sold investments."

"And where did you acquire the habit of asking so many questions?"

Natalie shrugged. "Same place, I suppose. I must learn what the consumer wants. Haven't you heard the expression, 'When the consumer controls production, production improves'?"

"Yet another question?" He filled her glass again. "Here. Take a break. It's a party."

"Will you show me the minks?" she asked, eager to deflect the cross examination she had brought down on herself with a careless mistake.

"It's dark. I'm sure you've seen plenty of minks."

"Actually, I'm embarrassed to admit I've never seen a live mink in my life. I've never been to a mink ranch."

"Is that a fact? Well, you must come back in the daylight. We'll give you a real tour. They're doing some interesting experiments. Meantime, I did invite you to dinner. Are you hungry?"

"Famished."

They walked through the house, their shoes echoing on polished parquet. Lapshin showed her a ballroom, a great hall, a billiard room, and a pistol range—elaborately sound-muffled with damask drapes. Through doorways Natalie caught glimpses of smaller, beautifully appointed sitting rooms and lounges. Lamps were on everywhere, although they seemed to be alone. It looked a little like the kind of place American corporations kept for executive retreats, but the fine antique woods, wallpapers, and carpets lent the house unusual substance.

A table had been laid in a cozy corner of the dining room, by a fire. Lapshin held a chair for Natalie, then sat opposite her, smiling when she exclaimed over the flowers.

"Does your staff automatically set two places when you take the helicopter?"

"My mess sergeant makes a head count when the ship lands. Usually we're four or five senior officers with enormous appetites. They'll eat well in the kitchen tonight."

Natalie, making an effort to turn questions into statements, said, "I'm having difficulty picturing the grizzled old Army cook who set this table."

"Here she is, now. Good evening, Nadia."

A petite young girl, eyes downcast, and strikingly pretty in a soldier's dress tunic, entered with a Limoges tureen and a covered serving dish.

"Mrs. Nevsky has come all the way from America to taste your soup," Lapshin said, causing the girl to blush. Natalie was reminded of Leo Margulies' story about the Red Army gymnasts performing for Wallace, and wondered how many little Nadias were stashed around the *dacha* for the pleasure of visiting officers.

"Sturgeon soup," Lapshin explained as Nadia first placed delicate sturgeon filets in their bowls. "Catherine the Great was partial to it, but it's quite rare now, because this particular variety has been made almost extinct by pollution. Fortunately, the Army has discovered ways to raise him."

Nadia ladled a clear broth over the filets and retired.

"This is spectacular," Natalie said, reassessing her opinion of Nadia.

"Best followed with champagne," Lapshin replied, indicating a fresh *Zolotoye* on ice.

The soup was followed by another fish—burbot, a nineteenth-century delicacy that Lapshin assured her was virtually unknown on the Russian table, again cultivated by the Army. Natalie complimented the walnut-fed turkey, but drew the line at suckling pig.

"Enough, thank you. Enough."

Lapshin, who, she noticed, barely touched his own food, offered a final toast. "In the nineteenth century, this was enjoyed by the millionaires of the Merchants Club in Moscow! 'To excess.' "

Natalie put down her glass. "Don't insult me. You're behaving in ways you would never act alone."

"My apologies," he said contritely. "Perhaps I'm trying to see how corruptible you are."

"I've had plenty to eat, thank you."

"Come," he said, rising. "Nadia's set coffee and brandy in my rooms." Natalie decided not to object when Lapshin started up the broad stairs, presuming that "rooms" meant they wouldn't enter straight into his bedroom.

They were at the end of a long second-floor hall, as lavish as everything else in the house, but more severe in design, though clearly a matter of taste rather than restraint. He had a parlor, an office, a bedroom with bath, and expensive Scandinavian furniture. Through the bedroom door she saw a queen-size bed with lacquered side tables and a mirrored headboard.

"If you'd like to freshen up . . ." he said, indicating the bathroom. Natalie hadn't looked at her face since Finny picked her up at the hotel. Her eyes gazed back, surprisingly steady considering that while she tried to pry information out of the Russian general, the question, Do I want to sleep with this man? had begun prowling through her mind.

She recalled the electric moment in her office with Stefan the model. Then she thought of Greg and how General Lapshin was built like him and how beautiful Greg's voice had sounded on the telephone. Funny how relieved she felt that Lapshin didn't know Wallace very well, that he had only met him through his father.

Lapshin was waiting in the bedroom with brandy on a tray. He intercepted her between the bed and the door. There were flowers beside the bed, faded, and a silver tray of perfume bottles on the dresser. A rack of antlers on the wall held a dozen silk scarves, trailing fringe. Natalie touched them. They were scented with Madame Rochas.

"Brandy?"

She said yes, for something to hold.

Lapshin splashed a little brandy into a pair of crystal balloons.

"*Na Zdorov'y.*"

Natalie caught the golden gleam in his eye. He looked a little drunk, quite sexy, and very determined. Seeking a diversion, she noticed an open book on the night table across the bed. Rescue. She walked past him, around the bed, and picked the book up.

"You're reading *Solzhenitsyn?*" she asked, and it wasn't hard to sound incredulous.

Lapshin followed her with a grin. "Don't tell Kirichenko."

"*The First Circle.* I should report you, General. No, wait, I just realized, this is legitimate research. Up that scientific sturgeon production." She put it down, dodged him again, and went back around the bed. Again Lapshin followed, shaking his head with a pleasant smile. "I am not studying science and you know it."

"Then what? Does decadence turn you on?"

As earlier on the helicopter, he turned suddenly serious. "Solzhenitsyn holds for me a vision of old Russia. Before all this. A time when men and women occupied a place bounded by the land beneath their feet and a spirit above."

Natalie had noticed at the Sojuzpushnina party in Leningrad, and earlier tonight with both Kirichenko and Lapshin, that the Russians pounced hungrily on ideas, falling eagerly into discussions one did not hear off-campus in America. She matched her tone to his, no longer mocking.

"But that's a Christian vision."

"Medieval," Lapshin agreed. "With all our modern thinking and all our fabulous machines we have never replaced the Christian concept of good and evil. It made them less vicious than we are, and much stronger. I know, you'll tell me about public executions and such cruelties, but in old Russia, one peasant hanged in the village quelled the unruly. In our century, we kill the entire village. What we've lost that the Christians had was a *belief* in good and evil. There is nothing to stop us anymore—and again, I mean all of us, capitalists, Communists, Russians, Americans—from being as awful as awful can be."

"Are you a Christian?" she asked.

"It's too late," he said. "I know too much."

He drifted into silence, gazing sightlessly at the bed. Natalie feared she was losing him at the very moment he might open up further, so she tried to bring him back. "I think you're trying to convince me you're an idealist."

Lapshin answered her with a gloomy smile and she knew she had failed. "I'm a soldier so I have to be an idealist."

Now his silence was like a wall. Boldly, she sailed around it. "Are you married, General?"

"No. I too am widowed."

"I'm sorry." She twirled the amber brandy. "At least that's what people say to me. Now I know why."

"It's such an intimate thing, yet you have to admit it when you're asked."

"You're young to be widowed— What am I doing? That's what they always say to me. How did it happen?"

"Relax." Their eyes met and Natalie said, easily, meaning it, "I thought we were connected. I felt something. . . . How did it happen?"

"The married officers' quarters were not so secure as we thought in Kabul. Our flat took a rebel mortar while she was cooking breakfast."

"My God." Natalie had a sudden, clear picture in her mind of tastefully decorated walls, like these, suddenly spilling to the floor. "How did you—"

"Actually, I was at the front. She was cooking for her lover. He was my regiment's KGB snoop—another wolf like Kirichenko—terrorizing my men, as if they didn't have enough to fear from the *mujahedin*. Cheka, OGPU, NUKD, KGB, they have plagued the Red Army since the revolution. . . . Scum!" He jerked his gaze up from the floor and cracked a smile. "Happily, he too was blown to bits. So I owe one to the *mujahedin*."

Natalie ran her fingers through the scarves again, shivering with a sudden, inexplicable insight.

Something in Lapshin's smile suggested it was not the *mujahedin*, but he himself who had blown up his flat, his wife and her lover.

"You think I'm terrible," the general said.

She said, "I think you've lost track. You owe the Afghans two, counting your promotion."

Lapshin laughed. "That's very funny. But why do you pretend to be hard?"

"I'm not pretending. I'm detached. You're putting me on."

"The story is true. It happened just as I said."

"Something's missing."

Lapshin shook his head. "I'm a fool to lie to a woman. . . . What isn't true is that I cared. I had married young and stupidly—against my father's wishes, I might add. The *mujahedin* saved me from a messy divorce, which wouldn't have done my career any good because an officer is expected to control his private life." He grinned again, slugged back his brandy, and reached for the decanter. "So I returned to Moscow a war hero who had made the penultimate sacrifice. Only you know my secret."

Natalie extended her glass, her eyes on his eyes, which had turned vivid gold in the bedroom's soft light. He steadied her glass as he poured. The dry tips of his fingers spread across the back of her hand and she felt the impression of each, warm and hard on her skin, and trembling lightly.

"Plenty."

Lapshin spilled a drop in the soft crevice where her thumb joined her hand. Before she could stop him, he bent his head and licked it away. Natalie jumped at his touch, splashing more brandy.

"Surprised?"

"Confused." She had been expecting some move from the moment his father introduced them at the Kremlin. But his kiss felt better than she would have predicted and made her vividly aware that it had been three months since anyone had touched her with intent.

Solemnly, he produced a handkerchief, mopped the dripping balloon, and asked, "May I dry your hand?"

"It stings."

"You're cut," he said, drying gently around a little scratch.

"Oh, I did a funny thing, today. I volunteered on one of the restoration projects, digging mud and smashing walls."

"Which one?"

Brilliant. She had come for his secrets and instead was spilling her own. "In the Kitai-Gorod," she answered vaguely, hoping there were others, as she scrambled to camouflage her mistake. "I love doing something local on a trip, like buying something you can't find in a hotel, or like this. Do you know?"

"I write poetry in London pubs. A pint by my elbow. They think I'm Irish." He was still holding her hand and at some point had begun backing smoothly toward the bed. She thought she could stop whenever she wanted. She got lost in his golden eyes and bumped against the side table. A picture clattered over. She picked it up. It was a photograph of a woman—a pretty face with wispy dark curls on a high brow, exotic-looking, self-absorbed, and determined. The woman of the faded flowers, the scarves, and the perfume. She looked familiar. Lapshin was watching her closely.

"Your girlfriend?"

"Yes."

"One of several?" Natalie teased. Who did the woman remind her of, staring so intently into the camera?

"Just one," he laughed. Natalie's pulse quickened. Lapshin's voice drifted to her from a great distance. "When I was married I used to think, God, when I get out of this I'm going to go wild. Turned out I'm a monogamous sort. We've been steady two years."

She freed her hand and tried to hide her shock by pretending to study the photograph, but surely the Russian could hear the startled breath storming through her lungs. Disguised in a blonde wig, Lapshin's girlfriend had shot Wallace.

23

"Where is she?"

"Away."

Lapshin took her hand again. Natalie willed it not to shake and it obeyed. Fear had not caused her to tremble, but anger. Cold, cold anger that she used to make her body obey like a machine. He kissed her fingers. She wanted to drive those fingers into his eyes, but she wanted more to keep him talking, so she allowed his lips to touch the machine. And she ordered the machine to smile while she tried to think what would be her next normal question if she hadn't seen the photograph and were only the widowed Natalie Nevsky, debating the pleasure of an evening.

"What's her name?"

"Dina."

"What does Dina do?"

"Do you really want to know?"

"Her boyfriend is kissing my hand. I feel a certain connection."

"Shall I stop?"

"I think so." She picked the frame up again and studied the face. Through the lens of what she knew, it appeared not so much a strong face as a willful face, stubborn, obstinate, with something perverse and wild in the eyes that made her wayward—a woman who would do what the hell she wanted for her own reasons. "Tell me about her. Do you get along?"

"Whenever she gets her way." Lapshin smiled. "She's like me, an heiress, as it were, to her father's accomplishments. He was on the Central Committee, until recently. She's mad for travel, especially since the new leadership has made it rather more difficult to enjoy the life she was accustomed to in the Brezhnev days."

"She can always come here, if she craves luxury."

"She regards my life-style as spartan. Decadent luxuries, for some, are like a drug. They live abroad and get addicted. Some come home whole, others, stunted."

"Is that what you think of her?"

"Dina is more than a simple *highlife-istka*. I enjoy her." His eyes flicked involuntarily toward the mirrored headboard. "And I admire her cold ambition."

"For what?"

"For me. She's ambitious for my career. There's a group . . . you see, we—the Army—we lost our seats on the Politburo. There's a group that thinks I'm the one to regain it."

She knew he would never answer if she asked what group, so she said, "Why you?"

"I'm young. I'm a hero. I'm capable. And I'm loyal."

"Sounds like she wants to marry you."

"I think she wants to see how far I get, first." He took the picture and put it in the drawer. "What about you? Do you have a boyfriend?"

"No. It's too soon."

"Did you have one while you were married?"

"No. I'm the monogamous sort, too. Besides, I was madly in love."

"Never tempted?"

Greg skipped through her head. "I'm not saying I never noticed a guy. But never one I'd trade Wallace for."

"My father says he was a good man."

"Goodness had nothing to do with it."

"Mae West said that, didn't she?"

"Where'd you learn that?"

"The flicks in Paris. When I was attaché, I saw a million old movies. . . ."

Now she could steer him gently toward his career, but he startled her with a question of his own. "Is it true your husband was shot?"

Natalie averted her face to hide the coldness that must surely glisten in her eyes.

"I thought everyone knew."

"I know what your newspapers reported, but it sounded so unlikely. A blonde assassin. Have the police found her?"

"They think she went to Europe."

"That sounds like a convenient excuse to stop hunting."

"I thought so, too."

"I don't understand how such a thing could happen."

What was he doing to her? Why play this game? Surely he knew what Dina had done. But he had let her see the photograph.

"She walked right up and shot him. By the time we realized what had happened, she had escaped."

Lapshin stared, then said, "I'm sorry. . . . Will you—do you imagine ever remarrying?"

"It's not high on my agenda. You're the first eligible man I've been alone with since he died."

"I'm not eligible."

"You act eligible."

"I didn't think you'd noticed."

Natalie looked him straight in the eye. She thought she knew what the colors meant now—hazel when he felt easy. Gold when he hungered. Black when he probed. They were black again.

"If your girlfriend Dina walked into this bedroom she would shoot you."

"No," said General Lapshin. "Dina would shoot *you*. I'm high on her agenda." His eyes stayed dark as the night.

"In that case, I think I better go home." She brushed past him, into the living room. Lapshin ran after her. "No, no. We're kidding. Besides, she's not here."

"Where is she?"

"New York. She's working for the Foreign Ministry."

"Well, if she comes to New York often, you ought to come along. The three of us can have dinner."

"This is actually her first trip to New York. She's preparing for the Gen Sec tour."

"When's he going? Maybe Dina will be there when I get home."

"February fourteenth."

"Valentine's Day."

"Your love day, isn't it? I've always thought we should adopt that holiday."

"It's time for me to go."

"Oh, stay. I'd be very happy if you could stay."

"I'm not ready. Besides, I promised David Finny I'd have breakfast with him." She forced a smile to her face. "I think he was afraid you'd seduce me."

"He intends to debrief you at breakfast. It's his job."

"What should I tell him?"

"Tell him the Soviet Army is on its knees. You've broken a general's heart."

The banter was getting impossible to bear, but Natalie took one more shot at it. "I'll tell him I did it in the interest of the Army getting back on the Politburo."

"I wish you wouldn't. I was rather indiscreet. But then again, I'm sure you will."

"I can't imagine a general officer of the Red Army ever being indiscreet unless he had a reason to be."

Lapshin's eyes turned golden. "That's a diplomat's answer. Come. I'll show you the minks."

"It's dark."

"They're best in the dark," he insisted. He rang for their coats and poured vodka while they waited. The outside lights were off and the night was bitter cold.

"I can't see," said Natalie.

"Light only makes the night darker," he said. "Take my arm."

She had thought of him as an invalid, still weak from his wounds, but rock-hard biceps swelled his greatcoat. He walked surely into the dark. Slowly her own eyes began to discern the shapes of walls and trees. The snow seemed to emit a bluish light. Ahead, across an empty field, she could see the long, low rooflines of the mink sheds. The wind carried a faint odor of musk and sweetness. She was under a roof before she realized they had arrived. The sheds had no walls.

"What's that noise?"

"They're nocturnal."

She heard several distinct sounds—the scuttling of claws on wire mesh, the thump of small bodies landing hard, and a busy squawking as the animals leaped about their cages.

"In the wild they'd be hunting at this hour. Even after forty generations in captivity, a loose mink runs for the river. They never forget."

Lapshin turned on his flashlight. Hundreds of eyes burned at her—black, green, and red.

He swept the beam down a long, long corridor between rows of wire cages piled one atop the other. From each cage, eyes glowed, close-set, forward-scanning, and predatory. There were wooden hutches in the cages, but the animals pressed the wire, watching.

Natalie shivered. "They're not afraid of us."

"They're not afraid of anything."

"But—"

"They don't know they're to become coats. All they know is they've never met anything they couldn't kill, except a larger one of themselves. The females are the more dangerous—they seem to enjoy killing. One escaped last month, swam the river, and killed fifty hens before we could get her out of the chicken house. She was drenched in blood."

"Their eyes are different colors."

"Genetics, the keeper tells me. We raise various fur colors. All based on the best American stock."

"Was Wallace ever here?"

"Can't you put him from your mind?"

"He's in my heart."

"That is a poignant answer," Lapshin replied. "I am touched." He started walking down the corridor and Natalie followed, afraid to be separated from the light. "Was he here?" she asked again.

"Of course. I told you, we consulted him about the design."

She breathed the animal scent and scuffed her boots in the wood shavings, close to him for a second of shared impression.

Why had Lapshin let her see Dina's photograph?

Lost in thought, she trailed her hand along a cage. Lapshin moved like lightning, batting her hand away as the mink hurled itself against the mesh with a flash of white teeth. Panicked, she jumped back.

"Careful, Mrs. Nevsky." He aimed the flashlight at the adjoining cage. The mink had no tail. "Lost it to her neighbor."

"I want to go now," said Natalie. "I'm cold."

He held on to her hand. "What are you doing here, Mrs. Nevsky?"

"Here?"

"In Russia."

"I told you, buying skins."

"How do these compare to what you have in America?"

"I can't tell in this light. And I'm not an expert. But they probably don't compare that well."

"So why don't you buy in America? Or Scandinavia? I would think with the falling dollar, you'd do best in America."

She couldn't see his face because he was shining the light down the rows of cages, but he sounded sober. Wondering what he suspected, she weaved a story around his objections.

"American and Scandinavian mink prices have jumped fifty percent this year. I'm hoping to fill some needs here."

"But you say our mink isn't as good. That doesn't answer why you're here. Is this a pilgrimage to your husband's past?"

"Do I need a reason?"

Lapshin was still holding her hand. He was silent.

"I do have another reason."

"Which is?"

"Just between us, since my husband died, the furriers on whom I depend for supply aren't sure I can take over our company."

"Because you're a woman?"

"Partly that. Partly because I'm an outsider. I'm here to wave the flag for Cotillion Furs. Show them I can do it. That's what they're waiting to see in Leningrad."

"Leningrad? But I met you in Moscow."

"I took the weekend off," she replied, and when he still looked dubious, she delved into her own fears for an explanation that rolled all too easily off her tongue. "I'm afraid. I don't know if I can do it without Wallace. I think I lost my nerve. Maybe I ran away to Moscow." She forced a smile. "Please don't tell anyone."

"What if you decided to stay here, with me, and didn't return to Leningrad?"

"They'd come looking for me. . . . I really am cold. I'd like to go home."

He brought vodka aboard the helicopter and got rapidly drunk. As the lights of Moscow hove into view, he started mumbling, "I don't want it."

"Don't want what?" Natalie asked, but General Lapshin merely smiled and fell asleep.

*　　*　　*

"How'd it go?" Finny asked at breakfast.

"I would give anything for a great cup of coffee. I have such a hangover. They drink."

Finny poured coffee. Natalie tasted it and gasped.

"General Lapshin warned me there'd be a debriefing at breakfast."

"Mrs. Nevsky, I enjoy breakfast with a good-looking woman as much as the next guy, but I'd like to get down to business. What the hell happened last night?"

"He's a mystic."

"Lapshin?"

"You should hear him talk about the war—have you ever spoken with a Vietnam veteran?"

"I am one."

Natalie covered her surprise. The Harry Truman impression made Finny seem older than he must be. "I was reminded of a vet. It's as if he doesn't quite fit in Moscow. He's putting up a front—carousing, what did you call him, 'rich kid'?—but inside he's on another planet. It's like talking to somebody who's stoned on dope—not that he was."

"Was he drunk?"

"After a while. Tell me, did you know my husband was a consultant to Marshal Lapshin's farm?"

Finny shrugged. "I heard they spent time together."

"He took me to the farm."

"Hell of a trip. Must be a hundred miles."

"By helicopter."

"You're kidding?"

"I couldn't believe it. We sailed out of the Kremlin in an Army helicopter."

"He's a nervy bastard."

"That's why he did it. He's needling everyone, daring them to disapprove. The guy's a child."

"Did he make any passes?"

"Shut up, Finny."

Finny's mouth popped open. "I'm just trying to get a profile on this very important Soviet general you had the good fortune to spend the night with."

"I didn't spend the night. I had a very nice time. You put in the profile that he's normal."

She broke off a piece of bread and buttered it. "He's got a girlfriend. Who's working as advance woman for Gorbachev's visit to the UN.

Her name's Dina. Another rich kid. Do you know who I mean? Works for the Foreign Ministry."

"Who's her father?"

"He was on the General Committee."

"Name?"

"He wouldn't say. . . . Could you find out?"

"I intend to."

"Could you let me know when you do?"

"Why?"

"I'm curious to find out how serious they are," Natalie said with a smile.

Finny responded as she wanted him to, with a conspiratorial grin. "I'll check it out. Where you going to be?"

"I'm heading back to Leningrad tonight. I'm staying at the Astoria."

"Seeing him again today?"

"No. I promised I'd help again at the restoration."

Finny had ordered eggs. They arrived with a slab of gray meat and Natalie felt her stomach roll over. "You going to order?" he asked.

"No. No, I'll just have cereal. No, just some bread." She broke off another piece, reached for the butter, shuddered again, and chewed it dry. "Finny? What's going on over here? My father said it's a civil war waiting to happen."

"Your father's exaggerating, unless he knows something I don't. Sure, there are factions: the old Brezhnev crowd, hanging in there; the Gorbachev reformers, convinced this is the Soviet Union's last chance to catch up, their last shot at change; the bureaucrats who know goddamned well that for them change means loss. Then there's the Army, that's already lost—guys like maybe Marshal Lapshin, sliding down the pole. And all the factions have one thing in common—fear.

"If you lose your job here, life stops. Compare what happens to a Soviet official and to a guy like your father. Your father gets his ass kicked out of State, finally. But he still has his apartment in New York, owns his car, keeps his pension; his daughter's free to get rich, and he can sell his talents teaching, writing. Life doesn't stop when it changes. Here it stops. If you're out, you're out. The average guy in the *Nomenklatura* has nothing but what the Party allows him. Fall out of favor with the Party and they take it back—the apartment, the car, the kid's school, the special shops. How long do you think Lapshin would keep that Army *dacha* if he got demoted?"

"He implied the Army's a kind of separate society."

"That's not how things work here."

"Do they talk about changing that?"

"Not to foreigners, they don't."

"They talked to me, quite openly."

"You might ask yourself why."

Natalie gave him an inquiring glance, and when Finny didn't respond, she said, "That sounds sort of enigmatic."

Finny poked dubiously at his meat.

Natalie said, "They knew my husband. And he knew everyone," she added proudly. "Do you think a coup is possible in the Soviet Union?"

"That's what you asked me last night."

"But seriously."

"A coup?" Finny snorted. "In Russia? Forget it. The Communist Party is the power and the KGB protects the Party."

"But with all the changes, and then the disappointments, you'd almost expect something to be brewing."

"There's no need for a coup. If they get tired of the guy at the top, they quietly remove him. The last leader to get shot here was Beria in '53."

"What if the Army made a move? There's plenty of frustration over Afghanistan. Right?"

"The Red Army wears a set of handcuffs called the Communist Party. The command structure is laced with CP officers whose sole job is to keep the Army under Party control. No, the only coup you'd ever see in Russia would be some broad-based group that somehow managed to infiltrate everything at once—Army, Party, KGB, bureaucracy—and any group that broad couldn't hide for long."

She was dismayed by how unlikely he made the Millionaires sound. Suddenly, he asked, "What are you doing in Russia, Natalie?"

"What?"

"What's this 'visit' all about?"

Finny was staring hard. He had bright, little eyes like a terrier and he was no longer smiling, and Natalie realized, too late, that in her excitement she had blundered badly. I *am* a bull in a china shop, she thought for the second time in twenty-four hours. I should have stuck to business.

"I'm here on business."

"So you said."

"It's difficult to expand on that, frankly, unless I can trust in your discretion."

"I can keep my mouth shut, provided we're not talking about threats to American security. And if we are, we'd better adjourn this discussion to the park."

"There's no need for that," Natalie replied, preparing to mold a lie that wasn't really a lie out of truth that was not the complete truth. "What I haven't said is that I'm in serious trouble. My company, Cotillion Furs, is in serious trouble." True.

"Oh yeah?"

"Wallace and I were partners. I'm on my own now, and I'm not doing so well." True and true again. "I came to Leningrad to make a splash for Cotillion." Half-true, until the Moscow trip turned it into a lie. "The afternoon I arrived in Leningrad I learned that the New York banks cut off my credit."

"So why don't you go back to New York?"

"Because I'm trying to put together a deal here that might save me." She hoped that was true, although so far this weekend the joint venture had been crowded from her mind. She vowed to read the material Rostov had given her on the flight back to Leningrad.

Finny smiled shrewdly. "Do the people you're dealing with know you're in trouble?"

"There are no secrets in the fur trade. Besides, there's nothing I can do about using their tapped overseas phones. But my problems are only part of the equation. What I'm hoping to convince them is that Cotillion Furs can offer something they need."

"Best way to deal with the Soviets, that's for sure." He sat back, apparently satisfied by her answer. "Good luck with it. Call me if you think we can help."

"Thanks. . . . You know, going back to what we were talking about . . ."

"The coup? What are you, a graduate student?"

"Come on, Finny. I'm my father's daughter. I'm curious. What's the United States' position on a Soviet, oh, say, upheaval?"

"Officially?" Finny looked at her as if she were crazy. "Good Christ, Natalie, they've got half the nuclear weapons in the world. We most certainly do not want upheaval in the Soviet Union."

"Unofficially?"

"The current crowd? This mob around the President?"

"People like Jeff Jervis."

Finny looked around the dining room. Then he winked at Natalie and rapped his knuckles on the table. "Comrade Bugsky, if you're listening, you'll like this. Dumping Gorbachev, who the American people happen to think is a pretty neat guy for signing the INF treaty, would restore the Russki boogeyman. The money slobs *need* a monster back in the Kremlin—another Stalin with dripping fangs—to frighten the American voter into accepting another arms buildup. Gorby's cute. Nobody wants to go to war with Gorby. Which drives the money slobs crazy, because in the end what this is really about is money, and this is an election year.

"But even better than a coup would be a botched coup. Now we're talkin'. Civil war. The money slobs would love a civil war in the Soviet Union. Blow the Commies away, divide Russia into a weak bunch of ethnic and national states, and open the entire region from Baltic to Pacific to the benefits of exclusive trade treaties with America. Yeah! Trouble is, the money slobs—and I put Jervis high on that slime list—the money slobs tend to forget political reality.

"The political reality is this: The 'Commies' keep our Chinese pals busy on their northern borders. The 'Commies' distract our Moslem enemies. And last but not least, they keep the Germans in check, which a glance at twentieth-century history will tell you is no small achievement. So I like the Soviet Union just the way it is, thank you."

She checked out of the National, left her bags, and walked across Revolution Square and through the old city wall into the Kitai-Gorod. At the Gladishev Warehouse, volunteers were swarming on the mustard yellow facade, and the garbage chute was thundering with falling plaster.

"*Natasha!*"

Natalie looked up at the urgent cry. Luba was waving frantically from the open loading bay where the chute entered the top floor. Natalie hurried into the building. Andrei waylaid her at the door.

"Where are you running, peasant woman?"

"I thought I would start on the fourth floor. Luba's there."

The architect leaned against the wall, blocking her way with a lazy smile. "If I were the Moscow boyfriend, you would not be up so early."

"Haven't been to sleep yet." She veered past.

"Ah, but—"

A woman screamed, a sound like metal scraping glass.

Natalie and Andrei looked at each other and ran into the street. The fourth floor loading bay was empty. From inside, the woman—it had to be Luba—screamed again.

"There!" said Andrei.

Luba staggered into view, clutching her head and reeling, dazed, toward the edge and the open chute. "Look out!" someone yelled. Luba caught her balance and backed away, still holding her head. Natalie thought she saw a flicker of movement behind her. Just then, Luba's back arched violently, as if someone had shoved her from behind. She reeled toward the edge. Someone screamed. Luba saved herself with an almost superhuman contortion, lost her balance, and pitched sideways into the yawning mouth of the chute. For a second there was silence. Then her screams sounded down the chute. Banging and thumping, she emerged at the bottom, skidding out and landing on a heap of broken plaster.

Natalie was first to reach her. Blood ran down her face and her body was still, arms and legs sprawled at sharp angles. Her eyes were open, fixed on the sky.

"Look!" a woman whispered.

"*Narkoman,*" said another. Drug addict.

Natalie, backing in horror from Luba's broken body, saw them pointing at a hypodermic needle that had fallen from her coat sleeve. The barrel was half full of a murky liquid suffused with blood.

Natalie felt the cool prickle of an interested gaze, looked up and locked eyes, for a split second, with a woman peering down. *Dina,* she thought. She might have imagined it, for she was gone in a flash, but Natalie was sure the woman had paused to pin her to the dirty snow with a look of cold disdain.

She climbed out of the dumpster, tapping Andrei's shoulder.

"Come on. She was pushed. Bring the others." She strode purposefully into the warehouse, motioning to a pair of burly college students. "You and you. Come on, let's go. Hurry." She started up the stairs. "Andrei! Come *on.*"

The architect shrugged and followed her, calling the others to join them. When Natalie looked back from the second floor landing, ten Russians were trooping after her. From the third landing she saw the group had dwindled to five, who were trading anxious glances. When they reached the fourth floor, she and Andrei were alone.

"I'll call the militia," he said, and before she could stop him he was clattering down the stairs.

"Where'd she go?" Natalie called to two volunteers who were staring down at Luba's body from the loading bay. "The woman? Where'd she go?"

Staring blankly, they edged past her, and ran after Andrei.

The entire space had been gutted, wall to wall, and she saw instantly she was alone. In the gloom, however, she noticed a ladder leading to an open hatch in the ceiling. She climbed it, cautiously, mindful that if she had seen what she thought she had seen, the woman would be likely to hurt her. But she was almost positive that she had stared into the face of the woman who had killed Wallace, so she climbed the ladder, poked her head above the opening, saw the roof was empty, and climbed out for a better look.

As on the street side, there was another sheer drop to the courtyard in back, but the warehouse stood against neighboring buildings on either side, their roofs a little village of shaft houses and skylights. She glimpsed movement—a figure tumbling over a low wall. Natalie lowered herself to the next roof. She found a metal stairway zigging down the wall and caught sight again of the fleeing figure.

She followed, slipping on the icy metal steps, clinging to the railings. Faster now, thinking less, Natalie ran down the final twist and landed hard on the cobbles. Rounding a corner, she saw Dina running toward a car that was parked across the mouth of the alley. A tall, heavyset man in a quilted jacket and worker's cap was holding the door for her. Dina jerked a thumb in Natalie's direction as she got in. The man closed the door. The car squealed away, and he started purposefully into the alley, toward Natalie.

24

She skidded to a halt.

A hundred feet separated her from the man in the high-walled alley. He broke into a run. She whirled, running back the way she had come. At the turn she lost her footing and windmilled into the rough stucco wall. He gained thirty feet.

When she reached the metal stairs, she saw he'd be on top of her in an instant if she tried to climb so she ran past the steps, praying the next turn in the alley wasn't a dead end.

"Help! *Pomagate!*"

Her voice echoed shrilly in the narrow space, but the man never slowed. Ahead was a wall, with a turn to the right. She ran into it. The alley ended at a wall. In the cul de sac was a single door. She tried to open it but it was locked. She pounded on the sturdy wood, screaming for help, hoping to frighten him away. Instead, he ran full tilt, straight at her as she backed against the door. He was big and broad-shouldered and filled the narrow alley.

"Help!"

The Russian balled his gloved fist and, to her utter astonishment, swung full force at her face. She hadn't an instant to think or react, but her tennis eye saved her. She was watching the man with one eye, focusing on his fist with the other, and at the last second she ducked. The fist flew over her head and smashed the door. She heard a grunt of pain, thrust through a tangle of legs and arms and ran, screaming.

He caught her at the turn. She felt a hand on her shoulder. Fear yanked her out of his hold, but another hand closed. He spun her around and cuffed her face hard, then wound up to punch her as he had tried to before. He's going to kill me, she thought.

Vainly, she tried to twist away.

The fist started coming again.

She heard a sudden explosive impact. The fist dropped and the man sank to the ground as another man stepped around the corner, swinging a short length of timber like a baseball bat.

"Greg!"

"Run!" her cousin said.

In Converse sneakers, gray sweats, gloves, a bright red ski cap, and a balaclava that hid most of his face, Greg Stuart looked like an American business traveler out for his daily run. Natalie would not have believed her eyes, were it not for the fact that Greg looked terrified. A loose grin was tugging his mouth and his eyes were unnaturally round, and fear had milked their blues so pale as to be almost white.

"How—"

"Later. He's got friends."

Greg reached for her hand. As he turned his back on the man on the ground, Natalie saw a flicker of movement from the corner of her eye. The Russian kicked with both legs. His boots slashed Greg's feet out from under him like a gigantic knife and her cousin fell hard. Before Natalie could move, the Russian pivoted on his side and kicked again. She felt a stab of pain in her ankle, lost her grip on the frozen mud, and flew into the air. The Russian was still in motion, turning onto his belly, reaching for the board Greg had hit him with. Natalie fell on him. Greg lunged to help her, but her full weight had slammed the Russian's head against the frozen ground. He groaned and went limp. Greg cried, "Run!"

He darted to the alley mouth where Dina had driven off, and motioned Natalie to wait while he checked the street. "Take my arm. We'll bluff 'em to the corner. If I say run, run."

They turned into the narrow street of shops. Two men sprang from a parked car. "Run!"

They tore through the lanes of the Kitai-Gorod, skidding on ice patches, banging into walls on the turns. Behind them two, possibly three, men pounded in pursuit.

"There!" cried Natalie.

Dingy steps emptied into a cavernous basement cafeteria she had seen the day before. They bumped between tables, burst through the cashiers' queue and exited across a street from the back of GUM, the department store that fronts on Red Square. They dashed in, mingling with the shoppers, and walked, as fast as they could without drawing undue attention, the skylit length of the store's main concourse. Outside, at the west end, they skirted hastily around a pair of gray-coated militia lecturing a frightened drunk, and plunged into the underground walkway beneath Revolution Square. Halfway through, Natalie looked back and saw their pursuers barrel down the stairs. They quickened their pace, dodged another cop, and emerged on Gorky Street, across from Natalie's hotel. They jumped aboard a trolleybus as it pulled out.

Natalie hadn't caught her breath when Greg dragged her off again at a side street that angled back to Marx Prospekt. They walked briskly, watching their backs all the way to Dzerzhinsky Square. Outside Detsky Mir, Children's World department store, he spotted a cab stand.

Natalie pushed him back into the doorway. "All right. What are you doing here?"

"What?"

"Who sent you? Jervis?"

"Natalie, could we just get out of here? That's the Lubianka Prison and KGB headquarters next door."

Wired from the chase and her close escape, and frustrated that she had lost the woman she thought was Dina, she felt no fear, only anger at being manipulated. "That man was not KGB. He didn't try to arrest me, he tried to kill me! I'd have been a lot safer with the KGB."

"And even safer with me. Shall we get out of here while we can?"

"Answer me. How'd you get here, Greg? I feel like I'm in a comic book and the artist just drew you in."

"People are staring."

"What are you doing here?"

"Attempting to save your ungrateful behind."

"How'd you find me?"

"Finny."

"I just phoned you yesterday in Washington."

"No, I was in Paris, already on my way here. I called you back, remember?"

"Doing what?"

"I happen to work for our government, Natalie."

"Yes, and?"

"You'd checked out of your hotel. Finny told me about the restoration. I just wanted to see if we could do dinner, or something. When I got there and heard what happened, I followed you to the roof. I heard you yell for help. I figured since I was already in the neighborhood and free for the evening, I'd save your life."

"Thanks a lot. If I hadn't fallen on him we'd both be dead."

"Next time you go looking for trouble, hire a professional bodyguard. . . . The important thing now is to get you back to Leningrad. You can say you're sick. And let Sojuzpushnina change your ticket and get you the hell out of the country."

He left her in the doorway and hailed a cab. Natalie followed, her thoughts a tangle.

"Help me tell this guy we want to go to the side entrance of the Leningrad train station."

"I already have my plane ticket."

"They'll be all over the airport."

"But they'll know you bought train tickets."

"Nobody tries to escape on a train. Trust me. We'll be fine."

"But the driver—"

"The driver just wants to get through the day. Ask for the side entrance."

Natalie was still debating whether to tell Greg about Dina's picture on General Lapshin's night table when the cab reached the station. Jervis was the problem. Whom did Greg serve?

"Greg, he was really trying to hurt me. He was trying."

"It's okay. It's over." He put his arm around her. Natalie shrugged it off. "He was protecting that woman."

"What woman?"

"I thought I saw the woman who shot Wallace."

"What?"

"I chased her."

"Are you nuts?"

"He was protecting her."

"And doing a pretty good job of it. I'm going to buy tickets. Why don't you go to the ladies' room and wipe the blood off your nose."

"Blood?" No wonder the driver was watching her in the mirror. Greg dabbed her face with his handkerchief and walked her to the bathroom. When she saw her face in the mirror she thought she would collapse. It was just a little nosebleed, but it recalled the man's intent. He had tried to hit her as hard as he could. He hadn't looked angry, though; it was as if he served someone who *was* angry and said, Hurt her, mark her, kill her. Cold water stopped the bleeding. Her expression hardened and when she walked back into the big station she half hoped to see her assailant waiting. Greg waved. "Tickets on the *Red Arrow* and your stuff is on the way from the hotel."

"I thought that was a tough ticket."

"I'm on a diplomatic passport. Let's find some dinner and a drink. Train leaves at midnight."

"Sounds good," said Natalie, having concluded that before she did anything about Dina, or figured out Lapshin, she first had to learn what role Jeff Jervis had played in Wallace's murder.

The *Red Arrow* sleeping compartment was like the inside of an expensive candy box, all velvet and plush, flowers and rich wood paneling. The beds were turned down.

"Top or bottom?" Greg asked as the wide Russian train glided heavily from the station.

"Top," she said. "You'd probably fall off and kill yourself."

They were reeling from the vodka they had downed at dinner. Greg had a friend in the Soviet copyright agency who had gotten them into the Writer's Union, which served a good meal. They had passed the time at the private club until eleven and shared an icy bottle in the taxi with another couple who cheerfully admitted they rode the *Red Arrow* whenever they could afford to escape a flat full of children and grandmothers for a private night on the rails.

Natalie undressed in the attached bathroom and emerged in a soft flannel nightgown. Greg was propped up in the lower berth, watching Moscow's lights slide by.

"That's cute. You look like Grandma Moses."

"I wasn't expecting a traveling companion."

He went into the bathroom and came out wrapped in a white towel.

"You look like a Roman senator."

Natalie passed him the water glass from which she was sipping vodka. Greg tossed back the liquor. She climbed up to her bunk and Greg lay down on his, filled the glass, and passed it up. They handed it back and forth for a while. Natalie playing the day over in her mind and wondering precisely where Greg fit into it.

"Thanks for the rescue."

"My pleasure."

"Is this the kind of stuff you did with—"

Before she could say Wallace he cut her off. "Let's not get specific aloud, shall we?"

"What?"

"They had plenty of time to make up our compartment."

"Oh. Well, you know what I meant."

"The answer is no. I was strictly a messenger boy."

"Greg."

"What?" He levered his body over the edge of his berth, folded his hands behind his head, and looked up at her. The towel had vee'd open to his waist and she could see a rippled line of stomach muscles straining to hold the position. She reached down and poked them.

"Don't ever lie to a banker."

Greg grinned at her and she smiled back. He said, "I'm not what you think. I'm just a messenger boy."

"Is that what you do for that slob billionaire?"

"Your gratitude takes strange forms, Natalie. I think next time I'll leave you to the wolves."

"I might be safer."

"What is that supposed to mean?"

"It's all too pat, you popping into Moscow when I'm here."

Greg shot the light fixtures a significant look. "Will you cool it?"

"Whisper."

"Go to sleep."

"No one's going to sleep tonight until I get the truth."

"Christ, Natalie." He tightened his towel and stood up and put his mouth to her ear. "I'm here," he whispered, "because I didn't trust my old dear friend's widow to stay out of trouble. I could ask you what the hell you were doing in Moscow for the *Leningrad* fur auction."

"I took a couple of days for myself."

"Oh, really?" He put his lips to her ear again. "Just popped down to Moscow a day after you hit Leningrad? Just happened to hit me for *blat* to get into a Red Army Kremlin party? Just happened to be volunteering on a restoration site where a girl is killed and a Russian thug tries to kill you?" He gave her an irritated look. "Give me a break, Natalie."

"I don't need a reason."

"But I do?"

"You followed me, Greg. What are you looking for?"

"Oh, boy." Greg raised his eyes to the polished wood ceiling. Then he whispered, "Do you know who you're playing with?"

"None of your damn business."

"Natalie."

"Greg."

"If you're not going to tell me, who are you going to tell?"

"Who are *you* going to tell? Are you going to go running back to Jervis? Or some lowlife in the White House basement?"

"What do you care?"

"Because you might get one of Wallace's friends killed," she said hotly.

"Is that who you saw? Wallace's network?"

"What's left of it."

"Or someone setting you up."

"What? What do you mean?"

"Oh, somebody like the KGB, say. Or the GRU. They're a fun crowd."

"They were Wallace's."

"I presume they showed you their official ring."

"Better, you sarcastic bastard. They used Wallace's book code."

"How'd you learn about book codes?"

"Margot Klein."

"What book do they use?"

"You don't know?"

"With Wallace, all info was 'need to know.' "

"Well, it's still need to know."

"Thanks. Didn't you believe us when we told you Wallace had retired?"

"I hoped you were wrong. I wanted them to contact me. I wanted Wallace to be working and you to be wrong."

"Why?"

"I didn't want him to be an old fool, which is what you and that slob Jervis implied."

"I did not imply that."

"Jervis did, and you went along with it."

Greg hung his head. "I'm sorry. I didn't want you mixed up in this. What did Wallace's people tell you?"

"I'm not sure that I want to talk to you. I don't know how you got here. And I don't know what you're looking for or who you serve."

Greg shrugged. "Rather than try to satisfy your laundry list of questions, I'll tell you what Wallace was up to, and you nod if you've already found out. Okay?"

"Okay."

Greg touched his lips to her ear again. He was still standing beside the berths, with his arms propped on her mattress. "Wallace was investigating a conspiracy he called the Millionaires' plot. Right?"

"You knew? Why didn't you tell me?"

"The leader is called the Boss. Like Stalin. But no one knows who he is."

"Why didn't you tell me this at home?"

"What you didn't know you didn't have to keep secret. Neither of us suspected you'd turn into Nancy Drewski as soon as you arrived here. Now feel my lips," he whispered. "There is no plot."

"There is so."

"No plot. It's over."

"I talked to Wallace's agents," Natalie insisted fiercely. "I met Soviet officers he cultivated. I saw the woman who shot Wallace. She killed Luba. Something is definitely going on. Wallace was right."

"Have they picked a date?"

"Valentine's Day."

Greg laughed. "Just in time for the Gen Sec tour to hit New York. They're probably dreaming he'll ask Mayor Koch for political asylum. Believe me, there is no plot."

"I don't believe you anymore. You've lied again and again."

"I've told you the truth, though not all of it. Wallace retired, just as Jervis said. Two years later, Wallace contacted me. He claimed he had discovered a Russian conspiracy."

"You told me this. You and Jervis."

"What we didn't tell you was that the Millionaires' plot was an Army and Defense Ministry conspiracy to overthrow Brezhnev. They had people in the entire state mechanism, including the KGB. It was heavy duty, no question about it."

"When was this?"

"Early '83, around the time you married. Brezhnev was losing his grip. Collapsing oil prices had hit the Soviets as hard as the Arabs, and the free ride was over. Corruption was out of hand, the comrades were howling for consumer goods, the Army was fighting for new weapons, and the economy was dead in the water.

"These so-called Millionaires had an idea to modernize the economy—decentralization, incentives, privatization, and applied technology. Their big thing was incentives. They had a radical idea to reward excellence with ownership. If Ivan doubled ceramic chip production at the Spark of Lenin Electronic Works, Ivan would receive title to a condo in Yalta. Real ownership. A deed to property that Ivan could keep, sell, bequeath. Needless to say, it was the *Nomenklatura*, not Ivan on the production line, who were going to reap condos.

"But even *discussing* reform was lethal without first ousting Brezhnev and his cronies. In other words, a coup, because Brezhnev had the Politburo in his pocket. Wallace was terrified of a Soviet coup. He said even a rumor of mutiny would start a KGB purge that would send the Russian people back to the Dark Ages. They'd remember Stalin as a human rights activist by comparison."

"What if it were successful?"

"Wallace said win, lose, or draw, a coup would unleash an entire generation of civil war. He said Russia had bled enough. He begged Jervis to let him persuade the President to quietly leak word to the Millionaires that we would not support them."

"Why not tell them himself?"

"He was not an operations man. He was an information gatherer. Besides, if he made the threat, they would write him off as part of a faction. Jervis finally agreed to bankroll an attempt to find out exactly who was involved."

"Taking Wallace's boat in the process."

"Give Jervis credit. He was serving the President well, protecting him from having to make a decision based on incomplete data. He could have turned it over to the CIA, but instead he honored Wallace's request to keep it secret. But Wallace didn't have the whole story yet. So he jumped back into Russia and threw his nets again. Suddenly it was all over."

"Why?"

"Two things happened at once. Just when Wallace discovered the name of the Millionaires' anointed leader, the supposed savior of the Soviet economy got himself killed in a helicopter crash. Wallace had his whole network investigate, but all he could ascertain was that legitimate, old-fashioned, shoddy Russian craftsmanship was responsible, not intrigue. Then, before the Millionaires could field a successor, Brezhnev upped and died.

"Plot leader dead. Reason for plot dead. End of plot.

"Andropov took over leading a KGB anticorruption purge. Luckily, he died. Now we've got Gorbachev rousting the Brezhnev crowd and pushing reforms that outstrip anything the Millionaires even dreamed of. If the bureaucrats don't get fed up and bounce him, we're going to have a strongman on our hands. But that is neither here nor there. The point is, the Millionaires' plot died with Brezhnev."

"But Wallace kept looking."

Greg sighed. He reached over Natalie, parted the curtain, and for a long moment stared out at the black Russian night.

"Wallace wouldn't stop. He asked permission to keep monitoring the Millionaires. Jervis gave it reluctantly. Wallace had the money anyway from the boat. He would report periodically, through me, but Natalie, he was spinning his wheels. There was no plot anymore."

"I met people he was investigating."

Greg closed the curtain.

"Sure you did. The fact is that the Millionaires have run out of steam. Gorbachev is more solidly in power every day. These old 'Boss' types must see that. The party's over. The new order is in. The Millionaires are too late."

"That doesn't mean they won't try."

"Not when push comes to shove. They're doomed. Don't you understand the KGB watches everything and everybody? The KGB has one job and only one job, to protect the Communist Party. The Party is the power, the KGB is the guard. Believe me, Natalie, it's over."

"Then why are the Millionaires attacking Wallace's people?"

"They're lashing out at their weakest enemy. The remnants of the Millionaires' conspiracy are battling the remnants of Wallace's long-abandoned and aging network."

"Those girls weren't aging."

"Children, by your own admission. Spoiled children making games of what their grandmothers did for real."

"They're being hunted."

"The games got out of hand. But no one is overthrowing the Soviet government."

"There's opposition," she persisted.

"Amorphous opposition, neither led nor organized. Not a plot."

Natalie thought of General Lapshin's *dacha*, multiplied it by the hundreds that must exist on Army installations across the Soviet Union, and wondered if Greg had any idea of the power and privilege the upper echelons of the Red Army had to lose. Thousands of high-ranking officers lived like kings on their research estates and arms factories, enjoying not only exotic luxuries, but the aristocratic power of an elite system within the system. Of course they and their counterparts in the bureaucracy were threatened by Gorbachev's repeated calls to end corruption. To them, openness and reconstruction had to be anathema. Proposals of withdrawal from Afghanistan—betrayal. The arms treaty and troop reductions—an attack on the source of their power.

Wallace had discovered that they had formed the Millionaires' plot to fight back. And if Luba and Elena could be believed, the Millionaires were waging a deadly fight. Well led, well organized, and most definitely a plot.

As if he could read her mind, Greg said, "Who'd you see at that reception?"

"Didn't Finny tell you?"

"Finny told me what you told him. I'm beginning to suspect you're a little devious, Natalie."

"At last, a compliment. Thank you." She patted his bare shoulder. "You're freezing. Get under the blanket."

"My neck's too short to whisper from down there."

"Put it over your shoulders."

Greg tugged the blanket off the bed and draped it over his shoulders. "My feet are cold."

"Come up here then." Natalie moved against the wall. Greg climbed up and settled down beside her. Shoulder to shoulder they were too wide for the berth. "I'm falling off."

"Here." Natalie slipped an arm under him and tugged his head to her shoulder. "Better?"

"Drink?"

"Sure."

They passed the glass of vodka back and forth again. "Whisper something," Natalie said. Through the double blankets, she could feel his body against her leg.

"You first."

"I feel like our parents are going to burst in any second. 'Turn out the light, kids.' "

"Shall I?"

"Leave it. . . . I told Finny the truth."

"What do you think of General Lapshin? Is he the one? Is he 'the Boss'?"

"I don't know. But I don't think so," Natalie said.

"Why?"

"I can't say. I just have a feeling he's not the type. He's a little spooky."

"So was Stalin. It goes with the territory. If you want to lead Russia, it helps to be a little twisted. You need a cold eye and a brain that works on slightly different angles than your subjects'. How's he spooky?"

"He just is. The biggest thing in his life is the Afghan war and I think it always will be. Like Vietnam is for Jervis."

"Jervis is a phony!" Greg retorted fiercely. "He hung out in Saigon, got his ticket punched in a sweep through friendly territory, and came home a veteran."

"Maybe for Jervis it's what he didn't do. For Lapshin, it's what he did do. He admits he enjoyed it."

"An honest man."

"But that troubles him. At any rate, he's too complex a guy to be the Boss."

"Stalin and Peter the Great weren't exactly simple souls," Greg argued.

"Their goals were simple. Lapshin's goals are all tangled up in his motives, and his motives are very complicated. Trust me on this, Greg. It's the same in business. The big stars are simple people. On target, dull, boring, and single-minded."

"How'd *you* get to the top?"

"With Wallace. Besides, we were never stars like that. We blew opportunities and dropped the ball as often as not. Why do you think I've got the troubles I do with Cotillion?"

"I thought it was because you're snooping around Moscow when you should be buying furs in Leningrad."

"Leo Margulies was ready to kill me," she admitted. ". . . Greg, what if you're wrong? Who will stop them?"

"Not my decision. It's up to the White House. I don't make policy. I'm no Colonel North. My orders are look, listen, and report. I obey orders and I intend to report what I've seen and heard."

"To whom?"

"What is that supposed to mean?"

Natalie chucked his chin again. "What's Jeff Jervis got on a nice guy like you?"

"Nothing. Jeff is a confidant of the President. I work for the President. We each serve in our way."

"You know, I'm pretty sure he sicced the Koreans on me. He's trying to destroy Cotillion."

"I can sympathize, but there's nothing I can do about it. I'm not his business partner."

"So what does he have on you?"

"Nothing. It's not State Department. It's White House cellar. You know how the game is played. This administration encourages private enterprise."

"Greg. We're alone in the night on a train in the middle of Russia. We've loved each other for many years and we've drunk more than enough vodka to tell the truth. Whisper it."

Greg whispered, "Nothing."

"If there's no plot, why did you lie to me?"

"Wallace taught me, Let sleeping dogs lie."

Natalie threw back her head. "I do love you. You make me laugh."

Greg touched his lips to her ear. "I love you, too, Natalie. Always have." To her astonishment, his tongue burrowed softly, parting the vodka fumes in her brain like a laser. She shuddered at first, on the brink of pleasure, but, startled and a little dismayed, she tried to pull away.

"Listen," Greg teased, holding her with unexpected force. "Listen." She felt powerless in his grip, which had the strength of certainty. He was as sure as she was hesitant. Her voice came thin to her, a reedy, doubt-filled protest that sounded as if she were waiting to be convinced by his reply. "I don't think this is a good idea, Greg."

Lovingly, with infinite, gentle precision, he rimmed the spiral of her ear. "Don't think. How does it feel?"

"Too soon."

"It's not like I'm a stranger."

She turned on her side to face him and try to explain that more than time held her back. Greg took the occasion to draw her to his mouth and brush her lips with his. Natalie trembled. There was a fragrance from him that lofted her back to the hot sun on the lawn of his house in Greenwich. Sally's house. Before Wallace. She got lost in the fragrance and in the warm, dry silk of his lips. Greg touched her surely through the flannel, nudging her from the shoals of indecision toward a sea of event. She thought she was safe with him. Yet this was a new Greg, more determined than she had ever seen him. She tried to stop thinking, and contrived to make her body press against his. She couldn't, and suddenly she knew exactly why.

What she had learned already in Russia—the book code, the Millionaires' plot, Wallace's struggling network, even the woman who killed him—had restored Wallace to her. She had her husband back. She believed in him again. And while she had no proof yet, she had reason to hope at least that he had been faithful to their marriage.

Greg was moving easily against her. But where with Wallace she would have felt her long, thin frame begin to triumph over gravity, here she was leaden, a skeleton of heavy bones. With comparison came a thousand overwhelming memories. Her heart swelled, hot and brim full, until a sob shattered in her chest.

"No! Please, stop."

Greg started to give her another teasing smile, but something in her eyes stopped him, and he released her. For a second his face was dark with disappointment. Then he smiled and patted her shoulder through the blanket. "I'm sorry. I shouldn't have."

"No, you shouldn't have." She looked away, angry and hurt, then thought maybe she wasn't being fair. They had been having fun. They were half bombed. She said, "I don't blame you. It's me. I'm just not ready."

"I thought with me it would be different."

"It's as if anyone who touches me is a stranger." She thought she should try to explain how she felt, that she had Wallace back and that she couldn't betray their renewed partnership, but suddenly that seemed too intimate, even with Greg, who was obviously relieved to smooth things over with a joke.

"I just wanted to get to the head of the line."

"Well. . . . I'll keep you in mind. Someday."

"Want to give me a ballpark projection on the month?" He grinned. "Or just let me take a number?"

For some reason that made her laugh, and she kissed his cheek with a combination of gratitude and relief. They lay silently awhile, until she said, "Can I tell you something?"

"Anything."

"Promise not to laugh?"

"Promise."

"I must be exuding some sort of chemistry. Last night I got into this same kind of situation with General Lapshin."

"A twosome on the train?"

"I got high enough to really want to sleep with him. Just to do it, end the past or something." And she just might have, she realized, had she not seen Dina's picture. Dina, ironically, was the one who restored Wallace to her.

"Seems I got here in the nick of time in more than one way."

"Shut up. . . . I knew I'd cry for Wallace. I'm really glad it's going to be you."

"Now?"

"Not now," she giggled, drying her eyes on her sleeve. "I can't tell if you're being kind or serious."

"Use my towel," Greg said, unwrapping it from his waist to dab her cheeks, and moving closer to kiss tears from the hollows beneath her eyes. Natalie pushed the towel back onto him, her eyes lingering a second on the smooth planes where his waist and flat hips narrowed into his thighs.

"I kept thinking of you last night with Lapshin," she whispered. "He's built like you, slim and fine."

"I'm beginning to sympathize with the Russki bastard," Greg sighed. "You and your chemistry must have left him chewing his mattress."

"He got drunk."

"Not an altogether bad idea," said Greg, reaching for their glass.

He had asked if he could stay in her berth for a "cousinly nap," and Natalie was glad she had said yes. Deep in the night, bundled cozily in nightgown and blankets, with Greg's head pillowed on her breast and the dark train rolling heavily beneath them, she whispered, "Someday, you will be my first major seduction."

"The major ones are best kept in the family."

"Stop that. We're hardly related at all."

"We're getting a lot more related now than we used to be, I'm happy to say." He snuggled closer and kissed her sleepily.

"Tell me something?" she asked.

"Anything."

"I asked you before, but you dodged."

"Consider me softened up. What do you want to know?"

"What does a slime like Jervis have on a nice guy like you?"

"Money."

"Money? You?"

"Money. I need a lot of money."

"But Sally."

"She wants to leave me."

Natalie's heart skipped a beat. "I'm kind of glad to hear that, I think." But there was honesty in the night and she added, "Actually, an available Greg is a heavy thought. . . . Are you sad?"

"It's fine with me, but she wants the kids. And she'll get them, because on paper she's as good a mom as the divorce court could want. I can't stop her, but I don't want to lose my kids. I can't get shared custody working in Washington, so I have to protect my visitation rights."

"You need money for lawyers." Who among us, she once heard Wallace laugh to another man, has not, while comforting a recently separated woman, said, My dear, you ought to see a lawyer?

"Lawyers are the least of it. Natalie, do you know how big money operates?"

"Not personally."

"I *mean* personally. I need enough money so that when Sally rents the villa in Bali for the summer, and I get 'Oh Greg, how could you deprive the children of summer in Bali,' I can rent the villa next door. Otherwise, when Daddy visits he gets stashed in the gardener's cottage a mile down the beach, while the current sailing instructor stays with Mommy and the kids in the big house. Thanks to Jervis I have a shot at the kind of money I need to be in Vail when they're in Vail, and Palm Springs when they're in Palm Springs. I'll be chasing them around the world on school vacations until they're eighteen or Sally gets bored and lets me have them. Capish?"

"That depends on what you had to do for the money, doesn't it?"

"I'm afraid the answer to that secret will require a seduction."

"Not tonight."

"Then no more secrets."

"Be my friend. Please."

Greg sighed. "I promise I'm not selling out. Things just worked my way. I'm Jeff Jervis's messenger boy because Wallace wanted it that way. He wanted me to watch Jervis. And he wanted me to keep a line open to the President, and to the next President, in case Jervis ever got out of our way. To do that I had to serve Jervis, too. Or at least seem to. We've got people running the government who aren't elected to the government. Some of them are billionaires."

"I hadn't realized until the funeral how close you and Wallace were."

"We kept our relationship quiet to protect Wallace in Russia. It would have been foolish to play up his White House connection. But the fact was, he was very much a father to me. Remember, my parents separated my first year at Georgetown. Then my father died. Suddenly Wallace was there when I needed him. He would visit me, take me to dinner. Then I started getting party invitations, often seated near the right admiral or some senior service guy at State. Then came the internship in the White House. And when that turned into a full-time position, Wallace introduced me to Sally's father."

"Was he grooming you to take over from him?"

"Maybe. But he was alone, too. No kids of his own. And I always knew that if I couldn't rise to the occasion—you know, dropped my tie in the soup, and blew the opportunity—that he would still take me to dinner, look out for me, help me, whatever."

"Did you have a plan when you introduced me to Wallace?"

"Very much so. The Jervis thing was getting him down and he started talking his age all the time. I thought you might perk him up. Did you ever."

Natalie smiled sadly. "Perked me up, too. . . . Are you saying that Jefferson Jervis is going to make you a wealthy man?"

"No way," Greg scoffed. "But through him I can earn enough to keep my kids *and* continue to serve my country—forgive the patriotic violins. But I mean it. I'm good at what I do. Wallace trained me well, and I've learned a lot more on my own. I could earn ten times my Civil Service salary in the private sector. Jeff's 'patronage,' shall we say, allows me to lend my talents and experience to a government that really can't afford people like me."

" 'Too prickly to eat and growing bigger every year,' " she quoted with a smile. "You told me that proudly, once."

"I *am* proud. And thanks to Jervis, this is one catfish who's able to work in the government pond."

"Did you speak to Wallace the day he was shot?"

Greg stared at the polished wood ceiling. "No," he said sadly. "I wish I had. Never got to say good-bye."

"Did he try to call you?"

"Not that I know of. I thought he might."

"So you don't know what he accomplished on his last trip."

"He accomplished nothing, dear. I'm sorry."

She cried when she realized she believed him. Greg kissed her tears and stroked her as mile upon mile flowed under the train. Eventually she fell asleep, dozing until a freight train racing to Moscow shook her awake. She lay thinking, then thrilled herself with a fantasy of climbing onto Greg, drawing, plunging, sculpting in cold passion a vivid substitute for her dashed hopes that Wallace had somehow transcended the sad and empty end of his life. But the fantasy had no life. The image blanked, suddenly, as if a curtain were drawn. She curled up as much as the space would allow and laid her cheek on his chest.

Greg watched through slitted eyes, affording her the privacy she craved, while he stroked her hair and talked to her. She thought it was as beautiful a thing as a man had ever done for her, and when he had said enough, she curtained his face with her long dark hair and kissed his mouth in gratitude.

"I want you to come home with me," Greg said. "Get you out of the country before something bad happens."

"Won't Sally notice a third place at the breakfast table?"

"What if that clown comes looking for you?"

"I still don't think he was KGB. He was with the Millionaires."

"Natalie, you are a startling combination of smart and dumb. What difference does it make who he was? He tried to kill you."

"In a police state I'm a lot more frightened of the government than of individuals. You can't run around waving a gun in the Soviet Union."

"The Millionaires still have clout in the government."

"No. I'm here as a furrier. The auction is big business for the Soviets. It's one thing to arrest a newspaper reporter or even some poor tractor sales rep traveling alone. Not me. I'm part of an important crowd."

"Your fur cover is about as bulletproof as a mink cape."

"It's not a cover. I'm here to save my business. I wish it were a cover, but the fact is, I'm on the brink. And if you tell Jervis that, I'll never speak to you again."

"Come home. Save Cotillion in New York. That's where the business is and the banks are."

"I'm staying," she repeated. "If they arrest me, you'll bail me out again. Won't you?"

"Not me, Sweetheart. I'm going home. I just came over to check you out. I've checked, I've warned, and I'm going home."

"Leaving me in the clutches of the Millionaires," she teased, her body warm and comfortable in his arms.

"More likely the KGB."

"What?"

"You'd be a fool not to assume that the KGB is investigating what's left of the Millionaires. The Committee for State Security investigates everything and everybody. It'll end up with the gulag and firing squads for anyone who's left, including any air-headed American widows they catch hanging around."

If Greg was right, and the Millionaires' plot was history, did she dare to ask Kirichenko's help in finding Wallace's murderer? She shivered, recalling the hopeless expression of the hotel manager cringing from Kirichenko's arrest party.

"Cold?" Greg whispered, holding her tighter. "Or sensible at last?"

"Goose walked on my grave."

"Come home with me."

"I still have business here."

"What kind of business?" Greg demanded.

Natalie's mind was roving far from the great train. She kissed his cheek reassuringly. "You ask a furrier what kind of business she has in Russia?"

But Greg had asked a better question than he knew. Had she become an amateur spy at the expense of her goal to save the company she and Wallace had built together? Would she return to New York clutching a few more details of his secret life to find she had lost the fruit of their shared life? She drifted back to sleep swearing that would never happen, but woke in the train station confused.

25

L eo!"

She jumped from her taxi and caught up with the furrier on the steps of the neoclassic Palace of Furs. "You look like you had some weekend," Leo greeted her. "Good time in Moscow?"

"Very nice. I met some of Wallace's friends. Look—there's Artie what's-his-name from *People*. Come on, we'll give him a picture. *Artie!*" she called, taking Leo's arm. "Here's a shot. Capitalists Quest Quality Communist Furs."

"What's got into you?" Leo muttered.

"Publicity, Leo. *Glasnost*. Take it where you can. Can you remember this guy's last name? Smile."

Artie, shivering in a shoddy Russian fur hat from the Beryozka tourist store, snapped a picture of Natalie and Leo and said, "More like bowling ball meets pin."

"How are you doing?" Natalie asked.

"We can't get a handle on the story. I want a cover, but I'm sliding down the tubes into 'Style.' "

"Glasnost. Perestroika."

"We done it already."

"Peace through commerce."

"Boring."

"Peace through naked self-interest."

314

"Closer. 'Bye, Natalie. Give me a call when you refine it."

Leo said, "I thought you were coming back last night. You missed a party."

"I took the night train. The sleeper."

Leo gave her another shrewd glance and said, "With who?"

"What do you mean, with whom? My cousin."

"Oh."

They exchanged their coats for smocks inside the auction house and headed for the mink room, where several hundred thousand sample pelts were hanging for inspection. Both Leo's sons were already at work. As they indicated a lot they wished to examine, pretty fresh-faced Russian coeds—fur girls, Leo dubbed them when he wasn't calling them honey or sweetface—took down the hanging strings and carried them to tables under strong fluorescent light.

"How's it look?" Leo asked, joining the examination.

His eldest son, his spitting image, tanned and portly, minus only a cigar, gave a Leo-like shrug. "Nothing I'd kill for."

Hands racing over the skins spread on the marking table, Leo began noting in his catalogue his opinion of their color, quality, how precisely the furs within the lot were matched, and finally, the price he hoped to bid. Natalie watched over his shoulder. She was dressed in Wallace's altered white bidding suit, and although the smock hid most of the brilliant red sash knotted at her throat, his trademark costume was still drawing looks around the Palace of Fur. While she still felt vaguely like a trespasser on Wallace's turf, it was Wallace's other turf that distracted her more. At precisely the moment she should be fighting to save Cotillion, her thoughts were dangerously scattered.

Dina loomed foremost in her mind. The night with Greg had honed her anger. Greg's attempt to reopen her, body and soul, had instead turned her back to Wallace. There flowered in her a purposeful coldness that scorned the risks and plotted revenge against Dina.

"Is old Harvey bidding for you, too?" asked Leo's son, glancing up sharply from a lot he had just tossed aside.

"Fox," Natalie said. "Maybe this evening you and Harvey ought to talk about pooling resources."

"Let's see what we have here, first," Leo interrupted. He drew her in beside him, and pressed her fingers to a pelt. He showed her that the long guard hairs varied in length. "You can live with these, but if they get any more uneven than this, the coat looks like a dog in the rain. Feel this."

He pronounced the short, wooly hair under the guard hairs sufficiently full and named two of the quality Canadian factories Wallace had contracted with as capable, with careful dressing, of making these skins into coats that met Cotillion's standards.

Natalie's eyes were burning. Every fur looked the same as thousands blurred into one gigantic mink. Finally, after hours of marking, Leo announced he needed a break. They went out to the hall and sat in deep overstuffed chairs, drank tea, and chatted with brokers Leo knew. Leo was restless, though he had to give his eyes more time to recover. "Come on, honey, I'll show you some real fur."

He took her to a hushed corner of another anteroom where snowy lynx hung in wild splendor. The fur girls put the lots he requested under the light. Leo pored over them, a smile dancing behind his cigar. "Gorgeous. Look, dear. Feel this. Silk!" He studied one particular skin for a few moments, examined some others, and returned to the first. Suddenly he slipped his hand inside the pelt and felt around. "Oh ho!"

"What?"

"What have we here?" He took Natalie's hand and thrust it inside the pelt. "Feel that?"

"This little rough spot?"

"That's a patch. The hunter missed, shot it in the belly by mistake. He fixed the hole."

"I can hardly feel it." On the fur side, it was invisible.

"Hey, these guys can sew." Leo pulled the skin inside out. The patch was a three-inch circle and almost invisible since the leather matched perfectly in color and thickness and was stitched with thread as fine as a single strand of Natalie's dark hair. "Nice work. Too bad he couldn't shoot this good."

Leo marked the lot in his catalog.

"Are you going to bid anyway?"

"It's a gorgeous lot. Best in the auction. I can work around it."

Natalie dialed 09 for directory information. Did Kirichenko even live in Leningrad? she wondered.

A huffy operator denied vehemently that any number existed for

Leningrad offices of the KGB. "The Committee for State Security," Natalie persisted.

"*Nyet.*"

"Please try a listing for Valery Kirichenko. . . . I don't know his patronymic."

"That number is not available."

"Do you mean—?"

The operator hung up. As it had taken forty rings to get her the first time, Natalie went downstairs to the Intourist desk and asked for a telephone directory. Much discussion and a long search of the service desk cupboards finally produced a four-year-old directory. It did not list the Committee for State Security. Expecting little, Natalie looked up Kirichenko. There were several, but only one V. Kirichenko, on Liteiny Prospekt. Her Falk Plan map showed it just east of the Fontanka Canal, which circled the downtown central city.

She got no answer in the afternoon and went on to other calls. She left another message for Stefan's Vera, her fourth, and then managed to get an overseas line to New York to talk with Bill Malcolm, who was yawning his way through a very early morning. Sleepiness did not hide the pessimism in his voice.

"I'm putting together a deal, Bill."

"What kind of deal?"

"I hope I can tell you tomorrow. I'm meeting with a senior trade official."

"Good luck."

That evening, Kirichenko himself picked up his telephone on the first ring with a brusque, "*Da.*"

"This is Natalie Stuart Nevsky, Comrade Kirichenko. We met in Moscow."

"*Da.*"

"Forgive me for interrupting you at home, but I knew no other way. I couldn't find a number for your office."

"What do you want?"

"I have to talk to you."

"About what?"

"I can't talk on the phone. Could I see you privately? I thought we could meet for tea or take a walk." Wallace had said the only place to talk frankly with a Soviet citizen was in the park or a loud nightclub. The Astoria's club was deafening, but not Kirichenko's style.

"I am an official of the Soviet government," Kirichenko replied coldly. "I do not talk privately with foreigners."

She wondered if even he feared a phone tap. He certainly sounded like a man talking for a recording. "Could we possibly have a personal conversation about an official matter?"

"No."

"Could we speculate, privately?" Natalie persisted, hoping he would appreciate a dash of humor, but he did not seem to.

"About what?" he asked, just as coldly as before.

"My husband's murder."

For a while the phone line buzzed emptily. Then: "You may come to my flat."

Her cab slowed on a seedy-looking, dimly lit stretch of the Liteiny a short distance from the bustling Nevsky Prospekt. She saw a block of store fronts tucked under old-fashioned apartment buildings with dark stone facades. A gang of teenagers were skateboarding and breakdancing outside a combination shooting gallery and video game parlor. They were hatless in the bone-piercing cold, showing off Mohawks and buzzcuts. Other than the boys, however, the sidewalks lay empty in front of darkened shops.

"Here?" she asked her driver, who pointed sullenly at the house number painted on the arch above a covered alley.

Natalie approached the alley cautiously, her street antennae sensitive to the stares she was drawing from the teenagers. Glancing back, she noticed a taxi she had seen leave the Astoria immediately after hers douse its lights and pull to the curb. The sight provoked a thin smile. Whoever had followed her, KGB or Moscow Millionaires, would be in for a surprise when they reported her destination.

The covered alley was dark. Recalling Wallace's descriptions of Russian streets, she had packed one of his miniature lithium lights, but instead of using it, she turned on her heel, crossed the street and went into the games parlor, where she found a pay telephone. The teenager using it, draped in chains and possessing spiky green hair, ducked his head and hung up almost immediately, honoring, like any good Soviet citizen, the three-minute rule.

Natalie dialed Kirichenko's number and covered her ear to block the noise of the pinball machine.

"*Da.*"

"It's Natalie Stuart Nevsky. Would you please meet me on the sidewalk? I'm a little nervous about walking down that dark alley."

"This is not New York City, Mrs. Nevsky. You'll be perfectly safe."

"I'd appreciate it very much if you'd walk me in."

"The *dvornik* will meet you," he said, and hung up.

She passed through the teenagers again, crossed the Liteiny behind the parked cab, and waited by the alley until the doorman appeared with a flashlight and led her silently into a courtyard, which was faintly lit by the glow that penetrated curtains in the windows overhead. Dodging garbage cans and piles of frozen snow, he indicated a dark hole in the wall that she hoped was a door, and faded back into the dark. "First floor."

Natalie started up the dark stairs, astonished that someone as important as Kirichenko lived in this modest neighborhood. On the landing, she shone Wallace's light on several doors, finally spying a printed name card. She knocked and waited, listening for footsteps within.

Kirichenko opened his door. She had forgotten how tall he was, and how thin. She thought of the wire sculptures of Don Quixote, though there was nothing naïve or innocent in Kirichenko's quick gray eyes. He ushered her into a small room.

"Give me your coat."

She shrugged out of it and had a look around while he hung it on a hook by the door next to his own coat. She was surprised again by the KGB officer's simple surroundings. Whereas General Lapshin had enjoyed the sort of elegant spartanism only money could buy, Kirichenko appeared to live like an ordinary Soviet worker.

His apartment consisted of this one room, with doors opening into a tiny pullman kitchen, a bathroom, and a separate toilet. Two beds against the walls, abutting and heaped with pillows, served as couches. A coffee table crouched in the corner formed by the beds, and she glimpsed a larger table folded behind a set of glass-doored bookcases. An office chair sat at a plain wooden desk, which held a manual typewriter and a telephone. At one end of the desk, and on some shelves affixed to the wall above it, was a clutter of framed photographs.

The flowered carpet was frayed, but like everything in the room, immaculate. The only luxuries, if they could be called that, were a color television tuned to an interview program—where an uncomfortable bureaucrat was attempting to answer complaints about housing—

and a large collection of framed posters from the Soviet Revolution that covered every inch of bare wall and lent fierce drama to an otherwise ordinary place.

Kirichenko turned off the television and asked, "What is this about your husband?"

Vague fears had been whirling like snow devils in her mind. What if, for instance, when she told him that Dina had shot Wallace, Kirichenko was more interested in learning from Natalie *why* Dina had shot Wallace? What if he had been watching her because he suspected she had taken up Wallace's spying? What if Greg was wrong and the Millionaires were in full flood? What if the KGB had forced someone to reveal the Millionaires' deadline? Kirichenko would be frantic. Valentine's Day was Saturday. This was Monday night. Under the gun, with less than five days to destroy the plot, he would stop at nothing to learn more from Wallace's widow.

"Well?"

She had to assemble her courage, but he hadn't even invited her to sit down. To buy time, she turned to the posters where the KGB officer's bony countenance was echoed graphically in the stern faces exhorting the Reds to fight the Whites, resist the allied interventionists, smash the capitalists. They were originals, the paper yellowed and holed at the edges where nails had been hammered with fervor and haste. "You're a collector?" she remarked. *"Objets de la Revolution?"*

General Lapshin or the foreign trade official Vladimir Rostov might have returned a self-deprecating smile, but Kirichenko did not. Expressionless, he watched as she continued to circle the room. It dawned on her that she had been misled at the Kremlin reception by his passionate defense of the Gorbachev reforms. He was the exact opposite of the sophisticated Lapshin or Rostov; he was what Wallace used to call a "real" Russian: suspicious, humorless about ideology, xenophobic.

Natalie peered in the glass bookcase where his collection included old handcuffs, a crude-looking revolver, and a short truncheon, its leather wrapping cracked with age.

He tracked her movements through slitted eyes and Natalie sensed his curiosity turn to menace.

"What is this white metal ball?"

"A hand grenade, painted to look like a snowball. When unarmed workers defended themselves with snowballs, an occasional one of these tended to make the czar's *gorodovois* wary of snowballs in general." A thin smile crossed his face and Natalie pressed her brief advantage, asking, "I wonder if I could trouble you for a cup of tea. I haven't had dinner and I missed lunch at the Palace of Furs."

Kirichenko looked surprised by her audacity, and Natalie was pleased that he actually seemed compelled to apologize. "I'm afraid my hospitality falls short of what you could expect in most Russian homes. In my Moscow flat I am better prepared. Here, I don't usually entertain."

"Then let me take us to dinner. There's a good restaurant in my hotel." She suddenly realized she would be very relieved to be out of here.

Kirichenko shook his head. "I have tea. And there're some biscuits in a box."

They were, curiously, from Fortnum & Mason. Later Natalie recalled that the imported delicacy ought to have tipped her to the fact that even Valery Kirichenko had contradictions in his life. For the moment, however, she chewed on the ginger cookie and continued her inspection of Kirichenko's posters while the KGB officer boiled water on a hotplate.

A smiling Lenin in suit and tie and working man's cap wielded a red broom with which he swept the globe clean of capitalists and kings. A czarist prison burned over the words *Hurrah for Freedom*. A peasant walking blindfolded off a cliff was urged to learn to read. A proclamation announced that the Petrograd provisional government had fallen to the Petrograd Soviet. Another hailed rural electrification. Yet another ordered *An End to Clemency and Slackness! All Social Revolutionaries Are to Be Arrested Immediately.*

"Did you have a pleasant night with General Lapshin?" Kirichenko called from the kitchen.

"I beg your pardon?"

"You left the Kremlin with General Lapshin, did you not?"

"Evening," she corrected. "I didn't spend the night."

"Where did you go?"

Reasoning that he knew anyway, she said, "We went to a *dacha*."

What else did he know? she wondered. Did he know she had met Luba at the restoration site? Did he know about her night with Greg on the *Red Arrow*? Or the men who tried to kill her? Or about Dina, herself? But, no. He could not know that.

He served the tea in glasses and offered a bowl with sugar cubes.

"Delicious. Thank you."

"What is this official matter about your husband?" He sat on a bed and indicated the other, but she moved toward the pictures on his desk, afraid to sit and instinctively aware that playing the confused widow was still her best defense.

"Mrs. Nevsky, you're trying my patience."

"It's terribly important," she answered. "But I'm afraid. In fact I was thinking of asking you to come to New York where I would feel safer."

"Your husband wasn't safe in New York," Kirichenko retorted brutally.

She looked away. "You're not making this any easier."

Abruptly, Kirichenko took a new tack, saying, "That may be, Mrs. Nevsky, but I cannot help you until you tell me what your problem is. I presume you need help."

"In a way, yes," Natalie replied, toying with the photographs and finally picking up the largest, an ornately framed picture of a young man in a leather jacket and a peaked forage cap pulled low over his eyes. He stood beside the driver of a World War I touring car, bristling with weapons. "Is this an ancestor? He looks very much like you."

"My great grandfather," Kirichenko replied with pride. "He was a hero of both the February and October revolutions. He'd been underground in Petrograd throughout the war. A very brave and committed Social Revolutionary."

"How did he fare when Lenin ordered the SRs shot?"

Kirichenko looked surprised she knew that much history and she kicked herself for saying too much, but all he said was, "Badly. He fared badly at the hands of the *Cheka*. It was a waste of a good revolutionary. Your husband had a connection to the SRs. His mother, wasn't it?"

"I think so."

"You're turning this request for a conversation into quite a mystery."

"No, I'm just being careful."

"Do you have reason to be?"

"I don't know," she said, replacing the picture of the revolutionary and glancing over the others, which formed a sort of photographic family tree of Kirichenko men in uniform: on a tank, beside an ancient airplane, standing in the shelled ruins of a European city, posed jauntily on the sandbagged walls of a Spanish town. This last had black borders—an International Brigadier, like Wallace—killed in the Spanish Civil War. There was a man in a police uniform who looked like Kirichenko.

"Your father?"

"Yes."

The son of a policeman, General Lapshin had sneered.

"Is this you with General Secretary Gorbachev?"

"Yes," he snapped impatiently. "When I was decorated. There's one with Andropov when I graduated and one with Mikoyan and another with Andropov. And there are more family, my mother and my sisters. Now what do you want?" he asked, as Natalie, still stalling, reached for another picture in a silver frame, separated from the rest and turned so he could see it as he worked.

Her hand froze in midair.

"Well?"

She forced her hand into motion and picked up the silver frame. "And who is this?"

"A lady."

"What's her name?" she asked of the dark-eyed beauty with the willful smile.

BOOK FIVE

THE COSSACK'S BRIDE

26

Kirichenko crossed the room in two swift strides and snatched the picture from her hand.

"Your request for a private conversation could not concern *my* personal life," he said, as he restored the photograph to its place. "Now what is this about your husband?"

The crazy laugh, which had not plagued her in weeks, began bubbling madly in her chest. She fought it down, at the cost of a weird grin tugging like something alive at her mouth. He was standing very close, looming over her. Natalie stared back, speechless.

Her mind was whirling, but she was no longer in such fear of him. Somehow the KGB seemed a little less omnipotent if General Lapshin's girlfriend could seduce its star officer. The Millionaires had infiltrated their worst enemy.

"Your husband," Kirichenko snapped.

"You know he was shot?"

"Yes."

"Can you help me find who did it?"

"I'm afraid I don't follow."

She played it out, striving for the proper balance between ignorance and illusion. "General Lapshin said you were a good policeman."

"What would a Russian policeman know about an American murder?"

"It's just that the police believe she was a foreigner and there's evidence she fled to Europe."

"So?"

"Wallace spent so much time in Russia. I thought, perhaps, you might know of a connection. Someone who hated him enough to kill him."

Kirichenko looked blank. "This is what you wanted to discuss?"

"What else?"

"What else, indeed. . . . No, I'm sorry, Mrs. Nevsky. I'm afraid I can't help you. I'm not really a policeman in the sense you need and—"

"But couldn't you ask certain policemen to investigate?"

"Investigate what?"

Here she was on thin ice because she certainly did not want Kirichenko's policemen digging deeper into Wallace's past and threatening the remnants of his network.

"I don't know what. I just thought—I hoped. I mean, I didn't know where to turn and you— This was a silly idea. I'm sorry I took your time. I'll go."

Kirichenko studied her thoughtfully, and she began to get the frightening impression that the KGB officer was debating whether he would allow her to leave. Enduring his silent scrutiny, as a numbing dread moved through her body, she grew aware of a cheap alarm clock ticking loudly beside his bed.

"You have not answered my question. Why have you chosen me?"

"I met you at the reception and—"

"You met dozens at the reception. Why not ask your husband's friends, the Lapshins, to help you?"

"But you're the policeman—"

Kirichenko shook his head. "There is more."

Terrified of getting caught in a lie, Natalie played on the truth. "I saw you at the Astoria. When I saw you again in Moscow it seemed too much of a coincidence."

"Nonsense."

"You *stared* at me at the Astoria. I thought then you were interested in Wallace's murder."

"What would I care about a Jewish–American furrier?"

"He was half Cossack, and he traveled here all his life," she shot back, resenting the anti-Semitic slur. Suspicion narrowed Kirichenko's eyes. Natalie used her anger, asking sharply, "Could you help me find a cab?"

Kirichenko's reply was a long, cold stare. Abruptly he came to a decision, at which Natalie could only guess. "There will be a taxi waiting for you on the street. The *dvornik* will take you." He handed her her coat, shouted a cryptic order down the stairs, turned silently into his apartment, and closed the door.

The doorman who had led her in walked her through the alley. At the curb was the cab that had followed her from the Astoria. In sudden terror, she thought she was being arrested. The *dvornik* held the cab door. She had no choice but to get in. The driver, his face muffled in hat and scarf and coat collar, careened through a U-turn and sped away.

At the Nevsky Prospekt, he turned right and headed down the boulevard, past darkened shops, with Natalie not daring to breathe until he turned onto Herzen Street, which led to the Astoria Hotel. He clipped her for ten rubles and stuffed them in his pocket. Natalie fled into the warm lobby, determined to find a drink.

As it had every night since her arrival, a band was playing in the dining room, led by a large, brightly clad, pink-haired woman banging a tambourine. On the dance floor, smartly dressed young Russians bobbed and weaved enthusiastically under the determinedly jolly gaze of older, well-off Party officials drinking at the tables with their wives. A mirrored revolving ball spun colored lights among the ornate crystal chandeliers and stroked the fluted columns and lofty rococo ceiling with shafts of red and green. Waiters plodded about with huge heaped dinner plates. A champagne bottle stood on every table and it was much too noisy to think, which was exactly why Natalie had come.

She bribed the maître d' for a table far from the dance floor. Sheltering behind a massive column that would hide her from cruising singles, she ordered chicken Kiev, the one reliable dish in the hotel, and vodka, and settled back to let the noise stop the churning in her brain.

Perversely, the noise had no more effect than a backdrop of soft rain, while the vodka, far from obliterating thought, unexpectedly lent order where chaos had prowled. Hardly conscious of her actions, Natalie pulled her notebook from her bag and began outlining the situation as she had on a thousand business trips before in a thousand hotel dining rooms. Her pen jotted abbreviations, codes, and symbols intelligible only to her.

Point One: Any plot whose conspirators could infiltrate the top ranks of the KGB was not exactly in tatters. Valery Kirichenko was too thoroughly awful for Dina to have fallen for him without a purpose. And that purpose was to penetrate the secret police investigating the Millionaires' plot.

Point Two: Therefore, Wallace Nevsky was not a fool. He had indeed been on to something very real with the so-called Millionaires.

Point Three: Dina had killed Wallace for the Millionaires. She was not the only one to blame, merely the most visible.

Point Four: ? What to do? Natalie left that blank and advanced to Point Five, which was the most intriguing.

Point Five: If Greg and Jervis had underestimated the Millionaires, it was because they had underestimated Wallace Nevsky. They could be forgiven, she supposed, but she could not. She had made the stupid assumption that her husband's entire network consisted of a bunch of flakes like Luba and Elena. What if his real net, his longtime agents, were still in place?

The band crashed into silence, announced a break, and trooped from the stage. A stray thought winged through the quiet. If she were Kirichenko, she too would have professed a total lack of interest in Wallace's murder. Why announce to anyone, particularly the widow, that he was intrigued by the possibility of a Russian killer?

Back to Point Five. Assume Wallace's net existed on a level above a bevy of miniskirted *highlife-istki*. Who? They would be survivors, cautious men and women, but watching her, for surely some must know that Wallace had smuggled something out of the Soviet Union, that it had not been found, and that the Millionaires had killed him for it. One of his agents might even know what it was.

In her bag were business cards, pressed upon her at the first night's dinner. She fished them out. The Cyrillic lettering reminded her how far she was from home, and she beat a hasty retreat back to Point Four. The question mark. What to do? She circled it repeatedly, round and round and round until it was black. But the question was less what to do than what did she *want* to do? What would Natalie Stuart risk to finish Wallace Nevsky's last mission, his calling, which late in his life had yielded something he regarded as sufficiently important to break his own forty-year rule against operations. Smuggling was an action, and by his enemies' accounts he had taken action.

She wished the band would come back.

It was one thing to seek to punish the woman who had killed him, quite another to pick up his cudgels. One thing to prove he hadn't betrayed their marriage, another to inherit his jeopardy. She had a business to run, after all, a business in perilous straits—was that too dramatic? Not at all—and a widow's life to live, and a past to put behind her. Wallace's fight was not, strictly speaking, her fight. Cotillion was her fight. As for Dina, Wallace himself had said that revenge was for fools who couldn't see the future for the past. Change is the best revenge, he had counseled their unborn children. She downed another shot *zalpon,* which caused her father to appear as her own private talking head, inquiring, Hadn't Wallace died to protect change? *Died* is the operative word, she replied, to which he responded, We are born to serve.

She could easily duck—bid at the auction, try to cut an agreement with Rostov, go home—and no one would ever know. Except, of course, ten generations of diplomats and missionaries chorusing from their reserved seats in heaven: If not Natalie, who? If not now, when?

She already had lunch scheduled the next day with Trade Minister Rostov. And she had arranged tea later that afternoon at Ivan Starkov's Amerika Institut. So that left, among Wallace's friends who had gone out of their way to make contact, only Fyodor Shelpin, the timid little Sojuzpushnina rep. She telephoned Shelpin from the lobby. Reluctantly, very reluctantly, he agreed to join her for an after-dinner brandy.

He arrived with his wife, a dowdy middle-aged woman who sat stiffly, would drink only mineral water, and shot frightened glances at Natalie and the band leader, who was regaling the nightclub with a sirenesque "Memories." If Shelpin had worked for Wallace, Natalie guessed his wife was unaware and that he had brought her along, as any sensible middle-level Soviet official would have, for a meeting with a foreigner.

Shelpin appeared nervous, and infinitely more Russian. He had exchanged the snappy Italian suit he had worn to greet the fur buyers for a heavily padded woolen sports coat, into which he seemed to sink like a cautious turtle. He stared morosely into his brandy as if he would rather be anywhere but talking with Natalie, who, in hopes of boring Mrs. Shelpin into wandering to the ladies' room, rattled on about Wallace, the fur trade, and her fond desire of getting a Cotillion coat on *People*'s cover. "I always dreamed," she gushed finally, "of coming to Leningrad with Wallace. To see the Russia he knew and loved."

Both Shelpins nodded vaguely. Mrs. Shelpin refused another mineral water. Fyodor, however, turned hungrily to the brandy, and Natalie asked the waiter to leave the bottle.

"Russia was such a part of his life," Natalie exclaimed. "And I've always believed Wallace gave so much back to the Soviet Union. Don't you think so, Mr. Shelpin? You worked with him. You know what I mean."

"He was a friend of the Soviet Union and Sojuzpushnina," Shelpin conceded with a nervous glance at his wife.

Natalie pushed him again. "And not just furs. He loved Russia and all it could be. He loved your diversity, the great differences between your nationalities, even your conflicts."

Mrs. Shelpin looked at her as if she were drunk, but Shelpin retorted with a distinct edge to his voice, "Western observers are obsessed by Soviet ethnic variety. You hope for conflict, even mutiny." His wife made a warning sound under her breath, which Shelpin ignored. "You simply don't understand that this is a nation that has routinely sent tanks into disturbed areas since tanks were first invented. So please don't talk to me about national quarrels. We are Soviets for six thousand miles from border to border."

"Wallace always said that the only factions that counted were at the top."

The colored lights from the reflecting ball revealed naked terror on Mrs. Shelpin's face, but she mustered tight-lipped dignity: "Is not Soviet way to discuss political subjects in nightclub," she replied in English. Shelpin himself looked as if he suspected that his old friend's foolish widow would next blurt, Done any spying lately?

"Dunya," he said to his wife. "Would you telephone the baby-sitter?"

Dunya turned to him in disbelief. He patted her hand and explained with a stiff smile to Natalie, "Our daughter is divorced. She's taken work in Novosibirsk. We have the children. It's all right, Dunya. Go telephone. I'll wait with Mrs. Nevsky."

As soon as she left, Natalie said, "I know you worked for Wallace." She stopped his denial with a gesture. "No. Don't waste your breath. I *know* you did. And tonight I know you're more afraid than ever."

"There is reason in Soviet Union to be afraid."

"I wouldn't deny it. But I have to ask—"

"I can't help."

"Just one question. Why did you do it, Mr. Shelpin?"

"Do what?"

He was clearly not a bold man. "What gave you the courage to help Wallace all those years?"

Shelpin hunched deep into his jacket. "He inspired me."

"How can *I* inspire you?"

"To do what?"

"The day he died—the day he was killed—Wallace smuggled something out of the Soviet Union. I don't know what it was, or where he hid it. Do you?"

At that moment his wife returned. She had scarcely had time to find a telephone, much less call a baby-sitter, but she reported that the baby-sitter was tired. Shelpin rose with apologies. Natalie jumped up beside him. The band was blasting through a Rolling Stones medley and for a moment, with the table between them and Mrs. Shelpin, they were alone in the cocoon of noise.

"Help me. What did Wallace smuggle?"

She never knew what she had done right. Maybe it was just that what she knew made her one of them. Whatever, she had reforged Shelpin's link to Wallace. Pumping her hand and smiling broadly, pantomiming an official Sojuzpushnina thank you and good night, he said, "When the sun rises go to the Peter-and-Paul Fortress. There's a man there swimming."

"Swimming?"

"The east bastion, by the Kirov Bridge. Open your coat so he can see your pearls. If you're alone, he may approach."

27

She started out at seven-thirty, two hours before dawn, criss-crossing the city on trams and trolleybuses to lose herself in the rivers of Leningraders traveling to work. After an hour she was still not sure she hadn't been followed. She was tired and her mind fuzzy. Gradually the bitter cold cleared her head. Hungry, she bought a roll in the Finland Station, ate it while walking briskly with the crowds, and jumped suddenly onto a departing tram. She changed conveyances six times in the next hour and got off, finally, on the north side of the Kirov Bridge, which overlooked the Peter-and-Paul. There she paused, leaning on the railing, waiting for the other disem-barking passengers to disperse.

The fortress's granite walls rimmed an island on the edge of the Neva, across the river and slightly upstream from the Hermitage. From its center a slim golden spire shot into the sky, which had dawned a cloudless blue. The price of this clear weather was an Arctic chill, and the air was so cold that the rising sun seemed to crackle against the golden spire. Men were swimming in the narrow arm of water between Natalie and the fortress, cavorting in a long slot they had hacked from the ice.

Natalie took one last look to be sure she was alone and scrambled down the embankment steps, past a rock wall bearded with icicles. Walking onto the frozen river, she joined the small crowd of specta-

334

tors in fur hats and sheepskin coats who were watching the swimmers. When she spread the fur lapels of her traveling coat, she thought her pearls would freeze to her throat. A pedestrian waved from the bridge.

An old man in a tank suit and green swim cap clambered out of the water and onto the ice at Natalie's feet. "Towel!" he called. Hoping this was Shelpin's man, she looked around, spotted a pile of rough towels, and handed him one. He dried his face, tossed it over his scrawny shoulders, and greeted her with a cheery, *"Do brave oo tra!"*

"And good morning to you, too, Comrade."

"Hot enough for you?"

"Sweltering. I wish I'd brought my bathing suit." He stared expectantly until she remembered to touch her pearls. The old man grinned with a toothless smile.

"I am Yulian. I am pleased to meet Vassily's bride. I am also surprised. I didn't think he would let you take the risks— Don't shake hands. We'll pretend you're curious about walruses. Quickly, what can I tell you? It's freezing in the air."

"What did Vassily smuggle?"

"I don't know."

Natalie's face fell. Yulian hastened to reassure her. "I mean he might have smuggled anything. But if he smuggled what I gave him, he smuggled a recording."

Margot Klein was right. "Of what?"

"A meeting. A Soviet officer and an American. I do not know their names."

"What did they look like?"

"Unfortunately, I was in the cellar." Yulian smiled. "Where I do my best work. I am what they call in English a 'bugger,' I think. When I told that to Vassily once, he laughed. I have no idea what he meant."

"An American and an officer? An Army officer?"

"I think so," said Yulian, jogging in place, rubbing his hands.

"What did they talk about?"

Yulian shrugged. "They spoke English. I don't."

Natalie was stunned. At such close range at last, she had expected so much more. "You have no idea what they said? Vassily didn't tell you?"

"It's better that way. Nothing to tell when the KGB asks."

"Have they?"

"No one who knows," he replied.

"Are you worried? Are they after you?"

Yulian shrugged again.

"I'm old. I've lived my life. And I've kept my tooth."

She thought she had heard his Russian wrong, until he opened his mouth and pointed at his empty gums. Way in back were two yellow molars, top and bottom. "One for the cap," he explained cheerily. "One to crunch."

"Cap?"

"My old cyanide tooth from the Great Patriotic War. For the SS."

All Natalie could think to ask was, "Does the poison last all these years?"

"Have you any more questions?"

"Yes. Did Vassily give you any idea what the recording was for?"

"For? What is any recording for? Blackmail."

Blackmail.

She climbed up to the Kirov Bridge. A taxi picked her up immediately. So excited was she to have proof, at last, that she didn't think about the cab until it reached her hotel. The driver, she realized with a sinking heart, could have been waiting for her on the bridge. Millionaire or KGB . . . What had she done to the old man in the river?

But that was paranoid. She knew she had not been followed. She was upstairs in her suite, dressing for lunch with Rostov, when paranoia assailed her from a new angle. If the taxi had been waiting, then Yulian was the one being watched.

"Are you familiar with the phrase *fat cat*?" Natalie asked the Ministry of Trade officials Vladimir Rostov had assembled at his *dacha*. Rostov, ever the good host, obliged with a friendly, "As in capitalist fat cat?"

"As in Hong Kong fat cat." Natalie was seated with the six men before a massive stone fireplace. Outside it was bitterly cold, sunny, and growing windy, but the house, which Rostov said had belonged to a Finnish baron before the Revolution, was warm and comfortable. Animal skins, including a bear Rostov claimed to have shot himself, were scattered on the floor. Natalie's chair was draped with wolf. They had had, upon arrival, an informal lunch around the *zakuska* table. Everyone had exclaimed over the plump ripe tomatoes. Rostov, who was wearing a French-made business suit and Adidas running shoes, had showed her around, taking particular pride in his Hitachi VCR and a vast library of Western tapes.

"Vassily always brought me videos," he said. They turned out to be Diana Darbee's *Parmalee Canyon*. Natalie had used the opening to test him about Wallace, but Rostov had not risen to her mentions of pearls or Wallace's "other interests." Now they were down to business, legitimate business, and she was winding up to pitch.

"What is this Hong Kong fat cat?" the Trade Ministry's finance man asked ponderously.

"Chinese Hong Kong businessmen who undertake joint ventures with the People's Republic of China. Manufacturers who supply the technology, the machines, and the training for the workers. The PRC extends the capital to build the plant, which they will eventually own."

"What sort of business?" asked a youngish aide, who had been friendly at lunch.

"Watchmaking, electronics assembly, plastics. And fur coats."

Natalie waited. They watched. Finally the Sojuzpushnina representative said, "I was not aware the PRC make fur coats."

"They are beginning to learn, with the help of Hong Kong furriers, who, as you know, learned the fur trade from American manufacturers."

"You gave away the technology?" asked the stolid man from Finance. Compared to the slick American investment banker who, these days, salivated to lend money, the Russian looked as if he would guard his funds with his life.

"We are an international business," Natalie replied, skating lightly over the bitter controversy in the New York fur trade. "For instance, after the Great Patriotic War, American mink ranchers sold breeders to the Soviet Union. Today we 'sell' our technology. Fortunately, fur coat retailing is a growing business. We've lost manufacturing jobs in America, but gained sales," she concluded glibly, cringing inside. Wallace would divorce her for talking like a Republican. She forged on.

"So, what Comrade Rostov has so generously invited me here for is to continue an interesting discussion we had the other night on the way home from the Sojuzpushnina auction party."

Several glanced at Rostov, who inclined his head with a proprietary nod and a little male joke, "I was going to be social, but Mrs. Nevsky would have none of it." His colleagues laughed dutifully and Natalie continued.

"I own Cotillion Furs, Limited, the largest retailer of fur coats in America. I also own several of the country's finest fur factories, as well as partnerships in many others. My mechanics have worked nearly forty years for my late husband. There are no finer craftsmen in the world and no finer coat for the price than a Cotillion fur." Disregarding her debts, her frozen credit line, her nagging supply problems, and the skepticism of every furrier in New York, she realized her company sounded rather wonderful, and the Russians looked suitably impressed.

"The Soviet Union is the world's leading supplier of raw material to the fur trade. Ten million ranched mink a year, many other furskins, both ranched and wild, including the finest sable and lynx. Yet, if a Russian woman wants a fur coat, she must buy from the Europeans, and it won't be half as good as an American coat. Somehow that doesn't seem right."

"Export business is more important than luxuries," the Russian finance expert intoned. Rostov turned to Natalie for her reply.

"Does the Soviet Union export iron ore? No. It makes steel, finished goods for its own use and exports steel. It seems strange that you don't reap the benefit of exporting finished fur coats."

They looked interested in where she was heading, curious how she intended to get there. "What do you propose?" asked Rostov.

"I propose a mating of Communist and capitalist fat cats. I propose a joint venture between the Soviet Union and Cotillion Furs."

The young aide started to ask a question. Both Rostov and the financial expert hushed him and motioned Natalie to continue. She said, "I will supply the machinery, the know-how, the management skills, and a core of skilled furriers who will both set up manufacturing systems and train Soviet workers to produce fur coats. You will pay for it. We will split profits."

They seemed willing to discuss forming a company for the *dzhoint venchur*. They wanted the *Amerikan no-khow* and Cotillion's *tekhnologiya*. At the point at which they had to consider money, however, they got restless, lighting cigarettes, gazing out the windows at the frozen gulf, exchanging glances. Natalie couldn't figure out what had gone wrong. She had pitched beautifully and still was selling her heart out. They liked the idea. But they didn't like her. Even Rostov looked perplexed, as if he wished he hadn't set this up. He was quite obviously the boss, but dragging top management from busy schedules ought to produce something of substance in the demanding new climate of *perestroika*.

At first she thought they were reluctant to deal with a woman, and indeed the finance man asked bluntly, "Is this Cotillion Furs what Americans call a one-man show?"

"One-woman show would be the correct term," Natalie retorted, mindful of Wallace's advice that the Russians admired strength. But there was her answer. It was less her being a woman than her being alone. Same problem she had faced in New York. Who was she?

She said, "I'd like to suggest a short recess so I could use Comrade Rostov's telephone. I'd like to bring my management team to Leningrad. You can meet them personally and see if they're the sort of people you'd like to work with."

"When can we meet these *menedzheri*?"

"Thursday."

They looked at the finance man, who looked at Rostov, who appeared intrigued. "In only two days? All right. We'll have tea. You can join us when you've finished your calls."

Rostov led Natalie to the sunroom. He spoke sternly into a bright green telephone, but after five minutes, he was still waiting for an international operator—time enough to remark on Natalie's triple strand of pearls, if he had cared to, or to acknowledge the code when she asked where she might buy pearl earrings. He did neither, however, joking instead about Soviet "idiocies," like the antiquated telephone system, his broken tape recorder, and the cracked runner on his iceboat, which was tethered to the shore like a frozen dragonfly.

"Have you telephone in car?"

"It's a great time saver," Natalie answered, fingering her pearls to no avail. Rostov got increasingly upset with the delay and suddenly snarled into the phone that it was a code 73 call. In seconds he had a line.

"Ah! Operator at last." He identified his ministry and placed the call to Cotillion's office, and waited some more. "Ringing!" he announced triumphantly, handing over the phone, and in leaving he managed to give her what by American office standards would be construed a pat on the ass.

"I don't like that," said Natalie.

Rostov left with an innocent smile.

"Joannie? How are you?"

"They haven't shut the phone off, yet."

Although the tinny-sounding telephone multiplied the distance, Joannie's brisk Queens accent seemed to pull Natalie all the way home to New York, through the wires into Cotillion's offices. For a grateful second, even in sight of the icebound gulf, she fancied she could smell the fur from the workrooms, coffee brewing, and Danishes on the morning cart.

"Okay, we're moving. I want Alex Moschos, Old Irving, and Pete Kastoria here in Leningrad, Thursday."

"Pete the foreman? What for?"

"To discuss manufacturing with the Soviet minister of trade."

"Manufacturing?" Joannie interrupted again.

"Do we have a supply problem?"

"Yes."

"Do we have a credibility problem?"

"Definitely."

"So?"

"Awesome, Natalie. Awesome."

"Tell them to keep it under their hats. I don't want anyone moving in on this deal before I've sewn it up. And call Lynn Brown—tell her I'll try to call her later—and tell her to prep with the accountant and get here Thursday, too. Tell her to bring at least one male assistant— it's got to be a male—a good details negotiator, well-dressed and sure of himself."

"Three furriers, one name-partner attorney, one hotshot male shyster. . . . Anything else?"

Natalie thought a moment. To impress the Russians, she needed more male window dressing closer to her level. She considered Bill Malcolm, dropped him as too detached from Cotillion Furs; thought about Greg, dismissed him because of the Jervis connection; and wondered, finally, whether her brother still remembered his Russian.

"Talk to Michael Stuart." She knew that Joannie, who had fielded Wallace's calls for years, would assume the line was tapped and understand why she had said Michael Stuart, instead of my brother Mike.

"Tell him the Russians want to meet Cotillion's deputy executive director."

"Wait a minute, Natalie."

"He'll do fine. I need a warm body here by Thursday."

"What about me?" Joannie asked harshly.

"You're not a money person."

"But what promotion do I get?"

Her protest brought Natalie up short. Joannie Frye had started with them at age seventeen as an intern from the City-As-School work-study program. She had been born forty-seven, Wallace used to say. A new title would make official what Joannie was doing already under the guise of administrative assistant, which was aggressively coordinating sales, distribution, and purchasing. Natalie made a decision she should have made when Wallace died. "You're my new co-chief operating officer. As soon as Cotillion is solidly mine again, we'll drop the *co*. Right now you're too young for the banks."

It was the first time in five years that Natalie had heard her sound astonished by anything.

"Natalie, I don't know what to say."

"So you better hire me a new administrative assistant and one for yourself, too."

While the command and communication lines between her, Natalie, Mike, and a yet-to-be-hired purchasing agent remained fuzzy, promoting Joannie was a step in the right direction. Natalie would try to rise above the day-to-day distractions to act as a proper chief executive officer, looking out for the investors' interests, running the company properly, and protecting it from larcenous manufacturing partners like Stevie Weintraub when they tried to dump garbage in Cotillion stores. Most important, she thought, Cotillion was moving again, not just reacting.

"We'll talk in New York. Don't forget to set up everybody at Pip." Pip Printing did their business cards. "Concorde them to Paris. Book them into an airport hotel. I want them here rested. I'll take care of visas on this end. Now, try to get Bill Malcolm into a conference call. Don't lose me. It's hell getting a line out of here."

She was in luck. Bill was breakfasting in the partners' dining room at Stuart, Malcolm and Hardy.

"Is a fifty-million-dollar joint enterprise with the Soviets new and noteworthy enough to raise venture capital?"

"What's the deal?"

"I supply machines, mechanics, and teachers. They do the factory, workers, and furs. I sell the coats."

"Terrific. Who do you sue if it goes sour?"

"I knew you'd ask that. They've got new laws about recourse. I can sue. Besides, the Soviet Union always honors contracts."

"What's to stop them from nationalizing you?"

"Self-interest. They'd shut themselves out of western deals for twenty years."

Bill agreed.

"Can you use it to get me new investors?"

"Let me talk to some people."

"Speed is everything. I need promises real fast."

She put down the telephone. Outside, the wind was whirling snow devils out of the dark stands of fir trees, down the slope, and onto the broad, frozen gulf, where they raced their sisters to the horizon. Rostov's iceboat seemed to beckon. She longed to hoist its sail and let the wind sweep her away. She ought to feel exhilarated, but instead, she hugged herself, suddenly aching with sadness; she was leaving Wallace behind.

A mirthless laugh from deep inside reminded her she hadn't left anyone, yet. Pip printed fanciful business cards every day. She had a long way to go before the titles meant more than words, longer before an organizational chart translated into quality goods bought and sold, and a long way to go to convince the Russians in the next room that Cotillion was real.

The afternoon sun was settling toward the ice. She made herself pick up the telephone. The operator reported smugly that the overseas circuits were busy. "This is a code 73, Comrade."

"Yes, Comrade. Immediately, Comrade."

Ten minutes later, Diana Darbee mumbled, "What the fuck time is it?"

"It's three o'clock in Leningrad. Do you know what I'm doing?"

"Natalie? Call me in the morning."

"I'm doing a deal with a Russian who loves your videos."

Diana's voice cleared up perceptibly.

"Better me than Joan Collins."

"*People* is covering the fur auction. I think they need someone beautiful and famous to hang it on. Better you than Joan Collins."

"You want *me* to go to Leningrad? In the winter?"

"I spoke with Artie what's-his-name. *People* needs a hook."

After a brief silence, Diana said, "I think I'll let Joan have this one."

Natalie's heart fell. "But this is a real shot at a cover."

"I've had *People* covers."

"No one's ever had too many covers," Natalie retorted. She took the ensuing silence for agreement and added, "You'll thank me for the favor."

"You say favor and I see fiasco."

"What do you have to lose?"

"Forget it, hon. Diana does not travel to Russia to look foolish."

"What foolish?"

"The big news out of Russia is political at the moment. They'll put some Soviet with a high forehead on the cover, not Diana, and Diana will stand around unnoticed, cold, and wet." Unspoken, Natalie guessed, and not open to discussion, was Diana's continuing fear of being linked to a messy murder trial if the New York Police Department arrested a "blonde."

"Diana—" Natalie had started to say she needed her, but that was no way to Diana's heart when the star was doing business. "Trust my judgment on this—I'm on the scene. The Russians are committed to this Gorbachev tour. He'll be in New York on Valentine's Day. They'll do anything for publicity. They're bending over backwards for me because I'm putting together a deal that's great for them. You can be part of it."

Diana's continued resistance was audible as satellite hiss on the empty lines. Natalie said, "Let me couch this in terms you'll appreciate. The Russians are willing to perform unnatural acts with Westerners who can help their economy. I can help them. You can help me help them. You get a *People* cover."

"And what will Natalie get?" Diana purred.

"Rich."

The actress laughed. "Let me think about it."

"I can't make a move without your yes."

"Call me tomorrow."

"I want your picture in a Russian lynx. If you give me a yes now, you can keep the coat."

"Yes."

Rostov stuck his head in the door.

"How have you fared on the phone?"

"No problems. As long as your ministry can expedite a half dozen visas."

"Delighted." The Russian trade minister looked both relieved and a little surprised.

"They're arriving Thursday, via Paris. Friday is the last day of the fur auction. Assuming all goes well, we'll get terrific publicity if we coincide our preliminary announcement with the departure of the Gen Sec tour."

"I am not so sure we can move that quickly," Rostov objected. "Today is Tuesday."

"We've got a great opportunity with the Gen Sec tour."

"The Gen Sec tour? What do you mean?"

"Gorbachev is promoting economic cooperation. Our joint announcement would support him vividly. In fact"—she sailed on boldly— "wouldn't it be wonderful if we could get him to visit the Palace of Furs this Friday on his way to New York?" A stray thought intruded on her pitch: by Saturday, if the Millionaires had their way, Gorbachev would be in exile.

The Russians were gaping. Natalie regained her focus.

"He could kick off his tour with our deal."

Rostov laughed at her audacity. "I imagine his schedule is already set."

"Still, he'll welcome our support. What more could he ask for than a Soviet–American business partnership the day he leaves?"

Rostov looked pained. "This mating of fat cats is very complex."

"There's another reason for a preliminary announcement on Friday," Natalie countered, stressing *preliminary*. "Diana Darbee is going to join me for the closing press conference."

"How wonderful."

"We're going to catch *People* magazine just before their guy leaves. *Bozhe Moy*, I hate to miss out on the publicity. We must remember the ultimate test of a deal like ours is to sell more coats."

"I hope I can meet her."

"Of course."

"But frankly, I still see no need to rush such an important announcement. So many details before we, as you say, do a deal. So much depends on so much. Yes? I propose we announce in July, at the next Sojuzpushnina auction."

They argued back and forth, but he wouldn't budge, which Natalie found baffling. Rostov was no old-fashioned, Brezhnev-era conservative bureaucrat, yet he was stonewalling her like an official whose job it was to obstruct. And that made no sense. Rostov dealt in America. He knew the need for swift movement, but he was fighting her every inch of the way.

She put herself in his shoes. Upon her broaching the joint venture she would have immediately checked Cotillion out with some of the New York furriers at the auction. Someone must have told him about the credit freeze while she was on the phone with Joannie and Diana. Which meant that he knew that unless she made a deal now, she would no longer own Cotillion come next July.

Shock them with the truth, she used to argue with Wallace, to which Wallace, as instinctively secretive as any furrier, had replied admiringly, How devious can you get?

"Comrade Rostov, before we rejoin your people, I must tell you one more reason to expedite our agreement."

"We have no agreement, yet."

"You've got competition."

"Oh?"

"A Korean furrier, with a very wealthy backer, is trying to take over Cotillion to get our urban retail outlets. They make junk, but they want my stores. They're putting great pressure on me. I don't know how long I can hold out."

"We are not the sort who rush into deals for any reason," Rostov replied blandly, but Natalie sensed she had scored.

"There is only one Cotillion Furs in America, Vladimir. No one else has such a retail network. I'm offering you the chance of a lifetime."

"You're offering me a chance to save your company."

"Someone's going to. I'd rather it be you." She turned to the windows to let him chew on it.

Rostov waited a long moment, then crept up and put his arms around her waist.

Natalie stood stock-still, absolutely frozen by the certain revelation that Vladimir Rostov was exactly the trade official he claimed to be, whose only ulterior motive had nothing at all to do with Wallace Nevsky's spy network or the Millionaires' plot. Rostov, evidently interpreting paralysis for acquiescence, nuzzled her neck and cupped her breast in a sure and knowing hand.

"*Let go of me.*"

She readied a sharp elbow. Rostov released her and backed up a step, smiling easily and asking, "Are not American deals lubricated in order to run?"

"You've done enough business in America to know how deals are lubricated, Comrade Rostov."

Rostov glanced at his Rolex, and the few Scots–Presbyterian genes in Natalie not already on alert stiffened to attention. Bribery was yet another area where he was going to find himself severely disappointed.

"The Wallace Nevsky I knew must have asked certain assurances of trust and mutual understanding before he joined your partnership. My old friend is dead and gone, so I do him no dishonor." He advanced again with outstretched hands and a confident smile. Natalie felt her temper getting away from her, but she owed herself one shot to stop him without souring her chances for a deal.

With the slightest of coquettish smiles—her only coquettish smile, in fact; one so reluctant that Diana Darbee might have deemed it a frown—she said, "Wallace and I waited months *after* we had closed our deal and signed our contracts."

"Vassily? Resistance to Vassily was like the matador's cape to the bull."

"We waited."

"At your insistence."

"It was mutual."

The Russian returned a baffled, "Why?"

Natalie hugged herself as she had earlier, turned her back on him, and gazed at the sunset, which was turning the ice violet. "For one thing," she answered, "Wallace was a hard-headed businessman. We were both risking everything to launch Cotillion."

She fell silent until Rostov prompted, "What is the other thing?"

"We both suspected, deep down inside, that we were in love, maybe from the first moment we saw each other. It was unspoken, but there. We both had a sense that we had all the time in the world." She turned around and gave Rostov the full force of her eyes. "We were companions before we were lovers."

A wistful expression crossed Rostov's face.

"Comrades," he whispered, shaking his head sadly and putting his hands in his pockets. "I know," he addressed the floor. "Vassily told me as much, while you were courting. We went right out and got roaring drunk, but it didn't help. . . . Well, the others are waiting. Why don't we go back in and tell them how you fared on the telephone."

On impulse, and quite uncharacteristically, Natalie reached out and touched Rostov's pink cheek. "Thank you. You're very understanding."

Rostov brightened immediately.

"You're still welcome to stay the night."

"And how was lunch at the Rostov *dacha*?" Ivan Starkov greeted her. He was waiting in the lavish chandeliered reception room of his Amerika Institut, which occupied a small, beautifully kept palace on the Moika River, not far from Natalie's hotel.

"Are there no secrets in the Soviet Union?" Natalie smiled, shaking his outstretched hand.

"Few, when it comes to international intrigue."

"What intrigue?" she asked, but Starkov only smiled. "My students are waiting anxiously to hear your pearls of wisdom."

She looked at him sharply, but Starkov merely started up the marble steps to the ballroom, where the *Institut*'s scholars waited at a long dinner table spread with an astonishing collection of American fast food. Natalie exclaimed at the pizza, tacos, fried chicken, hamburgers, and even sushi, in their original take-out containers.

"Where did you get this?" she asked.

Starkov smiled. "I have friends who travel."

His colleagues tended to resemble the rumpled old academic, affecting thick eyeglasses and threadbare tweed jackets. The young men had wispy moustaches. The women wore minimal makeup and prim dresses. She was reminded of the doctoral candidates in her father's seminar, except here in Leningrad the scholars were eyeing her like a butterfly pegged down for close analysis on the cutting board.

"*Do'bree den,*" she greeted them.

"English, please," Starkov retorted. "We can't study America without English. It would be like pizza without chili." He glanced slyly around the table until a student summoned the courage to correct him. "Oregano, Comrade Professor."

"Of course. English please, Mrs. Nevsky."

"All right. Good afternoon. If you're half as familiar with my business in the fur trade as Comrade Starkov is, there's little I can tell you about it that you don't already know. I've decided, therefore, to discuss banking, my former field."

Starkov nodded at a woman who immediately raised her hand. "We are wondering how American bank protects money from bad debt furrier."

"I imagine Comrade Starkov has explained the credit machinery." Starkov smiled back innocently, as if denying the rumor that in his KGB days he had purchased a Washington D.C. credit bureau.

Natalie explained that banks tended not to advance cash, but to pay invoices for goods received by the furrier, thereby being able to attach those goods. "In practice they don't want the goods, but they want to keep everyone honest."

"What are penalties for dishonesty?"

"Failure, if you're caught."

Only Starkov smiled.

"Can you describe the decision-making process in a limited partnership like Cotillion Furs?" a student asked earnestly. "And how the power is shared."

"Oh boy. My partner, of course, was my husband, which both complicates things and makes them easier. If we had a theme, at all—and I assure you there was less planning than you might suppose—but if we had a theme it was division of labor. Each of us had certain responsibilities. We kept it loose, particularly when we were starting out. Now that we're bigger we need systems and they can be a trap."

"Are there lessons we can learn from you that we can apply to *perestroika* and *uskorenie*?"

"When it comes to acceleration of the growth rate, our two countries are very much in the same boat. We are each old-fashioned economies pitted against adaptable new economies like Japan and Korea—dinosaurs in a world of sure-footed little mammals. You are held back by ponderous central planning— Is it all right to speak this way, Comrade Starkov?"

"*Glasnost* is a window into our own house," Starkov replied, adding with arrogant pride, "No one censors this Institute."

"But the United States is also hostage to its own sort of central planning. Our largest corporations move as ponderously as the most hidebound Soviet bureaucracy. They can't adapt to changing markets and techniques. Does anyone know, for instance, what has happened to General Motors?"

Twenty hands shot up. Starkov called on the obvious dunce of the class, but even he knew that General Motors had fallen from controlling half the American car market to less than a third.

"We've stopped listening to our engineers," Natalie explained. "And we've stopped respecting them. The best and the brightest become bankers, which is a waste of vital talent. The Japanese listen to their engineers and therefore build better cars and stereos. It has been said that if the American housewife ever saw a Japanese washer–dryer, every heavy appliance manufacturer in America would be put out of business.

"But you're not listening to your engineers either. Nor are you putting the effort into basic distribution systems. There's a Communist bias against the middleman. Like it or not, it's the middleman who ties the ends together. So what lessons can you learn from the United States? Get serious about distribution. And listen to your engineers. Don't blame the worker on the assembly line if the assembly line itself is poorly designed."

"That was a nice overview," Starkov complimented her as they drank tea in his office. "Though I had hoped for more specifics."

"I'll be back."

"Oh?"

"I'm hoping to make some more specific connections in Russia, myself." With that, she removed one of her earrings. "Excuse me. Wallace gave me these pearls. He did nothing halfway. They're so heavy, sometimes they hurt."

Starkov stood up abruptly. "I'm afraid my time is running short. I'll walk you out."

Startled, Natalie hurriedly screwed the earring back in. Starkov walked her to the foyer, where he helped her into her coat. Out of hearing of the babushka in the coat check, he asked, "May I give you some advice?"

"Of course."

"Stay out of your husband's footsteps."

Natalie forgot the KGB rumor about Starkov and seized his arm. "You're—"

Starkov pulled away, glancing anxiously at the babushka, who was watching. "You may be quite clever at business," he said, "but you'll never survive Nevsky's game."

"What are you saying?"

"We have an expression in Russia: what is in your heart is on your face."

"What is on my face?"

"Doubt."

"What am I supposed to do with that?"

"Do nothing," said Starkov, guiding her through the door into the cold, dark evening, and retreating into his foyer.

"Wait. I have to talk to you."

"Delighted," Starkov answered sarcastically. "Come back for the summer fur auction. We'll talk in July, if you're still alive."

"But you said you didn't know my husband."

"I didn't care to discuss him in the company we were with that night. And I don't care to discuss him now. My warning to you is my last gift to him, my final pearl of wisdom."

"Please," she whispered. "Help me find his friends."

"If Wallace Nevsky didn't know who his friends were, how can you?"

28

On the sidewalk, at the bottom of the steps of the Amerika Institut palace, Leningraders on their way home from work had gathered with their string bags around a battered panel truck where a man and a boy were selling haunches of meat frozen stiff from the cold. Natalie stumbled through the shopping queue, automatically looking around to see who was following. It had become a habit in only five days. The street seemed clear, which she took as an additional insult; they had decided she wasn't a problem after all. Her face burned, less from the cold than her private embarrassment. Starkov had dismissed her, an act as simply considerate as stopping the car to remove a turtle from the road. A kindness to an old friend.

She whirled about and ran back through the meat shoppers and up the palace steps. The babushka at the door ordered her away. She shoved past the indignant, scolding woman and demanded loudly to see Starkov again. He came down the curving marbled stairs, irritated.

"Who betrayed my husband?" she asked in English.

"Good night, Mrs. Nevsky."

"You just admitted he was betrayed. Who did it?"

"Good night."

"If you won't help me, there's someone else who will."

"Go to him then."

"His name is Valery Kirichenko."

Starkov reddened visibly. "I do not know this person."

"He's a high-ranking officer in the KGB. Ring a bell?"

"Help from the KGB could be fatally dangerous."

"I'll be safe," Natalie replied. "Armed with the truth, as it were."

"What truth?"

"*Everything I know.* I'll tell him that while trying to discover the truth behind my husband's murder, I found out he ran a spy network in the Soviet Union, and that he was investigating a conspiracy to overthrow the Gen Sec, which he code-named—that's a good spy word, isn't it?—code-named the Millionaires' plot. And I'll tell Kirichenko that my husband suspected Marshal Viktor Lapshin and his son Aleksandr were its leaders. And I'll tell him that the more I learned, the harder an American financier named Jefferson Jervis tried to stop my asking questions. Finally, I'll tell the KGB that my husband obtained a recording with which he intended to blackmail the plotters into stopping their coup, which is scheduled for Valentine's Day—this Saturday, Comrade!—when the Gen Sec is off in New York. Have I left anything out?"

Starkov had turned white.

"You foolish woman."

"I am not a foolish woman. I can tell by your face I just told you things even you didn't know."

"You foolish woman. Don't you realize that you'll destroy everything your husband worked for? You'll detonate Russia."

"I don't give a damn."

Starkov stared in horrified disbelief. He seemed so thoroughly shocked that Natalie was willing to bet the farm that he would never call her bluff. And, indeed, he attempted a weak appeal to sentiment, saying, "But Vassily died to protect—"

"He was killed," she shot back. "Who betrayed him?"

"I don't know."

"That's not good enough."

"But I *don't* know."

"You've got his network. You've got his sources."

Starkov started to protest. Natalie cut him off again. "You've got no choice but to help me."

Starkov hung his head. "We must go for a walk. . . . Come to my office," he said loudly in Russian. From there he led her down to a vaulted stone cellar room with a door to a side street. Checking the street first, he took her out and around a corner where they melted into the crowds on the Nevsky. "Take my arm, you'll look like my daughter."

She slipped her hand around his black wool sleeve. They started down the Nevsky toward the yellow and white floodlit Admiralty. Instinct told her that he would do all he could for her if she went softly. "Why did you serve Vassily?" she asked.

Starkov looked up from the pavement with a wan smile. "After years and years of studying the West, I came to see that we're moving quite naturally toward a single, economic world. Vassily's commitment to information was our best hope of getting there. I decided I'd spend my retirement helping him prevent accidents."

"Do you know Kirichenko?"

"*Bozhe Moy*, yes. He would torture his own mother in the name of *perestroika*."

"Who is his girlfriend?"

"I'm not aware that a woman of such tastes exists."

"Her name is Dina. She is also General Lapshin's girlfriend."

"The same woman?"

"It's my guess she's watching Kirichenko for the Millionaires."

A slow smile moved across Starkov's face like a fat summer cloud. "You've done remarkably well for an amateur."

"Thanks. I've had help and good breaks. But now I'm stymied. She shot Vassily to stop him from using the recording. I want to know who told her Vassily had it. Who betrayed him?"

Head bobbing as he nodded to himself, the old man weighed her question. "I understand that when you met Marshal Lapshin at the Kremlin you were admiring our painter Levitan."

"Who were you watching, him or me?"

"We've got some magnificent Levitans at the Hermitage. You must go to see them. The museum opens at ten in the morning. You might meet a friend of Dina's there if you show your pearls and talk about the babushki."

"No. No more cloak and dagger. You help me, yourself."

"All I know is that this man knew her once."

"But didn't you run Wallace's network?"

"Vassily ran his own network. I'm just a piece."

"Then who will take over for him?"

Starkov gave her a curious smile. "We've not been flooded with applications for the job."

"Well, can I at least come back to you if I need more help?"

"I wouldn't recommend it. That meat truck's been parked outside my institute for a week. And tomorrow I'm off to Moscow for my second interview with Kirichenko. I suspect he'll keep me busy for several days."

"Kirichenko *knows*?"

"No. Not about Vassily's network. Vassily did such a fine job of infiltrating the Millionaires that Kirichenko thinks Vassily was one of them. He's confused, and I'm doing my best to keep him that way. He suspects a few of our group of the same connection. Arranging to meet you at the Sojuzpushnina party and inviting you to speak to my students was as far as I dare go. Do you understand?"

"You're saying that knowing you is dangerous."

"Very."

"What will Kirichenko do to you?"

"Oh, I'm all right unless he finds proof. I've served my country long and well. And he's got to let me go by Friday because the Gen Sec is coming for a briefing on his way to America. So, without proof, Kirichenko will have to use much more restraint than he would with a powerless person like yourself."

"Are we back to you trying to frighten me?"

"I'd rather see you board a plane and go home. You've done well, but you are still an amateur."

"Is Rostov one of us?"

"Us?"

"I mean—you know—Vassily's group."

Starkov sighed. "Rostov can't help you. Vassily used him for information and introductions, but not directly. He's no agent. He's what he so cheerfully admits to be, a 'biznizmin' in the guise of a minister."

Natalie stopped at the corner of Gogol Street. Her hotel was around the corner. She extended her hand. "I'll see your friend at the Hermitage tomorrow morning. Good luck in Moscow. I'll talk to you when you get back. We'll compare notes and discuss our next move. Oh, by the way. You never told me Dina's name."

"Dina Feodorovna Golovkin," she told Finny on the telephone. She was running a bath when it occurred to her to get a leg up on the Hermitage meeting. Outside her windows it was dark and cold, and she was planning to order dinner in her room and get to bed early.

"Oh yeah," said the chargé d'affaires. "Sorry I didn't get back to you on that, by the way."

"Who is she?"

"Her father was *Marshal* Golovkin, minister of air defense until he bought it in a helicopter crash."

"Helicopter crash?"

"Yeah. Kind of ironic. Something broke and down she went. I remember it because when he died we got rockets from Washington. What was going on? Was it really an accident?"

"Was it?"

"Absolutely. Just an accident. But everybody wanted to be sure. Even the White House got into the act."

Her bath water had cooled in the time it took to get Finny on the phone, so she pulled the plug and tried the shower, which was uncharacteristically, blessedly hot.

She thought of Wallace because she was experiencing a sense of triumph similar to her husband's exultant mood the last time they made love so passionately on the yacht. She was very proud of the way she had handled Ivan Starkov. She had taken charge, toughed him out, and convinced the old Russian that she was worthy of his support. Not bad for an amateur.

But without Wallace's recording, her hopes rested with the man Starkov called Dina's friend. . . .

It sounded, she thought, as if Dina was the daughter of the original leader, the "Boss," of the Millionaires, the one who had died in the "shoddy workmanship" crash Greg had told her about. Finny had promised to run up a bio on her. She stepped out of the shower, reaching for a towel, and stopped dead. Someone had written four sets of book code numbers on the steamy mirror.

She wrapped the thin towel around her and ran into the bedroom and then the living room, but there was no one there. Suddenly remembering she had left the bathroom door open, she ran back and found the steam evaporating, fading the numbers. She traced them with her lipstick, got *The Pearl,* and opened it with shaking hands.

Page 149, line 7, word 1 was *I.*

241, 16, 7, was *want.*

347, 2, 1 was *your. I want your—*

"*Body* is the last word," said Greg Stuart, stepping out of the closet wearing a smile and a towel as thin as hers.

Two thoughts struck her at once. She was excited to see him. But how did he find out about *The Pearl* code?

"You weren't supposed to know—"

He stopped her with a cautionary finger and pointed at his ear. Natalie went to him. Greg hugged her warmly. She whispered, "You said you didn't know what book they were using."

"Obviously I do."

"But you said Wallace didn't tell you."

"Darling, of the four paperbacks beside your bed, one is *The Pearl,* wrapped in a Robert Ludlum jacket. Nothing that transpired between us Sunday night on the train suggested you read *The Pearl* secretly, so I drew the obvious conclusion. . . . You did tell me there was a book code."

"You're right. I did."

"Tell me you're glad to see me."

"Sorry. I'm just kind of stunned. I thought you were in Moscow."

"Tell me you would like *my* body, too."

"What are you doing here?"

"I telephoned Leo Margulies from Moscow. He said he hadn't seen much of you so I got worried about the company you're keeping."

"Greg, let's not get into this. Please."

"I reserved two seats on Air France tomorrow morning. I thought maybe we could hole up in Paris for a few days. Walk around, eat good food, and get to know each other. Or if it's too cold, maybe we could catch the train down to Marseilles."

"I can't leave early."

Greg picked her watch off the night table. "Let's talk about it later. Right now we have a date."

"I'm staying in Leningrad," she repeated. She started to explain that Cotillion's hastily gathered management was arriving Thursday, but she stopped herself. Her cousin did, after all, work for Jefferson Jervis, so she said only, "What kind of date?"

"I'm taking you to a *Pamyat* meeting. Get dressed and leave your brains in the hotel vault."

"Why?"

"You'll see."

The side entrance to the Russian Art Museum was strewn with mud and ice. At Greg's suggestion she wore a babushka, a simple scarf on her head. He had found a scruffy coat someplace, and as a couple they blended in with the crowds of young, old, and middle-aged citizens streaming into the museum's auditorium.

A lectern shared a bare stage with two VCR-driven television sets whose screens displayed the title: *What Russia Means To Us.* Two or three hundred people had filled the room to capacity. They squeezed between the standees lining the back wall, and moments later the crowd applauded a man who walked onto the stage. He wore a blocky wool suit and a dark shirt and tie, and launched into a speech that Natalie found notable for its openness and utterly remarkable for its lunatic theories of conspiracy.

"Lenin," he started off informing his audience, "owned three copies of *The Protocols of the Learned Elders of Zion.*"

Natalie looked at Greg. "The Nazis used that against the Jews."

"Sheer fiction," he whispered back, "forged by the czar's *okhrana.*"

A man turned and glared. Greg pressed her hand and Natalie fell silent as the speaker went on to warn against a Jewish conspiracy to turn the world against Russia. Among their dupes were Soviet bureaucrats, entrenched Communist Party officials, and even some of Mikhail Gorbachev's staff. He denounced Gorbachev's adviser on United States relations as an arch Zionist. Russian culture was being systematically destroyed, children corrupted, wives and daughters led astray. Moscow's grand subways came under fire as a plan fomented sixty years ago by the Zionist Trotsky to plant dynamite under the city.

Natalie glanced around. Here and there stood a policeman, although no move was made to stop the meeting, even when Gorbachev came under fire. "What can patriotic, tradition-minded Russians do to save the Motherland?"

"Return to their roots," was the answer.

"Here we go," said Greg.

On the television screen appeared a professional-quality film of rural Russian life. The camera panned empty village after empty village while a narrator lamented the rush to the cities, the destruction of the family, and the loss of the basic values that sprang from the land. Lapshin's theme on their helicopter ride, Natalie recalled. Another village appeared on the screen, prosperous and busy. Children played and smiling peasants went about their chores. Into their midst strolled a soldier, an officer with stars on his shoulders and battle ribbons on his chest. The audience rippled with anticipation. They knew him, Natalie realized, and indeed a deep hush fell over the auditorium as the camera closed on the stiffened cheek and dark eyes of General Aleksandr Lapshin himself.

"That's Lapshin," Natalie whispered.

"No kidding."

"You knew," she whispered.

"Just listen. You don't want to miss a word of this."

Lapshin spoke slowly, meditatively, echoing the things he had said to her in the helicopter skimming the dark countryside. She thought of the wolves, running in the light.

"I can always tell a soldier from the country. He is honest. He is loyal. He is brave. Physically, he's much stronger than the boy whose body was stunted in the city. One on one he'll always win a fight with such a lad. But as important as his physical strength is his inner strength, because the country boy knows what he is fighting for." He began walking down the dusty village street as the actors playing peasants smiled in the background. "He remembers his village. He fights for what he dreams to return to when his service is over, his pledges and obligations fulfilled. . . ." He faced the camera, suddenly, and Natalie, in spite of herself, shivered at the power he radiated. "I ask all true Russians to investigate those roots, consider them, and act. Young men and women, where do you want to raise your children? Do you choose the noisome slum or the steppe where Russian youth can flower?"

"This guy's going to rule the world?" Greg muttered.

The man turned again, glowering.

"Excuse me, Comrade," Greg apologized. "I was overwhelmed by fervor."

In the taxi Greg said, "I'm staying at the Leningrad. I've got a much bigger bed than yours. Why don't we get some champagne and caviar and talk about tomorrow?"

"I didn't realize you were so fluent in Russian."

"I'm not. I took a crash course when I started helping Wallace. No way I could pass like you. My accent is awful."

"The worst," Natalie admitted. "That guy looked at you . . . as if you were an American spy. . . . But you seemed to understand the speaker."

"I've got an ear for inanities. Besides, I've heard it all before. Come over to my place. We'll get drunk on champagne."

"No, thanks. I've got a big day tomorrow."

"What about Paris?"

A tram glided past as their cab slowed to turn off the Nevsky. Its windows flickered moving squares of light on Greg's face. His mouth was firm, his gaze unwavering. Natalie had never seen him so determined. She felt touched and even flattered by how deeply he seemed to care, but she would not leave Leningrad for him, or anyone, before she unearthed Wallace's murderers.

"Greg, I'm not ready for Paris. I'm really not."

"I'm not pushing you to sleep with me. We'll just spend some time together. It might be good for you and I know it would be wonderful for me."

"Not yet. I'll see you in New York."

"I'm worried about you here."

"Don't be. I'm doing fine."

"When are you leaving Russia?"

"Friday. Just a few more days."

Wednesday morning, in the semidarkness of a clear, iron-blue dawn, hundreds of shivering school children and Soviet tourists were climbing down from the Intourist buses that poured into the vast cobbled Palace Square behind the Hermitage. Unsure whether she had been followed from the Astoria, Natalie sheltered gratefully in the crowds until, at last, the babushki opened the museum doors. The old woman who checked her possum-lined jacket grumbled that it had no loop by which to hang it. Natalie mollified her with a discreetly exchanged ruble note and went in search of the Levitans.

The art museum was enormous—halls and vast rooms spilling one into the other—and she spent a quarter of an hour locating the landscapes in an empty gallery. Waiting for what seemed forever, she studied each until she thought she had memorized them. A Soviet tour group crowded into the gallery, listened to a brisk lecture, and trooped out. Natalie was about to give up when an artist hurried in and set up an easel.

Yawning, rubbing sleep from his eyes, he began to copy the outlines of one of the landscapes in pencil. A babushka had followed him in and now she stood by suspiciously. Natalie inspected the Levitans again, apologizing to the artist as she walked in front of him, fingering her pearls. He looked to be in his late thirties, dark-eyed and down on his luck. He wore a ponytail and a single pearl earring. With a glance at Natalie, he paused to sharpen his pencil with a pocketknife.

"May I see your work?" Natalie asked in Russian.

"It's only an exercise."

"The babushki are angry."

He flashed a smile and replied, in English, "The greatest empire on the face of the earth lives in terror of its grandmothers." As if on cue, the old woman came over and told him he should be careful not to drop pencil shavings on the floor. The painter ignored her, saying to Natalie, "I will show you the only way to frighten a babushka." He opened a notebook, poised his pencil, and demanded, "What is your name?"

The woman's tiny eyes, nearly lost in her plump cheeks, grew round with fear. She backed away and left them alone with the Levitans. "That," the painter said, "is the price of seventy years of barbarism."

"Who is Dina?" Natalie asked.

His face clouded. *He knew her.*

Natalie felt her heart clamor in anticipation. Unlike Dina's lovers, General Lapshin and Kirichenko, the painter had been instructed to help. But even as Natalie strained for his answer, his face turned blank; he seemed to close up and turn in on himself, as if the subject of Dina Golovkin was too painful to discuss.

"So that's it," he murmured. "I didn't think I would enjoy this meeting and I was right."

"But you were told to talk to me."

"It was suggested that things will go badly for me if I don't talk to you. On the other hand, I have every reason to presume that if the authorities catch me talking to you things will also go badly for me. We live in hard times for small people."

He raised pleading eyes to Natalie, as if begging for mercy. But he was directly connected to the woman who had killed Wallace. Natalie knew then what it was to be merciless. And with that discovery came the sure knowledge that a quiet threat would frighten him most.

"I'm sorry. But if you won't answer my questions I will complain."

"I'm here, aren't I?" he blustered, only to sink deeper into self-pity. "I thought I'd spend the morning with my own work. Instead I'm scribbling this boring Levitan."

"The sooner you tell me about Dina Feodorovna Golovkin, the sooner you can go home to your own work. *Who is she?*"

"Her father was Marshal Feodor Golovkin, an air defense minister."

"I know that."

"Dina studied law at Moscow State, and took a degree at the

Moscow Institute of International Relations. She served with the Foreign Ministry in Paris, Stockholm, and Rome. We met while she was modeling for a life class."

"Where'd she learn to shoot a gun?"

"Oh, you know her," the painter said, smiling. "She grew up with guns. The family had shooting estates, and her father was a great sportsman. They were very close. Mother drank and finally shot herself." His smile twisted into an expression of bemused awe. "I doubt they even noticed."

"Did you have a relationship?"

The painter sneered at the bland word. "It was not a relationship," he corrected Natalie archly. "We had a love affair. The old marshal was still alive. It was to spite him, I think, that she took up with a lowly painter. They loved each other, but contended mightily. There was always war in that house. Still, she went quite mad when he was killed."

"Who does she go with now?"

He shrugged. "I've hardly seen her since her father died. She's become intensely private. You used to see her around all the clubs in Moscow and here, too. But she's really dropped out of sight."

"I'm sure people mention her to you. Or you ask."

"Yes, I ask. . . ."

"What do they say?"

"I've heard she's involved with an officer."

"Who?"

"I don't know."

Lapshin, Natalie thought, concluding with a sinking heart that she knew more than the painter did.

"I hear she's working for the Foreign Ministry, again," he volunteered.

"Where?"

"I don't know. Last year she was dating an American. My friends saw them at his Moscow opening."

"An American? What's his name?"

"He didn't go up to her."

Natalie asked, "Was the American tall, an older man?" She was visualizing Jeff Jervis. "With a very thin face?"

"I don't know."

"Do they still go together?"

"I haven't heard him mentioned in a while. Only the Soviet officer."

"If you didn't meet him, how did you know he was American?"

"My friends said he was American."

"Businessman, diplomat, journalist?"

"Maybe journalist."

"Why do you say that?"

"He didn't spend any money at the show."

"Think," Natalie persisted. "This is very important. What else have you heard about the American?"

The painter shrugged. "Nothing, really. Just that they were around Moscow together for a while."

"Did she see him in America, too?"

"Why not? She travels freely."

"Who told you about them?"

"I am not involving my friend. It's just gossip. You know, people like to gauge your reaction when they talk about a woman you used to know."

"I know," she agreed, conceding defeat. She was getting nowhere with the painter. "Do you have any idea how I could get in touch with her?"

"Sure, if you have *blat* go to the Foreign Ministry and ask her whereabouts."

"I don't think I can do that."

"Then do what I do," he said sadly. "Go to every opening you can afford to get to in Moscow and hope to run into her someday."

"Does Dina work for the KGB?" Natalie was not certain which hat she had pulled that from, but she was desperate for any reaction.

The painter shrugged again. He was in full retreat now, and a relieved expression on his face suggested he thought he was home free.

"Do *you* work for the KGB?" she asked.

He laughed and raised his foot to the light. "Are these the shoes of a privileged man?" His shoe was constructed of some sort of plastic from which winter had peeled the veneer.

"Who made you talk to me?"

"My patron," he replied with a dismal smile. He began to fold up his easel. "If you'll excuse me, my studio has one small window that admits some light, this time of year, between eleven-thirty and one. If I hurry I can get home in time to do some work."

"Wait. Have you told me everything you were told to?"

"I was told you'd be persistent."

"What did you leave out?"

"Only personal thoughts, which are none of your business."

He tied a dirty string around the legs of his easel, stuffed his sketch pencil in a pocket, slung the easel over his shoulder like a rifle, and hurried from the gallery. "Wait," Natalie called. He shot her a look that said he was beyond responding to any more pressure; he had answered her questions and felt free to leave. But Natalie sensed something left unsaid, something in his personal thoughts that might somehow help untangle the chains of Wallace's past. She ran after him and caught up to him in a broad corridor with marble floors and windows on the left that stretched to the ceiling. Beyond them lay the frozen Neva, on which snow swirled in the wind.

"May I come with you?"

"What for?" He quickened his step and she noticed that he walked with a slight limp.

"To see your work," she replied, thinking to flatter him.

"You don't even know what I paint," he snapped back.

"I want to. What do you paint?"

"Men."

An uncomfortable image flashed through her head. She was standing next to him in a small dark room. Before them was a canvas in progress, in which naked men writhed together, limbs entwined, eyes daring her. An unmade bed took up one corner of the room, a table of dirty dishes another. He was staring at her as they walked along the bright corridor. Testing her? Testing her nerve?

"What color?"

"I beg your pardon."

"What color do you paint men?"

He laughed out loud, drawing immediate attention from the babushki who appeared from many doorways with censorious glares. "Very funny."

"I haven't the vaguest idea what you paint, but I really would like to see your work."

Apparently pleased that somebody cared, regardless of her motives, he said, "Perhaps you will buy something."

"Perhaps I will."

His name was Lev. His studio was in the back of a tenement in the industrial district south of the Moscow Station, and much as Natalie had imagined, minus the dirty dishes. Just beyond the single window rose a sheer stucco wall painted the ubiquitous dirty mustard yellow of Leningrad's poorer sections. As the stucco wall faced south and Lev's window north, the reflected sun suffused the room with a steady, muted gold light. A large easel stood in the light, empty, but on the walls hung a series of four oil paintings depicting the same two men, clothed, in various poses. Between the third and the fourth painting was an empty space.

"I like these."

"My two-guys set." Lev smiled happily. He walked her around the small room. "Two Guys on Line at the Green Grocer." Two young men were standing on line with empty string bags. Their gaze lingered despondently on a shelf of battered potatoes.

"Two Guys Waiting for the Tram." They were leaning over the curb. Behind them a shadowy line of people faded to the edge of the canvas. The men's faces were exquisite images of resentment.

"Wonderful," said Natalie, thinking this was one she might buy.

"Two Guys Entertaining in Their Flat." Here was a happier scene. The young men were setting a low coffee table for dinner and improvising furniture for the seating. Family photographs were set around their cramped room as she had seen at Kirichenko's. Their faces expressed happy anticipation, the optimistic hour before a party. Lev moved to the last in the series.

"Two Guys Applying for Emigration Permits." The faces had aged ten years, as if they had been standing at that high counter forever, surrounded by stacks of paper and watched by shadowy policemen with truncheons.

"They're all so personal."

"I'm good at faces. Bodies I'm poor at, so I leave their clothes on. You really like them?"

"Very much. I think you're best with their eyes. Their eyes make their faces. I feel really touched. Do they have names?"

The artist bristled. "They don't need names."

"No, I mean in your own head. Privately."

"Do they have names?" he mused, suddenly intrigued. "Call them Ivan and Alecksei."

Natalie returned to the space between "Two Guys Entertaining in Their Flat" and "Two Guys Applying for Emigration Permits." "Where's the missing one? Or haven't you painted it yet?"

Lev, who had been enjoying his brief exhibition, became subdued. "I sold it in Moscow," he said quietly. "It belongs to one of Dina's rich boyfriends."

"Which one?"

"I don't know. Dina bought it for him. . . . I had sent it down for a show. . . . And she bought it for him. . . ." Abruptly, he laughed. "That's irony for you. Great Russian irony. Chekhov would snicker."

"Why?"

"It is called, 'Two Guys Looking at the Girl They Love.' "

She moved into the empty space where the painting had hung and turned to face him. "Please, Lev. Tell me what you left out about Dina."

Lev's eyes drifted past her to the window and the golden light on the empty canvas. "Only that when we had our affair Dina threw herself mightily into advancing my career. She did everything she could, which was considerable. I had several one-man shows, thanks to her, and even today certain galleries still display my work for foreign buyers. Dina is that peculiar sort of woman who will submerge herself totally in a man she loves. Her ambition is boundless— for another. For her man. She would have made a grand czarina."

Natalie spent the rest of Wednesday in meetings with Vladimir Rostov's assistants, hammering out details of their proposed joint enterprise. She was racing the clock and the Gen Sec tour loomed, but movement was slow.

She put two full hours into defining the conditions in which Cotillion employees would live during their time in the Soviet Union, stressing repeatedly that they needed inducements like comfortable housing and the right to shop in the Beryozka stores and the Soviet elite scrip shops. Vital, too, were guarantees to former Soviet citizens who had emigrated to America. She had several former Russian mechanics whom Wallace had trained. Rostov's people accepted that émigrés could be very useful in overcoming the language barrier and promised to ease their temporary reentry and assure their exit. Whether they could deliver remained to be seen.

There were sticking points on money, and on the system of acquiring furskins. Natalie wanted her markers to acquire pelts before the auctions. The whole idea challenged the fur monopoly, the Soviets protested, which was precisely what she wanted to do. Timing was the worst sticking point. Rostov was still unconvinced that a Friday *press riliz* was either feasible or desirable. Natalie kept pushing for Friday. "And we need more than a press release," she argued. "We need a full-blown media event." But by the time they broke for the evening the best she could get was Rostov's noncommittal agreement to reserve judgment until he saw how well negotiations went the next day, when Natalie's staff arrived.

Exhausted, she declined his invitation to dinner, and staggered back to the Astoria, where the desk clerk handed her an envelope. She locked herself in the bathroom, praying for another snatch of *Pearl* code. But it was only a ticket for the evening performance at the Comedy Theatre on the Nevsky Prospekt, and a note in Russian: "Forgive me for not returning your telephone calls, Mrs. Nevsky. Come backstage after. I've told them you're looking to hire model. Perhaps you are, and I could certainly use the money. Vera."

Blocked in her negotiations, and stymied about the Millionaires, Natalie decided to accept Vera's invitation. A change of pace beat lying anxiously in bed, wondering if she should have gone to Paris with Greg.

Two Weeks from Ivan was a French bedroom farce *à la Russe*. Gigantic moving sets and spectacular crowd scenes supported a gossamer story about a married couple forced to take separate vacations due to a bureaucratic mistake at their electronics factory. Arriving unknowingly at the same Black Sea resort hotel, the wife became intrigued by a suave older man on the adjoining balcony, while on the next balcony, Ivan fell under the spell of the older man's beautiful companion, played by Vera. There was much mystery as to whether Vera was the suave lothario's daughter, wife, or mistress.

Natalie let her mind drift between new ploys to accelerate a bargain with Vladimir Rostov and the little she had been able to add to her understanding of the Millionaires' plot. Knowing who Dina was, and even her motivation, had been neatly counterbalanced by Greg's assertion at the *Pamyat* meeting that the Millionaires were a lunatic fringe. But, she reminded herself, Wallace had feared them enough to risk his life for Yulian's recording. A recording, she admitted bleakly, that might not even exist. At intermission, she joined the rest of the audience eating smoked fish and caviar sandwiches and drinking sweet champagne in the lobby.

Wallace loved the theater and was always visiting some actress he knew after a performance, so Natalie was accustomed to going backstage in New York, though she was never comfortable doing so. It was a private world, a mosaic of code words, reminiscences, and in jokes, and strident with the vulnerability of the people who had come offstage. In Leningrad it was much the same.

"I wish you had come last night," Vera greeted her.

"I thought you were wonderful," Natalie insisted, shaking the Russian woman's hand.

"*Bozhe Moy,* don't speak of it. Four entire lines. Gone as if the author had never dreamed them."

Vera did not specify who had flubbed the lines so Natalie said, "I'm so glad I got to see you."

Vera shut her dressing room door and turned up the jazz on a little radio beside her lighted mirror. "We can talk while I dress."

She had velvety blue eyes and a narrow face that might have looked pinched were it not for a full, smiling mouth. It was not hard to see what Stefan had fallen for.

She changed out of her costume into a snug thigh-length tunic. White over white tights, it had a mockingly military air, with epaulets secured by big rhinestone buttons. Over one shoulder Vera draped a double strand of costume pearls like a punk attaché's aiguillettes. The fringes of her black hair, which fell to the small of her back, were dyed flame red.

Natalie felt a twinge of envy for her boldness.

"Did you really like play?"

"Wonderful."

Vera chattered about the playwright as she worked on her face. She had a disconcerting habit of shifting in midsentence from her melodic Russian to fractured English, which reminded Natalie of someone seeking lost luggage in a bilingual hotel. She was finishing her red lipstick when she finally asked, in Russian, "How is Stefan?"

"Very anxious to hear from you."

"I started my English studies again," Vera replied vaguely. "From high school. What is 'wait tables'?"

"It means to be a waitress in a restaurant."

"I thought so. Stefan say he wait tables before he is modeling to earn money for rent. He tells me I do same." She turned from her mirror to stare at Natalie. "Here I am actress; in your country, a servant. Vera is not a servant. You see tonight. Am I servant or am I actress?"

"I can't answer that for you."

"I ask for visa, I am fired. My mother and father lose apartment. Move back to Gorky. Done. Do I give Nina to my rivals? Do you know what it is, Nina?"

"Yes."

"What do you think?"

"I think Stefan seems like a lovely boy."

"Vera is not sure she needs boy."

"Did you discuss this with my husband?" Natalie asked, wondering how Wallace had translated the news to Stefan.

Vera smiled. "Vassily was very understanding," she said, and a suddenly heart-wrenched Natalie thought, Oh my God, Wallace, you couldn't have. Could you? She wasn't exactly his type, but she was enchanting, if a man enjoyed flashing eyes and a ready smile. He had had a thing about actresses. Diana was hardly the first, though Natalie had always presumed, the last.

"I have to see my director for a moment. Then we can go and have supper or something."

Natalie said, "I'll meet you out front." She found her way out of the backstage caverns, retrieved her coat in the lobby, and changed into her boots. Outside, a tram was just pulling away with the last remnants of the audience. The street looked empty. Vera bounced down the steps a moment later, calling gaily that she was starving and hoped Natalie could afford caviar. But as she drew close, tears sprang to her eyes.

"What's wrong?"

The Russian actress removed her glove and stroked Natalie's Russian lynx. "Luba," she whispered. "It's Luba's coat."

29

I wondered who would get it." Vera whispered.

"Who," Natalie asked, carefully, "is Luba?" It had never occurred to her that Wallace had recruited Stefan's girlfriend into his
network.

"Wallace's friend from Moscow."

"What do you mean, 'friend'?"

"Friend," Vera repeated impatiently, wiping her cheeks as she
stroked the silky fur. A taxi veered toward them. Natalie waved it
away, fearful of breaking the tenuous link that had sprung between
them.

"Why are you crying?" she asked gently.

"I am crying because Luba ODed last *vikend*. Drugs. She was, how
do you say *narkoman*? Very mixed up girl. All the time new *shoozi*.
New *voch*. No art. No ambition. Only highlife."

"Luba was your friend?"

"What a waste, these women who drift."

"Let's walk," said Natalie, and turned away from the Nevsky into
a dark and snowy street. Vera followed obediently, and when they
had left the bright lights behind them Natalie asked, "Will you tell me
something?"

"Of course."

"Did you work for Wallace?"

Vera stiffened. When she spoke again her tone was conversational. "No. I am actress. You see tonight."

"I don't mean that. I mean, did you tell him things? Did you *report* to him?"

Vera considered the question for a while, glancing occasionally at Natalie as they walked. After several blocks, she linked her arm through Natalie's in the Russian manner. Natalie was uncomfortable with the intimacy, but made herself accommodate. Ahead, the dimly lit street arched on a bow bridge over a canal. Vera stopped in the middle and gazed down pensively, brushing snow off the railing onto the ice below. Natalie watched without a clue to whether the Russian woman was thinking about Luba, or Wallace, or the inconvenient Stefan.

"I'm hungry," said Vera.

"Come to my hotel. We'll have dinner."

They turned onto a brighter street and hailed a private car that was cruising for taxi fares. The Astoria's doorman demanded Vera's papers. Natalie said Vera modeled for Cotillion Furs and marched her in without further argument. Vera went to the pay phone to tell her parents she'd be late. Natalie ran her coat upstairs and joined her in the dining room, where the band's evening riot was going full blast.

The actress smiled knowingly. "Vassily preferred noisy restaurants, too."

"So you *did* work for him?"

"It wasn't work. I went to parties. I dated men he asked me to date. I reported things they said. It is an easy thing for a woman, particularly for an actress. Men boast, don't they?"

Not all men, Natalie thought. Some, like Wallace Nevsky, keep a very low profile, even while they act like the life of the party. They could fool anyone, even their wives. She ordered a bottle of Zolotoye. Vera applauded happily. "Vassily's favorite."

"Tell me about it. . . . Did you ever party at the Rostov *dacha*?"

"Comrade Rolex! But of course. He's a gas. Did he show you his pornographic videotapes?"

"He was Vassily's friend, not mine."

"Ah."

"So presumably Vladimir Rostov is not part of Vassily's group?"

"How would I know?"

"What," Natalie asked, "did Vassily want to know about Rostov?"

"Who did Rostov know in America? He wanted to know about his American friends."

"Who *did* he know?"

"Hundreds, it seemed. Thousands. So many I could never remember them all. Vassily was cross. He kept sending me back for more . . . it was fun."

"Do you remember any names that Vassily cared about, wanted to know more about? Jefferson Jervis?"

"*Da!*"

"Rostov knows Jefferson Jervis?"

"Apparently not."

"Are you sure?"

"I finally came right out and asked him. I said, Do you know this American I read about in magazine? Comrade Rolex knew the name but said, No, he did not know him. I was crazy."

"Why?"

"When Vassily heard this, he made me stop dating Rostov and go out with someone else."

Natalie was relieved. Cotillion's survival was riding on a deal with Rostov, best kept separate from Wallace's mission. Yet, at that moment, neither the deal nor Wallace's war with the Millionaires consumed Natalie half as much as the truth of her marriage. Vera was a hell-sent opportunity to settle the question most crucial to her, once and for all.

"There's something I don't understand," she said. "You're different from Luba. What did *you* get out of spying on Comrade Rolex?" Not the question foremost in her mind, but she had to build up slowly to asking if Wallace had been faithful.

Vera smiled. "Comrade Rolex is very generous. He is also quite handsome and a very interesting, how do you say it . . . well, very interesting. He concentrates, which is sometimes necessary when woman works as hard I work. It takes a while to relax, if you know what I mean."

Natalie nodded. "Changing gears."

"It is difficult to leave one and go to the other, sometimes," Vera continued. "*Patient*. That is what I mean. Comrade Rolex is *very patient*. In bed. Is there a word in English?"

"Yes," said Natalie. "But you couldn't have known ahead of time that Comrade Rolex was so patient. What did Wallace offer you?"

"Vassily offered to introduce me to Comrade Rolex."

"But why did you do it?"

Vera looked at Natalie as if the *Amerikanskaya biznizmin* was very dense. "An actress does not ordinarily meet trade ministers until she is far more famous than I. By then in her life she is probably married to some jealous actor."

Before Natalie could screw up her courage to ask what she had to ask, a man who'd been watching them from a nearby table came over and asked Vera to dance. She assayed his gold bracelets and necklace and rose smiling. Natalie poured herself another champagne and watched them foxtrot across the dark dance floor to an ear-splitting "What I Did for Love." A man asked her to dance, but she declined, in no mood to be touched by a friend, much less a stranger. When a second man gave her a hard time, she took the example of a Russian woman sitting alone at a nearby table, and stared moodily into her glass until he got bored and left.

Vera returned. Natalie poured more champagne. "How did you mean that Vassily was Luba's friend?"

"Friend."

Natalie gathered her breath. "I am asking you, did they have an affair?"

"*Vassily?*" Vera's eyes widened.

"Vassily. Wallace Nevsky. My husband. Did he have affairs with the women who worked for him?"

30

Vera picked up her champagne and gazed through it at the colored reflecting ball. "I will tell you how it was between him and me. When he brought me Stefan's message, the first time, he invited me to lunch. We have an expression in the theater—what's in a lunch? Of course I accepted. He talked all the time about you. The entire lunch. Natalia this, Natalia that. Natalia's so beautiful. Natalia is so intelligent. Natalia is elegant. *Très* boring.

"I had given up, when one night he invited me to late supper, after the theater. Here in this restaurant. Music. Dancing. Champagne. And I know upstairs he has his suite, so I think, here it comes, at last we rise to some higher purpose than discussing this woman I've never met. Do you know what he wanted?"

"Tell me."

"He wanted me to spy on Comrade Rolex."

Vera shook her head in mock astonishment and slugged back her champagne. She looked at Natalie and her smile faded into uncertainty. "Natalia? Why do you cry?"

"I'm not crying," Natalie replied, rummaging in her bag. "I'm not crying at all."

"Then I think you suffer a small eye infection," Vera said dubiously, handing over a perfumed handkerchief.

Natalie blew her nose. "You've made me very happy. Very, very happy."

373

"Well, he was happy too."

"God, I hope so. I know I made him happy. I can't tell you how confused I've been. People—here, let's drink more champagne." She seized the bottle and poured quickly, waving the empty at a waiter.

"To what do we drink?" Vera asked. "Do we drink to love?"

"We drink to trust."

Vera raised her glass with an odd smile that Natalie hardly noticed because she was determined to explain out loud what it had been like to mistrust her own deepest beliefs. "He made me feel valuable. He cherished me. Always. My friends, my girlfriends, would laugh at his manners—holding doors for me and walking on the outside of the sidewalk—and I thought it was funny too, at first, 'til I realized that it wasn't a demonstration, or just manners, but consideration. He made me know he thought of me. Do you know what I mean? If we met you at a party, he'd smile and flirt a little, but he would never, ever make me feel less than cherished. Do you know?"

"So now we drink to Vassily. Your Vassily."

"To Wallace."

They touched glasses and drank. "*Bozhe Moy,*" Vera said. "You have no idea, my dear, how much I've heard about you. So boring."

Natalie laughed and dried her eyes again. When she checked her mascara in her compact and met her own gaze, she was glad that she hadn't slept with Greg.

"He drove Luba *crazy,*" Vera laughed. "This jet-set woman had anything she wanted with a snap of her fingers—every man since she was fifteen. She mooned over him, followed him like a puppy. It was so funny. Once her little friend Elena almost had him. He was drunk and Elena is so feminine, but Vassily resisted."

Natalie couldn't stop smiling. She felt like running out into St. Isaac's Square and making angels in the snow. In a very real way she had gotten Wallace back again. His body might be gone, but her memory of him was intact.

Thank God she hadn't slept with General Lapshin either. Wallace had loved Greg, and while he would not have applauded her timing, he might have approved her choice. . . . *Or would he?* she wondered with a giddy smile. Maybe the old spymaster would rather she had seduced the Russian general to find out whether he was the Boss of the Millionaires' plot. No, she decided, she was not a spy. At best she might be an apprentice spymaster. What had Margot Klein said with her inimitable bluntness? "It's been years since Wallace had to do his own fucking." *Delegate.* She smiled again. *Delegate.*

"You said that Wallace had given Luba my coat?"

"I didn't know it was *your* coat. He brought it from America and gave it to Luba. She wore it to some parties and then again on their journey to New York."

"Wait. Wallace and Luba traveled together?"

"As I say, to New York."

"Together," Natalie repeated, beginning, finally—free of fear and jealousy—to understand what Wallace had done. "They traveled together."

"Well, I don't know that they sat next to each other, but they had tickets on the same jet."

Lowering her glass to contemplate the Russian actress's latest bombshell, Natalie was reminded of one spring when Wallace had returned from Tokyo with four speckled Japanese pond fish. They had darted from their plastic bag in separate directions and though she looked all that summer she never saw all four together again. Something similar was happening here, tonight. She had known a variety of unrelated facts about her lynx coat, unrelated and seemingly unconnected until suddenly Vera's information gathered them together.

Wallace had taken a Leo Margulies coat to Russia under the guise of promoting American wares at an important international fur auction. A common practice. She herself had Diana Darbee arriving Thursday, hoping to piggyback some terrific publicity onto her Russian deal. What she hadn't known, until tonight, was that Wallace had given the coat to Luba and Luba had worn it to New York *before* he had gift-wrapped it for his "Natasha"—a diminutive that he never called her. *Dummy.* She should have picked up on that clue alone—while wearing the gift, Natalie had nearly been arrested for shoplifting. Finally, Margot Klein had searched the coat, but found nothing.

"Vera," she snapped curtly, determined once and for all to get it straight. "How do you happen to know all these details?"

Vera wet her lips. "Luba was unreliable. Vassily gave me job to take to airport."

Natalie started to ask another question, but at that moment Vera's partner returned for another dance. The actress jumped up eagerly. Natalie grabbed her hand. "One more question," she whispered while the Russian boogied in place and admired his jewelry. "Did Luba travel on a diplomatic passport?"

She heard the answer she expected. "Of course. Luba had every privilege."

Of course. Of course. And, of course, if she had thought to tell Margot she had tripped the shoplifting alarm at Bonwit Teller, Margot might have found what Wallace had smuggled out of Russia. But the Englishwoman had missed it, fooled because the coat was American made—the trick Wallace had used to throw Soviet customs—and any suspicious Millionaires—off guard.

Yet, a man who had survived forty years of Soviet border crossings left nothing to chance. Thus, insurance: a second guise of having Luba wear the coat through the less rigorous airport inspection of privileged Soviet travelers.

Why the elaborate box and the stiff, flowery card to "Natasha"? Natasha was for the benefit of anyone who might be interested in what he was carrying. And maybe a hint to her? The box was to hold a second, similar-looking coat, Luba's own coat, purchased previously in New York, which she would then wear back to Russia.

Why not just smuggle what he smuggled in Luba's coat?

Because Luba was too flaky to count on her showing up at the airport without Vera's help. Vera got her there, Wallace switched coats for maximum safety, and succeeded in smuggling Yulian's recording out of Russia in the lynx coat.

"Why are you laughing?" Vera asked, sitting back down at the table.

"I'm not laughing."

But the joke was that tonight, three months later, the lynx coat was hanging right where it had started, upstairs in the Astoria Hotel, in the closet of Wallace Nevsky's favorite suite, because Natalie Stuart Nevsky had unwittingly smuggled it back into Russia.

"Can you sew?" she asked Vera.

"Does something need mending?"

"It's going to."

31

Vera ran after her, casting a little good night wave to her dance partner, who pouted at the actress's sudden departure. Upstairs in the suite, Natalie got a rudimentary sewing kit that had come with one of her toiletry bags, spread the lynx fur on her lap, and began sawing clumsily at the lining.

Vera kicked off her shoes, and if Natalie needed further proof that Wallace had never brought her here, she could take comfort in the way Vera wandered about the suite exclaiming at the furniture and the size of the rooms. The dull scissors parted some threads at last and Natalie peeled the silk out of her way, turning the lower half of the coat inside out and pushing aside the transparent organza that lay between the lining and the skins. With the coat exposed, she began to run her fingers over the hundreds of letting-out stitches and the seams between the skins.

Vera leaned over the back of the couch, breathing softly by her ear. "What are you looking for?"

Natalie stared. It had occurred to her, belatedly, that she was putting a lot of faith in Vera. The actress flushed and straightened up.

"I shouldn't be here. I am going."

"What do you mean?"

"Vassily said you should only know what you have to know. Can sew coat by self."

Natalie hesitated.

The fact was, she could *not* sew coat by self. She could barely baste a hem. And if she really made a mess of it, tearing it apart, there'd be serious inquiries at Soviet Customs when she tried to leave. Leo could repair it, but he'd be a fount of endless questions and would very likely innocently blab the whole story at the next cocktail party.

"Can you really sew?"

"Of course. I trained first as dancer. All dancers sew."

"Turn on the radio."

Vera found some old jazz on the console radio and returned to the couch, where Natalie explained, "I'm looking for a tape recording."

"Tape? What's this flat strip?" Vera pointed at one of the quarter-inch leather strips that connected the let-out skins. Natalie traced it around the bottom of the coat and up the back. But the leather was a single layer from inside to outside, where the silky fur hid it from view.

"Then that tape," said Vera, indicating a brown reinforcing tape basted around the inside of the coat about twelve inches above the hem. Basting, not heat binding, Margot had pointed out as proof the coat was American made. Natalie slid her nail between the basting stitches, twisted the tape, and showed the back to Vera. Silk, not plastic recording tape. The actress agreed and they worked their way up the circles of reinforcing tape, confirming that each was silk.

"The thread!"

Natalie would never have noticed if she hadn't been poring over the coat stitch by stitch, but above the first reinforcing tape, the basting thread felt slightly stiffer. Heart accelerating, she traced a thread to its beginning, snipped it loose, and began to draw it out of the tape.

"What it is?" Vera breathed.

"It feels like the invisible antitheft thread we sew into our coats. It sets off an alarm in the door."

"Invisible?"

"Almost invisible," she corrected, trying to remember Kenny Wilson's explanation of how it worked when the product first came on the market. "It's impregnated with something electrical, like a recording tape. It's given a code that reacts to a signal in the store."

Vera looked confused. "Like metal detector at airport?"

"Not really," Natalie said, drawing out several yards of thread and starting on another. "Well, sort of. I don't really know. If it were the same, the airport security would have detected it. But this is too long," she said, wrapping yard after yard of the fine thread around a spool from the sewing kit.

"A wire recorder!" Vera cried suddenly.

"What's that?"

"I don't know. It was in a play I did about Nazis."

"How do you listen to it?"

Vera shrugged. "I guess on wire player. I'll take it to the sound man at my theater." She picked up the spool. Natalie took it back. "Why don't you call him first?"

Vera looked at her watch. "In the morning. *Bozhe Moy*. It's late. I must go. I will call you in the morning," she promised, heading toward the door. Natalie ran after her. "Good night."

"Yes. Good night."

Natalie hugged her. "Thank you. Thank you again. You've helped in so many ways."

Vera returned another of her funny smiles. "Natalia," she said earnestly, "sometimes people do things they have to do. Sometimes they don't want to, but they must. Do you understand?"

"Perfectly. I will explain everything to Stefan. I owe you at least that much."

Vera hurried down the corridor toward the elevator.

"Vera!" Natalie called. "If you change your mind, you've got a coat modeling job as long as you need it."

"Thank you. Thank you," she whispered, and rushed away.

Natalie closed her door, locked it, and gathered up the reinforcing tapes. Vera had left before they sewed them back, but they weren't vital and the coat would hold together until she got back to New York. She couldn't wait to play the wire. She didn't relish hanging around while Vera queried her sound man, so she telephoned Fyodor Shelpin to arrange a meeting in the morning to ask him privately to meet Yulian again. The man who recorded the wire would be the one to play it.

"I'm terribly sorry it's so late, Mr. Shelpin. This is Natalie—"

"You have the wrong number," Shelpin said, and hung up.

Sure that something awful had happened to Yulian, and praying she wasn't to blame, she opened her *Fodor's* guide to find an electronics shop.

Vera had been a godsend. She might have worn the coat for years, never suspecting the secret, and Wallace's last triumph would have ended up in the Ritz Thrift Shop.

Natalie dropped the guidebook. Vera had left awfully fast. And with that funny smile. She went to the window, thought again, turned out the lights, and peeked out the curtain. A snow-brushing truck was circling the cobblestones; otherwise the square was still but for snakes of exhaust streaming from a parked car that had its engine running. Vera had twice given her a very strange smile. The first time when she proposed a toast to trust. What, she thought in sudden terror, have I done to myself?

She pressed against the glass to see the front entrance. Vera appeared, heading for the taxis, and Natalie felt a wave of relief. She was being paranoid again. But Vera walked past both cabs, lifted a pale face toward the hotel, and approached the car with its engine running. A window lowered. Vera spoke briefly, then crept, head down, into one of the taxis.

"People do things they have to do," Natalie whispered with a sinking heart. The taxi pulled away and when it had gone, three men got out of the car and hurried into the hotel.

32

She flung on the coat and threw her *Fodor's* guide and Falk Plan map into her shoulder bag, along with the wire tape. Nearly out the door, she ran back for her evening bag, which held her wallet, credit cards, passport, and Soviet hotel card. Halfway to the fire stairs, hugging the near wall so the *dezhurnaya* wouldn't see her, she remembered her hat. Too late.

She damned herself for a fool. Of course the Millionaires would have bought off or intimidated every contact of Wallace's they knew about. And Vera had even admitted how vulnerable a young Soviet actress was to pressure. And a very good actress she was: *"Can sew coat by self."*

Vy'khada net, warned a big sign on the fire door. No exit. Bells would sound if it was opened. They did not. She tore down the stairs, boot heels thundering. Sheer luck she hadn't changed into high heels when she went to the restaurant, but she'd been rushing to get back to Vera.

Three flights down, the fire door opened into a ground floor service hall. She glimpsed the lobby through a diamond-shaped window. People were leaving the club. Natalie turned in the opposite direction, down a corridor that was painted gray and scarred and chipped where carts had hit it. Ahead was the kitchen, dirty gray and poorly lit. She recalled she had seen from the street that it occupied a second smaller building attached to the hotel. She crossed the kitchen, still meeting no one, and found a narrow passage lined with garbage cans, at the end of which was a door. She pushed through it. The cold hit her like a fist and a startled *dvornik* whirled from the wall, buttoning his fly.

"*Do'bree ve'cher.*" She breezed past, bidding him good evening.

St. Isaac's was to her left. The car the men had come from was in the square. Ahead was the end of the building and around the corner a street that disappeared into the city. Her coat gleamed in the street lamps. She was nearly to the corner when the car started blowing its horn.

She ran. She heard its engine race. It was a little car. Three men had gone upstairs. One man left. She rounded the corner, bolted to the next, and raced down Dzerzhinsky Street. She heard the car turn the corner behind her before she reached the bridge over the Moika River. The river was thirty feet wide and six feet below the embankment. She jumped.

The ice held, barely. To her surprise it heaved like a waterbed as she fell and rolled in the snow. She rolled under the bridge, pulled her bag with her, and waited in fear.

Her head was freezing. The cold had sunk straight to her skull. By now the other three would be back on the street. The car had kept going a block or two. She looked down the river. The next bridge, which arched black across the snow-covered ice, carried the Nevsky Prospekt. Hugging the cut stone bank, she headed for it. Here the coat helped, being white as the snow. She switched to the south bank, whose wall was crusted by the last storm. At the Nevsky she found stone stairs, treacherously iced, and climbed to the street.

She was still only two blocks from the hotel.

It was very late. She hadn't heard the Astoria's band. What would still be open? Immediately up the Nevsky was the Kavkazsky restaurant, but it was closed. Further up, on the other side, was the Europe, a venerable relic like the Astoria. She had heard that its bar stayed open late. Before she could flash her hotel card at the doorman, he let her in on the strength of the lynx coat but the bar was just closing.

Revelers were reeling out to the sidewalk and someone shouted, "The tenth floor at the Leningrad. That's the place. Taxi!"

"Can I come with you?" Natalie asked, as a car that looked like the one chasing her cruised slowly by.

"Baby, you can come anyplace you want."

They were tractor salesmen from Indianapolis, she learned on the short ride across the Neva, assigned the thankless task of persuading the Soviets not to buy Japanese. At the Leningrad, an ultramodern hotel like the Pribaltiskaya, she rode up the elevator with them to the hot, smoky, tenth-floor currency bar, where, as the salesmen put it, "The joint was jumping."

"I love your coat," a woman said. She was Russian, which wasn't allowed in foreign currency bars, and Natalie realized she was a hooker.

"Are there other late-night spots like this?" she asked.

"This is it, after two, for people like you. The student places stay open, sometimes."

Natalie put down her drink and asked to buy a bottle.

"Is forbidden." She waved forty dollars. The barman palmed it and slipped her a long-necked bottle. Natalie stuffed it into her shoulder bag, eluded an amorous tractor salesman, and headed for the door. It wouldn't take the Millionaires long to find her in the only bar for foreigners.

The Russian woman trailed after her. "I'm going, too. I'll ride down with you."

Natalie eyed her nervously while they waited for the elevator. Was she, like Vera, in the Millionaires' pay? Had the word gone out already? Were they watching the bars and expensive hotels? In the elevator the woman repeated how much she liked Natalie's coat. Her own was a dyed brown kolinsky, a sort of poor Russian cousin of the mink.

"Would you like to trade?" Natalie asked.

"What?"

"Mine for yours."

"But—yes! Of course." The woman stripped off her kolinsky and reached for Natalie's lynx.

"I want your hat, too." It looked like squirrel, but at least it wasn't white.

"*Da. Da.*"

They left the elevator in opposite directions, the prostitute running out the door before the crazy *Amerikanskaya* changed her mind, Natalie burying her face in the kolinsky's perfumed collar as she crossed the deserted lobby to the front windows. From there she could see the car entrance and the road leading up from the river embankment. In the distance, across the snow-covered Neva, the lighted spires and domes and palaces of central Leningrad shone deceptively because the streets and squares were deserted. Taxicabs waited at the door. But she had no destination, nowhere in the shuttered city to hide the night.

Sheltering behind a marble column, she opened her *Fodor's*. She had just found the name of a late-night student bar, the Kafe Fregat on Vasilevsky Island, when a dull *boom* jerked her head up in time to see a squirming white mass sail eight feet over the driveway.

The woman landed in a parking lot, where she rolled in a grotesque tangle of arms and legs.

Natalie squeezed her eyes shut. The sight was replayed in the darkness of her mind. She opened them. A car sped away with its lights off. Horrified, she staggered to the front door where taxi drivers were staring uncertainly at the still form sprawled in the parking lot and edging toward their cars. Natalie jumped into the lead cab. The driver raced onto Karl Marx Prospekt without asking her destination.

"What happened back there?" she asked in Russian.

"Nothing. I saw nothing."

She had the *Fodor's* open in her hand. "Fifteen Petr Lavrov Street," she said. "The United States Consulate-General."

Giving up? she imagined Wallace asking. She could almost see him smile in the windshield and fancied he was sitting on the hood.

That poor woman—

One innocent, Wallace replied sadly. *In a country of three hundred million innocents.*

Give me a break, Wallace.

I miss you, he said.

I miss you, too.

Look! There's the Finland Station. Where Lenin stole the revolution. What's on the wire?

He was gone, leaving her shaken and drained and sure she would never, in what remained of her life, forget the sight of the Russian woman flying over the road in her white coat. Yes, she was definitely giving up. She would debate the niceties once she was safely within the walls of a small piece of United States territory.

But who was inside those walls? Who had Wallace telephoned in

New York? Greg? Jervis? Or, just as easily, some man or woman she had never heard of. An agent who had survived as long as Wallace had might well have contacts and colleagues even Greg didn't know about. So anyone could have betrayed him. Who was waiting at the consulate with a smile and a knife? We're getting dramatic here, she told herself, but her whole body was shaking and that was real.

The cab swerved, suddenly, throwing her against the door, and careened into a side street.

"You get out here!"

They had crossed the Neva and were now on the fashionable end of the Liteiny Prospekt where it passed through Embassy Row. "I'm not going down there," her driver announced. Looking back, Natalie saw why.

Petr Lavrov Street was blocked by police cars with flashing lights. "You get out here."

"No. I've changed my mind. Take me to Vasilevsky Island. Bolshoi Prospekt."

As the cab headed across the city, Natalie inventoried the contents of her bag, which she had grabbed without thinking to carry the heavy *Fodor's*. Her credit cards were dangerous if the Millionaires had access, which seemed likely, to reference checks. Also, the only computers she had seen in the Soviet Union were in the same hotels that accepted plastic, and they would certainly turn to them to track an American businesswoman. She had a couple of hundred in dollars, which was good, but only ten rubles: three cab rides. And she worried that the driver would remember her for paying in dollars.

Luckily, the shoulder bag held her gifts—pens, lighters, condoms, cigarettes, and, most important, four boxes of computer floppy disks, gold when it came to finding an electronics expert to play Wallace's tape.

But first she had to find someplace to spend the night.

"Where on the Bolshoi?" the driver asked. She had him drop her near the university.

"Ten rubles."

The ripoff inspired her to think larcenously: dollars would suck the driver into a conspiracy he would not want to admit to. The perfect cover. She gave him a five and received a happy smile.

The Kafe Fregat was hot and smoky. She bought a mug of thin beer at the bar and wandered among the wooden tables, hunting for a drunk. She found one with four friends, two women and two men, and boldly asked if she could join them. The men welcomed her. The women asked questions.

"I study at the Amerika Institut."

No one had heard of it. The boys were prepared to accept that she was a student, but the girls seemed to think she was kind of old. The drunk appeared almost comatose, though he responded to a smile and a glimpse of her bottle. By the time the waiters began throwing people out, she had an invitation to spend the night in what turned out to be as dirty a student room as she could recall having seen.

She had correctly judged the boy's condition. Talking up a storm, Natalie offered her vodka and in two slugs he sagged to the floor, snoring immediately. Natalie threw a blanket over him, turned on his desk light, and tried to feed the wire recording through Wallace's microcassette player. It took awhile, but she finally got the rollers to pull the wire. Despite this, however, it produced no sound, and after a frustrating hour she gave it up and ransacked the student's belongings for a player. She found an old reel-to-reel machine and spent another hour trying to make it work before she conceded it hopeless. Apparently she needed a wire player.

Exhausted, she collapsed on his reeking cot, fully clothed, and tried to sleep. His snoring woke her hourly. As the sky began graying through the window, she found the communal bathroom down the hall, washed her face, and repeated her Moscow light-eyebrow trick. Then she buried her hair under the student's ersatz fur hat and donned his thin wool overcoat, leaving the kolinsky, which he could trade for another coat, hat, and a pair of fine Italian boots. She kept the bottle. Head down, face muffled by his scarf, she joined the pedestrian stream on the Bolshoi Prospekt, blending in with the others queuing for the trolleybus, which she rode off the island to the Nevsky.

Too early for the better stores, she found a crowded cellar cafe and joined the Leningraders eating a stand-up breakfast. It was hot and smoky. Her stomach rebelled at the sight of eggs. She took dry bread and sweet tea and, restored slightly, started up the Nevsky, taking care to stick to crowds, and watching the intersections for her hunters.

The Nevsky was a combination of Fifth and Madison avenues, with the snazzier stretches of Broadway thrown in. Many of the buildings were converted palaces and mansions befitting the capital city of a great empire. In them now were airline offices, banks, museums, department stores, cheese shops, lavish delicatessens, and stores selling lace, crystal, china, perfume, prints, books, and wood carvings.

Fodor's listed specialty shops along the grand thoroughfare. Electronics shops were not included, but there had to be someplace that sold tape recorders. In that store she would find a service department employing technicians who supplemented their income with private black market work. If cars were fixed privately, then tape recorders and TVs had to be, too. And Natalie was sure that such a technician would gladly fashion a device to play Wallace's wire, for three or four boxes of Elephant Memory Systems certified 100% error free floppy disks.

Her first candidate was a Beryozka store, which surely sold the latest electronic gear available in the Soviet Union. A buxom matron wearing a cardigan stopped her in the foyer. "Foreign currency only."

Natalie had forgotten her student disguise. "I just wanted to look."

"Look where you can afford to look," the woman said curtly. Natalie started to reach for her hotel card, which identified her as a prosperous foreigner, when she noticed a man watching the door. He was standing beside the cash register, but he looked less like a clerk than a cop. There was something concentrated about his gaze that reminded her of Kenny Wilson. She backed out and hurried away.

She found an antique shop that advertised its own recording studio, but the operation was presided over by a bevy of middle-aged women who were clearly not technicians and looked unlikely to know anyone in the black market. She drew the same conclusion in an enormous record shop. A big department store, Gostinny Dvor, advertised, but did not display, color televisions. Another on a side street promised to sell personal computers, soon.

Long after she had presumed she would have connected with a technician, she was still wandering the Nevsky and its side streets. Time was on the Millionaires' side as every minute she wasted let them put more people on the hunt. Sometimes it seemed to her overworked imagination that a man or woman was watching every corner of every intersection. Her reflection jumped back at her from a shop window. The sight brought her up short, a frantic figure so stiff and angular, so hunched with fear, that were she the hunter she would have grabbed such a figure on the spot.

She straightened up, lifted her face to the overcast sky, tried some deep breathing, and deliberately slowed her pace. When she noticed many of the pedestrians licking ice cream in the bitter cold, she found an old woman selling it from a cart, bought some, and joined the throng. It was delicious, mother's milk for her hangover. Her emotions soared. Maybe it was due to a sugar high, but she plunged back into the crowds with a powerful feeling of, I'm here, I belong.

The Nevsky changed after a couple of miles—in Manhattan terms, from Fifth and Madison Avenue exclusivity to workaday Broadway or Lexington. The colonnaded theaters and libraries, pastel mansions, rococo palaces, churches, and cathedrals gave way to mundane five- and six-story commercial buildings. Shop fronts became more cramped and ordinary the closer the boulevard came to the Moscow railroad station. She was crossing a busy intersection, having attached herself temporarily to three women pushing baby strollers, when she recognized the Liteiny Prospekt, the avenue where Valery Kirichenko lived.

Bumping into Kirichenko while disguised as a student from Vasilevsky Island would provoke the KGB officer more than her abortive visit to his apartment two nights ago, but Natalie hurried into the Liteiny anyway. Nearing his block, she slowed down and sought camouflage on the ends of the lines of neighborhood women that trailed from the dusty food shops. She told herself that Kirichenko was the sort who left for work much earlier than noon.

Teenagers smoking cigarettes on the sidewalk marked the entrance to the video game store and shooting gallery. The store was closed, and judging by the hour of the day, the kids were dropouts, which could be a problem, because she needed a bright science major. They eyed her approach with the surreptitious and hopelessly hungry stare that a teenage boy turns on a woman too old to be available, yet young enough to stir the juices.

"Good morning," she greeted them cheerfully. Their eyes widened and one or two looked primed to bolt. Before they mistook her for the truant officer, she flashed a floppy disk.

"Anybody know what this is?"

"*Disketta!*"

"It's yours if you can show me where to find an electronics store." She backed into the doorway, and they followed, blocking her from view of anyone coming out of Kirichenko's alley. She opened her Falk Plan map.

"Outside," a boy said. "Further out."

She continued to unfold the map until it was entirely open and they pointed to the neighborhood around the Seaport Passenger Terminal on Vasilevsky Island, about a mile from the flat where she had spent the night.

The Number Fifteen Tram crossed the Nevsky and circled through the south central part of the city, over the Neva on the Schmidt Bridge, through Leningrad University, and on to its terminal near the seaport. She saw immediately that it was a logical district for a shop that dealt in black market technology because it had easy access to the sailors coming ashore to trade Western electronics.

The shop's window display consisted of a sturdy-looking portable radio, a squarish television, a large circuit board, and an electric typewriter of the vintage her father used. Inside, the shelves were almost empty, but for the occasional gray metal components, some plugs and wires packaged in plastic, and technical manuals in Russian. Behind the counter, however, a heavy iron gate suggested additional treasures in a back room.

The shopkeeper was engaged in argument with a red-faced customer who was pounding a television on the counter between them. The television screen was a gaping hole filled with blackened wires and broken glass. The owner smiled hopefully at Natalie, obviously glad of any interruption.

"What I am saying," the customer shouted, "and what you do not seem to understand, is that this TV exploded."

"And I ask, was it on?"

"It showered shards of hot glass on my wife's mother and burned holes in the carpet."

"But was it on?"

"Of course it was on."

"Well, there you are."

"What?"

"Obviously, you left it unattended."

"*Nyet!* I never left it unattended. I watched the evening news. I watched *Eleventh Floor*. I watched hockey. And then I watched General Secretary Gorbachev's pretour address to the Central Committee."

The shop owner picked up his abacus. "Evening news? One hour. *Eleventh Floor*. The one about the Aeroflot helicopter the hunters borrowed? One hour. Hockey. Two hours, at least. The Gen Sec speech ... " He moved the beads for a moment and announced, "More than five hours. You left it on *five full hours*? It is obvious,

Comrade, that you have had little experience in the operation of TVs."

He turned to Natalie. "May I help you?"

"Comrade," the angry customer shouted. "A TV should work five hours without exploding."

"You don't like your Soviet TV? Buy a Hitachi at the Beryozka."

"You need foreign money to shop at the Beryozka."

"That's not my problem, Comrade."

To Natalie's surprise, the man suddenly surrendered. His big shoulders slumped. He heaved the wreckage of his television off the counter and shambled out of the shop.

"And how may I help you, Comrade?"

Natalie opened her bag to give him a glimpse of a box of floppy disks.

"I'll bet you met a sailor," he said, smiling.

"Three sailors," said Natalie, showing him two more boxes.

"And what did they tell you they were worth?"

"I know what they're worth."

"I suggest the *glasnost* approach," the shopkeeper replied. "You tell me what you think they're worth. I'll tell you what I think they're worth."

Natalie showed him the spool. "They're worth what's recorded on this."

"What is this?" He unrolled several inches and held it to the light. "Recording? It's a wire. Haven't seen one of these in years."

"I need a player."

The shopkeeper handed it back. "And what do you play at?"

"Comrade, your shop fooled me. I didn't realize it was a police station." She stuffed the floppy disks in her shoulder bag and headed for the door, wondering what she would do if he didn't stop her. She turned the knob and started out.

"Wait!"

"No questions."

"That will be expensive."

"I've offered all I have."

"You've asked me to perform a special service," he said, licking his lips. "I want more." Her coat was still open and he was staring hard at her legs.

"Forget it." She turned away.

"You obviously have sources. You can buy again where you bought those."

"Buy what?"

"Genuine suede."

"My pants? You want my pants? What do *I* wear?"

"I give you my girlfriend's Yugoslavian *dzhinsky*."

"Can you play this?"

"I can try."

Olga, Sergei's girlfriend, was six inches shorter than Natalie and chunky, which meant that her jeans stopped midway down Natalie's booted calves, and left enough room in the waist to start a pregnancy. They were scratchy, but the short look worked reasonably well over her high boots. Olga started pestering Sergei for Natalie's boots, too, until Natalie informed them a deal was a deal and besides, her boots were impossibly narrow for the Russian woman's foot. Sergei was as good as his word. He tried.

Leaving Olga to tend the shop, he unlocked the iron gate and led Natalie back to his workroom, which was crammed floor to ceiling with old TVs and VCRs, ancient stereos, prestereo hi-fi sets, heavy portable radios, and box upon box of spare parts.

"It's almost certainly a dc biased recording," he said.

"Is that important?"

"It will hiss and the sound quality will be quite poor."

"I have to be able to understand what is said."

"You will, provided I can find the right playing head."

The problem, he tried to explain, was that the playing head had a little gap, over which the wire passed, which, to pick up the magnetized record on the wire, had to correspond in size and depth to the gap on the recording head. Natalie, a veteran of similarly earnest recitals by the gadget-loving Wallace, said, "I don't have much time."

With that Sergei began sifting through his boxes, which contained more unidentifiable junk than a Connecticut tag sale. Natalie sank into a musty armchair. She tried to rest while she watched him through slitted eyes, speculated what was on the wire, and worried how long it would take the Millionaires to figure out she had found a black market electronics whiz to play the wire recording.

Natalie dozed in the chair. Occasional bursts of high-pitched gibberish trilled from Sergei's workbench like birds at dawn. Suddenly she popped awake, wrenched from a deeper sleep by the sound of a familiar voice. Marshal Lapshin was speaking in slow, heavily accented English. "*I say the boy will do as he's told.*"

"*A full general's a little old to listen to daddy,*" countered a voice she did not recognize, though it sounded familiar. "*I want to hear it from the boss's mouth.*" American. With a trace of English accent.

Sergei was leaning over his bench, listening like a man who understood English. "Turn it off," Natalie snapped.

"But I just—"

Natalie jumped from the chair. "Turn it off, Sergei. You don't want to hear this."

Sergei moved a lever on the machine he had fashioned from an old reel-to-reel tape recorder similar to the player she had tried in the drunken student's room. It was a box about a foot square, with two reels on top, and wires leading to a round, black speaker. The reels, around which he had wrapped Wallace's wire, stopped turning. He stood up, wiping his hands on his smock. "I think perhaps I believe you."

"Just show me how it works, and leave."

"I am also thinking I wish you hadn't honored me with your business." He showed her how to back up the wire and how to insert the second length of wire after the first had played through. Impatiently, she hustled him out, making sure he locked the outer gate. Then she closed the inner door, ran to the jury-rigged player and rethreaded the first wire, her fingers fumbling with excitement.

33

First there was a noise like furniture being moved or people walking, then the American voice that had sounded familiar asked, "Where is the Boss?"

It was to that that General Lapshin replied, firmly, "*I say the boy will do as he's told.*"

"*A full general's a little old to listen to daddy.*"

The sound reproduction was poor. The American's sarcasm, however, and his put-on British accent, were pure Jefferson Jervis.

Lapshin said, "*Aleksandr is a good son. This is the last I will speak of this. A loyal officer, and a Russian patriot. Perhaps he thinks too much. He's a brooder. But he will accept his responsibility. On your side, however, is serious matter. Does your president know, yet?*"

"*I told you. I've kept him posted, in general terms, about your takeover.*"

"*Is not takeover. Is not mere change of government. Is return to older, Russian values.*"

"*The President is deeply in favor of older values, sir,*" the American replied smoothly. "*We'll fill him in on the details the second you and the 'boy' are in the Kremlin.*"

Definitely Jervis, thought Natalie, Jervis and Marshal Lapshin at the core of the plot.

"*Only then we learn if he will do as you promise.*"

393

"You have my word."

"Your word? You are not the United States government."

"You have the word of a man who is looking forward to becoming your business partner. Remember, I wouldn't be in the position I am in if the President and I didn't see eye to eye on the basics. You can count on his full cooperation, starting with a statement hailing your goal of private rewards. And we'll fight like hell until the Congress recognizes your new regime."

"The trade? The technical assistance?"

"Christ, Marshal. He would kiss your ass in Macy's window to finish up his term by signing trade treaties with a free-enterprise Russia."

"That is a foolish label for a socialist nation experiencing sudden change," Lapshin cautioned. To put it mildly, Natalie thought, wondering which of them Wallace had considered more dangerous.

"What is important is that we reward competence and discipline with ownership."

"Private property," Jervis agreed. "Name me an empire that's lasted without it. All the Bolsheviks ever did was stagnate the czar's gains."

"Don't think we need you," Lapshin replied coldly.

Jervis had apparently forgotten the depths of Russian xenophobia, yet Natalie was forced to admire his nerve, despite her loathing for his scheme to get richer quicker at the expense of the Soviet people. "Just as we don't need you, sir," the American went on. "But what an opportunity! Thanks to your movement, Russian technocrats and American businessmen will make each others' lives a lot smoother and one hell of a lot richer. This is the perfect business deal—a bonanza for both sides."

"For us it is more than business deal. Is better way for a nation to live. People need guidance in their values as well as more washing machines and computers."

"God knows the Soviet worker is going to need all the guidance he can get scrambling in a new economy. You supply the work force. We'll supply the products. And know-how. All we ask is you don't deal with the Japs."

"So long as you don't give us reason to."

"Which brings me to one last question. Gorbachev's going to be in New York on the tour and you've got people scattered all over the Soviet Union—Army, police, KGB, the ministries. They're going to *have to move fast. What's the signal? How do you coordinate the takeover?"*

"There will be clear, unmistakable signal for change on February fourteenth."

"A little hint would help me speed reaction time in Washington."

"You'll know it when you hear it," Marshal Lapshin replied loftily.

Jefferson Jervis laughed. *"We're going to get on together very well, sir. We don't pretend we like each other. It seems like the beginning of a long and profitable—"*

Lapshin cut him off. *"Don't make mistake. Don't think you're the only* biznizmin *we know in America. Don't think you're the only man we have in White House."*

Whatever Jervis replied to that threat she would never know, because the wire ran out at that moment, and the loose end began ticking from the take-up reel. Natalie lunged for the second piece.

Wallace had done it! This was proof. The Millionaires' coup was on for Valentine's Day. But Jefferson Jervis, whom he had trusted to bring him to the President, was in the thick of it.

Her cousin, she thought as she fumbled the shorter wire into the player, was out of his mind. The Millionaires weren't doomed. They were about to attack. Greg was also a bit naïve. His boss was making private deals around him. It was ironic, too, that Jervis had maneuvered himself into the Lapshin coup to do what she was trying to do with Vladimir Rostov, albeit on a gigantic scale, and by force. Takeover? Return to older values? She liked Luba's word better—coup. Then a bloody civil war and, as Wallace would say, poor Russia.

The second wire was only six feet long. She turned it on and was stunned to hear Wallace. He sounded as if a victorious grin were splitting his face from ear to ear.

"Nice try, Jervis, ripping off my information to slap together a sweetheart contract with a gang of Russian fascists. The Army runs the Soviet Union and the American businessman taps into Soviet national resources, three hundred million captive customers, a submissive, terrorized work force à la South Korea and Taiwan. More fool, this old socialist, for trusting a banker, but I've got you now. Voiceprint comparison will confirm that you and a group of dissidents led by Red Army Marshal Viktor Lapshin are plotting to overthrow Mikhail S. Gorbachev and install young General Lapshin as Gen Sec.

"Forgive the poor sound quality, incidentally. The old gent who tapped your meeting learned his trade bugging German Foreign Minister Ribbentrop's National Hotel suite in 1939. Unlike my sophisticated microcassette, which was totally erased by Lapshin's Red Army countermeasures, his primitive machinery picked up every word." The blank tape, Natalie remembered, that the police had found in his Panasonic.

"I can stop the coup—stop it dead—by mailing this recording to the KGB.

"But I would prefer not to, because of two basic facts about the Soviet Union that you and your ignorant President's men don't understand. One, the Soviet Union is riddled with potentially explosive factions. Two, the rest of the world will not survive Iran-like chaos in a nation that owns half the nuclear weapons on the planet.

"The KGB would use this recording to launch a worse purge than Stalin's—the very chaos I was trying to prevent when I first asked your help with the President. And let's not kid each other, this is your scam, not his. Doing nothing will be equally disastrous, because the coup is certain to explode into civil war. The Soviet people don't need this agony, and neither do the rest of us.

"Fortunately, your chat with Marshal Lapshin offers a better way to stop the insanity than either provoking the KGB or doing nothing. . . ."

Natalie felt a palpable menace fill the silence like air invading a vacuum. And when Wallace finally spoke again, it was in a voice she had never heard. Hard as stone, utterly sure, and merciless, it fused her gentle, lively husband to the secret man who had left her a widow.

"You, Jervis, will inform Marshal Lapshin that the clowns who 'run' our President have changed their minds and will expose him and his dissidents if they continue to plot against Gorbachev. A bluff, but a strong bluff, because whatever his many shortcomings, old Viktor Sergeivich Lapshin is a patriot who would never willfully destroy his country. Take my word on that, Jervis. It's not something you could understand. Just convince Lapshin the coup is hopeless . . .

"And, Jervis, if you think I'm bluffing, consider the place on the KGB's purge lis I can arrange for a certain American billionaire. That James Bond car you tootle around in ought to give their assassins a real chuckle. Or maybe for real laughs they'll send kidnappers. . . .

Stop them, Jervis. You lost. You tried to screw me and I screwed you instead."

"You show-off," Natalie whispered at the voice hanging ghostlike in the air, and again, aloud, *"You bastard,"* angrier at him than at Jervis or even Dina.

She thought she knew now the mistake he had made, the mistake Wallace himself had seen as he collapsed with Dina's bullets in his chest. Choking on grief and anger, Natalie gave a scream that ended in a hopeless whisper. "You show-off! You died for your ego. . . . What about me?"

He had called Jervis from the pay phone on his way to the yacht to gloat that he had the wire. But Jefferson Jervis had moved like lightning. The timing seemed tight, but Jervis must have suspected Wallace, and had Dina in place at the pier, waiting in one of the dozens of parked limousines, stolen invitation in hand, bewigged, and dressed to kill. Wallace had underestimated the financier's intelligence and courage. His first mistake in forty years? Perhaps. But not a mistake of age, a mistake of character.

"Did you think of me?" she asked the walls again. "Did you think about leaving me alone?"

Wallace, for once, had nothing to say.

His voice had made her crazy. She felt drained, as if they had had an argument—a row, as Wallace called it. She stopped talking to the walls, but she still directed her thoughts at him: *I'm just angry. I don't hate you. I love you. Don't worry. I'll finish it for you. But I'll do it my way.*

She checked her watch. One-thirty. In that other world that had died for her when Wallace died, she was supposed to be meeting Leo Margulies at the auction.

She unbolted the back door and looked out. A narrow service lane wove a crooked route between the backsides of old mansions that had been divided into flats. The residents used the window sills to refrigerate bits of sausages and cheese. A man reaching for a vodka bottle saw Natalie and quickly averted his face.

Think. Who are they? What are their resources? Who am I? What are mine? They're outsiders. They're dissidents. They're not official. They have contacts in the police, but they're not policemen. They're not militia. They can't arrest me. If I'm alone, they can hurt me. I'm safer in the crowds, safer in public, safer at the auction.

But she had to convince the Millionaires that she was not a threat. She found a bottle of alcohol she had seen Sergei use to clean the player's heads and dipped into her shoulder bag for Wallace's microcassette recorder and a gift cigarette lighter. Then she threaded the first wire into the player, turned it on, and set Wallace's machine to Record in front of the speaker. In this way she made a tape recording of the wire. She recorded the second piece of wire as well, and listened to be sure she had all of it on the microcassette.

Suddenly Sergei yelled in the electronics shop, anger that turned to fear. Olga screamed. Someone started pounding on the iron gate. Quickly, Natalie splashed the alcohol on the player. The second wire was still on the take-up reel. The first was on the sewing spool. She put it on the player and lighted the alcohol.

It burned slowly, with a low blue flame. She put on her coat and slipped her bag over her shoulder. The wire curled and blackened and vaporized in spots. The plastic reels melted like Dali watch faces. The wooden spool began to char. She heard metal screeching, and the pounding grew louder.

Natalie smothered the fire with the chair cushion and replaced the cushion upside down to hide the burn marks. The shop gate banged open. She tore out the back door and ran. Blocks away, she threw Wallace's recorder down a storm grate.

She telephoned the Pribaltiskaya Hotel from a phone booth in front of the department store where she'd hastily bought a dress. By then Cotillion's management team was meeting at the hotel with Rostov's people.

"No point waiting for you," said Mike. "It's pretty clear what you and Minister Rostov laid out. We're just humping the details."

"I'll be there soon."

"You're a pisser, sis. What a deal!"

"Let me talk to Leo." Leo would never know it, but he was going to help smuggle her copy of Wallace's tape.

"He's at the auction. Sojuzpushnina moved up the lynx sale."

"What?" she cried. "Up to when?"

"Right now."

"Bozhe Moy."

"What?"

"Keep going. I'll be there as soon as I can." She raced into the street and hailed a cab. "Quickly, Comrade. The Palace of Furs."

34

She was running up the steps of the columned facade, with Wallace's recording clutched in her hand, when she heard, "Natalie!"

It was Jefferson Jervis, climbing out of a black Zil limousine. "Wait a minute. I've got to talk to you."

She turned away, but he bounded after her, and blocked the door with his hand. "Wait a minute."

"We have nothing to talk about."

"The Soviets are not going to bail you out."

"They might, they might not," she lied calmly. "They're not my only iron in the fire. Will you please get out of my way? I've got an auction to go to."

"Mrs. Nevsky, I'm going to give you one last chance to save your company. I've got my own plane at the airport. We'll fly back to New York. We'll put together a deal that gives you total control of Cotillion."

"What about Hyndo?"

"They won't be a problem."

"Total control?"

"We'll sit down with my lawyers. We'll work something out."

She glanced down the steps at the Zil. Greg was in it, watching. She said, "Wallace taught me an expression that's very effective at a certain point in a negotiation. In five years I only heard him use it once. But it really cleared the air."

"What's that?"

"Fuck you."

She just had time to slip the recording into her dress pocket before Greg caught up to her at the coat check. "Natalie. This guy is dangerous."

"So am I."

"I mean it."

"What is he, a *mafioso*? Is he going to take my business by extortion?"

"He doesn't want your business. He wants you out of the Soviet Union. Right now."

"Why?"

"I don't know, exactly," Greg said, brushing a lock of blonde hair that had fallen to his brow. He looked genuinely frightened.

"You're just the messenger boy."

"Listen to the message."

Natalie pushed past him and headed for the auction hall. "You tell him that if he makes one more threat I will go to the police, *here*. I'll tell the KGB that Jervis is behind the Millionaires' plot."

"That's crazy."

"Let him explain that to the KGB."

"You'd blow the country up."

"It sounds like Jervis and his messenger boy have that in mind anyhow, doesn't it? Let go of me!" She jerked away and opened the door. "You really ought to think about whose side you're on, Greg. That man is a horror. God knows what he did to Wallace."

"What do you mean?"

"Think it through, Greg. Who do you think betrayed him?"

She turned away. She had said too much already.

"You really ought to come home with me, Natalie."

The truth suddenly burned like fire. Hot tears sprang to her eyes. "Is that what the train was about? And the other night, too? *Paris? Get to know each other?* Were you just trying to get me out of the way for Jervis?"

The peculiar perfume of newly cured pelts—astringent tannin and sweet decay—pervaded the great blue auction hall. Leo Margulies had taken the high ground, a desk in the top tier of the hundreds of brokers and mechanics bidding for Soviet furs. From that lofty position he glowered over the heads of his competition at the Sojuzpushnina auctioneers who were scanning the room hungrily for upbids.

Leo's sons were bidding for mink and shaking their heads at the prices. His own catalog was open to lynx, where he had marked his choices in pencil. The desk to his right was empty. Natalie slipped past old Harvey in his trapper's vest, sat down, and pretended to skim her messages while she dried her eyes.

Leo was pointedly ignoring her.

"Thanks for saving my seat, Leo."

"It was Wallace's. Where the hell have you been?"

"Taking care of business."

"I thought your business was buying furs."

"That's your business, and the boys' and Harvey's. I sell them."

The vaguest hint of an approving smile elongated the O around Leo's dead cigar. "Just remember, I'm a one-shot—"

"How are we doing?"

"Getting killed by the Japs, again." Leo scowled at the Japanese contingent in the next row. "And I don't know where the Italians are getting their money, but I could use the dollar to wallpaper my living room."

"What's with the lynx?" she asked, indicating his catalog.

"They bumped it forward. It's next."

"Leo, quick, I need another look at that lot you showed me. The one with the pelt the hunter patched."

"What the hell are you going to do with lynx?"

"You'd be surprised."

Grumbling mightily, Leo followed her out of the auction hall. "Hey, what the hell are you wearing?"

"It's a Zaitsev. Like it?"

The calf-length red dress had broad shoulders and dramatic lapels that plunged below the waist, which suited her height. Thick twists of costume pearls were massed at her throat like a scarf.

"Russian?"

"The saleswoman said he does Raisa Gorbachev."

"Terrific if you want to defect."

She had paid with American Express, reinforcing the message she had sent the Millionaires by burning Wallace's wire: Natalie Stuart Nevsky had no more interest in their plot or her husband's spying; she just wanted to buy furs, strike a deal with Rostov, and go home.

In the anteroom where lynx hung, the sight of the silken pelts brought a smile to Leo's face. He stopped complaining and breathed deeply as if the air in this small section of the Palace of Furs had superior qualities. The fur girls spread the strings he chose on the long table under the light.

Natalie hid in her hand a tightly rolled length of recording tape. Cut from the cassette used to copy Wallace's wire, it formed a cylinder slightly smaller than a pencil eraser.

"Show me the skin with the patch."

Like Wallace, Leo could recall individual pelts for months after he had examined them. He picked it without hesitation. Natalie put her hand inside and felt for the hunter's patch. Leo was watching curiously.

"How do you do that?" she asked. "How do you remember one skin?"

"How does Mama Lynx know her babies? What are you doing?"

She had found the patch and was trying to saw a path between the stitches with her fingernail. "Tell me about that lot." She nodded at the other.

"I told you the other day," Leo replied, fluffing the guard hairs on a pelt in the lot she had indicated. "The one you're holding is the best."

She worked a small opening between the stitches, slipped the cylinder of tape into the pocket between the patch and the skin, smoothed it shut, and withdrew her hand. "I want this lot."

"How many coats are we talking?"

"Two," she replied. A small buy might look suspicious. The more pelts she bought, the less likely they were to be examined by Soviet customs.

Leo whistled. "Bellies?"

"The best."

"Sixty skins. You'll need over a hundred just to match the sixty. We could be talking two hundred thou in skins alone. More like a quarter million bucks."

On her way back to the auction hall, Natalie tried to telephone Rhonda at Citicorp, but the international circuits were busy. Before she could try Rostov's code 73 again, an announcement came over the loudspeakers that reached every corner of the Palace of Furs. "Ladies and gentlemen. The lynx auction will begin in ten minutes."

Hurrying back, Natalie ran into Harvey, who announced he had made out like a bandit with fox and was going to celebrate. Leo's sons, however, were less ecstatic. They had managed to buy most of the mink Natalie wanted, but all at the top end of her price range.

She found Leo hunkered over his catalog like a cat about to kill. "I'm scared the Japs are going to buy skins, even though they don't know what to do with them. Christ, I wish Wallace were here. I hate doing this."

Leo wanted to buy the first lot of lynx. They were good skins and there was a certain status in winning the first lot, but he dropped out when he thought they were overbid. Gloomily, he watched a few more lots go, including another he had earmarked for a cape for a special customer. "The Italians are tap dancing. It's just us and the Japs. Here comes yours with the patch."

Natalie's lot was announced. Leo bid, drawing immediate fire from the two Japanese brokers and an Italian. "They don't know their ass from their elbow, but they know I do so they figure it's the lot to buy. *Up!*"

The Japanese raised again.

"*Up,*" called Leo to the auctioneer, and to Natalie, "Do you believe this? *Up!*"

The Japanese topped Leo's bid of two thousand dollars per skin, upping it to twenty-one hundred. Leo said, "Fuck them!" and shouted, "Twenty-five hundred dollars."

The Italian dropped out.

"Twenty-eight hundred dollars," called the Japanese broker.

"Forget it," said Leo. "It's not worth it."

"I want it."

"Natalie, a hundred skins at twenty-eight is two hundred and eighty thousand bucks. They're not worth it."

"Buy it."

"I won't bid any higher. This is crazy." He signaled the auctioneer that he was through. "The next lot is fine."

"I don't want the next lot."

"Going once—" the auctioneer called.

"Leo, for God's sake, get them for me."

"Forget it, honey. It's crazy."

"I need those pelts."

"Going twice—"

"What the hell for?"

"I have to pay top dollar. I want the most expensive buy, for the publicity. It pays for itself."

"That's ridiculous. You're not Revillon. What do your customers care?"

Natalie waved at the auctioneer, confusing him enough to make him hesitate. Several heads now turned toward Leo.

"I'm paying for image. The biggest buy!"

"Some image. A *schmuck* who pays too much."

"*I want those skins.*"

"Wallace would kill me. Natalie, these Jap furriers couldn't let out a Russian lynx if it jumped off a tree with a sewing machine. Bet you ten bucks they come to me in June, sell me those same pelts discounted fifty percent."

"I can't wait 'til June." By June, her hidden tape, which she needed in New York before Valentine's Day, would be long ago dissolved in the chemicals of a Tokyo tannery.

"What's the rush?"

The auctioneer raised his gavel.

"Diana! Diana. I need a coat for Diana Darbee."

"She can afford her own coat."

"I want her to wear the most expensive coat from this auction. *People* magazine is here, Leo. I want her on the cover in a Cotillion Fur."

"Why didn't you say so?"

"Buy it."

The auctioneer's gavel was plummeting toward his desk.

"*Up!*" called Leo.

The Soviets beamed. The other bidders applauded. Three hundred and fifty thousand dollars for one hundred skins was a record.

"Stand up," said Leo. "You paid for it."

"No, you."

"Stand up, you dummy. Wallace would have."

Artie from *People* loped up the stairs, shooting wildly. Natalie pretended Wallace was with her. She stood up, bowed, and smiled for the camera. Then she reached for Leo and signaled his sons to rise, too.

"Note," Leo muttered through his smile, "I haven't asked how you intend to pay for it."

"I'm putting together a terrific deal," she replied airily. But Leo's joke hit home. Without an agreement with Rostov in the next twenty-four hours, she was out of business, her reputation in the fur trade shattered forever, if she couldn't pay Sojuzpushnina.

Leo sat down, turned a page in his catalog, rubbed his hands together, and said, "Okay, now we get serious. There's some decent skins coming up for those little capes you wanted. Stick close, we're going to romp 'em."

But just as the bidding renewed, a fur girl came down the aisle with a message for Natalie. "This is Joannie calling," it read. "I am on the telephone, holding the line. Urgent."

"Tell her I'll call back."

"The circuits are jammed. We won't get through."

"Okay. Leo, I'll be right back."

"Wait a minute. I need you here. The capes are your idea."

"Right back. I've got trouble."

Natalie ran after the girl, worrying what disaster had driven Joannie Frye to call. She raced through the curving row of desks, around the other bidders, and out of the auction hall. "Where's the telephone?"

"Follow me, please." The girl led her through a door marked for staff, past some offices, and into a corridor.

"Where are we going?"

"Through that door," the girl replied, spinning on her heel and hurrying away. Natalie hesitated. It was the first time during the auction that she had seen a fur girl not smiling. She was already backing away, when the door opened suddenly with a blinding flash of sunlight.

Frigid air blew in. She saw the silhouette of a car on the street and the hard, black shape of a man running at her. Natalie whirled, running, but he caught her. She screamed and fought him, tearing at his powerful hand. He dragged her toward the door.

"*Natalie!* For Chrissake, what are you doing to me?" Leo bustled down the corridor, squinting belligerently into the daylight.

"Get help!" Natalie yelled.

"What's going on? What is this?" The old furrier grabbed the Russian's arm. The man was stopped in his tracks and turned smartly about as if a New York City fire hydrant had simultaneously grown a hand and turned obstreperous.

"What are you, a *schmuck*?" asked Leo. "Let her go."

The Russian raised his other arm high and smashed his fist into Leo's chest, immediately over his heart. Natalie felt the heavy thud. Leo formed his own fist. "Hey," he gasped, and suddenly clutched his chest. "Hey." His cigar fell from his mouth. His face contorted. His

lips were suddenly blue and he collapsed in a round heap on the floor.
"Leo!"

A group of fur girls rounded the corner, saw Leo on the floor and
Natalie screaming, and began screaming, too. The Russian fled. Natalie was barely aware of another blast of cold air and the door banging
as she knelt beside Leo. Car tires screeched.

"Get a doctor!" she yelled at the girls. "Get an ambulance."

Leo's entire face was blue. She pressed her ear to his motionless
chest, heard no heartbeat, and tried to remember the CPR drill she
had studied in the event Wallace had a heart attack. Breathing into
Leo's mouth and pounding his chest, all she could recall for sure was
the instructor's warning to expect to break some ribs.

Someone pulled her off him. "I'm a doctor," he said. "Get out of
my way." She rocked back on her heels and watched in disbelief and
growing horror as the doctor worked. Twice he got Leo breathing
again. The third time, he began shouting angrily for the ambulance. It
was nearly an hour before a crew arrived, jammed an oxygen mask
over his face, and bundled Leo onto a stretcher. "I'll come with him,"
Natalie said, but a uniformed militiaman blocked her.

"I'll ride with him to the hospital," she explained to the cop, who
was joined by a partner. "He's all alone. He doesn't speak Russian."

"You will come with us," was the cold reply.

"Get his sons. They're in the auction."

Only when he squeezed her arm hard enough to hurt did Natalie
realize she had been arrested.

35

She had read her Solzhenitsyn. She had written her undergraduate honors thesis on *The First Circle*'s antecedents in Pasternak, Orwell, and Koestler. Recently, she had discovered the exiled poet Irina Ratushinskaya. Yet none of them had prepared her for her own fear when the prison matron, a hulking woman in drab fatigues, ordered her to strip.

The fear filled her body violently, as if a firehose pumping terror had been rammed down her throat. Her face was numb and she could only think that Solzhenitsyn's, Pasternak's, Orwell's, Koestler's victims were innocent. Ratushinskaya was innocent. She, after all, was guilty.

"Wait," she said. "I am an American citizen. I want to see the United States consul—I mean, the ambassador."

She was no longer in Leningrad. They had bundled her into a sealed truck, then aboard a plane. Then another truck from the airport into Moscow. She had learned it was Moscow by accident. A shutter fell from an air slit and she caught a glimpse of the Children's World department store as the truck turned into the Lubianka Prison on Dzerzhinsky Square.

KGB headquarters. Safe from the Millionaires, in the hands of the secret police. It was two hours since her arrest. On the plane, handcuffed in a dark compartment, she had wondered if Leo was still alive. Now he was gone from her mind, erased by the fear.

"I demand to see my ambassador."

Never argue with functionaries, Wallace always said. They can't help you, but they can certainly hurt you. The matron was a hulking woman in drab fatigues, as expressionless as any Solzhenitsyn described. A little club wrapped in leather had appeared in her hand by dark magic. Face blank, eyes dead, she jammed the end into Natalie's stomach. She doubled up, gasping and crying. The pain, deep and ruinous, overpowered her.

"Strip."

She was still wearing her new red dress. Dead eyes watched her remove it. The matron pointed at her feet. Natalie stepped out of her boots onto cold cement. She hesitated with her bra. The club flicked painfully against her thighs. She unclipped it, rolled off her pantyhose and stepped out of her panties. Shivering, she removed her watch and earrings, pearls, bracelets, and a locket Wallace had given her, and finally her wedding ring, placing all of it in the outstretched hand.

The matron left her standing there, cold and naked. There was a light bulb in the ceiling and a television camera. "Wait," she cried, totally unnerved, but no one came.

Minutes passed, or seconds or hours. When her legs grew tired, she sat on the edge of the bunk, staring at the floor and picking nervously at the mattress. Every time she tried to fathom her situation, her thoughts scattered like leaves on a wind of fear. The door flew open. She jumped up. Another matron, almost indistinguishable from the first, handed her a white cotton robe. It smelled of a hospital laundry. The matron led her to a room with a table and a single wooden chair, and left her alone.

She tried to count time by her heartbeats, lost track, and waited, biting her lips. This time when her legs grew tired she was afraid to sit. A small voice said she should use this time to think. A louder voice argued that she had nothing to think about. The door opened.

"Thank God," she blurted.

Framed in the doorway was the tall figure of Valery Kirichenko, wearing a colonel's uniform and carrying a briefcase and a large, clear plastic bag with something white inside. Two people entered behind him, a man and a woman, who waited in respectful silence until he stepped aside. They looked vaguely familiar.

"It is her," said the woman.

"Are you quite sure?"

"Yes, sir. Quite sure."

"Dismissed, thank you."

They turned on heel and left, closing the door behind them, and Natalie felt her spirit crumble. They were the man and woman whose arrival at the Hopkins Inn had caused Luba to flee for her life.

Kirichenko, who was watching her closely, nodded with satisfaction. He put his briefcase on the floor beside the chair, opened the plastic bag, and dumped her bloodstained lynx coat on the table.

"If I were in your position, and I believed in God, I would be praying, rather than thankful."

She flinched from the rage in his eyes. "Save me time and yourself misery. Is this your coat?"

She had worried about the coat and had concocted a thin story. "May I touch it?"

"I've already asked you to save misery. Is this your coat?"

"It looks like a coat I gave a Russian woman in Leningrad." Thin as her story was, she clung to a desperate hope that the coat was all they had arrested her for.

"You *gave* her this coat? The police tell me it is very valuable."

"We traded coats."

"For one equally valuable?"

"Not quite."

"Matron!" he shouted.

The door crashed open. The heavyset matron marched in and dumped the Russian prostitute's kolinsky on the table beside the lynx. The dyed brown color alone made her last statement absurd. Worse, they had traced her to the student's flat. How much farther?

"I'm no expert at luxury, like you, Mrs. Nevsky, but even I see no comparison between these coats. You merely traded?"

"I was drinking. I was quite high. Frankly, I was drunk." She thought she could handle this coat thing. "We met in the elevator at the Leningrad Hotel, coming down from the currency bar."

"Did you see anything unusual after you traded coats?"

"I think there was a traffic accident. I got in a cab and left."

"Headed toward the American consulate, changed your mind when you saw police there, and ended up in a student's flat on Vasilevsky Island where you spent the night and traded this coat for his cloth coat, perhaps in gratitude for services rendered."

"I've been under a lot of strain. I admit I drank too much. I've purchased several million in furs and am at the moment in delicate negotiation with Vladimir Rostov of the Foreign Trade Ministry. I need to contact Comrade Rostov. We have meetings planned this evening and a media announcement tomorrow morning at the Palace of Furs to present a joint Soviet-American venture. We hope that as he begins his tour, the Gen Sec himself—"

Kirichenko cut her off, demanding scornfully, "Do you seriously believe you can do business in the Soviet Union if the word gets around that you are a KGB detainee? They'll flee, Mrs. Nevsky. Flee like rabbits. . . . Now, by your own admission you had quite a night in Leningrad. Hardly the demure widow I met at the Kremlin reception. Puzzling, though perhaps it explains this."

Studying her reaction, he opened his briefcase. Natalie tried, and failed, not to stare at his hand as he reached into it. He spread three copies of *The Pearl* on the table.

"This," he said, "belonged to a young woman who fell off a building. This, to an elderly gentleman who swallowed cyanide when my men tried to interview him. This, to a spoiled little brat who we're currently hunting in some of the better back alleys of Moscow. And *this*"—he reached in and pulled out a fourth book—"which we found in your hotel suite, looks like a popular novel you could purchase in any airport. But when we open it, we discover glued inside its covers the same pornographic filth."

Natalie was trembling.

"Or is it filth?" Kirichenko asked with heavy sarcasm. "Perhaps it is art? Perhaps an historical record of Victorian perversity, which helps us understand our pre-Revolutionary forebears. Which do you think, Mrs. Nevsky?"

"I want to see the American ambassador."

"And you will," he promised. "After we have a little chat—or two. Or three. Or four. Or as many as it takes."

"I don't understand what you're talking about, Comrade Kirichenko."

Violence flared in his eyes. "How dare you call me Comrade? How dare you. . . . Three people suspected of conspiring with your husband against the Soviet Union all possess *The Pearl*. Your husband is *shot*. You appear three months later with a crudely disguised copy of *The Pearl*. Are you familiar with the term *book code*?"

Natalie shook her head.

"No? Then tell me you indulge private sexual fantasies reading *The Pearl* and I will have you back in your hotel in two hours."

"I indulge private sexual fantasies reading *The Pearl*."

"May I presume your husband introduced you to it?"

"Yes."

"On which side of the chasm of abuse do you recline?"

"I don't understand."

Kirichenko picked up her copy and leafed through it. "Most of the scenes I read in your book are about sexual abuse. What is your pleasure? Giving? Receiving?"

Natalie was silent.

"Describe two or three of your favorite scenes."

"I can't."

"Shall I call the matron?"

"I can't. I can't do it. Please, it's too personal."

"You have no idea—yet—of the meaning of 'too personal.' "

He stood up.

"I've ordered that you undergo a medical examination. The doctor will need an hour or so. Use the time to think about your favorite scenes. We'll discuss them in detail when I return. When you have 'satisfied' me, we will go on to discuss a girl named Elena. Another girl named Luba. And then, we will discuss a conspiracy known to them as the Millionaires' plot.

"Think about the Millionaires' plot while the doctor examines you. Think about who is called the Boss. *Vozhd,* a term you bandied about the night I first met you. And think about your late husband's connections with the Boss and the Millionaires' plot."

"Why is the doctor going to examine me?" Drugs, she thought. The KGB uses drugs to make prisoners talk.

"A routine assessment of your strength."

"My strength?"

"To see what your body can take. We won't have you collapse midway through our discussion. . . . "

The full impact of that threat was still washing over her like an icy Atlantic breaker when Kirichenko said, "Here, I'll leave your copy so you can refresh your memory while the doctor takes your blood pressure. . . . Astonishing, the sexual habits of the Victorians. All these beatings. Rapes. Sodomy. I was reminded more of the Great Purge than making love. . . . I'll take your robe, now. You won't need it for the doctor."

"No."

He slapped her, lightly, a demonstration that he could do whatever he pleased. She backed away. He seized her arms, turned her around effortlessly, ripped the robe from her body. She stood stock-still, facing the wall. "Get away from me."

Kirichenko lifted her hair and trailed a cold finger down the back of her neck. "Enjoy your examination."

The KGB doctor was pale as a prisoner, with greasy hair and greedy eyes that lingered. He took her blood pressure, put her through a simple stress test of jumping up and down for two minutes, and took her blood pressure again. He listened to her heart and lungs, felt the glands in her neck, and watched, covertly, as she produced a urine sample. This he analyzed in a rack of test tubes. Musing over the results and shooting her an inquiring glance, he repeated the chemical analysis. Natalie huddled in a corner, shivering from the cold, and discovering that she felt curiously less humiliated than she would have predicted.

She had read her Solzhenitsyn.

Kirichenko had made an error in his choice of doctor. She almost smiled, thrilled by her first rational thought since she had been arrested. Faceless terror called for a bland, hideously ordinary doctor. Examining her routinely as if she were just one of a million faceless, nameless prisoners would have unnerved her to the breaking point. But this creep inspired more disgust than fear, and warring emotions cleared a little space for thinking.

She recalled that General Lapshin had described Kirichenko as incorruptible. His touch, his heavy hints of sexual assault, were perhaps deliberately designed to frighten her. He might not carry them through.

But there was nothing but his own moral code to restrain him. No one knew she was here. The Soviets could stall a search for weeks through channels, the bureaucrats claiming to be diligently hunting the missing American, while all the while the KGB would be free to brutalize her in these cellars in the heart of Moscow, less than two miles from the American embassy. She had to give them something.

What did the KGB want? What would they accept?

They wanted what Wallace had fought to keep from them—the Millionaires and an excuse to launch a fiery purge.

What did Kirichenko know?

Starkov had been right. Kirichenko still thought that *The Pearl* belonged to the Millionaires. Nor did he know as much about the

Millionaires as Wallace had managed to record on the wire. If he did, a thousand Army officers would be in prison, the plot extinguished.

She guessed that Kirichenko was still mired in rumors. That would explain his interest in her upon her arrival and his agents' overt attempts to frighten an amateur into making a mistake. Most important, he had not asked about Valentine's Day. Perhaps he did not know that the coup was two days off.

Ironically, after more than forty years, Wallace Nevsky's information network was still undiscovered. Now it was up to her to prevent the chaos that Wallace had lost his life trying to prevent. Her goal—extinguish the Millionaires' plot—was the same as Kirichenko's goal. But she had pledged her method to be Wallace's method—a quiet smothering of the rebel flame instead of the flood the KGB would release on the fractious land.

"I would seriously consider acquiescing to your interrogator," the doctor called from the table where he was still fiddling with his test tubes.

"Is that your medical or political opinion?"

"You run a terrible risk in your condition."

"What condition?"

He looked at her, surprise on his face. "You don't know?"

"Don't know what?"

"You're pregnant."

She was in that instant the happiest prisoner in the history of the Lubianka Prison. No hopeless soul unexpectedly released, no condemned woman ever pardoned, could have felt such joy. What she had lost forever was hers again, transformed.

Wallace was indeed with her, as she had so long imagined. She was carrying a finer secret than his recording, a glorious secret whose clues she had read all wrong—two missed periods attributed to the body-shattering agony of loss, sore breasts blamed on stress; mild morning sickness on travel, caviar, and vodka. She swore to stop drinking immediately, laughed suddenly when she remembered where she was, and just as suddenly burst into tears. But even crying, as the prison doctor leered, she knew that her body was in agreement, made for this, satisfied and complete.

The door banged open. A KGB officer, cold-eyed as Kirichenko, but younger and bearing a captain's insignia, marched in with a matron, who dumped her clothes on the table. "Get dressed."

"You," he commanded the doctor, "will present your full report to Colonel Kirichenko in one hour."

The doctor gathered up his things and left.

"Hurry up," snapped the captain, nodding at the matron, who flourished her club. Natalie dressed, quickly and silently, wondering what was in store for her, knowing they would ignore any questions.

"Move!" He pulled a set of handcuffs from his pocket, and clamped Natalie's arms tightly behind her back. The matron marched her out the door and down a long corridor, the captain trailing. They went through another door and up several flights of stairs. Natalie stumbled. The matron cursed and dug her fingers into her arm. They were stopped at a checkpoint at the top of the stairs. The captain produced a sheaf of papers and received a smart salute and passage into another hall. Natalie shivered. It was getting colder. Through another checkpoint, another salute, and a third checkpoint, where the guard officer personally read the papers and compared the mug shots they had taken when Natalie arrived, to her face. The matron dropped aside, and they passed into a courtyard surrounded by high walls. It was night and snowing. Natalie saw the outline of a large car.

"Here, take my coat," the captain said. "You must be freezing."

It was the first kind word she had heard since she was arrested and it caused her to blurt, "Am I free?"

"Hardly."

He opened the rear door and helped her in. No light went on inside the car. He got in front, started the engine, and drove out of the courtyard through a dark alley. At the end was a gate and as the car pulled into the pool of light that surrounded it, she saw the form of a man sitting across from her.

A guard shone a flashlight on the captain's papers, then turned it on Natalie. The light moved to the third occupant and instantly dropped away. The guard swallowed hard, saluted, gestured for the gate to open. The car eased into a side street. Motorcycles with blue flashers picked them up fore and aft and seconds later they were racing down a Moscow boulevard in the high-speed center lane reserved for the Soviet elite. As the street lamps flickered past she could see her captor's face. He was a changed man—troubled, cold, and remote.

"Where are you taking me?" she whispered.

"Out of the frying pan," old Marshal Lapshin said without a smile.

36

Incredible as it seemed, Natalie realized, the Millionaires had raided KGB headquarters, the heart of Soviet security. That they would take such a desperate chance could only mean that their coup was indeed set for Valentine's Day. That they had succeeded was a vivid measure of the rebels' power.

"How did you get me out? What pretext did you use?"

He laughed. "Pretext? We have no need for pretext in Soviet Union. Paperwork will open any door. The bureaucrats are boss, and we have many, many bureaucrats on our side."

Now, as the motorcade sped from Moscow center, Marshal Lapshin posed a question that destroyed her last illusion that she had been rescued.

"Do you believe in an afterlife?"

"My arms hurt. Could you remove these handcuffs?"

"I believe in an afterlife. I believe Vassily is looking down on us right now. Perhaps when he sees that your arms hurt it will teach him a lesson. Why did he betray Russia?"

"He loved Russia, Marshal Lapshin. He thought you would destroy her."

"That is not my intention," Lapshin snapped back.

"He meant you would fail."

"When did he say this?"

416

Natalie was appalled. He had tricked her into admitting she knew about the plot.

"When?"

"Last summer," she improvised hurriedly. *The widow. I am still the frightened widow.*

"He spoke openly?"

"Only to me and only in vague terms. He was worried about you."

"You'll have to be more specific."

"I can't. That's all he said."

"We shall see." The old Soviet marshal stared long and hard, then turned away, done with her.

Their helicopter was on a field outside the city this time, and manned solely by ranking officers. Even the steps were folded in by the captain who had engineered her release from Lubianka. "Keep the coat," he said gravely, and ran back to the car where Marshal Lapshin had rolled down his window to watch the takeoff.

The ship thudded into a snowy sky. The officers watched the windscreen in tense silence, leaving Natalie to brood on her fate. The captain, whose warm greatcoat was snug around her shoulders, had looked like a decent man who was sorry for what he knew was going to happen to her. The doctor had sent her soul soaring into territory she had never explored.

Natalie recognized the *dacha* by the jagged black loop of the river. General Lapshin was waiting by the helicopter pad. He stood erect and hatless as the ship descended, filled with cocky disdain for the spinning blades and the driven snow. Natalie was prodded toward him, her hands still clamped behind her back. The wind tore at the coat the captain had draped over her shoulders. Lapshin reached up and buttoned it with a gentle touch.

"You should have stuck to business."

"I did. I'm on the verge of a spectacular joint enterprise with a Soviet company. Can you get me back to Leningrad by tomorrow morning?"

Lapshin smiled, furrowing his stiff, reconstructed cheek. "Nice try."

"I don't understand. Why have you brought me here?"

"Someone wants to meet you."

He took her arm, but instead of heading to the house, guided her down the newly swept path to the mink sheds. Halfway there, they passed the soldier sweeping and trudged ahead in six inches of fluffy snow. Natalie smelled the minks on the wind, sweet and pungent. She shivered, imagining she heard them scurrying about their cages.

Lapshin continued past the sheds and Natalie thought suddenly of home, her memory keyed by a crisp scent of rushing water. They were nearing the river, she realized, and suddenly, crazily, when she saw its sharp black path in the snow, thought he was going to drown her. Bulk loomed out of the dark and materialized into a large, one-story building. It had no windows, only a heavily insulated door, which he opened.

A powerful mink odor gushed out, warm and gamey in Natalie's face. She tried to pull away. Lapshin dragged her inside and shut the door. Her breath came fast and hard as she felt herself assailed by a fathomless panic.

It was marginally warmer out of the wind, and dark, but the darkness was different from the gray glow of the snow. Electric lights dimmed very low simulated the blue hour of a late summer evening. As her eyes adjusted to the change, she saw a single room crammed with hundreds upon hundreds of mink cages stacked in long rows, three high, and separated by narrow aisles, which were lined with water pipes, feed chutes, and waste conveyors.

The animals had frozen, stock-still, when they entered. Now they started moving about their cages, darting in and out of their sleeping hutches, nosing the feed dispensers, testing the wire mesh with their teeth. Natalie thought of a Manhattan street as night fell, vibrant with expectation.

Lapshin was watching her.

"What is this?" she asked.

"A breeding experiment that your husband used to worm his way into my father's confidence."

"I don't understand."

"Minks breed once a year. We have one harvest, November–December. This is a controlled atmosphere. By manipulating the light, temperature, and diet, we hope to trick their biological clocks into breeding year round."

"Like battery chickens? You'll destroy the market."

"Your husband looked upon it as a socialist would—more mink for more people. But not to worry. America's best rancher has tried with no better results than ours, so far. The problem, of course, was that Vassily's real intent was to betray my father's movement."

"What does this have to do with me?"

"We want the wire recording."

"I burned it."

"What did it say?"

"I didn't listen. I burned it."

"You went to great trouble to play it. You played it."

"I heard the beginning," she admitted. "I heard your father speaking with an American. He mentioned you. I suddenly realized I don't want any part of this. I'm a businesswoman. I have a company to run. What Wallace did is past. He is dead. I am alone. Frankly, I couldn't care less what you, your father, or the American are up to. All I want to do is finish my deals in Russia and go home."

It sounded great, she thought. Independent woman makes her own life. Lapshin seemed to think so, too. He smiled faintly. "*Bozhe Moy,* I want to believe you."

"You want to believe every pretty face," said a woman behind them. "It's part of your charm, Aleksandr, and one of the many reasons I love you."

37

Natalie turned, ice in her heart, as Dina sauntered out of the gloom. She walked like a model, placing one foot directly in front of the other, with a languorous sway. It was an almost comical parody of Lauren Bacall, but General Lapshin couldn't take his eyes off her. She was slim and lithe, and without the blonde wig looked older, at least thirty. Her hair was different than in the two pictures Natalie had seen, straight and close cut, cupping her face, which was delicate and lively. Her dark eyes settled on Natalie and her willful smile turned cruel.

"You're lying."

Natalie couldn't look at her. She turned to General Lapshin. "She murdered my husband. Did you know that?"

"I suspected. I'm sorry for your pain. But he made himself our enemy."

"Where is the wire?" asked Dina.

"I burned it. I wish I hadn't. I wish I had it to do to you whatever it is you fear."

Dina smiled at that ruse. "You're lying," she said. "And we can't have that." She had a slight English accent with a world-weary, sarcastic lilt.

"You burned something, but not necessarily the wire in question. My personal feeling is you copied it. I've never met an American who didn't carry a vast array of gadgetry. Curiously, we find no tape recorder in your belongings. However, the customs form you filled out upon entering the Soviet Union listed a tape recorder. A Panasonic 111 Microcassette. Did you lose yours?"

"I gave it to a fur girl as a present."

"Where is the copy?"

"I made no copy. I didn't even hear the wire."

"Come here, Natalie."

Natalie looked at Lapshin. He nodded. "You have to tell us."

"I've told you."

"Come here, Natalie." Dina jerked hard on Natalie's elbow, causing the handcuffs to bite into her wrist. She dragged Natalie into a narrow aisle between two stacks of cages and pushed her up to one at eye level. "Look at the animal."

Natalie found herself face to face with a buff-colored female. It had a sleek, strong body, a small head, and fierce green eyes. Her stomach clenched. The mink stiffened, smelling her fear.

"You notice the lights are growing dimmer," Dina said. "The keepers have set the timers to simulate nightfall. The animals are waking up, getting ready to feed. They're hungry. And irritable. The water lines froze. They haven't had enough to drink. Aleksandr, give me a ruble note."

Lapshin pulled a money clip from his pocket and passed her a bill. Dina rolled it into a tight little cylinder. "Watch, Natalie." She slipped the ruble through the wire mesh. The mink attacked in a blur of sinew and flashing teeth. Natalie heard them scraping the wire. Dina withdrew the shredded bill and showed it to Natalie.

"Female, of course. You know the cliché. You could probably scratch some of these males behind the ears, if you'd a mind to. You don't, do you? I thought not. You're afraid of them. Odd, as they die for your coats, you'd think it would be the other way around. . . . Natalie, what did the tape say and where is the copy?"

"I didn't hear it. I made no copy."

"Aleksandr, free her hands, darling."

Lapshin produced a key and opened the handcuffs. Natalie started to massage her wrists. Dina took one of her hands in both of hers. She was strong.

"What did the tape say and where is your copy?"

"I heard nothing. I made no copy."

Dina moved suddenly and jammed Natalie's fingers against the wire. The mink struck.

Natalie screamed. The pain lanced from her bloodied finger to her elbow. Wildly she tried to pull away, but Dina threw her weight into a firm grip and shoved her hand back onto the cage. Frenzied by Natalie's blood, the mink attacked again.

Her hand burned like fire. Three fingers were bloody. Dina let go and she staggered away, gasping for air. A wave of nausea hit and her head was spinning. Dina watched, eyes aglitter.

"Bring her back, Aleksandr."

Natalie squeezed her wounded fingers and backed away. "There's no copy."

Lapshin blocked her escape. "Answer her."

"Help me," Natalie whispered.

"Sorry, Mrs. Nevsky. You're playing with the big boys now."

"He can't help you," said Dina. "You're in the way of events. You can't just stand there."

"I only tried to find out what happened to my husband."

"It was clear to most people what happened from the beginning."

"But it wasn't true."

Dina pointed at the blood dripping from Natalie's hand. "Can you honestly say you're happier for it? Tell me, where is the copy, or I will open this cage, put your hand in it, and hold it there until the animal can eat no more."

In that moment Natalie realized that she had never hated anyone before. She wanted to fly at Dina, hitting and kicking. But that was as impossible as escape.

"Tell us," Lapshin urged.

"Even if I had made a copy, which I didn't, you'd kill me after I told you."

Dina's eyes flared at what was almost an admission. Lapshin said, "We won't hurt you. We'll hold you, briefly, and let you go unharmed. You have my word."

"I'd prefer Dina's word."

"No problem," said Dina.

"Do you expect me to believe that? You killed my husband. You'll kill me, too."

"Give me your hand."

Natalie turned back to Lapshin. They were different. There was room between them. "I'm afraid. I'm dead either way. If you enjoyed the evening we shared, would you do me the one favor of making it quick?"

"Perhaps you need a little time to think about it."

Dina whirled on him, spewing rage. "Don't you see what she's done? She's hidden it. We can't do a thing until we find it."

Lapshin flinched. "All I'm saying is, maybe she didn't."

"We have to know for sure."

Lapshin took out a handkerchief and wrapped it gently around Natalie's fingers. "Natalie, we're contending for an empire. My father and Dina and I are just three among thousands. You've put yourself in the way. Consider your position."

"I'm attempting to make her position clear," Dina snapped.

"We'll give her an hour to think it over."

Dina started to protest, thought better of it, and acquiesced with a sullen smile. "All right, darling." Lapshin opened the door. Dina lingered to whisper, "He will not be coming back with me."

Natalie glanced at General Lapshin. He turned away.

She tested the door, but it was locked, firmly, from the outside. She sagged to the earthen floor, pressed Lapshin's handkerchief to her aching fingers, and pictured her hand closed in the cage with a frenzied animal.

It was not a matter of being brave. Dina would kill her either way. Until yesterday, she might have embraced the thought of being in some way reunited with Wallace. But today that was impossible because she was not alone.

In the dark, the minks had begun to stir. Natalie listened to their scuttling claws, the pouncing bodies, inquiring yelps, a sudden angry bang of teeth on wire, a threatening cry. They were hunters. They fed at night. Unique among domesticated animals, mink never lost their wildness. They killed as ferociously as if they had been captured yesterday, General Lapshin had marveled. Forty generations old, a loose ranch mink still ran for the river.

She stood up and ventured down an aisle, counting cages, and estimated the house held more than a thousand. She had an idea how to escape, but it scared her more than Dina. She tried the door again. No help there. She was out of options. Doing nothing was no longer an option, because she was not alone.

Natalie turned the crude wooden latch on a mink cage, opened the door, and jumped back. The animal flattened into an attack posture.

Sinuous as a reptile, long and sleek, it slithered toward the opening. Natalie backed away, her eyes locked on its eyes. They feared nothing, Lapshin had said. It was halfway out the door, stretching to sniff the air, like a smooth rope of muscle baring teeth.

Mesmerized, Natalie stared back. Her heart was pounding, her breath coming short, and all that kept her from slamming the door on it was the thought of Dina caught between the river and a thousand of its sisters.

She tore her eyes from it, pretended it wasn't there, and opened another cage. Again, the mink stalked the door, eyes alert, belly to the floor, and poised to spring. Shivering steadily, Natalie opened a third cage. The animal streaked out faster than her eye. It leaped onto her coat. She screamed. She felt the claws scrabbling on the heavy cloth, the sinewy strength of the body.

The mink dropped to the floor and vanished into the shadows beneath a waste conveyor. She whirled to see where the first had run. It too was gone, as was the second. An eerie silence settled over the building. The rest were waiting. She could see their eyes, and thought she felt their breath, warm with expectation.

She ran between a triple row of cages, flipping the latches, cage after cage after cage. There were ten rows of a hundred cages each. At two hundred, she stopped. The house was still. Something was wrong.

Peering down the row she had just opened she saw that most of the animals had scurried back into their hutches. A few watched apprehensively from their hutch openings. Others had disappeared entirely but for a tail or a quivering whisker. Puzzled, she checked the first row. Much the same. A few minks peered out from under the water conveyors, but most had stayed put.

"What? What are you doing?"

At the sound of her voice, many ducked out of sight.

"Get out!" she screamed.

That had the effect of chasing all but the bravest under cover. In disbelief, Natalie leaned against a wall, sucking her stinging fingers while she watched. Slowly, things returned to normal. The mink browsed about their open cages and now and then one wandered out and climbed down for a look at the floor. She was thinking they were not quite that frightening—though their reptilian movements were still the stuff of nightmares—when a demibuff snapped off the tail of a natural brown passing its open cage.

The wounded animal whirled in a murderous rage, attacking with teeth and claws. They fell, rolling over and over, broke suddenly, and disappeared. That fight seemed to provoke another and then another. Natalie felt a palpable rise in tension. It was like setting off a chain reaction. Quickly, she resumed opening cages, adding new combatants to a volatile mass.

When she had released them all, she retreated to the door and stacked some empty cages into a platform that allowed her to stand just inside the door and several feet above the floor.

The mink were fighting constantly, two and three battles at a time. She saw their eyes everywhere, glinting atop the cages, on the rafters, and massed on the floor. The noise grew louder, the yelps and growls constant, punctuated by screams. Now and then a single animal would tear across the room in a series of random attacks that left dozens tousling in its wake. Two such marauders clashed in the middle and suddenly all the animals exploded into full riot.

A battle erupted between her legs, demons tearing at each other, claws scraping her boots. Struggling pairs fell on her, squirming and clawing. Something caught her hair, tangled, snapped free, and tumbled down her back. She pressed against the wall and covered her face. Then, terrified they would smell the dried blood on her fingers, she shoved her injured hand in the greatcoat pocket.

The fighting stopped, abruptly. The mink house went silent. There was a noise at the door. A key. The latch snicked. A thousand pairs of eyes locked on the sound.

Dina stepped in and immediately spied Natalie on the cages.

"It's feeding time." She pointed the little silenced pistol at Natalie, shielding it with her hip. And in that practiced motion, Natalie suddenly saw how the Millionaires would launch their coup on Saturday. During a reception, at the Soviet New York Consulate or the UN, Dina Golovkin, a trusted Gen Sec tour advance woman, would emerge from the crowd to send Marshal Lapshin's "clear, unmistakable signal for change" by shooting down Gorbachev as coolly as she had murdered Wallace aboard *Panache*.

Snow blew in after her.

Natalie smelled the river, sharp on the wind.

Silent as spiders, the mink charged. Dina stepped back hastily, sensing something wrong, not knowing what. She was framed in the doorway when they hit her. Those in the lead tried to go around her legs, but quickly bunched in the narrow space, clawed up her coat, and tried to pass at her knees. Piling over one another, those behind climbed ramps of those ahead, rising instantly to her waist, her chest, her shoulders. Face to face with the frantic animals, Dina screamed and toppled backward, shrieking as they trampled her by the hundreds.

Natalie threw herself into the stampede, running on their bodies, stepping on Dina. On the snow a broad black channel of racing animals poured toward the river, a living arrow that pointed escape. She veered aside.

Dina was screaming. Natalie looked back and saw her stand, beating at the mink that clung to her coat and clawed her hair, screaming rage at Natalie, then pain as they bit her face and hands. She fell, and gained her feet again, only to be turned by the stampede and carried along. Frantically trying to run from them, she ran with them, herded like a blind giant to the edge of the ice where the mink were plunging into the water as smoothly and soundlessly as knives.

Dina couldn't stop. The ice crumbled. She pinwheeled the air and splashed into the river, her screams ending abruptly when the swift black current bore her under.

38

Horror threatened to overwhelm her. Staggering to the rim of the ice, Natalie felt the razor teeth slash again, smelled the animals in her hair, heard Dina scream forever on a squirming tide—abruptly silent, as if God had breathed His last.

A dim corner of her mind, not yet driven mad, whispered that the river was deadly. The weakened ice sagged beneath her weight, the water lapped her boots, but her knees buckled as she swayed on the brink.

Something was moving. Her eyes sought it, locked. A single animal coursed through the black water. Natalie backed away. The old, familiar fear jolted her back to sanity. She could feel the cold searing her nostrils. Icy water seeped through her socks. Her fingers ached terribly where they had been bitten, the pain a sharp reminder that she had much more to fear on the vast army reservation.

The snow had stopped.

Stars and a bright moon breaking through the clouds cast silver light on desolation that stretched as far as she could see. Twenty thousand acres. Fifty. Maybe more. Deep snow, numbing cold, and moonlight to track her by. Her senses quickened. She thought she could hear the wolves howling on the bitter wind.

She turned from the wilderness and trudged back toward the *dacha*, taking pains to step in her own tracks and then, after closing the door of the empty mink house, Dina's tracks, which she followed to a hedgerow fifty feet from the brightly lighted house.

If she had any hope at all it was in the telephone. The most private phone in the house was likely in Lapshin's own suite.

A soldier loomed out of the moonshadows, boots crunching snow. Natalie pressed into the prickly hedge. He strode by, heading toward the river.

She was summoning the nerve to dash for the French doors when a figure passed behind the glass. She spied another door further along and was about to chance it. She heard a whistle shriek down by the river. The sentry had found the minks missing.

A siren took up the cry, its howl dispersing soldiers from the house and outbuildings. Men pounded down the path. Flashlights darted yellow beams. A jeep roared by, General Lapshin at the wheel. Eight men raced after him and suddenly the house was silent.

Natalie ran for the French doors.

She expected a shout at any moment, but she made the house undetected and found herself in the book-lined room where Lapshin had first taken her from the party in Moscow. She started down the hall to the stairs.

A shadow appeared around the corner, quick light steps behind it. She hid in the nearest room, the plush target-shooting range with brocaded walls. Swinging the door partially closed, she watched through the crack. Just inside the door was a gun rack, open, and she realized that whoever was coming was likely coming for a weapon. She backed further into the room and knelt behind a wing chair.

Nadia, Lapshin's pretty little cook, burst in, ran to the gun case, selected a long-barreled pistol, slapped a magazine into the stock, and ran out. Natalie crept after her, found the hallway empty, and shambled toward the stairs.

General Lapshin's pillows reeked of Dina's Madame Rochas. His bed was wide and firm with a mirror across the room subtly angled to reflect the occupants. In it, Natalie saw a frightened, bone-weary woman clutching a telephone to her ear. The telephone rang with a purr like a cat. Between rings it popped and hissed. She counted ten rings. Twenty. Thirty.

Outside, cars and trucks roared, sergeants yelled, and snowmobiles buzzed. Search lights shot through the night and a helicopter clattered away like a china cabinet falling downstairs.

Her hopes rested solely with the telephone. Not that she could call anyone in Wallace's network. Of those she had discovered, Ivan Starkov must still be fencing with Kirichenko. Fyodor Shelpin had hung up on her the night before. Old Yulian the swimmer was a suicide. Luba was dead. Elena, hiding. And Vera had already betrayed her.

The operator woke up at last, surly and self-righteous. This was not Moscow, he reminded her, but an ill-equipped rural exchange. "Lady" visitors to the General's *dacha* had a lot of nerve expecting to ring up Leningrad at the drop of a hat in the middle of the night.

Vladimir Rostov's code 73 worked a minor miracle. She was, from the moment she uttered the magic number, Comrade-Of-Course and Comrade-Immediately. He promised to put her through to Minister Rostov as fast as his ancient equipment would permit.

Natalie, expecting soldiers to burst in the door any moment, could only wait. It was way too early to find Rostov in his office, nor was he at his hotel, which left his *dacha* on the Gulf of Finland, unless he was home with his wife in Moscow. Finally, the operator found him in the *dacha*. Natalie thought he sounded reasonably friendly, despite a sleepy whisper to someone with him.

"Do we have a deal?" she asked.

"Mrs. Nevsky. It's awfully late, or early, for business. It's still dark."

"In case we get cut off, please take down this phone number. I'm in a *dacha* owned by General Aleksandr Lapshin about a hundred miles north of Moscow."

"*The* General Lapshin?"

"The war hero. If we get cut off for any reason, call back immediately and insist on talking to me. Okay?" She gave him the number and made him repeat it.

"What is this about?" Rostov asked cautiously.

"Business," she said, climbing off the bed and straining at the end of the phone wire to wedge a chair under the doorknob. "Were you pleased with my people?"

"Well, we attempted to forge ahead without you after the authorities reported you had accompanied Mr. Margulies to the Kremlin Clinic. A wise move, I thought. Much better doctors. I understand he's still improving."

"I'm hopeful." Thank God Leo was still alive. "And how are our talks going?"

"Well . . . your people made a very impressive presentation. But it is hard to see how they can deliver such big promises."

I'm not up to this, she thought, sinking back into the pillows. I can't handle it. But the cold fact was she could not maneuver Rostov into rescuing her unless they had a deal. For if he didn't need her at today's press conference, Rostov couldn't care less when and how she got back to Leningrad. She was negotiating for her life.

"You're being very Soviet, Vladimir."

"I am not! Your people were very mistrustful."

He was either very angry or doing a fine acting job. She said, "There's no reason to make this complicated. These aren't disarmament talks. What did my people leave hanging? Let me clear it up right now. The Sojuzpushnina press conference is in twelve hours."

"Your people keep harping about assurances. Your attorney worries she won't be able to sue. Your furriers fear the KGB won't let them go home. Your brother demands guarantees he wouldn't dare ask a fellow capitalist."

"Don't worry about it. Americans are natural lawyers. We can't help ourselves. I will take your assurances as stipulated."

"You will?"

"Yes."

"How can you, just like that?"

"I'm the boss. Now what is hanging things up on your side?"

"We cannot possibly draw up contracts today. And even if we could, there's no way we would extend funds on such short notice."

"I'll settle for a letter of commitment."

"Perhaps such a thing could be expedited. Perhaps."

"Vladimir, I'm not going to beat around the bush. You know darned well you can save Cotillion by announcing a deal this afternoon. Otherwise I'm out of business and you're out of a partnership."

"We split sixty/forty."

So that was it. He had her helpless and he knew that in her position any deal was better than no deal.

"Vladimir, you wound me. Did we not agree to fifty-one/forty-nine?"

"Fifty-one/forty-nine next summer. Sixty/forty, today."

What's the point in arguing? she thought. Rostov fully understood that the value of their joint enterprise to her was the hook it gave her into American investment capital.

But she felt brave. "Fifty-five/forty-five, or you've got to start a new negotiation from scratch, with strangers."

"Done!" Rostov agreed.

Natalie sagged back on the bed. "There's just one further problem, Vladimir."

"No more problems or we won't make the press conference," Rostov said flatly.

"Transport."

"I don't understand."

"I need a ride to Leningrad."

There was a long silence. Finally the trade minister said, "May I ask why the general won't give you a ride?"

"We had a hell of a night, to put it bluntly. He's gone to sleep and I'm stuck. You must have some plane or something, don't you?"

"I wonder if I might speak with the general."

"A couple of minutes ago he didn't know his own name. If you want, I'll try to—"

"No. No. That's all right. Tell me—"

The chair she had wedged under the doorknob flew across the bedroom. The door banged open. Natalie shrank against the headboard. The telephone suddenly seemed a very small shield.

"Hold on a minute, Minister Rostov, General Lapshin's just walked in."

General Lapshin drew his gun, a motion as swift and easy as a cat opening its claws.

"Hang up the telephone. Hang it up!"

"Too late, Aleksandr. I know you want me to stay, but Minister Rostov is already sending a helicopter—aren't you, Vladimir?—Oh, a Sojuzpushnina ski plane. If I don't show up for our press conference in Leningrad, he'll be very upset."

Dina would have shot her dead and worried about the consequences later. But Lapshin, she prayed, was not as quick a killer. Besides, they shared a slight bond. He knew her, to some extent, thanks to their evening in the *dacha*. And he knew that she knew him, to some extent. Would it buy time to persuade?

He glided toward her, gun in one hand, the other extended for the phone. *"Hang it up!"*

She covered the mouthpiece and lied. "I don't care what you and your father are up to. All I want to do is make my deal with Rostov and go home."

"How do you expect me to believe that? I know you have the wire. I know you're going to use it."

"I cannot use a wire I don't have," she lied again. "If you won't trust me, consider what I could have told Valery Kirichenko."

"What?"

"That Dina was sleeping with him on your behalf."

Lapshin gaped. "What?"

"You didn't know?"

His face went white and Natalie realized he had not known, though his father probably had. He shook his head and gave a bitter smile. "For the cause? . . ." Then he looked puzzled. "Why didn't you tell him? You could have had your revenge, by telling Kirichenko."

"My husband died trying to stop a Russian civil war, not start one."

"What makes you think the KGB will let you leave the country?"

"*Glasnost*. Even Kirichenko won't risk another Daniloff fiasco at the start of the Gen Sec tour."

Lapshin lowered his gun, beyond caring, by the expression on his face. "You couldn't have stopped me with that wire anyhow," he said dully.

Natalie believed him. But if Wallace was right, the wire might stop old Marshal Lapshin. And he could stop the plot. For with Dina no longer alive to inspire the ambivalent young general, his father was the real Boss of the Millionaires.

39

If Natalie needed more proof of the *blat* Wallace had accumulated in his forty years in Russia, she found it on the dais in the great blue auction hall in Sojuzpushnina's Palace of Furs. A dozen high officials emerged from the sea of beaming Soviet officialdom to greet her personally, congratulate her on Cotillion's *dzhoint venchur*, and trade business cards while they waited for the signing ceremony to begin.

Natalie sat off to one side between Ivan Starkov and Lynn Brown, who was exhausted from jet lag and marathon negotiating sessions with Rostov, whom she had grudgingly dubbed Comrade Hardball. Natalie was tired, too, but her weariness seemed to hover in the distance. A sitting-up sleep on the bumpy ski plane had cleared her head a little. A quick bath at the hotel had braced, though hardly soothed, her aching body. And after disinfecting her mink bites in hundred-proof vodka, she had painted her nails bright red to distract from the cuts. There was still much to do this day, and for the moment she was glad to let Diana Darbee represent Cotillion at center stage. There were things she had to learn to do without Wallace, but seeking the limelight was not among them. Delegate, she thought with a smile, and Diana was perfect for the job.

The actress had draped herself in raw Russian lynx skins, and apparently little else. Leo Margulies—watching the event on Soviet

433

television from his hospital bed—was probably gnashing his teeth because mass-market Cotillion was getting mileage out of his pelts, but the bizarre costume had been Diana's idea.

Minister Rostov approached the lectern. His handsome pompadour gleamed in the camera lights. His treasured gold Rolex, Natalie noticed, was tucked discreetly inside his French cuff in deference to the Gen Sec, who, a hundred rumors promised, would stop by briefly.

The auction hall was packed.

The Soviets had filled the rows and rows of bidders' desks with teenage trade school students, fresh-faced boys and girls who watched in wide-eyed silence. In the front rows, the bemused employees of the Leningrad fur hat factories cast curious, if not apprehensive, glances at Natalie's team of New York furriers.

Pete Kastoria, her dapper foreman, was deep in whispered conversation with the hat factory managers. Nearby, Alex Moschos had spread his own mink jacket on his desk and was busily ripping out the lining to show the skinsides of the let-out pelts to a trio of suitably awed Russians. Old Irving, meanwhile, having dredged up the language he had not spoken since his childhood, was acting as translator and English instructor. He could not recall, it seemed, whether his family had fled Russia before or after the Revolution, and no one seemed to care. "Quality," he repeated, pointing at the mink jacket, at Alex Moschos, and up at Natalie on the dais.

Rostov rapped the lectern with the auctioneer's gavel.

Lynn Brown woke with a start. "I still don't know what you told Comrade Hardball on the phone," she yawned, "but I personally would rather negotiate the parochial school condom machine concession with Cardinal O'Connor."

Rostov banged his gavel again, tossed it aside, and launched into a speech predicting a big future for East–West economic intercourse. Then he called on Natalie to join him at the lectern.

Together, while the cameras clattered, she and Rostov put their signatures on a document that the cautious bureaucrats had titled "A Preliminary Agreement to Implement a Joint Enterprise Between a Proposed Soviet Company—*Furmak*—and Natalie Stuart Nevsky, for the Purpose of Developing a Soviet Fur Industry." Her brother had fought to the mat for that last phrase, explaining to Natalie that now anyone who resisted the agreement would be put in the position of not wanting a Soviet fur industry.

"Congratulations," old Starkov commented dryly when she returned to her seat. "If I understand Wall Street, your future is assured."

"The word 'preliminary' is going to cost me two points in interest."

Starkov's shoulders were sloping from exhaustion, having endured two days of Kirichenko, followed by a four-hour Amerika Institut briefing of Gorbachev, who, Starkov had related, had been as demanding as the KGB officer. She could see Kirichenko himself, lurking in the auction hall, but with the international media in such heavy attendance for the start of the Gen Sec tour, and the televised signing, Natalie felt reasonably sure she could leave the Soviet Union unmolested.

At that moment Mike strolled into the auction hall, gave Kirichenko a friendly nod—having no idea who he was—and nodded again to Natalie, confirming that her lynx skin buy had cleared Soviet customs on its way to Finland, the first leg on the trip to New York.

There was a moment's confusion after the signing and some of the press began trickling away when suddenly a dozen large men in suits and sunglasses took up positions. Seconds later, Gorbachev himself entered with a flourish and commenced a swift hand-shaking blitz of the dais.

Natalie saw Artie of *People* trampled by the wire services when Diana Darbee suddenly slipped like a snake between Gorbachev's bodyguards and aides and aimed a kiss at the General Secretary that landed, in a blaze of camera flashes, on his pink round cheek.

"I think," said Ivan Starkov, "you have just regained your interest."

Natalie whispered, "Can you get a message to Marshal Lapshin to meet me at the airport?"

"He won't talk to you in such a public place."

Natalie named another. Starkov said he would try.

The air in the games arcade was thick with cigarette smoke and alive with the bonging, chirping, and ringing of video games and pinball. A young marksman with a green ponytail opened fire on a row of ducks, his rifle cracking sharply as Marshal Lapshin walked in with Starkov.

Lapshin was wearing a civilian overcoat over a business suit, tailored to his girth, and a fedora, which he removed as he approached the dirty, wooden table where Natalie had arranged three glasses of tea. The courtesy, she saw, was automatic. His eyes were cold and she knew, again, his was one face she could never read.

"*Na Zdorov'y*," she greeted him.

"What do you want?" Marshal Lapshin asked, still standing.

"Vassily's recording is safe in New York. It is absolute proof that you are plotting to overthrow your government. It even reveals you conspiring with a foreigner."

Lapshin nodded at the street outside the dirty window. "On my signal four men will come in here and shoot you down like an animal."

"One hour later, copies of Vassily's recording will be released to the Soviet embassy in Washington, the Soviet UN mission, and the media, in case you've managed to subvert your embassies."

"Am I supposed to be frightened?" he asked heavily. Natalie noticed a black Chaika parked on Liteiny Prospekt, shadows in its windows.

"Not for yourself, Marshal Lapshin. For your country. Vassily knew you so well."

"*Da?*"

"You're a patriot. The old-fashioned kind. Stop the coup, Marshal Lapshin. Stop it now. Ease your people out of the ministries and the Army. Let it die gently."

"Vassily was wrong. I've done what I've done for my son as well as my country. For him I will risk chaos. The Gen Sec is already airborne. I have merely to pick up a telephone to accelerate our schedule."

"I doubt you can kill him while he's in the air. And if you don't kill him, he'll come back."

"We never intended to kill him."

"And what exactly was Dina Golovkin's role to be?"

At first, Lapshin said nothing, and Natalie thought she had scored. Then she saw his eyes shift to the Chaika. "I can beat you to the punch," he said. "It will be a bloody fight—blood on *your* hands— but I will win it for my son."

Natalie took her last shot.

"He doesn't want it."

The marshal looked away. His gaze collided with the boys in leather, chains, and colored hair playing the video games. "My country—"

"He doesn't want it," Natalie repeated. "And you know it. That was Dina's real role, wasn't it? Fire Aleksandr up to be the Boss. He's not the Boss. You are. And you're too old to win a civil war, much less lead a country." Victor Lapshin started to cock a finger at the street and Natalie thought she would die. Then she saw his shoulders sag. He dropped his hand, asking dully, "Why do you do this? All for Vassily?"

She gave him an answer he would understand, an answer that would persuade him to surrender.

"All for Vassily."

40

Finnair was the carrier preferred by the New York furriers rushing out of Leningrad when the auction had ended, but Natalie flew Air France to connect with the Concorde in Paris. Speed was all. The faster she got home, the sooner she could personally tout the Soviet joint deal to her creditors and board of directors. Diana Darbee joined her, wielding her celebrity clout to obtain last-minute seats in first class.

Their fellow passengers, mostly French, heading home for a weekend respite from employment in the Soviet Union, were a somber crowd. Rigorous airport embarkation procedures had cast a pall on the airliner, and even lifting into the sky had done little to dispel the gloom of oppression. Natalie, however, was exhilarated. She had much to celebrate and the ebullient Diana was the perfect person to share it with. Some of it, at least.

"Guess what?"

"What, Star?" The actress had taken to calling her Star since the press conference.

"I'm pregnant."

"I didn't realize you were dating."

"Diana!"

"Wallace? Really?"

"We did it the day . . . You know, the day he was sh—killed."

438

"That is terrific. You *did* feel him inside you. Remember, you told me you felt him inside of you. Jesus, that's great."

"Thank you."

"What are you going to call it?"

"Vassily, if it's a boy."

"That'll go over big in the playground."

"But if I name him Wallace, he'll end up Wally. I don't want a Wally."

"How about Greg, after the cute cousin?"

Natalie hesitated.

"Or Mike, like your brother. There's a name for a kid."

They settled on Vassily Michael Stuart Nevsky.

"And Diana if it's a girl," said Diana. "After her godmother."

"Godmother?"

"Well, who the hell else? Listen, when a young actress auditions, she should always have something special to talk about with the casting people. Like, 'Hello, I'm Diana Nevsky. I'm named after my godmother, Diana Darbee.' I guarantee the casting agents will remember the godchild of Diana Darbee."

"I guess I hadn't realized she was going to be an actress."

"If she gets Wallace's personality and your face she'll be an actress. . . . The other way around, God only knows. But either way, we've got a responsibility to this child. Which brings me to a piece of not so nice news."

"What?" said Natalie, expecting another joke.

"You know, when I was first selling my name, Wallace taught me that deals that collapse usually fall apart *after* initial agreement."

"You sound serious."

"I am, Star. Sorry to say, but you gotta know that both Al Silverman and Jefferson Jervis telephoned Comrade Rostov last night."

"*What?*" Al Silverman was on her board.

"They're moving in on your deal. Jervis formed a syndicate out of your creditors. The pitch was that Cotillion's management problems would get in the way of your joint agreement."

Natalie sank into her seat. "They didn't waste any time, did they?"

"What did you expect? Now that your deal is public knowledge, anybody with a retail chain and an uncle in the fur trade's going to try to move in on it."

"I should've guessed."

"You've been a little spacy," Diana agreed. "Like something else was in your head. I figured you were still having a hard time with Wallace, but maybe it's because you're preggers. Anyway, Rostov played it cool. Didn't close any doors, didn't burn any bridges. He is not committed to anyone, yet—including you."

"Wait a minute. How do you know who called Rostov?"

"Let's just say I owe you one."

"One what?"

"Several, actually." A little smirk popped onto Diana's face, and melted into a contented smile.

"What are you talking about? Am I missing something?"

"You missed your chance with Rostov, I can tell you—or did you set me up? I wouldn't put that past you."

It dawned on Natalie that Diana had been with Rostov last night when she called from General Lapshin's *dacha*.

"I thought he'd like you, but I hope you don't think I expected you to sleep with him on my behalf."

"*Nyet problema*—are all Soviets like him?"

"I wouldn't know."

"The guy is . . . he's so very, kind of . . ."

"Patient?"

"*Yeah!*"

Just then the pilot made a brief announcement in French. Applause sounded through the airliner like a collective sigh of relief.

"What did he say?" asked Diana.

"We just flew out of Soviet airspace."

The dour French broke into open smiles. Animated conversations sprang up between strangers. Cabin attendants rolled bar carts down the aisles, champagne corks popped, and the air was suddenly thick with the scent of cheese and pâté. The purser appeared beside Diana with a bottle wrapped in white linen.

"What's that?"

"Champagne, mademoiselle."

"No alcohol. And tell them down the aisle to bogart those cigarettes. We've got a pregnant woman, here—hey, you okay, Star?"

Diana had caught her staring out the dark window. "Fine. Just thinking."

"Think fast. I'd guess you have about two days to derail the Soviets' second thoughts."

"It's going to be a busy weekend," Natalie agreed.

"You've got no time to be busy. You've got to think."

*   *   *

Monday found her addressing a joint shareholders' and creditors' meeting in Cotillion's crowded boardroom. All had come, even, to her shock and dismay, Jefferson Jervis, who listened with his chin on his fist and a smug look in his eye. That they had agreed to attend could be regarded as a victory in itself, but lobbying as hard as she knew how all day Saturday and Sunday, she still had far from enough support to retain control.

When she finished her presentation of the Soviet joint venture, Jervis stood up, uncoiling his bony frame like a snake. "Speaking for my partners, Mrs. Nevsky, I congratulate you on cobbling together a glitzy package, but from where we stand, Cotillion is right back where it was three months ago. Who's going to manage the company? Who's going to make the coats?"

Instead of replying, Natalie took a long look around the room at Jervis's creditors' syndicate, Mike and Bill Malcolm's competing creditors' syndicate, and her shareholders, several of whom were firmly in Jervis's camp. She tried to put a name on them, tried to pinpoint a villain. But all she saw were rows of anxious faces—foreheads wrinkled in consternation, eyes opaque with worry, mild fear, and a burning desire to avoid even the possibility of an eventual problem. There were two exceptions—Jervis, out to get her for stopping the Millionaires, and Mike, grinning his encouragement. The rest just didn't want any grief.

Bill Malcolm stood up, walked the length of the table, and dropped ostentatiously into Wallace's chair. "Listen," he whispered. "Take the money and run. I'll negotiate you a hell of a management contract. You can use the opportunity to gain management experience and learn more about making coats. If you're unhappy in a couple of years, I'll back you in a new project."

"It's not only that you're afraid to take a chance with me," she said softly. "You've found an excuse to demand guarantees. Not just you, Bill. All of you."

"What's that, Natalie?" Jervis called from his end of the long table. "Can't hear you."

This time she stood up.

"I said I'm through apologizing. I said I'm tired of being told I don't know furs. I said I'm not an outsider."

One or two mouths dropped and some nervous glances were exchanged.

"I said that distribution—such as the franchise chain I created with Wallace—and promotion—such as the ad campaign we wrapped around Diana—are the future face of the fur trade. I said the fur trade is becoming a modern business, like the rag trade. I said I'm fed up with being told I don't have the expertise. I don't have to know how to build a fur coat. I hire furriers to build them for me."

She gazed down the yew wood table into a satisfying silence. A few people traded furtive looks, but most stared at their fingers or found new interest in the polished marquetry. Natalie loved the silence. It was like a vote of approval for what she had become. From the workroom on the floor below she thought she heard ghostly applause, but it could have been the smooth rumble of the sewing machines.

Jefferson Jervis broke the spell. "Tell it to your creditors."

Natalie shifted her attention from Jervis to her intercom. "Joannie. Do we still have Wallace's speaker phone? . . . Bring it here, please."

She waited, not speaking, until Joannie brought the matte black box and plugged it into a telephone jack. She dialed. Two rings. Then, "Edward R. Mayall Capital," said the secretary Eddie shared.

"Mr. Mayall, please. Natalie Stuart Nevsky calling." She cast a smile to Jervis, who was drumming his fingers at his end of the table, affecting great boredom.

The speaker phone was an attractive little instrument that Wallace had found in one of his high-tech catalogs—American-made in the Midwest—with a carrying handle, connecting wires that retracted automatically, and a tone as clear as a fine stereo. Eddie Mayall sounded exactly like paratroop boots crunching on wet gravel:

"Welcome home, Natalie. Congratulations on bringing capitalism to the masses."

"I hope it's something I can sell."

"How's that?"

"I want you to reorganize Cotillion Furs." Jervis looked up sharply. "Underwrite a holding company to pay my creditors and buy out my shareholders at par value."

Eddie said, "Darlin', I will guarantee you a bridging loan to the maximum of your needs, on the strength of your Russki deal, but only if you agree to climb into bed with the unwashed."

"I understand it means going public."

"Like right away."

"I said I understand. Put together a deal to go public on the best basis." Eddie would lend her the money she needed until he could bring the deal to a Wall Street brokerage house that would sell her initial public offering.

"What changed your mind?"

"I don't like it, but I'd rather control a public company than lose a private one. Do you have any more damned questions?"

"One. How come you're not blessing Bill Malcolm with this opportunity?"

"Whoever helps me will be going against Jefferson Jervis."

"Ah so."

"Still interested?"

Eddie chuckled. "I've got an item or two on Jervis in my files. There is a blunt flagpole outside my office on which he is welcome to rotate."

She switched off the phone and sat back. Her brother was grinning, Jervis's thin lips were compressed in an angry line. The rest looked puzzled.

"What does this mean?" asked Wallace's old friend Al Silverman, who had thrown his support to Jervis.

"It means I will own and control fifty-one percent of a new firm. Anyone who wants to convert their Cotillion shares and join me can. Joannie, fax Eddie a confirmation. Call the holding company NSN."

"What is this NSN?"

"Natalie Stuart Nevsky."

"Mr. Jervis," Silverman called. "Perhaps you would be interested in purchasing my shares for something over par. You could buy control."

Jervis stood up sneering and headed for the door. "You dummy. I'm not buying into an empty shell."

"What shell?"

"She's left you an empty shell. Her new company will control the assets of the old company. It's perfectly legal as long as she can pay for it. And thanks to her Soviet joint venture, she can sell stock to pay for it. You got balls, Natalie. Wallace would have been proud."

Change, Wallace always said, was the best revenge. Success, Natalie suspected, was even better. It certainly felt good to beat Jervis at his own game. But in fact, she needed all the strength she had gained from that victory not to scream after him, How dare you speak Wallace's name? How dare you speak of the man you betrayed?

Evening found her alone in the boardroom.

The shareholders had dispersed, most promising to come into the new company. Lynn and Mike had hurried off for strategy drinks with Eddie Mayall. Even Joannie had gone home, after failing to persuade Natalie to join her for dinner.

She sat caressing the smooth surface of the yew wood table Wallace had attached for a bad debt. Almost at peace, she let her mind wander, wondering, idly, whatever had happened to that bankrupt Canadian. Back in business under a new name the next day, she supposed, if he was a real furrier.

"Knock! Knock!"

She looked up to see her cousin Greg tentatively rapping the door. He looked wary. His face was a little drawn, which made his eyes enormous—stormy pools of emotion that she couldn't identify. Regret?

He said, "Joannie told the security guy I was okay."

"How would she know?"

A wan smile acknowledged her jibe. "She said you beat Jervis."

"In a way."

"Congratulations."

"Thanks."

"May I sit down?"

She felt sufficiently pleased with herself to try a small joke. "I won't shoot the messenger boy."

"I cannot bear that you hate me."

"I don't hate you. I'm just deeply, deeply disappointed."

"I can't change that. I did what I thought was right. And remember, Wallace had died already. I couldn't change that. Could I?"

"No. But you could have served me better. You are my cousin. You were my friend. And Wallace's friend."

"I will do anything to make it up. Anything you want."

"Why?"

"I know I lied to you about Wallace. But I never lied about anything else."

"You did," she retorted fiercely. "You lied to me on the train."

"I never lied about us. I wanted you to come away with me."

"So where does this go?" she asked, surprised how much she cared. "What do you want?"

"You."

"Why?"

"I love you very much. I've probably been in love with you since you were fifteen."

"Stop it, Greg. I'm not ready for this."

"But the clock is running, Natalie."

"What do you mean?"

"Diana Darbee called me."

"Why would Diana call you?"

"We've known each other for years. She was Wallace's girlfriend and I was almost like his adopted son."

"I didn't realize you were close."

"More competitors than close. Now we're just remnants of the past."

"Was it a motherly call?" Then the penny dropped. "*Wait!* What did she tell you?"

"I know you're pregnant."

"I don't *believe* her!" Natalie exploded. "It's nobody's business but mine. She had no right."

"She thought I could help. And she's right."

"How? I don't need help."

"Let me atone," Greg pleaded. "Let me make it up."

"How?"

"I'll help raise Wallace's child. I owe him so much. And I owe you."

"What about Sally?"

"I've already moved out. I got a place in town. . . . Can we talk at dinner?"

She agreed to dinner, because before she could talk to Greg about the future they would first have to recapture the essence of their friendship, if that were possible. So she treated dinner like a first date. She ran home to change her clothes and made sure she was already downstairs in the lobby when he picked her up.

"Let's walk."

They spoke little along the twelve blocks to the Parker Meridien. Family gossip, news of the world, love, death, movies—nothing sparked a conversation. Greg had reservations for dinner in the Maurice.

Natalie preferred, however, to start their evening across the lobby in the somewhat brighter, more public lounge where a pianist was playing Alec Wilder songs. Ensconced on a soft banquette, she drank Perrier, enjoying the music, the bustle of the lobby, and the agreeable sight of Greg Stuart in a blue suit.

The hotel only added to the impression that she was sitting next to a handsome stranger.

"How's business?" he managed as the set neared completion.

"You heard from Joannie. I won. I won it all."

"And remain so modest."

At last he had pulled a smile out of her.

"Can one presume you're a wealthy woman?"

"Not 'big money' by your standards," she replied, regretting slightly how sharp it must have sounded to him.

"Darn. For a second there I thought I might tumble from one well-endowed bed into another."

"All other things aside, Greg, I won't sleep with you for a million years if you ever allude to Sally's body again."

"Worth the wait." He grinned. "You know, you look wonderful. Something in Russia must have agreed with you. Really wonderful."

She could say the same for him, she thought. In repose his face was classically handsome, but the smile fairly ignited his features. His hair seemed to glow and no sea on the planet had ever been bluer or deeper than his eyes.

"What's this song?" she asked.

Greg rose in a single, fluid motion, conversed with the piano player, and returned to Natalie. "Still Mr. Wilder: 'Where Are the Good Companions?' "

She started to say that Wallace had liked the song, but changed her mind. Before the silence turned significant, Greg said, "Let's eat."

Three days back from the Soviet Union, she was still ravenous for fresh green salads. Then she had a sudden passion for oysters. Squeezing lemon over a second plate of Belons, she asked about Sally.

"Sally gets the kids. I get the lawyers."

He had rented a place on East Seventy-first, even though he worked in Washington, to have a home his children could visit on weekends. Russia skewered her thoughts. Weekends became *vikends*, Vera crying that Luba had ODed on the *vikend*.

Greg ate with grace and precision. She found her gaze lingering where his cuff revealed a glimpse of downy gold hair, felt his eyes on her, looked up into his smile. Flustered, she tried to say something, anything. Greg came to her rescue.

"Rainbow Room," he said. "We'll steal a dance."

Natalie looked blank.

"Don't you remember? A whole bunch of us went up after a Christmas party. I was the oldest. You were about fifteen. We stole a dance. Hello? Natalie? God, you were naïve. There's a music charge in the main room. So we went to the bar first, had a drink, and then wandered over to the main room and stole a dance."

"I didn't realize."

"The trick is to check your coat so you look like you belong."

They had fox-trotted twice around the dance floor and Natalie had just allowed her cheek to settle against Greg's shoulder when the waiters caught them. A stern-looking captain informed Greg in Germanic tones that dancing was for dinner patrons only and would he and the lady please quit the floor?

Greg winked at Natalie. "What would Nancy Drewski say to the KGB?"

Down on Fifty-first Street, he hailed a cab. "Your place or mine?" he teased, and she could have responded in kind.

"Show me your apartment."

Greg Stuart looked a little surprised. "There's no rush."

"I just want to see where you live. I mean, I don't feel like going home yet. That's all."

"You're the boss."

He had rented the parlor floor of a wide graystone with a bay window that swelled into the branches of a Callery pear tree. "How did you find this?"

"Sheer luck. One of our guys got bounced from the UN mission. I can almost afford it. Wait 'til you see the inside."

He led her up a flight of stairs, unlocked his door, and turned on the lights. The living room was empty, but for a lamp that gleamed on the parquet floors and a dozen paintings on the walls. "I furnished the kids' room first," he explained. "Come in."

"I could lend you some furniture. I've got more rooms than I know what to do with."

"The art helps," Greg said. "But I sure could use a couch."

"I didn't know you collected," she said, shrugging out of her coat as she commenced a quick round of the framed oils.

"Sally—God bless her—started giving me paintings for my birthdays. Probably sleeping with some artist, but it got me in the habit. I bought a few myself."

Natalie stopped short.

"I picked that one up in Moscow a couple of years ago."

"I like it."

Did the empty room echo? Or was she talking too loud?

"Would you know it was Russian if I hadn't told you?"

"Definitely."

Her face had frozen like a mask, but Greg didn't notice as he ducked into the pullman kitchen, saying, "By no coincidence at all I stashed a bottle of champagne in the fridge. Like some?"

"Perrier," she breathed, approaching the Russian canvas.

Greg looked up from the half-refrigerator. "I'm told it's one of a series. I hope to pick up the rest when I can afford them."

"What's it called?" she asked when she could trust her voice not to betray her.

"Two Guys Looking at the Girl They Love."

"Of course," she whispered. "I should have guessed."

Ivan and Alecksei looked back at her, gazing as Lev must have gazed at Dina Golovkin, with awe in their eyes.

In the corner of her vision, Natalie saw Greg approaching with the bottle. She tried to turn so he couldn't see her face, but she was paralyzed by the enormity of his betrayal, overwhelmed by shock and bitter rage.

He waved the champagne under her nose. "Are you sure I can't persuade you?"

The innocence in his voice was frightening. He sounded carefree, as if he had already forgotten that he had virtually murdered Wallace, betrayed his country, and duped her, the woman he claimed to love.

"Not even a glass?" Greg coaxed.

Mute, she shook her head.

Much of her heart had died with Wallace. But a new spirit had taken life in Russia. She felt it stir within her now—quick and strong, even predatory. She realized that Greg was teasing her openly, mocking her with his eyes and knowing smile. Greg had not forgotten; just the opposite, he reveled in his victories. But if he was so sure he had gotten away with it, his arrogance thrust upon her a fabulous opportunity.

"Perrier," she repeated firmly. "For both of us." Her heart stumbled, for only a second, and she pressed on. "We're going on a health regimen until the baby is born."

"We?"

Natalie faced him with a smile. "Both of us, Greg. You're right. I can't do it alone. I need your help. I'd like to take advantage of your kind offer."

EPILOGUE

NATALIE

N atalie cast an anxious glance back at the Rose Garden, where an English pram, dark blue, and nicked and scratched from being passed around a large family for many years, was parked beside a leafless tree. The weather was warm for early December, even by Washington standards, and the President had left the French doors to the Oval Office open. But Vassily had just shaken a cold.

"I covered him," Greg assured her, catching up as she stepped through the doors.

"There you are," the President greeted them.

The old man was puttering happily with ice and crystal, mixing a bourbon and soda for the President-Elect, who glowered warily at the intrusion. Natalie thought the new man looked as if he had had a gruesome day and had hoped that a private drink with the outgoing President meant the worst was over. She offered a sympathetic smile. If she were about to assume office, the sight that would haunt her long after inauguration was the expression on the face of the President whose term was almost over. He looked as happy as a man who had found the exit from a burning building.

The President introduced them as "Natalie Stuart Nevsky and her cousin, Greg Stuart."

The President-Elect responded with a politician's memory for faces and Natalie saw in his eyes an all-too-familiar spark of recognition

451

followed by an embarrassed search through his memory for some better connection than the widow whose husband had been shot by a blonde.

"Saw your picture on the cover of *People. Time,* too. *Newsweek.*"

"Pleased to meet you, sir. Congratulations on a very impressive victory."

"You looked great. You and that actress, what's-her-name, and Gorbachev. What a shot!"

He turned to Greg, remarking that they had met once at a White House intelligence briefing and again while playing golf with Jeff Jervis at Burning Tree.

The President handed him his bourbon, Greg his scotch, and Natalie a neat vodka he had poured from a frosted blue bottle. Greg offered a toast to a smooth transition and then the President told the President-Elect that Natalie and Greg had something to tell him about the Soviet Union.

She described the private intelligence network Wallace had created for Harry Truman and how every President since had used it. Now, she told him, it was his turn.

He interrupted with a tart remark about democratic checks and covert imbalances, and it was obvious that visions of nationally televised, hostile inquiries danced in his head.

Natalie bridled. "We're not 'spooks.' We don't do operations. We offer only information about the Soviet Union. Unbiased and deep inside."

"I already turned down a similar deal from an American business-man who does fifty times the business you do in Russia. He offered to keep me posted with his impressions. Your friend, Mr. President, Jefferson Jervis."

She took a single minuscule sip of the still icy vodka and put the glass aside. Vassily objected to the taste in her milk. "I would sooner appoint a convicted rapist headmaster of a school for runaway girls."

The President nodded rueful agreement. "There's a fella turned out to be a disappointment."

"Jervis," she said, "is convinced he is the greatest intelligence officer on earth, and in fact he is a rank amateur. He hasn't the slightest inclination to separate information from ideology and—be warned—he is operation-oriented."

Greg added, "If you sent him on a friendship mission to Tashkent, the folk dancers would end up spearing their camels."

"Is there some kind of personal animosity between you and Jervis, Mrs. Nevsky?"

"No. Jeff and I have tangled in business, and elsewhere, which I can fill you in on later. But I bear no personal animosity toward him. I have no reason to." True. Jefferson Jervis, for all his wheelings, dealings, and machinations with the Millionaires, had never betrayed Wallace, because Wallace had never given him the chance. Far from being an old fool, he had outmaneuvered Jervis at every turn, and of that she was very proud.

"Well . . . I'll have to think about it."

"It's up to you, Mr. President. I would only add that I am not offering to 'post' you with my 'impressions.' My network has been in place nearly forty-five years."

"What will you do if I don't accept?"

Natalie laughed. "Breathe a sigh of relief."

From the garden came a plaintive howl. Natalie bolted out the door. The carriage stood serenely in the Rose Garden, but the little face within was screwed up in an expression Natalie knew meant Vassily wasn't sure whether he wanted to sleep or cry. Her instinct was to pick him up, but he liked motion almost as much as being held, so she checked her first impulse and tentatively rocked the carriage. After a tense moment, he opened his eyes with a smile of recognition that made her knees go weak.

The President and the President-Elect stood by as Natalie, flushed and a little frazzled, wheeled the pram into the Oval Office.

"He doesn't like being alone," she explained. " 'Bye-bye' is his least favorite expression. I'm sorry. What I was starting to say is I'm busy. I'd be on maternity leave if I worked for a corporation, but I work for myself so that's not an option."

"Surely you have managers—"

"There's a limit to what I can delegate. I've learned it's the nature of the fur trade to skim the brink of disaster. Today, for instance, my friend Diana Darbee, who is the star of my ad campaign, is threatening to go into partnership with one of my competitors if I don't put her name on all my labels. I'm suing a crook who failed to deliver eight thousand fox jackets he promised. My salon owners are demanding thirty percent more coats than last season, but it will be at least two more years before my Soviet enterprise begins to produce the quality and volume I need. In other words, sir, I'm busy. I don't need the job."

"But—"

"I will serve, if asked," she replied, aware that her father and grandfather echoed staunchly in her brain.

"Well, dammit. Impress me. Blow me away with some great piece of information. The Director of Central Intelligence told me a top KGB officer got killed the other day in a suspicious car crash. What do you know about that? The CIA is predicting some sort of Kremlin purge."

Natalie glanced at the President, who summoned up a vague nod of permission to continue. "It wasn't a car crash, sir, and there will be no purge, though some Army officers and Ministry of Defense officials are retiring earlier than they had planned. It was apparently an Afghan mortar attack on the officer's hotel room in Kabul, where he had gone to interview an Army general—a very convenient mortar attack for the general who, with his father, a marshal, was leading a plot to overthrow Gorbachev."

"Beg pardon?"

"Greg, please."

She went to the pram, while Greg related the story of the Millionaires' plot. He concluded, "Kirichenko played his investigation very close to the vest, not knowing who to trust, even in his own KGB, so it dies with him."

"Lapshins still fanging about?" asked the President-Elect.

"Marshal Lapshin shot himself," Natalie answered. "His son, the general, is happily fighting the rearguard action in Afghanistan. The plot is over."

"Your husband was killed as part of this?"

Natalie nodded and concentrated on keeping her voice neutral. "He apparently made some sort of a mistake and somebody got to him. Possibly an old KGB rival."

"He was at it forty years," said Greg. "The man had a right to get tired."

Natalie looked down at Vassily, who was nearly asleep. "It's not a forgiving business. . . . But at any rate, the Millionaires are through. And the Soviets have a chance to accomplish lasting changes, some of which are likely to benefit us as much as the Russians."

Bending to kiss Vassily, she whispered, "Bye-bye."

Vassily whimpered.

Greg shot to his feet. "I got him." He scooped the baby out of the carriage, cradled him confidently in his arms, and commenced a soothing walk out the door and across the lawn.

"Is he warm enough?" she called after them.

"Yes, he's warm enough."

The President-Elect said, "You're tempting me."

"Before you get too tempted, please understand that spying is a confusing business."

"I imagine it is."

She gazed after Greg, her eyes hardening. The worst part of all, the crime she would never forgive, was that Wallace had missed out on his child.

"You couldn't begin to, sir. For instance, Mr. Stuart is a Soviet agent."

"He is *what?*"

"We are still dredging up details, but apparently, he reports to a section of the GRU—Soviet military intelligence—that the Million-aires had infiltrated. He originally hired himself out as the Million-aires' watchdog, hoping for a piece of their action, like Jervis. He is immensely talented and I suspect he's become indispensable to the Soviets. Ultimately he betrayed my husband."

"He *what?*" The President-Elect shot a black look at the garden.

"Betrayed her husband," said the President. "Told the blonde to shoot 'im."

"Why?"

The old President gave the new man a look that said he had better get used to reality real soon. Natalie said, "He saw a chance for what he calls 'big money,' by breaking in on the scheme Jefferson Jervis was working with the Lapshins. Whoever brokers the big technology and material exchanges with a new Soviet regime stands to make enormous fortunes."

"So he did it for the money?"

Natalie reflected on his question. Greg was bigger than that. The money was part of it, but he was driven to excel. He liked the game. And yet, she knew with cold certainty that Greg had been aware that one day, somehow, his own ambitions would throw him against Wallace.

"It's more complex than that. There came a moment where my husband threatened what Greg wanted. . . . But don't you see, sir, the important thing is, he doesn't know we know. It goes without saying, don't tell him anything you wouldn't tell your barber."

"But—goddamn, he's holding your child. I gather you're involved with this man."

"He is good with children. He is *not* my lover."

"Of course not, but—"

"My point," Natalie continued evenly, "is that if you allow him to continue to liaise between Wallace Nevsky's network and the White House, he offers all sorts of opportunities to deceive Soviet intelligence."

"Deceive is right! He knows about your network. What's to stop him from passing their information back to the KGB?"

"He knows about my *husband's* network," Natalie corrected.

"Beg your pardon?"

The outgoing President wandered over and splashed fresh bourbon on his ice. "She's offering to build you a new network."

"What?"

"Like her husband did for Truman."

"How?"

"I've made my own contacts. I have Soviet partners in business. I cultivate officials on my trips. I've been back to Russia four times already. In a few months, as soon as Vassily is old enough, we'll go back together. It will take me years to build a network as fine as Wallace's, but I have a base I can build from, if you want."

"What about that son of a bitch holding your baby?"

"We use him. We use him to send false information to confuse the Soviets. We let him think I'm bumbling around like a bull in a china shop trying to reactivate Wallace's old net."

"How long can you keep the charade going?"

"Until I have a few people solidly in place, I hope."

She glanced at the garden. She felt no particular hurry. Greg *was* good with children. For love, she had Vassily. Occasionally, already, she could see Wallace in his eyes, and she was never alone. The day would come when she would have to make a new life, if only to save the boy from a crazy single mother, but that day would dawn obvious and she would deal with it then.

"But, Mrs. Nevsky, you're playing footsie with the man who practically murdered your husband."

Natalie silenced him with a glance.

In her mind's eye, she sometimes saw Wallace as she had first seen him, a tall man in a white suit loping toward her with an expectant smile. Most often, she remembered him the last day on *Panache,* telling his Russian story with a straight face and mischief in his eye.

"My husband," she told the President-Elect, "would love it."

ACKNOWLEDGMENTS

I am especially indebted to Robert L. Mayall of New York—private banker, dealmaker, Vietnam veteran, and raconteur—who steered me through the rapids of fur finance, merchant banking and business ethos and showed me the sights along the way.

Furriers and bankers who were generous with information and introductions in New York, London, Montreal and Idaho include Arthur Frayling, OBE, of Hudson's Bay London, Ivy Sharp and her *Fur Review*, Ernie Graf of Ben Kahn, sable coat makers George and Patty Moschos, Zelda Salzberg of Lenore Marshall, Marta and Lee Moyle of Moyle Mink Farms, and Jennifer Mayall. Victor Shvalbe and Eian Zaydelman allowed me to observe the wary mating dance of furrier and money lender. Janet Brown shared the insights of a young investment banker. And the myths and habits of the business world were dissected by Eddie Pollitz, novelist and plutocrat-at-large.

Valery Moskolenko was a stalwart guide to Brezhnev's Moscow, and the Taubman tribe of journalists, scholars and world travelers—Lori March and Howard, Philip, William, and Jane—helped me keep abreast of changes in the Soviet Union, both real and apparent. Reportage by Martin Walker of the *Manchester Guardian* and Felicity Berringer and Bill Keller, *The New York Times*, portrayed the old and new faces of Russia. Melissa A. Simmons wrote a splendid book called *Buying and Caring for Your Fabulous Fur*. I thank Lawrence Block for Wallace's Russian story.

When asked which word processor I prefer, I praise the infinite memory, boundless energy and editorial talents of Ms. Sharon Nettles.